D0189588

LARISSA IONE

THE MOONBOUND CLAN VAMPIRES

chained by night

POCKET BOOKS

New York   London   Toronto   Sydney   New Delhi

Pocket Books
A Division of Simon & Schuster, Inc.
1230 Avenue of the Americas
New York, NY 10020

This book is a work of fiction. Any references to historical events, real people, or real places are used fictitiously. Other names, characters, places, and events are products of the author's imagination, and any resemblance to actual events or places or persons, living or dead, is entirely coincidental.

First Pocket Books paperback edition October 2014

POCKET and colophon are registered trademarks of Simon & Schuster, Inc.

For information about special discounts for bulk purchases, please contact Simon & Schuster Special Sales at 1-866-506-1949 or business@simonandschuster.com.

The Simon & Schuster Speakers Bureau can bring authors to your live event. For more information or to book an event, contact the Simon & Schuster Speakers Bureau at 1-866-248-3049 or visit our website at www.simonspeakers.com.

Cover illustration by Craig White

Manufactured in the United States of America

10 9 8 7 6 5 4 3 2 1

ISBN 978-1-4767-0018-2
ISBN 978-1-4767-0020-5 (ebook)

For Doug. You touched everyone you met, and the world just isn't the same without you. You are missed.

1

I N A SECRET club blaring rock music and laughter, raised shot glasses brimming with whiskey clinked together like death knells.

"Dude, it's your last night as a single male. Why aren't you starting drunken brawls or banging that female you just sucked?"

Hunter glared at his blond companion from across the scarred tabletop. As a human-turned-vampire, Riker held on to some strange human rituals, like the thing called a "bachelor party."

"I don't fuck outside my species." Unlike Riker—and most vampires, for that matter—Hunter had never swum in the same gene pool with mankind. Thank the Great Spirit for that. "And it's not my last night," he muttered. "The mating ceremony doesn't take place until next month."

Riker gave Hunter a *bullshit* look. "She arrives at MoonBound tomorrow."

Hunter groaned at the reminder that his future mate was arriving courtesy of an ancient vampire custom that required a "trial run" before a clan leader could be bound to his mate forever.

Forever. Sounded like way too damned long to Hunter.

He downed his shot of Jameson and changed the subject. "Where are Baddon and Jaggar?"

Riker's leather bomber jacket creaked as he propped his hip against the table where they'd been standing for the last two hours. "They're making up for your picky ass." He jerked his thumb in the direction of one of the private rooms down the hall in the back. "They took off with that purple-haired chick and her friend."

Hunter cocked an eyebrow at the sea of purple-haired humans milling around, all victims of the newest hair-color craze.

Riker clarified. "The one with the dog collar. The *metal-spiked* dog collar."

Why did groupies think vampires liked dog collars? Not to mention the fact that they sort of interfered with the whole bloodsucking process.

With a sigh, Hunter shoved away from the wall he'd been leaning against. He was done with this cesspool of sex, drugs, and blood. He'd never liked the underground vamp-worship scene, and while this was one of the classier Seattle clubs that secretly catered to vampires, it still reeked of desperation.

The humans who came here to give their blood and bodies to vampires were desperate to be turned someday. The vampires who frequented this kind of club were also desperate, either for food or to reconnect with the humanity they lost, and Hunter was neither. As a born vampire, he'd never been human, and as an experienced warrior and leader of one of the largest vampire clans in the Pacific Northwest, he hadn't wanted for food in a long time.

He strode across the blood- and drink-stained concrete floor, barely registering the way the crowd of humans and vampires parted for him. Technically, in a club setting, he was on equal footing with all vampires, but as a clan chief and one of the oldest born vampires in existence, Hunter was given a wide berth and undeniable respect.

Of course, it didn't hurt that he was six and half feet tall and wearing an arsenal of weapons under his leather duster.

He broke away from the crowd and shoved open the first door he came to. Dim light from behind Hunter flooded the private room, spilling onto a stained sofa and an ancient, sagging bed in the corner. The heady scents of blood and sex billowed out into the hall, overpowering the lingering odors of stale cigarette smoke and grease from the boarded-up old burger joint next door.

A spiked dog collar rested on top of a messy pile of clothes on the floor.

"Yo," he called out to the pair on the mattress and the other pair on the sofa. "Finish up. I'm outta here."

The naked human female tangled on the mattress with Baddon moaned. Baddon, his chest plastered against hers and his fangs buried in her throat, didn't look up, but Jag did from the sofa, long enough to acknowledge his leader with a slow nod.

Hunter closed the door and returned to Riker, whose smirk of amusement didn't quite hide the concern in his silver eyes.

"Knock it off," Hunter growled. "I don't need a pity party."

"Your future mate is from ShadowSpawn," Riker said, handing him a fresh glass of whiskey. "A clan that has been waging war against us for centuries. They have artwork made from MoonBound scalps and bones. And I've met Rasha. Trust me, pity is the least of what you need."

Hunter pressed his spine to the wall and kicked his head back hard enough to hurt. It had been two months since he had struck a deal with the enemy clan's brutal leader to mate with his daughter in exchange for the return of Riker's mate, Nicole.

But Hunter had told his own clan about the deal just two days ago.

Riker was still pissed that he'd been kept in the dark, but Hunter had kept quiet for the guy's own good. Riker and Nicole would have stewed in guilt or tried to do something stupid to break the arrangement.

"I'm sorry, Hunt." Riker looked down at his steel-toed boots, his hair falling forward to conceal his expression. "This is my fault. What you did for me and Nicole—"

"Don't." Hunter cut his friend off. "I said I don't need your pity, and I don't need your apology, either. I made a choice, and I have to live with it. But I'll tell you what I do need," he said, focusing on the tense stirring in his muscles. "A good fight."

Riker lifted his head and flashed fangs. "Maybe we'll get lucky and run into some poachers on the way home."

"Or," Hunter suggested, "we could hunt our enemies here in the city." The very thought of taking on the role of a predator, the way it used to be—the way it *should* be—drew a rumble of anticipation from deep in his chest.

Riker's gaze cut sharply to the front door as two young male vamps entered. The guy didn't miss anyone coming or going. "No way. It's too risky."

Hunter drained the glass of whiskey. "That's the point. And it's not that risky."

"I said no. We can't let our chief get killed. Or worse."

Yes, there was worse than getting killed, and Hunter knew it. Humans loved their vampire slaves, and if he was captured alive, he could very well end up mopping some human asshole's floor after a year of "reprogramming and training." More likely, though, because he was a born vampire—distinguished by the fact that his eyes were the same black-brown that they'd been when he was born instead of the silver color that defined a turned vampire—he'd spend the rest of his life in a Daedalus lab.

Nicole, former CEO of Daedalus, the company that had revolutionized slavery, had been clear about what happened to born vampires in the human world, and it wasn't pretty. The poor bastards were in for a lifetime of being poked and prodded, studied, tortured, cut open, and possibly used for breeding. Hunter would rather die.

He swirled the ice cubes around in his glass. "You know I can do what I want, right?"

"And you know why you named me your second in

command." Riker waved off an approaching human female whose bite scars and lack of panties under a short denim skirt announced her availability for any vampire pleasure. "To stop you from doing stupid shit."

Hunter snorted. "To *try* to stop me from doing stupid shit."

"I do have backup, you know." He jerked his head toward Baddon and Jaggar as they emerged from the bedroom looking sated and relaxed. But they were warriors through and through, and beneath their loose-gaited swagger was a deadly alertness that no amount of sex or blood could diminish. Their assessing gazes took note of every individual in the place as they made a beeline toward Hunter.

"How is it," Baddon drawled as they approached, "that this is Hunt's party and *we* got all the action?"

"Not me." Riker held up his hands in denial. "I fed, but I have a beautiful mate I'm going home to."

Jaggar punched Riker in the shoulder. "Lucky bastard." He eyed Hunter. "I saw you with that busty brunette. Did you get some?"

"Depends on what 'some' is." Hunter started out the door without explaining himself.

For the first time ever, he'd actually considered throwing all his crazy into the wind and doing the female who had crawled onto his lap and rubbed herself against him as he fed, but his impending doom—also known as mating—had weighed too heavily on his mind. He detested the ShadowSpawn female, and the mere thought of her put him in the mood to do anything but have sex.

Then there was the curse. Oh, and the possibility

of a spy inside the clan who might be feeding info to ShadowSpawn.

Hunter was so screwed.

"Hunt!" Riker jogged after him. "No stupid shit."

"Yeah, yeah," he muttered as they scaled the stone steps up a poorly lit passage that came out into a dark alley. The narrow street, cluttered by Dumpsters and crates, was otherwise clean and, even better, deserted.

The club sat on the outskirts of Seattle in a posh neighborhood the cops and vampire hunters left alone. It was possible that they were aware of the existence of the club, but as long as no wealthy humans were harassed or killed, the law tended to stay away. No sense in bringing attention to a "vampire problem" if there wasn't one.

Except that there *was* a problem, and soon it would spill over into even the areas that had been ignored for decades. It was a storm Hunter had seen coming for years, one that had been brewing since the day humans discovered that vampires existed.

The smell of approaching snow rode the wind as they strode through the streets, mixing with the crowds of humans enjoying the 24/7 nightlife that kept this part of Seattle hopping even in the cold winter months. A siren blared in the distance, so distant that none of the humans milling about would hear it.

How these weak humans had conquered and enslaved the vampire race continued to baffle him. Sure, they had an advantage when it came to weapons, and they outnumbered vampires by a bazillion to one, but Great Spirit above, they were *stupid*.

Baddon took the lead as they approached the mall

parking lot where they'd left the clan's Land Rover, his hand tucked beneath his biker jacket, ready to draw a weapon. *Eager* to draw a weapon, probably.

The parking lot's lights went out, shrouding the SUV in darkness, courtesy of Baddon's ability to mentally manipulate electricity. The lack of light gave them an extra edge over human vampire hunters, and while Hunter figured that the heightened caution Riker insisted on was a waste of time and effort, he never argued. Rike was hypervigilant, and when the safety of clan members was at stake, wasting time and effort was a better alternative than being dead.

Jag and Baddon ranged out ahead to secure the immediate area around the Land Rover as Rike lagged behind, remaining at Hunter's back. When Bad gave the all-clear signal, Hunter dug the keys out of his pocket.

"I'm driving. No arguments."

There was some grumbling but no formal protests as they piled into the vehicle. Rike took the passenger seat and plugged classic Creedence Clearwater Revival into the radio, and Hunter got to listen to three big vampire warriors sing at the top of their lungs during the entire thirty-mile drive. Finally, as "Bad Moon Rising" faded out for the second time, they reached the private gravel drive that led deep into more than a hundred acres of land owned by the clan. The property was used for storage and hunting, and it also contained two small cabins that any clan member could use as getaways.

Or as hideouts.

He parked the truck inside the barn, where other vehicles were stored, from snowmobiles and four-wheelers to Jaggar's classic Corvette and Baddon's Harley. From here, the snowmobiles or four-wheelers could make it through the forest to the public lands where their headquarters were located in less than half an hour.

Unfortunately, a recent increase in human activity in the forests meant that vampires had to be more cautious. Now Hunter and his clan mates had been reduced to traveling on foot both for silence and to minimize the chance of leaving tracks that would lead humans to headquarters.

"Fucking humans," Baddon muttered as they trudged through the woods.

There was a murmur of agreement from Jag and Rike, and then Hunter caught a scent that raised the hairs on the back of his neck.

"Everyone . . . stop."

Already on high alert, they drew weapons and squared off in fighting stances as Hunter lifted his face to the breeze. The stench of unwashed skin, alcohol, tobacco . . . and stale vampire blood drifted in the wind, mingled with the tang of distant campfire smoke.

"Poachers," he whispered harshly. "At least a dozen."

"Shit." Baddon, his black hair longer in the front than the back, shoved his bangs out of his eyes as he flipped the safety off his crossbow.

They kept moving, taking it slow and quiet. But as they approached the edge of the lake that the clan used for swimming and fishing during the summer, a shot rang out. A bullet punched into a tree trunk mere feet from Hunter's head.

"Stake Reapers!" Baddon shouted, and fuck, this was not good.

Vampires had been plagued by hunters and poachers for decades, but Nicole's messy defection from Daedalus—and humanity—to join MoonBound and become a vampire had caused a shitstorm. Humans had begun to call for the extermination of free vampires and tighter controls on enslaved vamps. Now every sleazeball on the planet was out to bag a vampire, and some, like the Stake Reapers motorcycle club, were cashing in on the rush to grab as many vampires as they could sell before wild vampires became extinct.

Worse, the Stake Reapers had proved to be the most dangerous organized group Hunter had come across, and Baddon's speculation that the outlaw club had a vampire at its wheel was even more disturbing.

Two big dudes broke out of the brush, one armed with a machete, the other with a baseball bat, and both carried pistols. Hunter spun, taking out the machete guy with a kick to the throat. He whirled again, narrowly missing having his head bashed in with the bat. He threw a right cross and knocked out a few of the bat-wielding bald guy's teeth.

As he grabbed the guy by the collar, a metallic snap echoed through the trees, followed by a blood-curdling scream.

Hunter wheeled around, tossing the bald dude against a mossy boulder hard enough to knock the guy out. Several yards away, Jaggar was clutching his leg and groaning in agony as he writhed on the ground. A massive leg trap, built either for bears or specifically for vampires, was clamped around his lower leg, its vicious spikes shredding flesh and likely breaking bone.

Hunter ran toward Jag as Riker and Baddon took down two more humans. Another shot thundered through the air. Riker jerked and clapped his hand over his bloody shoulder.

"I'm cool!" Riker shouted, and with a nod, Hunter scrambled next to Jag.

The trap, coated in Jaggar's blood, was slippery as shit, but Hunter managed to pry it open without damaging Jag's leg any more. Hissing in pain, Jaggar yanked his leg free, and when he was clear, Hunter let the metal jaws snap shut.

"Hold on, buddy." Hunter ripped a thick strip of fabric from his T-shirt and hurriedly tied it around the gaping wound and the exposed bone in Jag's leg just below the knee.

Once the makeshift bandage was tied off, he hooked Jaggar under the arms and hauled him to his feet, but getting him back to clan headquarters wasn't going to be easy. Jag's leg was mangled, definitely broken.

Riker and Baddon had the last remaining human against a tree, and while Hunter was aware that there were more of them deeper in the forest, he and his boys had no choice but to make a break for home.

Quickly, he threw Jaggar over his shoulder. "Let's go!" he shouted. "Bring the human."

"Roger that!" Riker shouted back as Baddon flipped the poacher around and punched him hard in the head, knocking the guy out. The dude crumpled to the wet forest floor with a satisfying thud.

Baddon effortlessly mirrored Hunter and tossed the human over his shoulder before jogging ahead to scout the path. Riker fell in behind Hunter, protecting his back. A hundred yards from the scene of the battle, two MoonBound warriors, Takis and Aiden, joined them, bows drawn.

"We heard a fight," Takis said, eyeing Jaggar. "Hunters?"

"Stake Reapers," Baddon growled.

"Shit," Aiden breathed. "You guys okay? Rike?"

Riker cut a sharp nod at Aiden. "I'll be fine. We need to get Jag help."

They moved faster now, with Aiden and Takis clearing the way, and had no more trouble. Still, it was unsettling that the Stake Reapers had set their traps so close to clan headquarters. MoonBound's mystic-keeper had warded the area to passively repel humans, but either the wards had been destroyed or the Stake Reapers possessed some ability that rendered the wards useless.

Either way, the clan could be fucked. Their headquarters was concealed by ancient magic, so if the wards could be neutralized, it was possible that the invisibility spell could be, too.

"Baddon." Hunter shifted Jaggar's weight to relieve the pressure that was making his right arm go numb. "See if you can do some more digging into the Reapers. If they can neutralize our wards, your theory that they have a vamp in their ranks might be dead-on. Riker, I want extra patrols assigned for the next few days, and tomorrow I'll personally meet Rasha's party at our territory's border."

Baddon gave a crisp "Yes, sir," but Riker glared. The guy would no doubt give Hunter an earful about how it was too much of a risk for him to leave headquarters, but Riker's efforts would be wasted. Hunter wasn't going to take any chances with his future mate. He didn't like her, didn't want this, but if something happened to her inside MoonBound clan's territory, her father would mount every MoonBound vampire's skin on his walls.

So yes, he would make sure his future bride and his clan were safe.

His fate, however, was very much up in the air, and as they covered the final miles to headquarters, the voice of the demon who had come to Hunter two months ago rang in his ears.

Before the winter ends, you will be dead.

2

Fate was following Aylin Redmoon like a wolf on the trail of an injured deer. With every step closer to MoonBound clan's territory in the rugged Cascade Mountains of Washington State, the sense of impending doom grew.

Very soon she was going to be mated to a brutal male, her virginity taken against her will, before being cast aside as garbage.

But first, her twin sister was to be mated. And unlike Aylin's future mate, Rasha's was handsome and respected by his clan members, and he believed in bathing more than once a year. Aylin had never seen Hunter up close, but she'd heard the chatter, which, if it was to be believed, made him out to be some sort of vampire Adonis.

Patches of melting snow from last night's storm crunched under Aylin's hiking boots as she and her sister made their way along a winding riverbank. Rasha's boots didn't make a sound.

Aylin cast a sideways glance at her twin. Rasha's blond hair was pulled into a severe ponytail, while

Aylin's waist-length locks were bound lower and looser with a leather thong, but aside from that, they were identical. Even their clothing matched, but not out of some silly twin-sisterhood thing. No, Aylin had been set up as a decoy so that Rasha, the firstborn and ShadowSpawn heir, would have a better chance of escape in the event of an attack by humans or a double cross by MoonBound.

As they walked, Aylin was careful to stay behind her sister and to the right, the submissive position she'd been taught to take with every male and some females in her own clan. It didn't matter that she was the daughter of the clan chief; her status as second-born twin ranked her below all males, and her physical flaw automatically made her inferior to healthy females.

But that didn't mean she didn't sometimes "forget" her place. She always paid for it, but those few minutes when she mouthed off or outwitted one of her "superiors" were worth it.

A deer bounded across the trail a few yards in front of them, its nimble steps lending to a nearly silent run through the trees. How Aylin envied that deer its freedom and agility.

Rasha moved just as gracefully, every step deliberate and soundless, one gloved hand clasped firmly around her crossbow, the other poised over the hilt of the dagger at her hip. Her blue eyes scanned the forest ahead, cataloging every windblown leaf, every bird flitting from tree branch to tree branch. Rasha was in calm, cool warrior mode . . . even though she was on the way to mate with the enemy.

"Aren't you nervous?" Aylin asked.

"Why should I be?" Rasha signaled one of their six escorts to range out ahead. They should be coming across MoonBound's warriors at any minute, and they wanted no surprises. "I'm about to be mated to the leader of one of the largest and oldest vampire clans this side of the Rockies. I'll be a queen. And Hunter is fucking hot. I could be mating an ugly monster with a harem of females."

"Like I am?" Aylin looked up at a squirrel scolding them from the branches of a tree.

You should be hibernating, buddy.

The squirrel didn't hear her thoughts, of course. But deep inside, like shadow wings fluttering against her soul, Aylin's totem animal, her mourning dove spirit guide, awakened, preparing to deliver the message to the little rodent if needed.

"Exactly." Rasha leaped across a narrow in the river, but Aylin had to use a fallen log to cross. "I know it's not what you want, but you need to make the best of it. Isn't that what you're always telling me?" She cast Aylin a teasing grin. "It's annoying, isn't it?"

Aylin tossed a pinecone at her sister. They had an easy relationship when they were alone and Rasha wasn't being scorned for being nice to her crippled, cursed sister.

"Telling you to make the best of mating with Hunter is a little different from you telling me to make the best of mating with Tseeveyo," Aylin pointed out. "You actually *want* to mate with Hunter."

"For the good of our clan." Rasha swatted a branch out of her face. "But he doesn't want me."

"And Tseeveyo only wants *me* because he needs our father as an ally."

Rasha averted her gaze. They both knew there was another reason Tseeveyo wanted Aylin, but neither wanted to go there. "You need someone to take care of you, Aylin. You're lucky Tseeveyo wants you, and at least this way, you get to be a clan chief's mate."

One of his mates. "I can take care of myself." She definitely didn't need a male whose evil deeds had given birth to the Hopi legend of the child-eating ogre known to many as Cheveyo.

"Really." Rasha cast a skeptical glance at Aylin's crooked right leg, which nearly buckled as she stepped off the log. "You can't hunt, and you can't compete with other females. Without me at Shadow-Spawn, it won't be long before you'll be shoved to the fringes of the clan and begging for scraps. And if something ever happens to our father, your last line of protection will be gone. The clan will either shun you or kill you."

What Rasha was saying was true, but that didn't mean Aylin wanted to hear it. "Thanks for the breaking news," she muttered over the incessant squirrel chatter.

Rasha looked completely perplexed. She never had understood that she shouldn't say every little thing she was thinking. "I was just being honest."

"You were reminding me where my place is in the clan."

"Because you never learn," Rasha said, glaring up at the squirrel. "You're always bucking the system, and believe it or not, I don't like to see you punished. If you'd just accept your place in society, your life would be so much better."

"If I accepted *my place*, I'd be dead, and you know it." How often had she heard not only clan members but her own father say that she should have been drowned before she took her first breath? Aylin wondered what offended everyone most—that she was the second-born, the "cursed" twin, or that she'd had the audacity to be born with a deformed leg in a survival-of-the-fittest world.

Rasha sighed. "Just, please, will you behave with Tseeveyo? I know he's a bastard, but if you lie low, follow orders, and do what he says, it'll be okay. Just do your best—"

"Enough!" Aylin bit out. "The last thing I want to talk about is how I've been sold to a clan that is, somehow, worse than ShadowSpawn. So will you shut up about it, already?"

No one else in the world could have said that to Rasha. Not if they wanted to walk away with their teeth intact. But Rasha, for all her faults, hadn't physically harmed Aylin since they were children. Not seriously, anyway. No, Rasha had other, more effective ways to put Aylin in her place, and Aylin had learned long ago never to let her sister know what was important to her. Rasha knew too much about Aylin's soft spots as it was . . . as she proved now by raising her crossbow and taking aim at the noisy squirrel. "*That* thing needs to shut up."

"No!" Aylin struck out, slamming the weapon up as it fired. The bolt went wild, and the squirrel skittered into a hole in the tree trunk.

Rasha snarled, baring her fangs. "Dammit, Aylin. Animals are food, not pets."

"Spare me," Aylin said, starting toward Moon-Bound's territory again. "You weren't going to eat the squirrel. You were going to kill it to hurt me."

"Not to hurt. To *help*. Do you see what I mean about you not learning your lessons? I do these things for your own good. I wish you'd see that." Rasha shoved past Aylin to take the lead. Aylin nearly fell over, her bad leg shifting awkwardly as she tried to regain her balance, but Rasha's hand snapped out to catch her.

Aylin shrugged out of her grip. "Oh, I learned very well not to keep a pet." At ShadowSpawn, compassion for animals was considered a weakness. "I was only going to ask that squirrel what brought it out of hibernation. I think it was trying to tell us something."

Hissing, Rasha rounded on Aylin. "Shut your mouth," she whispered harshly. "If any of the warriors had heard you—"

"They didn't." Aylin bent to tie her bootlace. "And I'd have been careful."

"It doesn't matter. Communicating with animals is forbidden, and you know it."

Of course, she knew it. Every vampire was gifted with a special skill or two, but Aylin's talent of using her totem spirit to talk to animals was considered taboo for reasons Aylin had never understood. But then, much of what went on in the ShadowSpawn clan didn't make sense to her. And because of that, because she questioned the ideology of the Way of the Raven, the other clan members thought she was either stupid or a troublemaker. Usually both.

They continued through the forest in uneventful silence. Then, as they dropped into a valley that bordered MoonBound territory, Benito, one of their young scouts, stumbled out from the shadows, his face streaked with blood, his black clothing shiny with wet splotches.

"Fucking . . . humans," Ben gasped.

He coughed, spraying pink mist as he collapsed onto the fern-covered ground. A thick wooden handle rose from between his shoulder blades, and it took Aylin's brain several precious moments to realize a hatchet was lodged in his back.

Suddenly, the woods exploded with movement and the sounds of battle.

Rasha spun in a blur, and Aylin felt a sharp sting in her right thigh. Rasha's blade slipped silently into its sheath; Aylin hadn't even seen her sister remove it.

"Aylin, run!" They'd prepared for this scenario, but now that it was real, Aylin froze, paralyzed with terror and pain. "Dammit, Aylin, go!"

Blood dripped down her leg from the shallow cut Rasha had made—again, part of their contingency plan. Aylin was a decoy, the cut intended to explain her limp and fool anyone who captured her into thinking she was Rasha, injured by an enemy blade.

Spurred by a series of gunshots and screams, Aylin ran as fast as she could in the opposite direction.

Tree branches slapped at her face and arms. The ground slipped out from under her as she scrambled up the hillside. The sounds of fighting seemed to be right on her heels, but when she glanced behind her, there was nothing but forest. Relief that no one was chasing her veered sharply into terror when a man wielding a steel pipe topped the ridge just a few yards ahead.

Cursing, she fumbled for one of the two throwing knives at her hip. Her hand closed on the hilt, but before she could set her stance to throw the blade, a burly human male burst out from the trees to her right. He swung his crossbow up, training it on her chest.

She let the dagger fly. Thanks to countless hours of training when she was a child, she could hit a wasp in the air at thirty yards, but this guy's eye was a much better target. He went down with a grunt.

"Vampire bitch!" The pipe-wielding maniac dived at her, smashing the pipe into the backs of her legs.

Agony shot through her, and she crashed to the ground. The bastard kicked her in the ribs, knocking her onto her back. The air exploded from her lungs in a painful burst. His boot came down on her throat, pinning her to the ground.

His ugly, gray-bearded face stared down at her as she clutched at his ankle in a futile attempt to dislodge his foot. What little air she could suck in felt like whips of searing fire.

"Aren't you a pretty one?" he said. "And going by those blue peepers, you're purebred, too. You'll fetch a fortune in the sex-slave market."

Terror made her clumsy, but by some miracle, her fingers found the second blade at her hip. *Hurry . . . hurry . . .*

The knife slipped out of her hand. *Dammit!*

The pipe man's foot crunched down with more pressure, and black spots floated in her field of vision.

Concentrate. You know how to handle a blade.

Forcing herself to stay calm, she palmed the knife. With as much strength as she could muster with the crappy leverage she had, she stabbed the dagger deep into his denim-clad calf. The man screamed and fell back, but as she struggled to her hands and knees, something pierced her shoulder, and instant sizzling cramps seized every muscle in her body.

Shock dart.

Her fuzzy thoughts understood what he'd nailed her with, but her body no longer functioned, and as she lay on the ground, seizing and shaking, she could only pray that Rasha had gotten away and would come for her.

Please, please, save me, Rasha.

Because, spirits knew, no one else would.

3

THE PRISONER WAS defiant. Hunter might have appreciated that quality in a vampire, but from a human . . . it just proved how stupid they were.

"You're in a vampire stronghold, chained in a prey room, and you still can't say anything except 'Fuck you' and 'Fuck off'?"

"Fuck you," the human snarled. "I ain't afraid of you."

"Your scent says otherwise."

The human, stripped down to his Harley-Davidson boxers, spit a bloody wad onto the dirt floor. "I said I ain't scared."

So. Damned. Stupid.

"You *ain't* scared?" Aiden, whose usual mild manner and surfer-dude good looks concealed a dark talent for torture, ran his thumb over the sharp edge of his favorite skinning blade. "We'll see what we can do about that."

Hunter stomped on the chain looped around the human's wrists, yanking his arms hard behind his back and wrenching this shoulders in their sockets. The scumbag gritted his teeth but didn't make a sound.

"How many Stake Reapers are there?" Hunter asked. "Who's hiring you to poach us?"

The gang member, whose black leather jacket's name tag read "Chem," bared his red-streaked teeth. "We don't need no fucking money. We'd string up your kind for free."

Hunter kicked at the bag they'd found slung over his shoulder beneath the jacket. "So the vampire fangs and scalps in here weren't going to be sold?"

Chem's lip curled. "Didn't say we don't make money doing what we love."

Rage swept in, swift and hot, and Hunter's hand snapped out to catch the fucker around the throat. "Listen to me, you piece of shit. We can do this the easy way or the hard way. Aiden prefers the hard way. He has an unholy love for his knives. Me? I've got better things to do." Like prepare for his mate to arrive in the morning. "So why don't you save us both a lot of time and pain and tell me what you know? Because you *will* talk eventually. I promise you that."

"Fuck. You." Chem grinned, his lips pulling back from yellowed, chipped teeth. "You leeches have no idea what's coming, do you? A storm, man. A fucking slaughter, and by the time it's over, you parasites will be extinct in the wild. The rest of you will be slaves . . . just like the pretty young thing we pass around in our clubhouse."

How did people who despised vampires justify using them for sex? Fucking assholes.

A low growl boiled up from Hunter's chest, and his hand tightened on Chem's throat. Deep inside, the desire not just to kill the thug but to do it in the cruelest way imaginable writhed like a demon trying to break out. Hunter's father would have displayed Chem in the common room and let everyone watch as he jammed sharp objects into sensitive orifices. Then he'd spend days divesting him of body parts, starting with his balls and cock.

A surge of excitement rolled over Hunter as that evil demon thrashed at its restraints.

No.

Sweat broke out on his brow, and beneath his palm, his fingers squeezed harder. Chem's face turned a brilliant shade of purple, made even more colorful by the veil of crimson that formed across the field of Hunter's vision.

No!

Hunter refused to turn into his father, but the darkness ran through his veins like a malevolent sludge, infecting his thoughts. *Do it. Cut him. Open him from crotch to sternum, and let the clan's children play with his innards. Do it!*

Nausea churned in his stomach. Releasing the human, he stepped back and forced himself to calm down.

"Jesus Christ," Chem rasped, his bloodshot eyes wide as he gaped at Hunter. Wetness bloomed across the front of his boxers. "Jesus . . . the *fuck*?"

Aiden was staring as intently as the human, but in an instant, he blinked, collected himself, and slammed his fist into the human's jaw. "What, never seen a pureblood vampire rage out? The red eyes and four-inch fangs are just the beginning, asshole."

"You goddamned freaks!" The stench of Chem's

terror burned Hunter's nostrils and got his inner monster excited again. "Die, all of you!"

Hunter needed to get out of there before two hundred years of self-control, of carefully distancing himself from the male his father had been, went out the window. No way was this smelly, vile poacher going to be the one to undo a lifetime of restraint.

"He's all yours, Aiden." Hunter tapped on the cell door, and Katina opened it, her silver eyes glittering with bloodlust at the sight of the poacher all strung up like a side of beef. "Find out what he knows. I don't care how you do it or how long it takes. I'll send in Baddon to help." Baddon was their resident expert in all things gang or motorcycle-club related, and he no doubt knew more than Chem would like.

Plus, Baddon got off on torture as much as Aiden did. He just didn't hide it as well.

Aiden's cold smile dropped the temperature in the cell. "Yes, sir. Don't worry, I'll have this bastard singing like a canary in no time."

Hunter didn't say another word, afraid that if he did, he'd tell Aiden to get the hell out . . . and then there'd be nothing to stop Hunter from giving in to the desires his father had encouraged.

Desires that, once released, could never again be controlled.

4

T ODAY WAS DOOMSDAY.

Okay, maybe it wasn't as bad as that, but if Hunter had to list his top five most dreaded things, mating with a female he hated would be near the top. Right behind losing a child and being forced into slavery. And if bringing his future mate and current enemy into his clan's home today wasn't enough, there was another tempest racing in on the heels of last night's blizzard. He felt it as a deep buzz in his bones and a weight on his soul.

This storm was going to be about more than the weather, and he wondered if it had something to do with the humans, as their prisoner had suggested. As soon as he'd checked up on Jaggar, he would pay Aiden a visit, hoping he'd gotten something useful out of the scumbag.

Cursing to himself, he shoved open the door to the infirmary, a newly expanded room off the lab. Grant, a salt-and-pepper-haired male who had been a microbiologist in his human life, looked up from where he stood at Jaggar's bedside. Nicole, a vampire physiologist and the closest thing they had to a medical doctor, had worked late into the night to repair Jag's broken tibia, and now the injured vampire was sitting up, his lower leg wrapped in bandages, his scowl more than hinting at his irritation at being immobile.

Next to him on a rolling equipment tray was an untouched sandwich and a half-empty pouch of human blood. Chances were, it was Jaggar himself who had stolen the blood off a delivery truck bound for a vampire slave supply shop in Seattle.

Grant hung a clipboard at the foot of Jag's bed. "Hey, chief. Your boy could use an attitude adjustment."

He gestured to Jaggar, who snarled. "Tell Dr. Horrible to let me recover in my own chamber." Jag shot Grant a nasty look. "He keeps trying to inject me with shit."

Hunter crossed to Grant, his nostrils stinging from the harsh chemicals Nicole insisted on using to keep the lab and the infirmary clean. Not that Hunter was going to complain. Nicole's obsession with cleanliness was far better than Grant's clutter and disorder, which bordered on chaos.

"Are you trying to give him antibiotics?"

Grant shook his head. "Most antibiotics don't work on us, something I discovered, quite tragically, a few years ago." Clearing his throat, he jammed his hands into his lab coat's pockets and pulled out a couple of syringes. "I want to test the effects of colloidal silver on broken bones. Analysis indicates that silver might make our bones heal faster and stronger."

"Fuck that." Jaggar ran his hand over his short-cropped brown hair with an angry jerk. "I'm not going to be the guy who gets turned into the Hulk because of a lab accident."

"Please," Grant drawled. "If anything, you'd end up like Wolverine. That would be cool. Stop whining."

"That *would* be cool," Hunter agreed. Jaggar muttered something under his breath and reached for his bag of blood. "What does Nicole say about your experimental treatment?"

Grant shrugged. "She doesn't think the healing process will hurt." He thought about that for a second. "Well, not for long. The injections are likely to be excruciating. I'd never try it on myself. That's why I need volunteers."

Jaggar cursed and then threw down with one of Myne's favorite Nez Perce insults, calling Grant a crazy sack of elk balls.

"Yeah?" Grant grabbed his crotch through his khakis. "You can suck on my crazy sack of—"

The lab door slammed open hard enough to put a dent in the wall behind it. Myne burst into the room and zeroed in on Hunter. His dark eyes glinted as fiercely as his titanium fangs, and Hunter went on instant alert. By mutual unspoken agreement, Myne never dealt directly with Hunter if it wasn't important.

"Humans are attacking ShadowSpawn's bridal party." Blood streaked Myne's cheeks and neck, but it wasn't his. Hunter picked out the stench of three different humans in the blood Myne was wearing like war paint. "They're fucking everywhere. Takis and I took out a few, but we couldn't help Rasha and her sister."

Rasha had brought Aylin? Hunter had never seen

Rasha's twin, who was rumored to be hideously deformed. But Aylin had helped Riker and Nicole when they'd been held captive by ShadowSpawn, so Hunter didn't care if she was a pox-ridden troll. MoonBound would get her back along with Rasha.

"Let's go." Hunter started toward the door, but Riker jogged inside, the thick layers of bandages from last night's bullet wound visible beneath his black T-shirt.

"Stay here!" Riker barked from near the doorway. "We'll handle it."

"The hell you will," Hunter growled as he pushed past both Myne and Riker. "This is my future mate the humans are fucking with."

Riker caught up with him at the door to the clan's armory. "It's too dangerous."

Hunter cast his second in command a pointed glance as he ripped weapons from their racks, the clang of metal against metal jacking him up even more. "Would it be too dangerous for you if it was *your* mate who had been captured by humans?"

It was a low blow, given that Riker had lost his first mate to humans who had captured and forced her into slavery decades ago, but Hunter wasn't above reminding him how desperate the situation could be.

"Screw you, Hunt." Riker loaded himself with even more weapons than he already had, shoving dozens of blades into sheaths all over his body. "This is different. I'm not a clan leader, and you aren't imprinted on Rasha. This is hardly a love match."

No, it wasn't. If anything, it was about two enemies with nothing in common sharing a bed while pistols were pointed at their heads, the irony being that vampires couldn't even fire guns without being disfigured by the gunshot residue. Still, Rasha was to be his mate, and no one fucked with what belonged to Hunter.

"I'm going," Hunter said in the *I'm the chief* tone that shut down all arguments.

Riker unloaded a litany of curses but then kept his mouth shut as they finished weaponing up and jogged through the warren, raising the alarm and rousing the fighters. It took mere minutes to pull together a lead party of six. Myne would follow within ten with a larger second team.

Once Hunter and his boys hit the cold outside air, they put on their vampire speed and raced toward the scene of the ambush. What would take humans days to reach took them only hours, but they were still too late. The bloodied battlefield was empty of even the dead.

Which meant that either ShadowSpawn had cleaned up . . . or the humans had. As he tracked the battle, studying footprints and blood, an icy knot formed in Hunter's chest. The humans had outnumbered ShadowSpawn's team, and while most of the blood belonged to the humans, it was ultimately they who had carried the vampires away . . . dead or unconscious.

If Rasha and Aylin were dead, they'd right now be getting butchered for parts to sell on the black market. If they were alive, they were suffering at the mercy of barbarians who would use them for sport until it was time to sell them into either the legal or the illegal slave trade.

"Split up," he called out. "Find Rasha and her sister. We're looking at a couple of dozen male humans, so don't engage until Myne gets here with backup." He bared his fangs in anticipation. "And then they're all yours."

Riker flanked Hunter as they followed tracks and blood trails. The humans hadn't even tried to conceal their movements, at one point even dragging one of the ShadowSpawn males along behind them. Hunter paused now and then to scent the air, and when he finally caught the unmistakable fragrance of an injured female, he growled. She was bleeding badly, and he was going to make every human he found pay for that.

"Shit." Riker sprinted ahead, halting at the top of a ridge that looked down on a thickly wooded river valley. Smoke spiraled up from the trees, and raunchy laughter came with it. "Their camp is down there. Isn't that Yakima Indian land?"

"Yep." And didn't that just figure?

Native American reservations were off-limits to vampires. Didn't matter that Hunter was full-blooded Cherokee. Ever since scientists had discovered that the virus that caused vampirism had originated in Native American tribes, the Native Americans had been trying to distance themselves from vampires and shed the negative stigma. Now vampires were killed on sight on Native American land.

The human poachers were well aware of that fact and had no qualms about taking advantage.

Too fucking bad.

Using dense brush and thick tree trunks as cover, Hunter and Riker crept to the very edges of the surprisingly organized camp. A hound tied to a stake leaped to its feet, but Riker stared the animal down, and the dog, falling victim to Riker's ability to hypnotize, settled on its haunches and panted quietly.

From behind, Hunter heard Myne's whispered voice, and a moment later, he joined them with Baddon and Takis. "I've got three warriors closing in from the west," Myne said softly. "Aiden, Tena, and Harleigh will come in behind us."

Riker gestured across the way to four positions where the warriors who had accompanied Hunter and Riker were waiting for the *go* signal.

Hunter peered down at the camp, the odors drifting from it indicating the presence of at least twenty human males and five vampires, two of whom were female. The three males were hanging upside down from tree branches as their blood drained from gashes in their throats. Nearby, several human males were guzzling beer and telling jokes as they sharpened their butcher knives.

Rage turned Hunter's vision crimson. As much as he despised every ShadowSpawn clan member in existence, he hated the humans more. No vampire, Shadow-Spawn or not, should be treated like a side of beef.

"Hunt," Riker whispered. "We're outnumbered. I strongly suggest you hang back."

Outnumbered and outgunned. The humans definitely had the advantage here. Oh, his warriors would take down the humans, but the hunters were heavily armed with weapons that were extremely lethal to vampires. The potential for one of them to be injured or killed was real. And there was no way Hunter was sending his warriors into battle without him.

He was about to tell Riker as much when a burly human emerged from under a shelter of camo netting, his meaty fist clamped on the back of a blond female's neck. Her wrists were bound with duct tape, and blood seeped from a nasty wound in her right leg, but she held her head high as the poacher shoved her, limping and stumbling, toward an iron cage large enough to hold a bear.

"Release me!" she snapped. "Do you know who I am?"

"Bitch, I don't care who you are." The man backhanded her, sending her reeling into a tree. Blood sprayed from her nose, and Hunter's rage turned as cold as the knot in his chest.

Snarling, the female swung her bound arms around and managed to punch both fists into the guy's beer-swollen belly. The man *oof*ed and gripped her neck hard enough to make her wince.

"My father is the most powerful clan chief on the West Coast," she said, and although she sounded calm, there was a slight tremor in her voice. Fear wasn't something he'd expect from Rasha, an experienced warrior and ice-cold killer . . . so was that Aylin? "He'll pay you three times what you'd get for me on the underground market."

The human stopped, shifting her around so she could see the bodies of her male companions. "Is that so?"

"Yes." She swallowed sickly and averted her eyes as the men with butcher knives began their gruesome task. "If you send Aylin with a message, he'll bring payment. I promise. As his heir, I'm worth a lot to him."

So that *was* Rasha. Which meant she was worth far

more to Hunter than she was to her father. Rasha was going to bring peace to his clan, and these human scum weren't going to get in the way.

The man leered at her. "Your daddy won't want you back after we're done with you." He pawed at her ass with his free hand, and Hunter decided it was time to make that cockroach stop breathing.

"Come on, boys," Hunter whispered. "Time for poacher blood to flow." Fisting his favorite bone-handle knife from the sheath around his neck, he tore through the underbrush, his sights fixed on the son of a bitch dragging Rasha toward the cage.

He hit the poacher with a punch to the throat, as all around him his warriors took down several more humans with their surprise attack. Hunter's poacher crumpled to the ground, his windpipe crushed beyond repair. Hunter wished he could have made the guy suffer more, but with humans swarming out from their tents, Hunter would have to be satisfied that the asshole was going to spend a couple of minutes suffocating slowly.

Rasha braced herself against a tree, her injured leg barely holding her upright. Quickly, Hunter slashed the tape around her wrists.

"Are you okay—"

"Shit!" Riker's shout came from behind Hunter. "Humans coming from all around. There's too many."

Hunter launched his blade at a poacher who was taking aim at Katina with a rifle. The knife punched through the guy's temple, dropping him like a brick.

He grabbed Rasha's arm and spun her around to him. "Where's your sister?"

Rasha blinked at him as if she didn't understand the question. Had the humans drugged her or whacked her over the head? Dammit, he didn't have time for this. Shouts and gunfire came from all directions, and Hunter barely avoided being brained by a tire iron that came out of nowhere.

He dragged Rasha behind a tree. "Answer me," he snapped. "Where's your sister?"

"The . . . the far tent, I think," she finally blurted.

"Rike!" Hunter gestured accordingly. "Grab the female and get out."

"Roger." Riker clapped him on the shoulder. "Good hunting."

As much as Hunter hated to leave his warriors behind, Rasha was the priority right now. If anything happened to her, ShadowSpawn would blame Moon-Bound, and the war Hunter had tried so hard to prevent would destroy his clan. He wasn't going to let anything jeopardize the mating that had to take place. Taking Rasha's hand and ducking low, he led her away from the camp.

Luck was on their side, and they managed to slip past the humans, but Rasha's injured leg made her clumsy and slow, and worse, it made her noisy. Charging bears made less of a racket.

Using a blackberry thicket as cover, he drew her to a stop. Her long hair was a tangled mess, completely the opposite of how he'd seen it in the past, when she'd pulled it back in such a severe ponytail that he figured she should be bald. He also didn't remember her being so . . . pretty.

Or so pale.

"Hey." He waved his hand in front of her face, but her glazed eyes didn't track. "You okay?"

"I think . . ." She swallowed sickly, and sweat beaded on her forehead. "I'm bleeding again."

Even as she said it, the scent of blood flooded his nostrils, and his gut sank when he saw a heavy stream running down her leg. She was in shock, wasn't going to last long, and between the humans crawling around the forest like locusts and the new snowstorm he felt coming, he knew they weren't going to make it back to headquarters this way.

Quickly, he gripped her shoulders and braced her against the nearest tree. The thuds of running footsteps and crunching snow in the distance made his heart race in an urgent rhythm as he held her steady.

"I'm going to stop the bleeding. Hold still."

He didn't wait for permission. He dropped to his knees and ripped the torn fabric of her jeans away from the injured area. The laceration looked like it had been made by a blade, but some sort of impact had torn the flesh and widened the gash. Oddly, the wound wasn't deep, so why was she bleeding so badly?

A distant shout made her blood loss a question for later.

His fangs elongated, and his mouth watered as he leaned in and swiped his tongue along the ragged seam of the cut, and instant, hot pleasure jolted every nerve ending. Didn't matter that they were in a critical situation and that Rasha wasn't exactly in the mood for a male's mouth on her flesh; she was a born vampire, and the purity of her blood was a powerful drug like no other.

She gasped softly, her leg trembling under his palms. He sensed her surprise and anxiety, but she didn't protest.

He suppressed a moan as he dragged his tongue over the laceration again. His body sang with energy, and okay, he supposed that feeding from her was going to be the one good thing to come out of their mating. Nothing compared to the decadence of a born female's blood, but, like born males, they were nearly as rare as albino deer.

He risked taking time for one more healing lick, and then, with her sweet, smoky taste swirling in his mouth, he popped to his feet.

"Do you think you can run?"

She just stared at him, her gold-spoked blue eyes wide.

"Hello?" He waved his hand in front of her face. "Can you run?"

"Y-yes." She took a single step—and passed out.

"Son of a—"

He caught her before she hit the ground, threw her over his shoulder, and asked the Great Spirit above for a safe journey. They had a long way to go and no guarantees that they'd get there.

A YLIN WOKE TO the sensation of cool water caressing her forehead. She opened her eyes and nearly screamed at the sight of the huge vampire hovering over her, but a heartbeat later, she recognized the strikingly handsome face of the MoonBound male who had rescued her from the humans.

His sculpted, rugged features, combined with skin the color of rich sandstone, announced his Native American heritage, and he radiated a deadly aura even though she didn't see a weapon on him. Well, those massive fangs were weapons, and from a feminine standpoint, so was his tongue.

That tongue had soothed the cut on her thigh.

An intense, heated shiver went through her at the memory. She'd been woozy and nauseated from blood loss and pain, and yet when his warm tongue had stroked her skin, he'd simultaneously eased her hurt and awakened something sinful inside her. She'd been both afraid and fascinated, and for a moment, she hadn't cared about her future or her past. Hadn't even cared about the present, where humans were hunting them. All that had mattered was the fact that for the first time ever, a male had tasted her blood.

What had Riker called him? Roland? She frowned. That didn't sound right.

Roger, Riker had said, clapping him on the shoulder. *Good hunting.*

Okay, so . . . Roger wasn't much better. Strange name for a born vampire with Native American heritage.

"Hey," he said gruffly. "I was starting to worry. You've been out for hours."

Hours? It had been *hours* since they'd fled from the humans? She sat up with a start and nearly whacked her head on the wooden frame of the bunk bed above her. Where were they, anyway? Where was Rasha?

"My sister—"

"She's fine." Roger's deep voice rumbled through her in a wave of pure pleasure as he held up his cell phone. A text message from someone named Takis flashed on the screen.

Female is safe. Recovered their belongings as well. We lost George, but we got the heart of the fucker who killed him. We're holed up in the caves for now. Stay where you are until the storm passes.

"Thank you. For both of us." Relieved that Rasha was safe, she released the tense breath she'd been holding. "I'm sorry about George."

Roger snorted. "Are you? Your clan nearly tortured him to death fifteen years ago. We had to trade a month's worth of packaged blood to get him back, and his jaw never did heal right."

She remembered that now. His pain had been

the dinner entertainment for weeks, and she'd had nightmares for months. Since there was no good way to reply to what Roger said, she changed the subject. Fast. "Where are we?"

He lounged back on the mattress, propping his shoulder against a wooden bunk support post. "One of MoonBound's hunting cabins."

To keep from looking at him and the way one long leg was cocked up with his booted foot on the bed frame and the other was stretched out to the floor, she checked out the cozy one-room building.

Sparsely decorated, it contained the log-frame bunk bed she was currently in, a beat-up futon, an icebox, a wood stove, and, on the walls, dozens of weapons that ranged from bows and arrows to hatchets and daggers.

She smoothed her hand over the fur bedcover. "Aren't you concerned about humans finding it?"

"The cabins are warded to repel humans, but that's mostly a paranoid precaution. This is private property."

She eyed him warily. Was he trying to trick her? "Vampires can't own property."

"No," he said bitterly, "because to humans, we *are* property." He shifted, cocking his knee up even more, revealing a tantalizing bulge between his legs. Aylin, who always felt cold, began to sweat. "We own land under the name of a dummy corporation. It's where we store our vehicles and meet with our human courier."

"Human . . . *courier?*"

He nodded. "He brings us things we can't get ourselves and sets up services like cell-phone accounts."

Completely floored, she just stared. "So you have

vehicles and a human servant?" She'd heard of such things, but as followers of the Raven way of life, Shadow-Spawn didn't believe in most human conveniences, and they certainly wouldn't *work* with humans.

"Our human agent comes from a family that has been helping us for centuries, since before humans even learned of our existence."

"Oh." Interesting. And practical. Her father scorned vampires who relied on humans for anything but blood, but Aylin figured that staying current with the ways of the people who outnumbered vampires so badly was smart. She'd even said as much once.

Once.

She could still feel the sting of her father's back-handed blow for that error in judgment.

Roger's hand bumped the bandage he must have wrapped around her thigh while she slept, and she nearly jumped out of her skin. Males never touched her. Especially not her leg. Even an accidental touch got extreme reactions, as if her birth defect was contagious. But this was the second time he'd put his hands on her, and he'd done it without freaking out.

"Sorry," he said, pulling his hand back. "Does it hurt?"

"No," she lied. Oh, the wound itself felt fine, and thanks to Roger, it was probably nearly healed by now. But a deep ache had settled into her bones. Winter storms always affected her leg like that. On the coldest days, she sometimes couldn't even walk. Since clan law stated that anyone unable to make it on his or her own to the dinner table couldn't eat, she would have starved if Rasha hadn't smuggled food to her bedchamber.

He gestured to her leg. "It bled a lot for such a shallow wound. You remember Nicole? Our female your clan threatened to hold prisoner? When we get back to MoonBound, I want her to take a look at it."

Yeah, she wasn't real proud of how her clan had treated the female, but she doubted that apologizing would do any good. "That's not necessary. I'm fine."

"It's not a request."

Anger flared, bright and hot. She was used to having no freedom of choice at ShadowSpawn, but immediately after Rasha mated with Hunter, Aylin was going to become a prisoner in a harem. Which meant that for the next month, she wasn't going to put up with being ordered around. "Look," she said firmly, "I'm grateful for all you did to rescue us. But that doesn't give you the right to make decisions for me. MoonBound isn't my clan."

Roger's black eyes went utterly flat. "So that's how this is going to go? Life at MoonBound is going to suck for you if keep the ShadowSpawn princess attitude."

ShadowSpawn princess? She barely contained hysterical laughter. Instead, she clapped her hand over her abdomen as a hungry rumble rose up.

Roger lost a little of his angry edge and glanced at her belly. "We keep emergency food supplies here. I have hot water on the stove . . . I think we have soup packets and hot cocoa, too." He shoved to his feet and popped the lid off a chest at the foot of the bed. "And we have enough alcohol to start our own vampire nightclub."

Unaccustomed to such attention, Aylin could

only shake her head, even though her stomach was growling.

He swiped a bottle of whiskey from the chest and twisted off the top. "Are our emergency supplies not up to ShadowSpawn princess standards?"

"Yes," she said dryly. "That's exactly the problem. No caviar and champagne."

"Maybe you should feed." He took a massive swig from the bottle, and she couldn't look away from the play of his throat muscles as he swallowed. "You lost a lot of blood. It'll help you heal."

Her fangs punched down, and her mouth watered madly. No one had ever offered his blood to her. Hell, at moon-fever time, the males drew straws to see who *had* to feed her. Short straw was the loser, the person who had to offer his wrist. It was humiliating. She'd always dreaded that one day a month during the new moon when the thirst for male vampire blood became an urgent and life-sustaining requirement.

And on the night of the full moon, when males must feed from a female vampire, Aylin never had to participate. ShadowSpawn males would sooner starve than stick their fangs in her flesh.

Drinking cripple blood is bad luck.

The Great Raven cursed her in the womb. Those who feed from her will suffer the same curse.

You shouldn't touch her blood, let alone drink it.

Yep, she'd heard it all.

"I . . . ah . . . I'm fine." Determined to prove her point, she swung her legs off the bed and stood. So far, so good. But when she took her first step, her right foot caught the edge of an uneven floorboard, and her leg, already compromised by the cold and the injury, buckled.

Arms came around her, and in a dizzying flash of speed, Roger plopped her down onto the futon and kneeled on the floor in front of her. Damn, he was gorgeous. He was beautifully male, built of lean muscle and sturdy bones, a perfect blend of sleek athlete and powerful warrior.

And his hair . . . good Lord, she'd never seen hair so black and glossy; in the weak light from the corner lamp, it shone blue. His eyes were nearly as dark, but what they shone with was anger.

"You aren't fine, and you're an idiot if you let pride keep you from accepting help."

It wasn't pride, but she wasn't about to tell a complete stranger that she didn't know how to handle his overtures. Usually, if she was the focus of attention, it was the negative kind. "I'm not an idiot."

"You're a warrior," he said gruffly, "and in my clan, any warrior who refuses help when they need it takes a month of kitchen duty and skips a moon feeding. Because they were idiots."

He thought she was a warrior? Clearly, Roger hadn't heard that Aylin was a curse on her family and the shame of ShadowSpawn. And kitchen duty as punishment? *Pfft.* Slaving in the kitchen was her full-time *job.* Punishment at ShadowSpawn was swift and brutal, and she couldn't remember a single year that hadn't seen at least one execution. "I said—"

"Yeah, yeah," he drawled. "You said you aren't an idiot. Prove it." He tilted his head to the side, exposing his vein. "Feed."

Every cell in her body quivered with excitement at the prospect of nourishment and healing. "Fine," she said wearily. "Give me your wrist."

One ebony eyebrow shot up. "I don't do wrists."

He cupped the back of her neck with his big, warm hand, and pleasant tingles spread across her skin as he gently but firmly drew her head toward him. His gaze held her in place even more effectively than his grip, and she swore she even saw a glint of anticipation in his espresso eyes.

"Take it." His voice was soft, but there was a guttural undertone in it that made her shiver with feminine appreciation.

Her heart pounded, and her pulse raced as she got closer. She thought about fighting him . . . but it dawned on her that there really was no reason to do that. Just pride, as he'd said. And the truth was that she was hungry, not just for blood but to know the feel of a male's hard body against hers, even if it was only because she was drinking from him.

Leaning in, she tentatively gripped his shoulders to steady herself. He slid his hand up, tangling his fist in her hair as she put her lips against his smooth skin. Her fangs tingled, and when she opened her mouth over his vein, they throbbed to the beat of his pulse.

She was really going to do this, wasn't she? For the first time in her life, she was going to feed the way vampires were meant to. She'd waited so long for this, hadn't been sure it would ever happen. Not when every male she'd ever fed from had literally kept her at arm's length.

Suddenly, she jerked back. "Why?" she rasped.

"Why are you doing this? I'm your enemy. And I'm . . . cursed."

"Cursed?" He smiled tightly. "We'll share curse stories when we get back to MoonBound. As for the rest? We might be enemies, but now I'm responsible for you. You need to be at full strength for our trip to headquarters after the storm lets up." He urged her mouth down to his throat again. "I won't let my clan down."

Aylin wondered if any of the males at Shadow-Spawn would say something like that, about not letting the clan down. Then she realized she didn't care. Not when the biggest, most handsome male she'd ever seen was holding her against him, urging her to sink her fangs into his vein.

She didn't need any more urging. This was her moment. Closing her eyes, she tapped her tongue on the roof of her mouth behind each fang, releasing a chemical that numbed the pain of the bite and intensified the pleasure. The tips of her fangs punched through his skin, and he hissed. His hiss trailed into a groan that mingled with hers as his essence flowed over her tongue.

Great Spirit above, she'd never tasted anything like this. He was smoky and rich and electric, as if power flowed in his veins instead of blood. A jolt of pure energy sang through her, making her body buzz to vibrant life. Her skin prickled, her breasts ached, and between her legs, wetness bloomed.

Closer. She had to get closer to him.

Moaning, she dug her nails into his shoulders and tightened her thighs around his waist. He stiffened, and for a split second, she thought he'd pull away.

She dug her nails in harder. No way. She might not be a warrior, but she could still plunder. She was a female who had been let off her chain for the first time in her life, and she was going to take everything she could in the short time she had.

Everything.

6

Damn, but this female was not what Hunter had expected. He'd seen Rasha a couple of times, had also been on the receiving end of her sharp tongue. He'd hated her instantly, and the feeling had been mutual, so when he'd grabbed her at the humans' camp and brought her to the cabin, he'd expected her to fight him about everything. Hell, he'd expected her to wake up swinging. He'd figured he'd have to watch his back for months. Maybe years.

Instead, so far, she'd been almost . . . pleasant.

It had to be a trick.

Or maybe now that she was away from her clan, and her father, she was a different person.

Hunter understood that more than he'd like to. His relationship with his own parents had been rocky at best, filled with hate at worst.

She arched her back, driving her pelvis into his, and suddenly, he didn't care if it was a trick or not. He'd have been happy never to have sex with her, but hey, if she wanted to start this relationship now, he could deal. Fucking was fucking, and clan business was clan business. He'd been prepared to separate the two for the rest of his life with Rasha, but maybe, just maybe, they wouldn't have to live like two angry cats in a cage.

The caress of her mouth as she sucked on his neck felt connected to his cock, and behind the fly of his jeans, he got rock-hard. The scent of her arousal, sweet and musky, rose all around him, ramping up his desire to toss her onto the futon and drive into her until they heated up the tiny cabin with the fury of their lust.

With one hand still tangled in her silky hair, he dropped his other to her butt and hauled her more tightly against him. His erection met her core as he lifted them both onto the futon, being careful not to jostle her mouth away from his throat. He wanted her to take as much as she could, as much as she needed, and nothing was better than sex during feeding. When two vampires were connected that way, it was a closed circuit that delivered full-body orgasms like nothing else.

"Keep feeding," he whispered.

She moaned in response and shifted her body so they were stretched out on the hard mattress, him on top of her, rocking his sex against hers to the rhythm of her pulls on his vein. Heat roared through him, searing him from the inside out, and when she dug her nails into his shoulders, he growled in approval.

She was being much gentler than he thought she'd be. Rasha had always struck him as the sex-is-a-battle type of vampire, a female who would never give any male an inch of advantage, even in bed.

Especially in bed.

Cradling her head against his throat, he smoothed his hand up to her slim waist and over her rib cage. Her warmth radiated through her T-shirt, and her desire radiated from her entire body as he swept his thumb across the swell of her breast.

She gasped, breaking the seal on his throat, and a wet rivulet flowed down his skin. Her tongue flicked out to catch the stream, licking upward in a lazy, sensual stroke. When she reached the puncture from her bite, she latched on again, drawing like she was starving. He shouted at the ecstasy of it and thrust against her as though he was already inside her.

"Keep doing that." His voice was a guttural rasp he could barely hear over the sound of his pulse drumming in his ears. "Harder. Suck me harder."

A petite snarl rose in her throat, and if he thought he'd been hard before, now he went painfully rod-stiff. His balls joined the party, throbbing and aching inside the prison of his denim pants.

"That's it, Rasha." He closed his palm over her breast. "Fuck, yeah, just . . . like . . . that."

She went taut. Her lips quivered against his throat, and then suddenly, she was wedging her hands between their bodies and shoving against him. "Get off me."

Baffled, his brain clouded by lust, he blinked. "What?"

"Get off me!" she shouted.

Whoa, what had triggered her psycho switch? He reared back onto his knees, and she scrambled out from under him until she was backed against the log wall. Panic and fear and . . . hurt? . . . turned the blue of her eyes murky.

"What's the matter? Did I hurt you?" He reached

for her, but she rolled off the futon and landed awkwardly on her feet.

Her hair was as wild as the feral look in her eyes as she stood there, panting and staring at him as if he were a grizzly bear and not the male who had saved her life and would soon be her mate.

"Dammit, say something." He stood, and his sudden movement sent her scooting sideways toward the bed, as far away from him as she could get. Her limp made him curse inwardly. He *had* hurt her. He was such an asshole. "You're still in pain. With the feeding, I figured your wound would have been mostly healed by now."

"It's not the wound." She swallowed hard, and he abruptly got a very bad feeling. "It's me."

The bad feeling widened into a cold, dark, gaping cavern, and his temper, fueled by unquenched lust, jumped in to fill the void. "Explain!" he barked. "What's wrong with you?"

"What's wrong with me?" She made a harsh sound that was somewhere between a laugh and a sob. "It's the same thing that's *always* been wrong. I'm not Rasha. I'm Aylin." She jabbed her finger into her sternum. "You've been making out with the wrong twin."

AYLIN COULDN'T REMEMBER the last time she'd been so humiliated. She couldn't remember the last time she'd been so *stupid*.

She'd always prided herself on the fact that out of everyone in the clan, she was the most educated. Most of the other clan members, even those who had been born human, were too old to have benefited from modern education. But even those few who had gotten a decent education didn't have a chance to keep their minds sharp. Her father didn't permit anything but the most basic literature to be brought into the clan.

Aylin alone had been allowed to have books, and that was only because her father couldn't read English beyond an elementary-school level and wanted Aylin to be useful. But when she'd started questioning his decisions, the clan's dependence on the Raven way of life, and the world around them, he'd suddenly forbidden her to read.

Rasha had smuggled books to her every time she went to a human settlement. It had always been worth the beatings when she got caught with a book, whether it was a dime-store Western or a college text about physics. Aylin might not have been able to understand everything between the covers of the technical books, but she read every word. Ultimately, just flipping through them gave her pleasure.

So no, she'd never considered herself to be stupid.

Until now.

She'd just been so happy to find a male who wasn't completely repulsed by her. She'd been so thrilled, in fact, that she was prepared to take things as far as Roger would go. Especially because if she lost her virginity, there was a chance—a slight one, but a chance nonetheless—that her mating with the chief from NightShade would be called off.

"Aylin?" Roger stared at her, obviously horrified. "You're *Aylin?*"

Then his horror and surprise veered sharply to anger, and in a move so fast she could barely track it, let alone prepare for it, he had her by the throat and backed against the wall.

"What game is this? A ShadowSpawn plot to derail the mating? Or is this some twisted twin prank?" He squeezed so hard she coughed, and then he let up, allowing her a huge gulp of sweet, fresh air. "Answer me."

"How dare you," she ground out. "How dare you accuse *me* of being deceptive. I thought you knew who I was. But you . . ." She sneered. "You believed I was Rasha. So what game are *you* playing? Either you're disloyal to your clan and are willing to bed the female who is going to be Hunter's mate, or Hunter wanted you to screw her so he could call off the mating and save face. So which is it, Roger? Were you risking death by betraying your leader with his future mate, or are you following the orders of a coward with no honor?"

"Coward? No honor?" He released her and stepped back, his expression a deadly mask of cold rage. "Maybe there's another explanation."

"Such as?"

"Such as the fact that I thought you were Rasha . . . and I'm *Hunter*."

Oh.

Oh, shit.

"But I heard . . ." She trailed off, her argument unformed and unimportant at this point.

She'd just done something she'd never done before, and she'd done it with the one male on the planet she shouldn't have done it with. The male who would, in a few short weeks, belong to her sister.

It didn't matter that it was to be a mating of convenience and that Rasha didn't even like Hunter. Hell, Aylin had overheard Rasha and their father planning for the future of MoonBound after Hunter's death— and it hadn't sounded like they were thinking *far* into the future.

No, none of that mattered. Rasha might not even care about the fact that Aylin damn near screwed her mate-to-be, but their father . . . if he ever found out, he'd kill her. Literally. Without Rasha around to moderate his punishments, he could very well end her.

"I'm sorry," she said. "I didn't know. I thought your name was Roger."

He scowled, and it wasn't fair that he was handsome doing even that. "Why the hell would you think that?"

He made it sound like she'd pulled the name out of thin air. "I heard Riker call you Roger," she said, a little irritably.

"Not Roger. *Roger*. As in, affirmative." Hunter dragged his hand over his face. "He was giving me a positive response to my order."

Well, sure, it all made sense *now*. Now that they were away from her human captors and she was no longer afraid for her life.

Hunter shifted his stance, and Aylin made the mistake of dropping her gaze. It was impossible to miss the impressive bulge behind the fly of his jeans. Part of her wanted to groan with embarrassment. But a larger part of her wanted to puff up with pride for being the one to put it there.

"Why did you tell that human scumbag that your name was Rasha?"

Ah, so *that* was why he'd thought she was her twin. "I hoped that if he thought I was valuable enough, he'd let my sister go to arrange a ransom payment."

"And then your father would come and rescue you."

"Exactly." Although, to be honest, she wasn't sure Kars would have done that. If he had, it wouldn't be to rescue his precious daughter. It would be for the opportunity to butcher humans and to punish the people who took something of his. Even if that something was Aylin.

"Is that why you were traveling with Rasha? To act as a decoy?"

Yes. But she wasn't going to tell him that. Who wanted to admit to being disposable? "I'm attending her until your official mating ceremony."

"Fuck." Hunter swiped the open bottle of whiskey from the table where he'd left it. He drained fully a quarter of the deep amber liquid before finally lowering it from those full, sensual lips. He held it out to her. "Want some?"

With the electric effects of his blood coursing through her system, she didn't need the alcohol. But she snatched the bottle anyway and took a sip.

Big mistake.

She might as well have been swallowing kerosene. She coughed and wheezed, her eyes watering madly.

"Not used to drinking, huh?" He took the bottle from her.

"What was your first clue?" she rasped. "The choking or the crying?"

He laughed, a deep, masculine sound that vibrated the air and her blood. "The whiskey face. Best one ever."

"I'm not used to whiskey," she said. "At Shadow-Spawn, everyone drinks hollywine." Everyone but her, anyway. She had so little control over her life as it was; she didn't need to give up more by drowning her senses in alcohol.

Hunter's laugh died away. "Hollywine?" He shook his head. "That shit is bad news."

Yes, it was. Made from holly berries that were toxic to humans, hollywine hit vampires fast and hard, and while it had the effect of delivering a massive dose of euphoria and enhancing sexual appetites and performance, it made some vampires rage out. She was pretty sure the liquor was also responsible for making a few of their clan members insane.

"So MoonBound doesn't make it?"

"Hell, no." He swigged from the bottle, and she wondered if he realized the irony of scorning one type of alcohol while scarfing another. "You need to stay away from it."

She crossed her arms over her chest. "And there we go again with you ordering me around."

His gaze dropped and flicked back up to her eyes, but she could have sworn he'd been looking at her breasts. And dammit, the very thought made them ache all over again. "Nothing's changed," he said gruffly. "You might not be Rasha, but I'm still responsible for you while you're a guest of my clan."

"Yes, well, since you already said your clan doesn't serve hollywine, it's pointless to order me not to drink it, isn't it?" She cocked an eyebrow. "Unless you think your order will stand after I leave. Which is pretty arrogant."

He narrowed his eyes at her, and she wondered if she'd just pushed him too far. "I don't care what you do after you leave. But while you're with my clan, you do as we do."

She sank down onto the futon again, hoping to ease the throbbing in her leg. "And what is it that you do?"

One shoulder rolled in an easy shrug. "We hunt, feed, train, play . . . we do what everyone does."

"Play" was what ShadowSpawn members did with their food. "I don't like to play."

Hunter frowned, the dim light putting deep shadows in the hard-cut planes of his face. "How can you not like to play?"

She shrugged. "I just don't." Best not to explain that she didn't like to see anyone or anything suffer. Not even humans. Too many years of being at the mercy of others had given her too much insight into how terrifying it was. She was a terrible vampire.

"Then you're doing it wrong." He pivoted around and opened a cabinet that held a small television and something called a Nintendo 5th Dimension. He tossed her a controller thingie. "Let's kick some classic Super Mario ass."

Video games? That was what he meant by playing? She couldn't help but laugh.

Oh, Rasha, you are really going to hate this male.

And didn't it figure that Aylin really liked him?

7

MYNE STRODE THROUGH the candlelit cavern with purpose, thinking that the only way there could be more tension in the cave was if they were sharing it with a bear. And actually, Myne would rather deal with a bear than with the ShadowSpawn wench.

Riker and Katina had laid out supplies from one of several stashes hidden throughout the system of tunnels that MoonBound had long ago appropriated for use during emergencies, and while a blizzard counted as a crisis of sorts, Myne figured it was nothing compared with the chaos that Hunter's mating with Rasha would bring. Myne wasn't sure if his ability to sense impending doom was a gift, a curse, or just his imagination, but he *was* sure that the pressure in his chest was a warning. Of what, he had no idea.

She was crouched down in the dirt at the rear of the cavern, pawing through a backpack. As always, the sight of her kicked off a Pavlovian response, and his mouth watered. He hated that about himself, that his body could betray him so blatantly.

"Hello, Rasha."

Standing, she smiled. At least, he was going to call the slight baring of her teeth a smile. "I was wondering when you'd acknowledge my presence."

"Had to happen eventually."

"And best not in front of Hunter, right?" She brought her hand up to her throat, where she trailed her finger along the pulsing vein in her neck. "How are you feeling, by the way? Coming up on month four without a moon feeding, aren't you?" She flicked a fingernail against her throat, and a drop of blood welled on her lightly tanned skin. "Moon-blood deprivation is setting in, isn't it? I'll bet you get cramps at night and your vision is starting to blur. You feel like your body is caving in on itself."

Spot-on. And holy shit, he wanted to lick that drop.

"Are you afraid yet? Afraid you'll be so crazed on the night of the full moon that you'll attack any female you see?"

As a matter of fact, yes, he was.

"You know why I called things off, don't you?" she asked.

"I'm guessing it's because you found out you were going to be mating Hunter?" At her nod, he hooked his thumbs into his jeans pockets. "I'm going to tell him about us."

She snorted. "Tell him what? That for years, every couple of months, we meet secretly on the night of the full moon? That you have . . . special needs that only I can fulfill?"

"That pretty much covers it."

Ice glazed over her eyes. "I don't think so."

"I didn't tell you to get your blessing," he said. "I told you because I at least owe you a heads-up."

She flipped her long blond hair over her shoulder with a brisk shove. "You owe me more than that."

"The hell I do," he growled. "You got as much out of our arrangement as I did."

"Yes, but I *wanted* what you gave me. You *needed* what I gave you."

So utterly expected of her to point that out. "And that's why I'm letting you know what I'm telling Hunter. I've done that. So have a nice life. I'm sure you two will be very miserable together." Deservedly so.

He started to turn, but Rasha sank her nails into his forearm and yanked him around with a hiss. "You will not tell him about us, or I'll tell everyone in your clan about your time as a slave for the humans."

"Nice try." He jerked out of her grip, leaving deep gouges in his skin from her sharp-ass nails. "But you don't know a damned thing." Turning his back on her, he started toward the front of the cave.

"Mr. Pritchard."

Myne froze. A hot load of adrenaline dumped into his veins, even as a chill swept over him. "What did you say?"

"You heard me."

He pivoted around slowly, afraid that if he moved too fast, he wouldn't be able to stop until Rasha was dead. "How do you know about Mr. . . . him?" The human who had given Myne his name.

You're mine, you fucking cur. That's your name from now on. Myne.

Rasha's gaze was unflinching, brimming with the

kind of confidence that came from knowing you'd won. "When I learned I was mating with Hunter, I made it my mission to find out everything I could about everyone in his inner circle."

"If that were true," he gritted out, "you'd know I'm not in his inner circle."

She gestured toward the front of the cave, where Aiden and Takis were laughing about something. "I know they're lovers, but Aiden sometimes wets his wick with a female. *Tsk-tsk.* Poor Takis." She pointed to Katina. "And I know she was kidnapped as a human child and raised by wealthy people who paid a lot of money for her. When she saw her face on a billboard, she ran away, but before she could go to the police, she was turned into a vampire." Rasha smiled. "Shall I tell you what I know about what they did to you inside that Daedalus lab? How they experimented on you? Removed one of your kidneys while you were still awake? Defanged you? Subjected you to humiliating research? Forced you to fuck—"

"Enough!" he barked. Everyone in the cave turned to stare. Lowering his voice, he ground out, "I get it. I won't say anything to Hunter. But don't you ever bring that shit up again, and if you use your ill-gotten information against anyone in the clan, I'll break your legs and leave you on Daedalus's doorstep so you can get some firsthand experience with what you think you know about me." He jabbed his finger into her breastbone. "Stay the fuck away from me."

The cavern felt suddenly devoid of oxygen. He practically ran out of the cave, and when he hit the outside ledge, he inhaled huge gulps of frosty air as snow and wind battered his face. He scooted to the side, where a crevice and an overhang sheltered a cove large enough for five. But he was alone, thank the spirits. Putting his back to the rock, he closed his eyes and concentrated on keeping his shit together.

Not a day went by without him thinking about his time as a human slave, but usually, it was in conjunction with memories of his brother. They'd both been captured and sent to Daedalus for the three T's, "testing, taming, and training," as Daedalus staff called it. Myne preferred the more accurate "tattoo, torment, and torture."

Myne and his brother, Cloud Walker, aka Subject 212NP, eventually escaped, but Cloud had been recaptured, and Myne had been wounded badly enough that he would have died if not for Riker.

So yeah, Myne's time in captivity was always with him, but Rasha had dug up shit he'd thought he'd buried a long time ago.

Footsteps put him on alert, but he relaxed when Riker ducked into the little cove with him. "Hey."

Myne acknowledged him with a nod. "You want to know what happened with Rasha."

"I'm guessing she didn't like the idea of you telling Hunter about your full-moon meetings?" Riker was the only person besides Rasha and Myne who knew, and that was only because he'd caught them.

"I'm not telling him. She isn't, either. So as long as you keep your mouth shut, we'll be fine."

Riker's eyes flashed. "As long as you never feed from her again, your secret is safe with me. But why the change of heart?"

"Blackmail," he growled. "She knows shit she shouldn't know. About my time in captivity. My kidney. My . . . fuck it. She just knows shit, okay?"

Rike's eyebrows climbed. "Your kidney?"

"Don't ask. But, buddy, watch your back, because she claims to have dirt on everyone."

"Know your enemy," Rike murmured. "She's a bitch, but she's not stupid. What can we do about your moon feedings now?"

We? An uneasy sensation wound its way through Myne at the way Rike had worded his question. The male was a friend, the best Myne had ever had, and the clan had become the best thing ever to happen to him.

Which meant that it couldn't be long before everything went to shit.

He looked out at the wall of snow beyond the cover. "I made arrangements for a female in the city."

"Have you had her before?"

Myne shook his head. The number of females who had let him feed more than once could be counted on one hand. "She thinks she's into pain."

What a joke. It took someone mentally twisted, with nerve damage, or both to be able to withstand the pain of Myne's titanium fangs.

The things had been great—at first. They'd punched through human flesh like nails through water. But then he'd discovered that the agony they caused vampires was nothing short of horrific. He'd tried to have them removed, but the titanium had fused to his bone, and the vampire-sympathizer dentist who installed them didn't know why they caused pain to others but not him. It wasn't until Nicole came along that he got his answer.

Turned out that vampires who had once been human were allergic to even the smallest exposure of their blood to titanium. About half of the born-vampire population also had a sensitivity to it. So Myne, in order to feed from a vampire female on the night of the full moon, had to find either an immune born female or a turned female who didn't mind a little *oh, my God, I'm going to die* agony. Unfortunately, few of either existed.

Rasha was one of the few. A chance encounter at a vampire club in the city had turned into years of meeting every two or three months on the night of the full moon. She wasn't immune to titanium's pain punch, but for her, it also carried an erotic blow, one so intense that she would have met him monthly if he'd asked. But screw that; the only reason he stomached being with her at all was that he liked not being dead.

"For what it's worth," Riker said, "I don't think Hunter would care about your past with Rasha."

"Oh, yeah," Myne muttered. "He would."

Rike knocked his head back against the rock wall. "Dammit, Myne, just tell me what the fuck went on between you two."

"It's between me and Hunter."

"You know you can trust me, right?"

He knew. He had opened his mouth to say as much when an angry scream, a shout, and a clatter broke through the snowstorm. Myne and Riker bolted into the cave, skidding to a halt as a pan lid sailed over their heads.

Rasha stood near the far wall, armed with the pot Riker assumed went with the lid. Aiden, Takis, and Katina were staring at her.

"What the fuck, bitch?" Katina yelled.

"I told you guys to stay out of my bags!" Rasha yelled back.

Aiden held up his hands in a *screw it* gesture and turned to Riker. "Chick is crazy. We weren't looking through her shit. She's delusional."

Myne just shook his head. He didn't like Hunter, but even *he* didn't deserve Rasha. He thought back almost two hundred years and changed his mind. Hunter deserved her.

Unfortunately, the clan didn't.

HUNTER AND AYLIN had played video games for two hours before she fell asleep, and Hunter wasn't ashamed to admit he was disappointed when she'd dozed off. He'd planned to use the game to lower her defenses and start earning her trust. As Rasha's sister and the daughter of ShadowSpawn's clan chief, she was potentially an invaluable source of intel. But he hadn't expected to enjoy her company.

After a few minutes of jaunty Super Mario music and gathering gold coins, he'd found himself drawn to her easy smiles. She'd learned quickly, and when he'd assured her she'd be able to play anytime she wanted while she was at MoonBound, she'd actually bounced in her seat.

But how much of that was an act? Nicole had credited Aylin with helping her to escape Shadow-Spawn's clutches, but even that could have been a setup. Nicole's jailbreak had kicked off a battle that ended only because Hunter agreed to mate Rasha, and Hunter had wondered, more than once, if the entire thing had been orchestrated by Kars to get

what he'd wanted for so long: influence inside Moon-
Bound.

So Hunter had played video games with Aylin,
using the time to lure her in and build a bond of sorts.
But now that the storm was over and they were tramp-
ing back to MoonBound through the snow, he figured
it was time to do a little prying. See how well his plan
to win her over was working. Any insight into Rasha's
and Kars's minds would be helpful.

Especially since he'd just gotten a text from Takis
that read: *We'll meet you outside headquarters. Hurry. I'm
ready to hand off Rasha to you. She's . . . something else.*

Something else? Hunter texted back.

Yeah. Something else besides civil.

Hunter cursed silently. He couldn't believe he'd
actually let himself think Aylin was Rasha. Maybe
deep inside, he'd been hoping. Because Aylin . . . she
intrigued him. She was an impossible combination of
wary *and* unguarded, as if she didn't trust others but
wanted them to trust her. Her spirit seemed desperate to burst from her with an explosion of energy, but
something was holding it back. She reminded him of a
bird with clipped wings or a wolf on a chain, wanting to
be free but unable to make it happen.

Of course, it could all be an act. Her father had
once hamstrung one of his own young warriors, a male
not even fully grown, and sent him to beg MoonBound
for sanctuary. Hunter had taken the youth in, and the
clan had nursed him back to health, only to have him
poison their water supply.

Seven clan members had died, and now, forty years
later, three still suffered from the effects of the poi-

son. The kid escaped before MoonBound could catch him, but he'd fared no better when he arrived back at ShadowSpawn. Kars had reportedly wasted no time in slaying the male, whose injury had left him unable to hunt or fight.

No, Hunter wasn't prepared to trust any Shadow-Spawn member, and that included Aylin.

"I really need you to see Nicole when we get to MoonBound," he said to her. "You're still limping."

They trudged through the snow more slowly than he'd have liked, given that the woods were full of humans, but clearly, her injury was still bothering her.

She'd been following in his tracks, but now she eased up next to him, her face partially covered by the hood of the jacket he'd scrounged from the cabin's supply closet. He barely felt the cold, but she'd been shivering since she woke up.

"It's not the wound," she said. "I mean, the wound took longer to heal than it would for most of us, but I've always been a bleeder." Her cheeks flushed, and he wondered if it was from the cold or the subject. "The limp is something I've had my whole life. I was born with a twisted thigh bone."

"A twisted thigh bone?" He laughed, and Aylin stopped dead in the snow.

"You think that's funny?"

"Hardly. I'm laughing at the rumors about you."

She stiffened. "And what have the rumors said?"

"That you're a hideous, deformed hunchback."

A blast of wind blew her hood off, and she pushed it back into place with an irritated shove. "How very Shakespeare." Hunter had heard of Shakespeare, but he had no idea what Aylin was talking about. He must have looked perplexed, because she added, "Shakespeare made Richard III of England out to be a deformed hunchback, which wasn't true. He had a curved spine, but he wasn't a Quasimodo."

There she went surprising him again. "You must like to read."

"Very much." Tucking windblown strands of golden hair inside the hood, she started walking again. "You?"

He shook his head. "I can read, but I'm more of a video games and movies guy." He offered her a hand to leap a narrow stream, but she waved him off and carefully stepped on stones to cross. "Do you like movies?"

"I haven't seen many. Rasha brought a human movie device to the clan, but my father broke it." Her voice took on a bitter note. "People were getting too many dangerous ideas, apparently."

Using the opportunity to dig a little deeper, he asked, "And you don't agree?"

She appeared to consider that. "I think," she said slowly, "that when leaders control what their people see, hear, and do, they create an environment of fear and anger. Chained dogs turn mean for a reason."

Either Aylin was a whole lot smarter than her father, or she was telling Hunter what he wanted to hear. In any case, he'd be wise to not underestimate this female. "That's not much of a Raven way of thinking," he pointed out.

"My clan follows the Way of the Raven. I don't." She glanced over at him. "Do you follow the Way of the Raven or the Way of the Crow?"

"Crow," he said, but both were bullshit.

The myth of the raven and the crow had been fabricated by the original twelve vampires to explain their origins and hide the truth. To this day, many believed the story of how a raven and a crow battled atop the bodies of two dead Indian chiefs until the blood of all four mingled and the chiefs rose as vampires.

But those who thought the raven and crow fable was a load of crap sought answers in the scientific theory that involved a mutated virus within the Native American community. Which was true. Scientists just didn't know that the virus had originated with a demon named Samnult.

"Rasha won't like that," Aylin murmured. "She's as Ravengelical as my father."

Not a surprise. That Aylin didn't feel the same way was. Unless, of course, she was fucking with him.

"What can you tell me about your sister?" he asked.

Aylin jammed her hands into her coat pockets. "She's older than me by seven minutes."

"That's not what I was looking for, but okay."

She sighed. "Why don't you just ask me specific questions instead of fishing?"

Well, she'd called him on that one. He wasn't comfortable beating around the bush anyway, wasn't sure why he'd even gone down that road. "Is she bitter about this mating?" he asked, putting it all out there. "Is she leaving a lover behind at ShadowSpawn?"

Aylin took a long time to consider her answer, which didn't bode well. "Bitter? No. As for lovers . . . I don't know."

She was lying, but he couldn't expect anything else from a sister trying to protect her twin. Or from a ShadowSpawn clan member.

"Are *you* bitter?" She scooped up a handful of snow and ate a bite. "Or giving up a lover?"

Fuck yes, he was extremely bitter. "I'm doing what I have to do in order to protect my clan." Which meant giving up all his lovers.

He knew many clan chiefs, including his father, who either had multiple mates or one mate and multiple lovers, but Hunter had always believed that a leader was strongest when his attentions were focused only on one mate. And since he would never tolerate another male with his female, he couldn't be a hypocrite.

No matter how much he despised Rasha.

Or how much he found himself liking Aylin.

9

WE'RE ALMOST THERE."

"Great." Aylin feigned a smile at Hunter's announcement. She should be thrilled to get out of the cold, but for some reason, she dreaded their arrival at MoonBound.

"You must be anxious to see your sister."

"Of course," she said, but her response was more automatic than genuine. She cared about Rasha, but the thought of seeing her sister with Hunter made Aylin's stomach sour.

They dropped into a narrow valley, and ahead, standing in a group near a cliff of moss-covered rocks, were several MoonBound warriors, including Riker. Draped in rich furs, Rasha stood apart from them like an ice queen, her expression carefully neutral, her posture stiff.

Riker acknowledged Aylin with the shallowest of nods, and she wondered whether he held his brutal treatment two months ago against her, even though she'd done nothing to cause him pain. In fact, she'd helped his female, Nicole, to escape.

Aylin hung back as Hunter broke away to meet

Rasha. Rasha watched him approach, and Aylin didn't like the calculation—and hunger—that gleamed in her sister's eyes.

"Rasha." He halted a couple of feet away, and Aylin experienced a shameful flicker of joy that Hunter wasn't looking at Rasha the way she was looking at him, as if she couldn't wait to see him naked.

Rasha inclined her head in greeting. "Hunter."

Fat snowflakes began to fall from the featureless clouds above as he gestured to Aylin. "Obviously, I've met your twin sister."

Rasha waved her hand dismissively. "*Second*-born."

Hunter's full lips curved into a tight smile. "Thank you for making sure I don't mistake her for being first-born. That would have been a disaster."

His sarcasm was lost on Rasha, who nodded as if she'd just saved him from some sort of life-altering social faux pas.

"Did she tell you she's staying until after the mating ceremony?" Rasha asked.

"She did." Hunter gestured for them to follow. "Come on. The entrance to our warren is just a few yards away. We'll have a celebratory meal prepared for your arrival."

Rasha fell into step next to him, and Aylin took her place behind her sister as they moved toward a massive rock face. Three warriors remained outside, melting into the forest, while the other three brought up the rear, their hands hovering over the blades at their hips as if they expected Aylin or Rasha to attack Hunter.

"Will there be humans?" The eagerness in Rasha's tone made Aylin cringe.

Hunter scowled. "Humans?"

"At the meal."

"Ah. Fresh out. Venison is on the menu."

"Disappointing." Rasha sniffed with disapproval. "But I trust we'll have humans for our mating celebration?"

"Why don't you put in a request with our head chef. He's very accommodating." Hunter picked up his pace, but if he thought he could outrun Rasha, he was very mistaken. More than a century of living with Rasha had taught Aylin that lesson well.

He slowed a moment later, gesturing to a slab of moss- and vine-covered stone set deep into the side of the mountain. "You can't see it, but there's an opening here. The entrance is warded, so even if you know where it is, it'll be invisible to you if you don't have a MoonBound tattoo." He glanced at Aylin, his gaze so much softer than when he looked at Rasha, and her heart fluttered stupidly. "I'm guessing you have a similar system in place at ShadowSpawn?"

"We do," Rasha said. "If you're lucky, you'll see my access symbol soon."

Aylin wanted to gag. Rasha's tattoo was on her inner thigh, which meant that if Hunter saw it . . . yeah. Aylin didn't want to go there.

Aylin hadn't been as bold as Rasha. Or, more accurately, she hadn't been given a choice about either the placement or the method of permanently etching the symbol into her skin. Her father had held her down and carved the raven's skull into her back with a dull blade dipped in acid.

To Aylin's surprise, Hunter didn't respond to Rasha's suggestive offer other than to say, "You'll need to get a MoonBound glyph. I'll have our mystic-keeper mark you on the day of our mating ceremony."

A subtle tautness in Rasha's jaw hinted at her annoyance with Hunter's lack of interest in the location of her tattoo, but he didn't seem to care about her irritation. He led them through hallways that grew wider, lighter, and cleaner as they went. Hard-packed earth gave way to stone and wood flooring, and the walls went from being little more than rough-cut rock and dirt to smooth surfaces made of sanded logs and polished stones. Native American artwork and carvings lined the walls, along with chalk drawings that looked like they were made by children.

Aylin trailed her fingers over the edges of a deer hide that had been used as a canvas for a painting of wild bison. "This is amazing," she murmured.

Rasha snorted, no doubt preferring Shadow-Spawn's sparser and more gruesome decor, which, more often than not, included the bones and skulls of their victims—animal, human, and vampire.

"You like art?" Hunter glanced over at Aylin, and she couldn't help but be pleased that he used a different tone of voice when he spoke to her than when he spoke to Rasha.

"No," Rasha blurted, once again cutting off Aylin before she could so much as open her mouth.

"Somehow I guessed that of you. But the question was for Aylin." Hunter didn't even look in Rasha's direction, his gaze fixed firmly on Aylin. She wondered if he could feel the daggers Rasha was staring into the back of his skull.

"I love art," Aylin said, leaving it at that. Rasha already looked like she was on the verge of a volcanic eruption. She hated to be ignored, hated it even more when Aylin got attention that Rasha believed belonged to *her*.

A female Aylin recognized as Lucy, a youth ShadowSpawn had captured and held hostage with Riker and Nicole, crossed in front of them at a fork in the passage. Wearing baggy cargo pants and a bright orange hoodie that matched her short, spiky hair, she smiled shyly at Aylin, but when her dusky silver gaze lit on Rasha, she bared her fangs and scurried into the darkness.

Sudden tension bloomed, thick enough to burn her nostrils. Hunter wheeled around to Rasha, his sensual mouth little more than a grim slash. "What did you do to her?"

Rasha rolled her eyes. "We put her in her place. Simpletons are meant only for menial labor and pleasuring warriors. You can't allow them to run free. It's for their own good."

Hunter's expression turned thunderous, and a chorus of low growls echoed through the halls as Riker and the other two males inched closer. Anxiety spiked, and Aylin wondered if she was going to be made to pay for what ShadowSpawn had done to Lucy. Aylin had tried to help the girl, but Lucy had been held either in the dungeon or in the fighters' quarters, and the best she could do was slip Lucy extra food and send her one of her own threadbare blankets for her bed.

Very slowly, Hunter moved toward Aylin's sister. Rasha held her ground, chin up, shoulders squared, but it didn't do any good when Hunter's big body bumped up against her and backed her into the wall. The sounds of his hands slapping the wall as he slammed his palms down on either side of her head rang out like gunshots.

For the first time in recent memory, Rasha looked afraid.

"Lucy hasn't spoken a word about what happened at ShadowSpawn," he said, his voice as still and cold as a grave. "But eventually, she will. And if I find out that she was violated in any way, I *will* castrate and kill whoever did it."

Rasha batted her eyes, all innocence and sugar, but Aylin knew her sister well enough to recognize genuine worry in the set of her mouth. "Do what you must. MoonBound is my clan now. ShadowSpawn deaths aren't my concern."

Snorting, Hunter shoved away from her. "We'll see."

They continued down the hall in strained silence until Hunter stopped at a huge oak door. "These are my quarters," he said, still sounding like he'd eaten brimstone for breakfast. "You're both welcome at any time." He moved to a door a few feet away. "Rasha, this apartment will be yours."

Rasha's mouth puckered with disapproval. "I assumed we'd live together."

"Our quarters are connected by a door between the bedrooms. I thought you'd want privacy until we're mated." He threw open the door, and Aylin nearly gasped.

Plush rugs covered the polished wood floors, and coffee-colored leather furniture created a cozy living space in the living and dining rooms. The kitchen was small but clean, and instead of traditional art, the walls had been decorated with colorful stones set into the plaster in wild circular patterns.

Not even her father's quarters at ShadowSpawn were this nice.

"It'll do," Rasha said, sounding utterly bored.

"If it doesn't meet your standards," Hunter said, his voice as smooth and sharp as a velvet-covered blade, "I can arrange for a cell in the dungeon. I'm sure it'll be closer to what you're used to at ShadowSpawn." Rasha's face went crimson with fury, and Hunter smirked as he turned to Riker. "If you'll show Aylin to her quarters, I'll get Rasha settled in."

"Roger that," Riker said. "Their bags are already in their rooms."

Relieved to escape the mounting tension, Aylin gladly followed Riker to an apartment a few doors down and around a corner. She expected him to drop her off and get away from her as fast as he could, so she was shocked when he came inside with her.

"I wanted to thank you for helping Nicole back at ShadowSpawn," he said, inclining his blond head. "She was grateful for your friendship."

Very rarely did anyone thank her for anything, and never had anyone called her a friend. At a loss for words, Aylin merely nodded.

Riker made an encompassing gesture around the room. "This was where Nicole stayed before we were mated. You should be comfortable here."

That was when Aylin finally took a look at the accommodations she'd been given. It wasn't a dirty, tiny cell with a mat on the floor, which was what she'd had at home. This was a suite, with a small but practical living area containing a sofa, a two-seat table, and a human device she thought was called a TV, and in another room, she could see the edge of a bed and a dresser. It was nicer than anything she'd hoped to sleep in, even in her wildest dreams.

"I . . . yes, thank you."

Riker started out of the room, pausing in the doorway. "Nicole would love to see you. She hangs out in the lab. If you need anything in the meantime, just ask anyone. I promise, we're all on our best behavior."

This was so bizarre that Aylin wasn't sure what to say. All she could do was utter a raspy "Thank you" again.

"You're welcome. Dinner's in an hour."

10

I F HUNTER HAD been at all unsure that he wouldn't like his soon-to-be mate, he was now completely, 100 percent certain that he'd kill her within a year. Except that, with his luck, he'd probably imprint on her and be unable to strangle her the way he wanted to do right now.

But if he found out that Lucy had been harmed and Rasha had something to do with it, he'd overcome the imprint bond and put her out of everyone's misery.

He'd left her to settle into her quarters, and five minutes later, she'd barged through the door connecting the bedrooms and announced that she'd rather stay in his room. In his bed. With him.

Yeah . . . no.

She hadn't argued with his decision, but steam had practically whistled from her ears as she wandered around his private quarters and office, making disapproving sounds every time she came across something she didn't like. Apparently, she thought books, artwork, movies, and sports magazines were a waste of time. She even gave Monty Python a disdainful snort. Who the hell didn't appreciate Monty fucking Python? Now, as she eyed the video games, she huffed in disgust.

"Game consoles aren't allowed at ShadowSpawn," she said. "My father thinks a warrior's time is better spent hunting or training for battle."

Your father is a dickhead. Somehow he managed not to say what he was thinking. "We all need downtime. Recharges the batteries."

"We recharge the batteries with fights." Her gaze raked boldly over him, so different from the way Aylin looked at him with furtive glances. "Or fucking."

Okay, so Hunter was all about rest and relaxation with a female or two, and sure, a good fight could release a lot of tension, but sometimes mindless entertainment was a release of its own. Most important, mindless entertainment didn't come with complications.

She sauntered up to him, her hips swaying, her breasts bouncing freely against the olive tank top she wore. "Bet you're wondering if you're getting a virgin mate."

Not by a long shot. He watched her come closer, the blatant heat in her blue eyes growing into an inferno as she got closer. No, that was the walk of a female who knew damned well how to take what she wanted from a male.

He stood his ground, wondering if her touch would light him up the way Aylin's had. If it would make his skin heat and tingle and send blood pounding through his veins like a river after a dam breaks. When she planted her palm on his chest, he got his answer.

His skin crawled. His blood froze.

"I'm not a virgin," she said in a smoky, sultry voice. "I hope that doesn't disappoint you."

"There's something to be said for experience," he said, letting her interpret that however she wanted to. He wondered how much experience Aylin had. The way she'd clung to him at the cabin while she fed, the way her body had fit against his as she arched against him . . . shit, she'd been eager and unrestrained, and he bet she'd be a wild thing in bed. And wasn't *that* thought inappropriate as all hell?

"I like the way you think." Rasha trailed her hand down and hooked her fingers under his waistband. "Because I'm going to blow your mind." She batted her eyelashes coyly. "Along with other things."

Her words were enough to make his balls shrivel. "Great. Looking forward to it after we're mated." Grasping her wrist, he lifted her hand away and ignored her furious glare. "Now, if you'll—"

"Show me the rest of MoonBound!" she snapped, her command grating on his last nerve.

"I have things to do," he said, forcing his teeth to unclench so he could get the words out clearly enough that she'd understand he wasn't fucking around. He had to get away from her before he killed her or threw her out on her ass. Either would kick off a war with ShadowSpawn that they couldn't afford. "I'll have someone else show you around."

Rasha made a sour face, but to his surprise, she nodded. "Of course. You're a chief, and you have a lot of responsibilities." She looked over at the three pairs of doeskin baby moccasins on his mantel and smiled tightly. "I look forward to sharing them, to sharing *everything*, with you after we're mated."

Like hell. She wasn't going near his responsibilities. Or the moccasins his infant sons and daughter hadn't lived long enough to wear. If she so much as touched them . . . He suppressed a growl and fished his phone out of his pocket, hesitating when the screen lit up. Who should he get to give Rasha the grand tour? Probably someone who already hated him.

Grinning, he texted Myne, who must have been practically outside the door, because thirty seconds later, Hunter recognized the male's heavy, rapid knock. Leave it to Myne to impart impatience and irritation through a simple rap on wood.

"There's your tour guide." He tried not to seem too eager to have her gone as he threw open the door, happy, maybe for the first time ever, to see Myne standing there in jeans and a black Henley. "Myne, this is Rasha." He gestured between them. "Rasha, Myne."

Myne was his usual unfriendly self, and he merely stared, lip curled to show a hint of titanium fang.

Rasha at least dipped her head in acknowledgment. "We've met."

"Excellent." Hunter nudged Rasha toward the doorway. "Myne, show her around the place. I'll meet up with you both in the dining room."

"I live to do your bidding," Myne drawled.

Hunter closed the door with more force than was necessary, glanced at the stack of paperwork on his desk, and shrugged. Fuck it. He could catch up on clan business later. He'd always had a talent for procrastination, and the time spent with Rasha had brought out his restless side.

Besides, he needed to catch up with Aiden. By

now he should have gotten some good intel from the human poacher.

Hunter hoped so, because in the darkest corners of his mind, his father's ghost was urging him to take matters into his own hands, to get them bloody.

Far better if Aiden was the one getting his hands wet.

He found the male talking with Baddon outside the human's cell. Both warriors sported grim expressions, and both had blood on their hands.

"Tell me the human talked."

Aiden nodded. "He's a low-level scumbag, doesn't know much, but he said a lot of gangs, motorcycle clubs, and gun clubs are in a race to see who can bag the most vampires."

Baddon growled, his tattooed hands clenching and unclenching. "I talked to some of my Gravedigger boys. My VP, Han, said someone contacted him yesterday, wanting to know if the Gravediggers wanted in on some poaching action. Didn't say who he was, but Han got the impression the guy was from the government. Whoever the dude was, he offered ten thousand bucks for every vampire scalp and set of fangs delivered."

Hunter cursed. Wasn't that just fucking great? Hold on to your hats and teeth, boys and girls, because humans were getting serious.

"This is worse than I thought." Hunter scrubbed his hand over his face, wondering how it was that shit always hit the fan all at once. "Did you get anything else out of the bastard?"

Aiden shook his head. "Dude is dry. But he did tell us how he got his name."

A hiss and a curse came from Baddon. "Chem. So fucked-up." He glared at the cell door as if imagining ripping apart the human on the other side. "Apparently, he's some sort of amateur chemist. He used to develop designer drugs for his club to sell. When hunting vampires became more profitable than drug dealing, he started using his talents to create chemicals that can knock us out, poison us, and even fucking *melt* us."

"Kill him," Hunter growled. "I don't want that trash fouling the air anymore."

He didn't wait for the show. Instead, he headed toward the weapons storage area to check out the loot his warriors had gathered off the dead poachers who kidnapped Rasha and Aylin. Hanging out with sharp objects always calmed him down.

Sensing a presence ahead, he rounded the corner, and his breath caught at the sight of Aylin. She was freshly showered, and her hair hung in a damp curtain against a green and white flannel shirt that was long enough to cover her denim-clad ass.

Barely.

A hint of her heart-shaped bottom peeked from under the shirt's hem, and Hunter's fingers curled into his palm at the memory of grasping those firm cheeks as he held her against him in the cabin last night. How could one twin so easily heat his blood while the other chilled it?

He approached as she studied the carvings in the walls, her slender fingers tracing the patterns that had fascinated Hunter as a child.

"I used to spend hours making up stories about those pictures," he said.

Aylin jumped, and it struck him then that she truly wasn't a warrior. Not like her sister, anyway. He'd bet his Xbox that Rasha would never have been caught by surprise in an enemy stronghold. But just because Aylin hadn't been trained to be a fighter, that didn't mean she couldn't play an effective role in a plot against his clan, and he wasn't ready to let his guard down with her yet. If ever.

"You shouldn't sneak up on people like that," she said breathlessly.

He grinned despite his misgivings. "I'll try not to walk anymore."

The smallest hint of a smile turned up one corner of her mouth as she went back to looking at the wall. "A long time ago, I saw a picture book of drawings like this. The book said they were carved by ancient people."

"They were," he said. "These drawings were here long before our clan moved in."

"When was that?"

He eased up next to her, inhaling the fresh scent of her clean skin and apple shampoo. Great Spirit above, she smelled . . . edible. "Hundreds of years ago."

"How long have you been chief?"

"Almost two centuries," he said. "Before that, my father was chief."

She turned to him, her azure eyes glittering with curiosity. "What happened to him?"

"I killed him." At her raised eyebrows, he cocked his head. "Didn't you learn all of this when you were growing up? I can't believe your father wouldn't school you on vampire history and the histories behind all the clans."

"Oh, we learned all of that," she acknowledged. "My father believes in knowing his enemy."

"Then if you know my clan's history, why the questions?"

"Because," she said crisply, "history is rarely written without bias, and there are always two sides to a story. I learned about MoonBound's past from my clan's point of view. Your version of events could be very different."

Smart girl. He wondered if Rasha was so astute and open-minded. He doubted it. She struck him as the type never to question the belief system in which she was raised. "Has anything I told you been different?" he asked.

"Not so far." She regarded him thoughtfully for a moment. "But you haven't told me much."

This female was as fascinating as she was beautiful. And so very different from her sister. Rasha wore hard years on her face, giving her a harsh appearance, while Aylin's features were softer. More refined. And their eyes . . . where Rasha's glittered with a keen, shrewd intelligence, Aylin's were watchful, as if she didn't waste her IQ points on getting one step ahead of everyone else but instead waited for others to fall on their own.

Rasha was a warrior, but Hunter was willing to bet that Aylin was the more intelligent of the two. He checked his watch. "It's almost time for dinner. Want to walk with me? I can give you a tour on the way."

Aylin caught her bottom lip in her teeth. Pristine white fang tips pressed into her plump flesh, and Hunter's body hardened at the memory of having those fangs in his throat.

"Where's Rasha?" she asked.

"She'll meet us in the dining hall." When Aylin didn't respond, he said, "Are you worried she'll be jealous?"

Aylin snorted. "Rasha has never been jealous of me, and she never will be."

Rasha was a fool. She should be jealous of everything about her twin. "Then why the hesitation?"

She appeared to consider her answer. Finally, she blurted, "Because I don't trust you."

Interesting response. And a smart one. "What have I done to make you not trust me?"

"Nothing." She shrugged. "But I've never met a clan chief who wasn't a ruthless son of a bitch."

Hunter blinked. Then laughed. "Do you always say what you're thinking?"

"Hardly ever."

"So I just bring out the worst in you?" He stepped closer, drawn by her scent, her smile . . . hell, he was drawn by everything about her. "Or do you feel like you can get away with being mouthy to a chief because your sister will protect you?"

A barely audible growl rumbled deep in her throat. "I would never hide behind my sister."

"Then I bring out the worst in you."

"I guess that's it," she said, and this time, her growl was a little louder. A little more guttural. A *lot* sexier.

He halted a mere foot away, close enough that her heat scorched him in all the right ways. "Aren't you afraid of me?"

Aylin looked at up him, her big eyes going right through him. "Yes. But I've never had anything to lose." She stepped back and gestured down the hall. "Are we going?"

Nothing to lose? She was a chief's daughter, and even as the second-born, she should hold a high rank in the clan. Except . . . clans that followed the Way of the Raven often drowned the second-born twin at birth, and they usually didn't tolerate birth defects in any child. He wondered how badly she was treated in the clan, even though her father was the clan's leader. Maybe the fact that Kars was the leader was the only thing that was keeping her alive at all.

It's not your concern. Let it go. Rasha is enough to deal with as it is.

Mental pep talk delivered, he gestured for Aylin to follow him. She stayed behind him for a few paces, so he slowed to accommodate her limp, but she only slowed more.

Finally, he stopped in the middle of the hall. "Am I walking too fast for you? I can slow down."

Startled, she blinked. "I can keep up."

"Then walk next to me."

She opened her mouth as if to argue, and then, after a furtive glance down the hall, she stepped beside him. But still, as they walked, she seemed uncomfortable, slowing every time anyone looked her way. Was she honestly expecting someone to chastise her? In front of him? What the hell was going on in the ShadowSpawn ranks that had made her this way?

Probably the same shit that went on at Moon-Bound when Hunter's father, Bear Roar, ran the clan. The memory of that set his temper on edge. He never wanted to be associated with that kind of brutality toward his own people, had worked hard to eradicate every trace of his father's legacy.

You're my blood, his father had once said. *You can never escape that.*

Maybe not, but Hunter could sure as hell try.

"I'm only going to say this once," he said, his gaze fixed on the training room ahead, because he was afraid that if he looked at Aylin, his anger would scare her. "In my clan, everyone is equal. You don't have to look at anyone's back when you're walking."

She didn't reply, but he sensed turmoil coming off her, as if she didn't believe him but wanted to.

He let his words sink in as he showed her the training room, the main living quarters, and the armory. When he got to the library, he thought she was going to stroke out.

"A library," she whispered as she entered. "A real library."

"You don't have one at ShadowSpawn?"

She trailed her fingers along the book spines as she wandered around the room. "My father thinks reading is a waste of time."

Hunter thought her father was a waste of space. And now he knew where Rasha's attitude came from. "So you have no books at all?"

"We have books for children to teach them to read at a very basic level, but aside from a few history or warfare books my father keeps in his chambers, no." She pulled a Harry Potter book from the shelves and smiled as she smoothed her hand over the cover. "Sometimes when Rasha goes to the city, she'll bring me back some books. I hide them under my mattress."

"You have to hide them?"

She nodded. "Only senior warriors are allowed to have books. Approved books."

"Your father is a shitty leader." He waited for her to argue, but she merely moved to another book section.

"This is amazing," she said. "Can I borrow a book while I'm here?"

"Borrow whatever you want. That's what the library is for." He watched her gaze flit around the room, and he wondered what made books so magical for some. "Who are your favorite authors?"

Closing her eyes, she lifted the Harry Potter book to her nose and inhaled. "All of them. You?"

"Like I said, I don't read much," he said. "But I like a good political thriller or horror novel now and then. Can't beat the oldies—Stephen King, Tom Clancy, Steve Berry, Brad Thor . . . but there's that new guy, Croft, who writes thrillers with a vampire protagonist. The vampire fights slavery while pretending to be his human partner's slave. I hear there's even a movie coming out soon."

Nicole said that the popularity of the Croft books was a good sign. She was convinced the tides were turning in human society as more and more people spoke out in favor of vampire rights. He hoped she was right, but history showed that not only were humans slow to change, but they quickly forgot the errors of their past.

Aylin sniffed the book again. "I prefer fiction from the old days, before humans knew we existed."

Hunter did, too, but it was clear that Aylin truly

appreciated everything. She was like a kid in a candy store as she flitted from section to section and pulled out books to flip through or just touch. The touching was the worst. Every time her slender fingers caressed the fragile pages, his skin tightened and warmed as though remembering how they felt on his body.

Finally, as she carefully replaced a beat-to-hell copy of *The Pillars of the Earth* on the shelf, she sighed. "I suppose we should go. We'll miss dinner."

"It doesn't start without me," he pointed out. "We can be late."

For a long moment, she stared at him as if he were a big jigsaw puzzle and she was trying to put the pieces together. He wished her luck, because he'd never been able to do that himself. "You aren't what I expected," she said. She pulled a mystery novel from the shelves and brought it to her nose. A smile spread across her face as she drew in a deep breath. Someone needed to create an air freshener in "musty library" scent for people like her.

"What did you expect?"

"A hideous, troll-like tyrant."

"Hideous?" Hunter feigned offense. "You thought I was hideous?"

She laughed, a light, happy melody that made him think of springtime, which was strange, because vampires rarely evoked images of sunlight and butterflies and chirping birds. "Okay, no, I lied. Tales of your virility and Adonis good looks reached even my ears." She straightened a dog-eared page in the book. "But you *are* supposed to be an unpredictable tyrant with delusions of grandeur."

"Screw the tyrant-grandeur crap," he scoffed. "As long as everyone knows about my virility and handsomeness, I can live with the rest."

She rolled her eyes, but she was still smiling. "Everyone needs priorities, I guess."

"And what are your priorities?"

"Probably the same as everyone else's." She eyed the rows of books the way a starving vampire stared at an exposed throat. "To stay alive."

What a strange answer. To him, staying alive wasn't a priority; it was a given that you did what you had to do in order to not die. To focus on it meant you were currently in danger or expecting danger. So which of those was affecting Aylin?

She popped the book back onto the shelf and turned to him. "Speaking of staying alive, should we go to dinner? I'm famished."

As much as he'd love to hang out a little longer, he wasn't going to let her go hungry. He led her toward the dining hall, detouring to take them up a ramp and along an open hall that looked down into a massive living area filled with couches and tables, a television with a massive collection of movies, a Ping-Pong table, and a kitchenette.

"That's where most people spend time when they aren't in their quarters." He pointed to an open doorway on the opposite wall. "There's a game room, too, with pool tables, a foosball table, and, thanks to Baddon's crime network connection, four classic video arcade games. Gotta love Pac-Man."

Aylin seemed completely lost. Maybe she'd never heard of Pac-Man. "Where's your fight arena?"

"Fight arena?"

She looked at him as though he was a moron. "You know, the room where fights take place."

"We have a workout room for sparring. It's next to the gym."

"No, I mean *fights*. Our fight arena is where disputes are settled, innocence or guilt is determined, and sometimes a hunter or poacher is brought in for a special gladiatorial battle to the death."

Dark memories flitted like shadows on the edges of his mind. "We haven't had one of those in a very long time."

"Good. It's barbaric. And ridiculous to think that a person who wins a fight is automatically innocent of whatever crime he's been accused of." She snorted. "That's why my father has banned most books. He'd rather keep his flock uneducated and in the dark."

Yes, very dark memories. Before Hunter had taken over his father's position, the clan had been a violent, dangerous place. His father, a first-generation vampire descended directly from one of the Originals, had led MoonBound by the Way of the Raven. He'd believed, like so many chiefs, that stricter rules and harsher lifestyles would keep clan members safe and in line.

It was Bear Roar's very beliefs that had been his downfall, with Hunter being the one to topple the bastard.

"My father ran MoonBound the same way," Hunter said, unable to keep the bitterness out of his voice. "Even my mother approved."

"What happened to your mother?" Aylin asked.

He cocked an eyebrow. "Don't you know?"

Aylin ran her palm over the wooden banister, which was worn smooth by countless other hands over the decades. "The story I heard was that you traded her to humans in exchange for your life."

"That's pretty cowardly." The scent of roasted venison wafting from the kitchen got him moving again. "Do you think it's true?"

"I thought it might be, but now I'm not so sure." They passed a couple of young females coming from outside, their coats dusted with snow. "Well?"

"Well, what?"

"Is it true?"

Before today, he hadn't thought about his parents in so long that their memories were practically covered in dust and cobwebs. As far as he was concerned, they could stay that way, and he bit out a clipped, "No. I exiled her. And if humans have her, they're welcome to keep her."

11

THE MORE TIME Aylin spent with Hunter, the less she felt she knew about him. So much of what she'd learned as gospel was wrong, and as they entered the dining hall, she wondered how many more surprises he had in store for her.

She glanced around the well-lit, cavernous room at the long tables packed with food and people. But something wasn't right. Where was she supposed to sit?

Hunter guided her to a table where she was relieved to see two friendly faces: Nicole and Riker. Rasha was already seated, her posture stiff and unyielding. Aylin would bet that the wooden goblet in her hand was either filled with alcohol or already emptied of it.

"Here," Hunter said, gesturing to the chair next to Nicole and across from Rasha, who suddenly looked as if the cup was filled with lemon juice.

"I don't understand," Aylin said quietly. "Where's the table for people like me?"

Hunter frowned. "People like you?"

"Defective," she said, hating that she had to spell it out when it should be obvious.

A shadow passed over Hunter's expression before he forced a smile. "You sit here."

She hesitated until she realized that at this same table, there was a male with only one eye. At a nearby table, Lucy, wearing Mickey Mouse ears, was chatting animatedly with another female, and across from them was a male with a missing hand.

"Is this a special occasion?" Rasha asked. "Is that why there's no table for . . . *them*?"

The shadow came again, but this time, it was accompanied by a flash of fangs. "Sit. Down," he said to Aylin. He turned to Rasha. "We always eat like this. No one is shunned."

Rasha's chin came up, her expression sour. "I see."

"I don't think you do." Hunter waited for Aylin to sit before sinking into the huge oak chair draped with deer hides at the head of the table. "I don't run things the way your father does." He looked out over the room full of people. "And I'm sure everyone here is glad of that."

"Really." Rasha took a sip from her cup. "Would those who were here under your father's rule agree with you?"

Hunter stiffened, and Aylin braced herself for his wrath. If the stories about Hunter's father, Bear Roar, were true, he had been a leader much like Aylin's father, with a temper that left people maimed or dead. "Those who had a problem with my leadership style have long since left."

"Yes," Rasha purred. "They defected to Shadow-Spawn."

"And ShadowSpawn is welcome to them." Hunter

held up his goblet, and everyone in the room followed suit. "Today we're celebrating the arrival of my future mate, Rasha. Our union will secure peace between our clans, and I expect you all to make her feel welcome. Same goes for her sister, Aylin." He glanced over at Rasha, whose cold smile chilled even Aylin. "To peace."

Rasha clinked her cup against his. "To peace and the merging of our clans."

A vein in Hunter's temple throbbed, but he held up his goblet once more, and the rest of the clan shouted, "To peace!"

Hunter leaned toward Rasha and in a low voice said, "Our clans aren't merging. They will never merge."

"Of course not," Rasha said. "Poor choice of words. I meant uniting. Now, instead of fighting each other, we can fight humans."

Feeling like an eavesdropper, Aylin turned to Nicole, whose fair skin glowed with her pregnancy. "It's good to see you." She took the platter of carved venison that Nicole offered. "You're just starting to show."

Riker, on Nicole's other side, palmed his mate's belly. "It's happening too fast."

"Too fast?" Aylin plopped a well-done slice of meat onto her plate.

Nicole patted Riker's hand reassuringly. "He's worried because we don't have a gifted midwife, and I haven't determined how to make labor and birth less dangerous. But I'm working on it, and I still have six months to do it."

Vampire pregnancies used to be rare, but Nicole, with her background in vampire physiology, had discovered a way to change that. Unfortunately, giving birth often ended with either the mother or the baby dying, sometimes both. Born vampire females had the highest survival rates, but even so, it was always best to have a gifted midwife present.

"Could you do like the humans and take the baby out with surgery?" Aylin passed the tray of meat to Hunter and tried desperately to ignore the electric current that sizzled up her arm when their hands brushed.

Sighing, Nicole shook her head. "Unfortunately, cesarean sections aren't practical for vampires. There's no known anesthesia that can knock out a vampire without being fatal to the baby, and epidurals don't work to eliminate the pain of the surgery. Besides, I think the problem with the birthing process is uncontrolled bleeding. A cesarean section would only make things worse." She squeezed Riker's hand. "But I'll figure it out."

Riker swore quietly and stabbed the slab of meat on his plate with his fork as laughter broke out in the back of the room.

Hunter tapped Aylin on the shoulder and said in a low voice, "Watch this. It's a little dinner entertainment."

"I love a bloody fight at dinner." Rasha grinned. "Whets the appetite."

Aylin's stomach turned over. She'd always felt like something was wrong with her because she couldn't get into a brutal battle during a meal, so she took a relieved breath when Hunter scowled at Rasha and said, "We stopped doing that a long time ago."

"Disappointing."

Hunter eyed Rasha from over the rim of his cup. "I have a feeling you're going to find a lot of things around here to be disappointing."

"I'm beginning to see that."

Hunter didn't have a chance to say anything else. Someone tossed an apple from one side of the room to the other, and in an instant, a young male popped out of thin air to catch the fruit in one hand.

Aylin gasped, sure her eyes were playing a trick on her. "Where did he come from?"

"Just watch." Pride glowed in Nicole's expression. "Bastien is amazing."

Someone else hurled an empty bowl in the opposite direction, and Aylin could hardly believe her eyes when Bastien flashed invisible and reappeared on the other side of the room to catch the bowl before it hit the wall.

Rasha stared at Bastien in utter disbelief. "But how—"

Hunter cut Rasha off with a gesture as a dark-haired born vampire dressed from head to toe in leather rose from his seat to meet Bastien in the middle of the room. When one tattooed hand produced a massive blade from under his jacket, Aylin's heart stopped.

"That's Baddon," Hunter said. "He's our fastest warrior and a helluva fighter. He blooded that blade when he was eight. Took down two humans who were attacking his mother."

The guy was twice the size of the kid, and Aylin didn't care what Hunter had said earlier about no bloody fights. Baddon looked like he could crush Bastien with his pinkie.

Riker leaned across Nicole, a proud smile on his face. "Bastien is my son. He's only been training for a couple of months, but he's a fast learner."

Only a couple of months? Aylin glanced at Baddon's hulking form. And they'd pitted him against . . . *that*?

There was a hushed silence, and then Baddon struck out at the younger male. The blade slashed a path across the very place Bastien's neck should have been. But the boy was gone, and when she heard a chorus of claps, she followed the sound to another table, where Bastien stood on top, his feet straddling a giant bowl of bread.

Two more males, both different shades of blond, and a dark-skinned female joined the chase with their own weapons, and soon Bastien was disappearing and materializing all over the room. Aylin couldn't even keep track. She watched in fascination as the kid dodged knife attacks and punches simply by disappearing. Twice he materialized behind his attackers and *thunk*ed them on the head with his thumb and forefinger before laughing and disappearing again.

"I didn't think that talent existed anymore," Rasha said, her voice as full of amazement as Aylin had ever heard it. "We need to breed him. As much as possible. Right away."

A low, rumbling growl came from Riker. "There will be no breeding. Especially not anytime soon."

"Clearly, he's old enough—"

"I said no!" Riker snapped.

Rasha's toothy smile was too calculating for Aylin's liking. "That's up to your leaders, isn't that right, Hunter?"

"Leader," Hunter said coldly. "Not leaders. And Riker's right. We don't breed people, and Bastien has a long way to go before he's ready for any kind of relationship."

Rasha let out a sound of disgust, and Aylin knew this wasn't over. But she did have to wonder what Hunter meant by Bastien not being ready for a relationship. He was young, but he had to be at least in his early twenties. Since vampire aging and maturity slowed to a crawl around that age, he could be as old as forty. Maybe even fifty.

The show went on for a few more minutes, and then, after a round of applause, everyone settled in to eat. Bastien took a seat next to Lucy, who kissed him on the cheek and made him turn the color of a ripe apple.

The tension between Hunter and Rasha made for an awkward start to the meal, but it wasn't long before the warriors at the table started telling jokes and reciting stories, and Aylin found herself enjoying not only the food but also the company.

As she set down her fork and breathed a heavy sigh of contentment, Hunter stood.

"I know some of you are wondering what's going on with the situation outside our walls," he said, his voice carrying as if he were using a loudspeaker. "Human hunters are suddenly everywhere, and the emphasis now seems to be less on capturing vampires and more on killing us. Humans outnumber us ten thousand to one, and their weapons are getting more sophisticated and efficient. But we're not helpless, and we're not going to sit back and let them exterminate or enslave us. Our joining with ShadowSpawn will clear a path toward peace talks with other clans, and it's my hope that instead of fighting each other, we can concentrate on dealing with the humans."

He gazed out at the clan members, and Aylin wondered if everyone was as mesmerized by his commanding presence and deep, authoritative voice as she was. She could listen to him talk all night. Of course, that thought had her thinking about talking all night in bed, and she had to take a gulp of ice water to cool down those errant thoughts.

"We're all going to be in this together," he continued. "And we each have different skills and backgrounds that can be of use in the months and years ahead. I invite you all to bring your ideas to me or to one of my senior warriors." He stepped back from the table. "Now, if you'll excuse me, I have clan business to take care of."

Two big males, including the one Aylin had been afraid would kill Bastien, rose from their seats and joined Hunter as he strode out of the room. The moment he was gone, the atmosphere became charged with tension as Riker braced his forearms on the table and addressed Rasha, his body practically radiating hate.

"I've been on my best behavior, because I respect Hunter and don't want any of this to be more difficult than it already is," Riker growled. "But I won't forget what you and your clan did to Nicole, Lucy, and me. And I won't let you hurt anyone in this clan again."

Rasha's lips turned up in a cruel smile that Aylin knew too well. Shit, this was going to get bad.

Clutching the table edge with both hands, Rasha shifted forward so she was practically nose-to-nose with Riker. "I liked you better when you were chained in our dungeon, bleeding and begging for us not to hurt your precious Nicole."

"Rasha!" Aylin hissed, just as Nicole burst to her feet, knocking her chair over with a crash that silenced the entire dining room.

"Rike might be on his best behavior," Nicole snarled. "But I'm not."

Heart pounding, Aylin leaped to her feet, desperate to stop the confrontation before it took a violent turn. "It's been a long day," she said quickly. "Rasha, we should get settled in." She grabbed her sister's arm and pulled her away from the table, shooting Riker and Nicole apologetic glances as she did.

Surprisingly, Rasha went without an argument, squaring her shoulders and lifting her chin as if she was a queen lording over her subjects.

When they were in the hallway, Rasha jerked out of Aylin's grip. "I hate it here."

Aylin loved it. The floors were clean, the food was good, and the people were . . . happy. Oh, and they bathed. Bonus. "Maybe if you'd quit being a bitch, you'd like it more," she suggested.

Rasha started in surprise. "What did you just say?"

Yeah, Aylin kind of surprised herself with that one. But something about this place made her feel safer than she'd felt in a long time. "You heard me. And don't sound so shocked. You know I'm right. You're going to be mated to this clan's chief for a long time, so you might as well try to make some friends." She reconsidered that. Finding a friend here wasn't going to be easy for Rasha. "Or at least try not to make more enemies."

Aylin hoped the bitterness in her voice was audible only to her own ears. Rasha was getting everything Aylin wanted, and she was too damned stubborn and mired down in the ShadowSpawn way of life to appreciate it.

Rasha started down the hall toward their quarters. "Silly, naive Aylin." She patted her on the shoulder as if Aylin were a small child. "Leave the politics to me, and go back to looking pretty. I'll handle Hunter and the clan my way."

An unsettling sensation of doom settled over Aylin like a death shroud. Rasha's way was *always* the violent way. Aylin had only been at MoonBound for a few hours, but she already knew Rasha would never fit in with these people.

Unless . . . what if Rasha didn't plan to fit in? The invisible death shroud closed around Aylin like shrink-wrap as a horrible thought formed in her brain. The only reason Rasha wouldn't care about forging relationships was that she had something else in mind.

Rasha didn't *want* to fit in at MoonBound. She wanted to take over.

12

HUNTER HAD NEVER been so glad to be done with dinner in his life. Rasha was the most obnoxious, nasty female he'd ever encountered. How was he going to live with her for a lifetime if he could barely tolerate spending an hour with her?

He'd grown gradually angrier every time she opened her mouth and revealed her thoughts on "merging" the clans, the seating arrangements for "the defective," and breeding Bastien. It seemed they were never going to find common ground, and he wondered how futile any efforts to deprogram her would be. Maybe Riker, who had military experience, or Jaggai, whose time in the CIA when he was human had benefited the clan greatly, would have some insight into bringing Rasha over to their way of thinking. He hoped so, because as it stood now, she had her head up her ass.

Granted, the clans did need to work out some sort of relationship, and the thought that Riker's son might pass on his ultrarare talent of invisibility to his offspring had crossed Hunter's mind, but hoping for kids with his gift was different from breeding for it. To do that would make MoonBound no better than Daedalus, which Nicole said had been planning to do exactly that with Bastien.

Bastards.

The bastards were, even now, planning more ways to destroy vampires, and as Hunter stood in his office with Riker and Nicole, he shared the latest.

"You need to watch this." Hunter hit the button on the TV remote, and the video from a Seattle news station started up, releasing the paused image of a male reporter standing with another human male in front of a modern building with a huge glass front that, frankly, looked like a pain in the ass to keep clean.

"I'm here on the grounds of Daedalus's main office with CEO Charles Martin." The reporter turned to a towheaded man who appeared to be in his late thirties. "Mr. Martin, you've led the charge to eradicate wild vampires despite resistance from vampire-rights groups. Can you tell our audience why this is so important to you?"

"We've proven with decades of research and experience that vampires aren't capable of coexisting with humans unless they're tamed and collared," Martin said. "What these vampire-rights fools don't understand is that vampires eat us. They're stronger, faster, and they have no sense of morality. To them, we're nothing but food. Imagine if lions and bears ran loose in the streets. Vampires are a hundred times worse. We can't allow predators of that caliber to walk among us. They killed my sister and destroyed one of our labs, killing dozens of humans and even other vampires."

Nicole growled. "That's not true. He's lying. That bastard."

Hunter nodded. "His crusade is starting to drown out the vampire-rights groups. There's a growing call to exterminate us. The human poacher in the prey room said as much."

Nicole's lips pursed, and for a long time, she just watched as the reporter asked Charles more questions before moving on to state representatives who were apparently considering expanded measures to "reduce the vampire population," which included targeting clans, open hunting seasons in all federal and state forests, and Vampire Strike Force sweeps through city slums and sewers. If what the Stake Reaper said was true and Baddon's intel was good, it looked like the government was already working to reduce the vampire population . . . but they were doing it secretly, right under civilians' noses.

"We can't fight that kind of targeting for long," Riker said. "If they have the ability to destroy our wards, they'll locate the clan eventually."

Nicole blew out a long breath. "What if we go a different route? What if we sabotage Chuck with Daedalus's own practices?"

"I'm not sure I follow," Hunter said.

Nicole grinned. "We leak Daedalus's practices to the media."

"No one will believe you," Riker said. "You're a vampire. They'll say you're making stuff up, and no one will blame them."

"But I have records," she said. "Remember the files we stole from the lab? Grant and I still haven't gone through all of them, but we've got a lot of information I'm sure the media would love and the public would find horrifying. Breeding experiments, dissection of conscious vampires, cruel death trials . . . If we can make the public aware, maybe we can generate some sympathy."

Hunter eyed the female, who until just three months ago had been human. And, as the CEO of Daedalus, vampire enemy number one. Now she was the clan's doctor and a huge asset to the vampire race.

"Do it," he said. "Let's stir up some shit."

Nicole grinned, but Riker's expression remained battle-hard. "There's something else," he said, and Hunter went cold. "Rasha knows some things she shouldn't know, and she claims she has dirt on pretty much everyone close to you."

"Like what?"

Rike bared his teeth. "She knows about Katina's past and Aiden's . . . indiscretion with females. And she somehow dug up details about Myne's captivity by the humans."

Nicole frowned. "Who has Myne told? You said he hasn't even talked to you about it."

"Exactly," Riker said. "He hasn't told anyone. Which means she got the info from Daedalus."

As disturbing as the news was, there was an upside. "ShadowSpawn must have someone on the inside," Hunter said. "Which means we might not have a spy in our midst."

"How so?" Nicole asked.

Riker turned to her. "You remember the midwife we borrowed from ShadowSpawn?"

"How can I forget?" Nicole said wryly. "Daedalus captured her, and she's the reason you kidnapped me."

Unfortunately, even with Nicole's help with the rescue plan, they'd been too late, and Neriya had died in a Daedalus lab.

"ShadowSpawn knew she'd been captured," Hunter said. "And we didn't tell them. We knew they either had a spy in our clan or one inside Daedalus. This new information could confirm the Daedalus theory."

Riker nodded. "It's good news. And who knows, maybe Rasha can actually be of use if she can help us strike at the humans from inside."

Maybe. But Hunter wasn't going to count on her for anything. And he definitely wasn't going to trust her.

What a great way to kick off a forced mating.

13

HUNTER INHALED DEEPLY as he stood inside the ceremonial teepee outside MoonBound clan's headquarters. Myne and Baddon had accompanied him to perform the ritual necessary to summon his totem animal, and as blood from their cuts ran down his chest, he wondered if they even suspected the true reason he'd come.

He wasn't here to have a chat with his spirit bear. No, he was here to talk up the demon who had created the vampire species. A demon who had long ago made clear that if anyone spoke of the truth of their origins to another vampire who wasn't an Original or a first- or second-generation vampire, he'd destroy their entire race.

Message received, and even though Hunter hated doing it, hated pretending he believed the absurd story about the raven and the crow, he'd spent his entire life quashing rumors that even hinted at a demonic hand in vampire creation.

Smoke from the fire in the center of the teepee swirled all around Hunter, wrapping him in tingling warmth as he opened himself up to the spirit world. A mist of gray clouded his mind, and a great pressure swelled under his breastbone, until it felt as if he was going to collapse in on himself.

"Samnult," he called out the moment before the pressure became unbearable. "Yo, Sam, you around?"

A blast of heat seared his back. "You're late."

Wheeling around, Hunter stared at the being who had appeared in his tent. No human appearance for the demon today. Nope, his gunmetal skin was spiderwebbed with pulsing crimson veins. His twisted, blackened horns jutted a good eighteen inches into the air, and filthy claws tipped his freakishly long fingers.

"Only by a night," Hunter said. "Why does it matter?"

Samnult snarled, his chapped, scaly lips revealing a mouthful of sharp gray teeth. "You don't get to question me. I'm your god."

"You're our breeder," Hunter bit out. "Not the same thing." *Arrogant ass.*

The demon's claws struck Hunter across the chest, adding four more ragged gashes, from his left shoulder to his right hip.

Pain screamed through him, but he clenched his teeth and managed not to strike out in retaliation.

"Do you want to go through the trials or not?" Sam growled. "It makes no difference to me. I'm more than happy to take the firstborn child from your mating."

Hunter inhaled deeply, forcing himself to remain calm. If the demon decided he didn't want to let Hunter take the tests, Hunter was screwed. Time to suck up.

But only a little.

"I want this. I was hoping we could do it after the full moon." Mainly, he wanted more time to make sure Rasha would be on board with taking the demon's test with him. He couldn't do it alone, and Hunter couldn't risk Rasha's refusal.

"No."

Hunter stared. "No? Just . . . *no?*"

Sam casually picked at his teeth with those sharp, black-tipped claws. "You hard of hearing?"

"Fuck," he muttered.

"Maybe later."

Hunter wanted to punch Sam in his ugly face.

The demon flicked tooth crap onto the ground. Disgusting. "Remember, you can take either twin with you."

Aylin would definitely be the more pleasant traveling companion, but he needed Rasha's fighting skills. Besides, Rasha would likely be more willing to fight for her own child. "When we first spoke, you said they'll both be the death of me," Hunter said carefully. "But one will choose to save me. What does that mean?"

"That's for you to figure out."

Were all demons so cryptic? What assholes. "Can you give me a hint about which one will save me?"

"I'd look at which has more to lose if you die. Or if you live." Sam shrugged. "But then, you may not have a choice. If I were Aylin, I'd tell you to take a hike. She's not the one who will give birth to your firstborn."

That was along the lines of Hunter's thoughts. "So when do you want this to happen?"

"Day after tomorrow. There's a portal near Lake

Chelan. You and the female will meet me there." Hunter quickly calculated the drive time, but Samnult dashed his hopes of hopping in the Rover by adding, "You'll go on foot."

Great. An added element of danger. "We'll have to leave tomorrow."

"Then you'd better get ready."

"How will I know where to go?"

Samnult moved in a blur to slap his palm on Hunter's forehead. A throbbing rattle banged around in Hunter's skull. "You'll feel it."

The demon stepped back, flashed a grin full of sharp teeth, and disappeared, leaving Hunter with a vague awareness of the portal in the distance, a pounding headache, and a sinking sense of doom in his gut.

He'd made a deal with a demon, and now he had to go make another.

14

AYLIN FOUND THE lab exactly where Hunter said it would be. She'd gone back to her own room following dinner, but now, after ten minutes of restless pacing, she decided to see if Nicole was working.

The pretty, strawberry-blond female was in the lab, bent over a rack of test tubes. When Nicole saw Aylin enter, she grinned. "It's good to see you again. We didn't get to talk much at dinner. How are you doing? Is your room okay? Everyone treating you well? Can I possibly bombard you with more questions?"

The other female's concern for her welfare left Aylin momentarily flustered. "Ah, yeah. Everything is wonderful." Her smile faltered. "Too wonderful, I think."

Nicole gave Aylin a troubled look. "You don't want to go back to ShadowSpawn, now, do you?"

A shiny, sharp scalpel on a tray next to a microscope caught Aylin's eye, and out of habit, she nearly swiped it to stash under her mattress. But she wasn't at ShadowSpawn, didn't need to squirrel away items

simply to have things to call her own. Still, the tempta-
tion had her flexing her fingers until she moved past
the table. "Would you want to go back?"

Nicole didn't need to answer that, and they both
knew it. "Maybe you can stay. Hunter could negotiate
with your father to let you move here. Or you could
mate one of the clan members."

"Those are good ideas." Aylin meandered through
the lab, marveling at the equipment and furniture. The
"lab" Nicole had used back at ShadowSpawn was little
more than a cobwebby closet. "But none of it is possible."

"Why not?"

Aylin considered whether or not to tell Nicole
the truth about her betrothal to Tseeveyo. She was so
ashamed to have been mated off that way, without her
consent and to a monster whose brutality was legend.
But Nicole had been nothing but supportive from the
moment they'd met, had never treated her like an
enemy. Maybe it was time Aylin finally confided in
someone as a friend.

A friend. Something she'd never had. "My father
already arranged a mate for me. I'm to be given to him
after Hunter and Rasha are mated."

Nicole sank down on a rolling stool and invited
Aylin to do the same.

Even though restless energy vibrated through
every cell in her body, Aylin pulled up a seat next to
the other female.

"Who is he?" Nicole asked.

"He's a clan chief."

"Like Hunter?"

From what Aylin could tell, no one was like Hunter. "Like my father."

"Oh, Jesus." Nicole reached out and took Aylin's hand. "I'm so sorry."

The other female's pity was exactly the reason Aylin hadn't wanted to tell anyone, but at the same time, Nicole's kindness made her eyes sting with gratitude. "Can we keep this between us? I don't care if you confide in Riker, but I'd rather no one else knew."

"Of course." Nicole gave Aylin's hand a gentle squeeze and then released her. "But isn't there any way you can get out of it?"

Fat chance of that. Aylin had lain awake many nights thinking about it, and she'd come up with far too few options. "There might be a couple of ways, but one is iffy, and the other is too dangerous."

"After seeing what you had to deal with at Shadow-Spawn, I think I'd be willing to try anything." Nicole placed her hands protectively over her belly, and Aylin wondered if she even realized what she was doing. "What's the dangerous idea?"

"MoonBound could offer me sanctuary," Aylin said. "The problem is that my father might not honor it, and even if he did, Rasha could revoke my sanctuary status once she's mated to Hunter."

"Rasha wouldn't do that." Nicole frowned. "Would she?"

"I doubt it," Aylin said, but she wasn't so sure. Rasha would do anything to protect her status as First Female, and if that meant getting rid of Aylin, she wouldn't hesitate, sister or not. "But you never know with her, and if my father didn't honor sanctuary or

Rasha revoked it, my father would be very . . . unforgiving. He might even kill me."

"Son of a bitch." Nicole's eyes flashed silver fire, and Aylin suddenly wondered what color they'd been when she was human. "What if we mate you to a MoonBound male?"

Aylin appreciated Nicole's outrage, but it wasn't that simple. "Without breaking off my betrothal to the NightShade clan chief first?" She laughed bitterly. "Then both ShadowSpawn and NightShade would wage war against MoonBound until my mate was dead. At the mating feast with Tseeveyo, I'd be forced to drink my wine out of a bowl made from my dead mate's skull."

"Ew."

"Yeah." Clans that followed the Way of the Raven had such wonderful traditions.

"Okay, so what's the iffy way?" Nicole asked.

Aylin's cheeks heated. "I . . . ah . . . lose my virginity and have my first, um . . ."

"Orgasm?" Nicole's reddish eyebrows shot up. "You've never even had one by yourself?"

Truly, this couldn't get more embarrassing. "You're a vampire physiologist," Aylin pointed out. "Didn't you know that born vampires require a sort of sexual awakening with a member of the opposite sex before they can feel pleasure? We call it the *salisheye*."

"Damn," Nicole breathed. "That's a new one. But born vampires are so rarely seen in captivity that humans haven't studied them much. It's why they're so valuable to Daedalus." She gave a shake of her head as if to clear it. "I hope this isn't a rude question, but how old are you?"

"I was born in 1910."

"Wow. I realize this might be a delicate question, but . . ."

"Why am I still a virgin?" At Nicole's nod, Aylin sighed. "You've seen the males at ShadowSpawn."

Nicole grimaced. "Gotcha. But still, in all that time, there was no one even a little decent you were attracted to?"

Of course there was. Aylin once had a huge crush on a young warrior who had been sent to ShadowSpawn by another clan. He'd even flirted with her—until her father made an example out of them both. Aylin could still hear the male's grunts as he was beaten by the clan's most brutal warriors, could still feel the lashes she'd gotten during supper.

"My father threatened every male with a fate worse than death if any of them touched me. Remember when I said I'm not allowed to breed?"

The computer next to Nicole beeped, but she stopped it with a few clicks on the keyboard. "Because your father says you're defective."

"That's part of it," Aylin admitted. "But it's also because my virginity is the only thing I can bring to the mating table."

Nicole exploded to her feet. "Bullshit. What about Rasha? Is she a virgin, too?"

Rasha, a virgin? Hilarious. "She's the firstborn. She's more valuable to a mate if she's experienced. Extra valuable if she's given birth." She glanced at the test tubes. "Thanks to you, though, the rarity of pregnancy is no longer a concern." In the last three months, four ShadowSpawn females had announced their pregnancies. In the past, no more than one female per year had done that.

"I knew I shouldn't have given the formula to your father. Not that I had a choice." Anger seethed in Nicole's gaze. "This is crap. We'll find you a male. We'll get you out of this."

While Aylin loved Nicole's fierceness, she couldn't quite get there. She'd tried too many times to escape the life she'd been born into, and each time she failed, she lost confidence that it would ever happen. "I appreciate the offer, Nicole, but remember the iffy part? Tseeveyo will be furious, but he might take me anyway, just to keep a peaceful alliance with my father. He could toss me into a chamber with the rest of his harem and forget about me." Which would actually be a good thing. "Or he could torture me every day for denying him my *salisheye*. And if he rejects me, it just puts me back into my father's hands again."

"That's sick," Nicole spat. "And I know sick. So what are you going to do? What do you *want* to do?"

Hunter. His named popped into her head like it belonged there. Which was ridiculous. He was mating with her sister, and even if he wasn't, he'd never take someone like her as First Female. "I don't know what I can do, but I know I need to be healthy to have a chance at doing anything," she said. "That's why I'm here. Hunter said you could help me with something."

Nicole frowned. "Is everything okay?"

"For now. I was injured during the attack on our party, and it wouldn't stop bleeding. Hunter was concerned."

Nicole reached for a box of surgical gloves. "Let me take a look."

"It's fine. Hunter . . . fixed it." *With his tongue.* Even now, the memory made her squirm on the chair. "But it's been going on for a long time. The bleeding, I mean. It's like my blood doesn't clot."

Abandoning the gloves, Nicole grabbed a pad of paper and a pen. "Have you fed recently?"

More squirming. This time accompanied by her mouth watering. Hunter's blood had been the most amazing thing she'd ever tasted. "Yes."

"When?"

Aylin cleared her throat. "Last night."

Surprise flickered in Nicole's expression. "When you were with Hunter?" At Aylin's nod, Nicole bent over the notepad and scratched something on the paper. "Do you feed regularly on the night of the new moon?"

"Yes." If sucking on some reluctant jerk's extended wrist could be called feeding. Really, it was charity, and Aylin hated every second of it.

"When did you last feed a male during the full moon?"

"Never."

Nicole's head came up sharply. "Never? As in, never in your life?"

Heat prickled Aylin's cheeks. "Never." No one wanted her contaminated "cripple blood."

"Jesus," Nicole whispered.

"Don't do that." Aylin stood, suddenly very uncomfortable discussing her private shame. "Don't pity me. It's how things are. I don't like it, but I deal."

"I'm sorry." Nicole's voice was soft but firm, a curious balance of sympathetic and professional. "I don't mean to pity you. I know what it's like to feel different." She cast a furtive glance around the lab, but they were alone. "I don't have a vampire gift like everyone else. Riker said sometimes it takes a while before it manifests, especially in turned vampires," she added quickly. "But it still sucks when everyone is wondering what you can do, you know?"

"Yeah," Aylin muttered, thinking that everyone at ShadowSpawn wondered what she brought to the table. "I know."

"Well, I do have good news." Nicole cleared her throat. "About the bleeding, I mean. It's not your fault. We've discovered a chemical reaction in vampires that takes place when they feed from the opposite sex during moon phases. Those chemical reactions are vital to survival. If males haven't fed from you, it's been affecting your body chemistry, and one of the effects is a decreased ability for the blood to clot."

Huh. That explained a lot. *You don't even bleed like a normal vampire, you freak.* She'd heard those words a million times from her father and other clan members. Now she wanted to throw those words back into their faces. Their prejudices had caused her condition, and all this time, there'd been an easy fix.

"Could I die from this chemical reaction thing?"

"Not from being, ah, moon-blood celibate, for lack of a better term," Nicole replied. "By itself, it won't kill you. But it compromises your circulatory system, and if you take a bad enough wound, you could bleed out. Basically, on the next full moon, you need a male partner."

Easier said than done. "No one will feed from me."

Snorting, Nicole threw her pen down on the counter. "MoonBound isn't like ShadowSpawn. Trust me, if you let the word out that you're willing to feed a male, you'll have a line at your door."

Aylin doubted that. But even if it was true, there was only one male she could picture at her throat.

And he was the one male she couldn't have.

15

AYLIN WASN'T READY to go back to her chambers. She'd spent too much time alone in her life already, and what she wanted now was company. She'd have loved to spend more time with Nicole, but Riker had swept in like an erotic storm and carried Nicole away in a whirlwind of whispered promises. Nicole had offered to stay and talk, but there was no way Aylin could interfere with what was clearly going to be some much-needed private time for the couple.

It was for the best, anyway. Aylin had a few questions for her dear sister.

She found Rasha where she'd left her, in her room, pacing like a madwoman, her boots striking the hardwood floor with hammer-like thuds. Maybe she'd just learned that she was suffering from a preventable health condition caused by ignorant clan members, too.

Inappropriately cheered by that thought, Aylin chirped, "What's up?"

Rasha rounded on Aylin with a snarl. "Hunter is with another female."

An abrupt stab of betrayal pierced her in the chest,

which was absurd, given that Hunter didn't owe Aylin anything. He certainly didn't belong to her. They'd spent a brief night together in a cold cabin and shared some blood. No big deal.

Don't forget the steamy make-out session. Don't forget how he thrust between your legs, his erection sliding over places no male has ever been.

He'd thought she was Rasha.

As if she'd been doused by a bucket of icy water, Aylin cleared her head of thoughts she had no business thinking. "What makes you say that?"

"I can't find him." Rasha swiped a ceramic cup off the counter. It broke into a million shards, splashing a sharp-smelling clear liquid onto the floor. "Someone said he left the warren but wouldn't say where he went."

"There are a lot of reasons he might have left."

"Not when he should be with me."

Aylin rolled her eyes. "You don't want him anyway."

"Of course I want him."

How had Rasha said that with a straight face? "You want the status and power he'll give you. You don't want *him*." Not the way Aylin did.

Rasha kicked at the shattered remains of the cup, sending pieces bouncing off the walls and furniture. "It doesn't matter. I don't share. *I* need to be the sole female influence on him. So much around here needs to be changed. Have you seen the way he runs this clan? This isn't a den stocked with sturdy, battle-scarred warriors," she growled. "It's a playground for pampered, soft-skinned children."

"Is that so?" Hunter's deep voice boomed in the

small space, and as Aylin wheeled around with a startled hiss, the room grew even smaller.

His masculine presence filled every corner, every nook and cranny, as he stood just inside the doorway, his ebony hair held back by a leather thong to reveal his sharp cheekbones and unforgiving, square jaw. He wore only a pair of jeans and a massive mantle of black fur draped over his broad shoulders. The ceremonial pelt gaped open in the front, revealing a thickly muscled chest and hard-cut abs. Two thin cuts slashed an X in his chest, and four evenly spaced lacerations sliced diagonally from shoulder to hip. Thick smears of blood coated his skin and pants.

Dear sweet spirits, Hunter could have stepped fresh out of a battle in primitive times. Gone was the video-game-playing, whiskey-swigging male with the gorgeous smile. In his place was a vampire who was a chief from head to toe, and the cold sheen of ice in his eyes said he was comfortable in that role.

"Yes," Rasha said, an uncharacteristic hitch in her voice. "It's so."

Hunter slammed the door closed behind him, turning the room into a tomb. "Examples."

Rasha hesitated, something Aylin had only seen her do when confronting their father. A heartbeat later, Rasha's superiority complex kicked in, and she met Hunter's angry gaze with a scornful one of her own. "You have a library and a game room." She made a sweeping gesture around the chamber. "Your residences are plush and warm, all of it encouraging laziness and soft warriors. You allow the injured and weak to sit at tables with people who are healthy and worthy.

You allow them full portions and the same choice food everyone else eats."

Hunter's expression was utterly flat. "And you disagree with all of this?"

"Warriors shouldn't be coddled, or they'll lose their edge." Rasha glanced at Aylin. "The infirm need incentives to overcome their weaknesses."

"All here pull their own weight," Hunter said. "Without the fear of being punished for things that are out of their control."

Rasha snorted and waved her hand in dismissal, clearly done with trying to convince Hunter he was wrong. "Where have you been?"

If Hunter was irritated by the question, he didn't show it. Then again, he was already irritated. "I was meeting with someone about our future."

His boots crunched on shards from the broken cup as he came closer, the movement causing his fur robe to part, and Aylin got a glimpse of a ceremonial blade tucked into his waistband. The bone handle rested against rippling abs streaked with blood, and Aylin's fangs throbbed. But did she want his blood . . . or his body? And did it matter? She couldn't have either. Both of those things would soon belong to Rasha, and it was time she stopped obsessing. Besides, she had no desire to listen to her sister plan her future with a male she didn't even like.

She inched toward the door. "I'll just go—"

"Stay." Hunter's deep, rumbling command might as well have been an invitation to bed, because suddenly, her pulse was pounding in her ears, in her chest, and all the way into her pelvis.

As if he knew, Hunter's gaze snapped over to her, pinning her in place with the efficiency of an arrow through the sternum. "This concerns you, too."

"Me?" she croaked. "Why? What's going on?"

Hunter shrugged out of his furs and laid them carefully over the arm of the sofa, the powerful muscles in his back flexing under smooth skin made for a female's nails to dig into. "What do you know of our origins?"

"Vampirism is caused by a virus," Aylin said, wondering where this line of questioning was leading and wishing he'd cover himself again. Those broad shoulders and thickly muscled arms were way too distracting. Even Rasha kept stealing glances.

Which annoyed Aylin more than it should.

"A virus that was created when the blood of a raven and a crow mixed with the blood of two fallen chiefs," Rasha added, as if Aylin didn't know the lore that was drilled into all vampires from the moment they were born or turned.

Aylin shrugged. "Scientists think the virus mutated from an already-existing virus in ancient Native American tribes."

Rasha threw Aylin an exasperated look. "Who the hell told you that?"

"I read," Aylin shot back. "You should try it sometime."

"Both theories are bullshit," Hunter said gruffly. "Vampirism *is* caused by a virus, but it's not a naturally occurring one originating with mutations or birds. It was created by a demon asshole named Samnult. It's forbidden to speak about and something only the

Originals and first- and second-generation vampires know. I'm telling you both because Samnult gave me permission."

Demons? So . . . Hunter was crazy. Maybe Rasha would be a good match for him after all.

"I don't expect you to believe me right now," he continued. "But I'm still going to need you to listen." Inhaling deeply, he looked up at the ceiling, as if searching for his next words in the rafters. "Hundreds of years ago, twelve tribal chiefs met in a peace summit. The white man had invaded and defiled the land, and the chiefs wanted it to stop. They summoned the crossroads demon Samnult, who promised them greater strength, speed, and special gifts to fight against their enemies. In return, the firstborn children of all mated chiefs through two generations must be given to the demon."

Hunter paused, maybe to give her and Rasha time for their brains to catch up, but Aylin didn't see that happening anytime soon.

"This," Aylin muttered, "is insane."

Hunter's intense gaze met hers. He might be crazy, but he believed what he was saying. "I thought so, too, until I met Samnult in person."

So he truly thought he'd come face-to-face with a demon? "After inhaling what herbs?"

Rasha stared at Aylin, in shock that she'd spoken to a chief that way, considering her lowly status at ShadowSpawn, but something about Hunter . . . and maybe this clan . . . brought out Aylin's voice. Hunter was dangerous; of that Aylin was certain. But she was also certain that he wouldn't hurt her. In the short time she'd been at MoonBound, she'd seen too much evidence that he wasn't a brutal leader.

And sure, she'd been outspoken with her father, too, but she had long since learned to choose her battles very carefully. She'd also learned that when you didn't hold a lot of power or physical strength, you had to use patience and brains to get what you wanted.

Right now, though, patience was in short supply, and she tapped her foot while she waited for Hunter to respond.

He studied her, his eyes going dark with warning. Had she been wrong to think he wouldn't hurt her? "Are you calling me a liar? Or are you saying I was hallucinating in a drugged stupor?"

"Uh . . . ignore her." Rasha stepped between them the way she always did when Aylin got into it with their father. "She doesn't understand a chief's responsibilities and rituals." Rasha glared at Aylin. "And she sometimes forgets her place."

Yeah, Rasha's methods of protecting Aylin could use some refinement. The *my sister is an idiot, so give her a break* thing might work, but it was getting really old.

"I don't need your help, Rasha." Aylin pivoted out from behind her sister to face Hunter again. "If what you're saying is true, then explain to me how Rasha isn't with this Samnult demon. She's firstborn. Why didn't he take her a long time ago?"

"There's what Samnult calls a 'warrior's worth clause,'" Hunter said. "If the chief passes a series of tests, he and his mate can keep the baby."

Horror and disgust made her stomach churn as endless scenarios involving demons and innocent children played out in her head. Great Spirit above, it would take more than a demon to pry her child out of her hands.

"That's sickening," Aylin hissed. "Tell him to go screw himself."

"Aylin!" Rasha gasped. "Never speak that way about a demon. He could be listening."

"Then he shouldn't be eavesdropping," she shot back.

Hunter cursed. "It doesn't matter what I tell Samnult to do. He'll still take my child. I won't let that happen." He shifted his focus to Rasha. "But there's a catch. I need you to accompany me."

His announcement fell like an ax, along with a long, tense silence. Finally, Rasha said, "I need to think about this."

"*Think?*" Hunter asked, as incredulous as Aylin was. "You need to *think* about making sure our child will be safe?"

"That's what I said." Rasha's gaze was cold as ice. "Can you give me a minute?"

Hunter's expression went thunderous, his hands fisting at his sides, but he gave a curt, shallow nod and left. The moment the door closed, with an ominously soft click, Aylin rounded on her sister.

"You're kidding, right?" Aylin snapped. "Tell me you're just screwing with him." That would be cruel enough, but at least Rasha wouldn't be a complete monster.

"No," Rasha said, almost offhandedly. "I really need to think about it."

If Rasha had spontaneously sprouted wings, Aylin

wouldn't be more stunned. "What's there to think about? If what Hunter is saying is true, a *demon* wants your firstborn child."

"It's true," Rasha muttered.

So . . . Aylin was wrong about not being more stunned. "You . . . you *knew*?"

"Father told me everything before I left," Rasha said slowly. "He expected Hunter to ask this of me."

Aylin rubbed her temples, as if doing so would make all of this go away. Hell, she'd be happy if it simply made sense. "Okay, so you've had time to think about it. Tell him yes."

Rasha sank down on the back of the sofa with a sigh, as if the conversation about saving the life of her child was exhausting. "It's not that simple."

"But you're not thinking of refusing, are you? I mean, obviously, our parents went through the trials even though our mother was a young vampire—"

"They didn't do jack shit," Rasha interrupted. She paused before saying in a clipped tone, "We had a brother."

Aylin's gut dropped to her feet, leaving her off balance and reaching blindly for the wall for support. "You're lying."

"He was born three years before we were." Rasha bent to unlace her boots with jerky motions that seemed more than a little angry. "Samnult came for him while he was still wet with birth blood."

Oh, Great Spirit, no. "Our father told you this?"

"Yes," she said as she kicked off a boot. "When he was explaining Samnult and our origins."

Son of a bitch. "So our parents willingly gave up

our brother to a demon? Did they fail the quest or something?"

Snorting, Rasha went to work on the other boot. "They didn't go on the quest. Father didn't think our mother would survive."

So he hadn't thought she was strong enough. Like mother, like daughter, Aylin supposed.

"Still, I can't believe our mother would have gone along with this."

"What choice did she have?" Rasha made a helpless gesture. "If even half of the gossip about how our father treated her is true, she had little say in the matter. He told the clan the baby was stillborn, and she went along with it, probably out of fear."

That made sense. From everything Aylin had heard, their mother had been little more than a prisoner of Kars's obsession.

"I still don't understand why you have to think about this," she said. "You aren't a newly turned vampire like our mother was. You're a warrior, born and raised. You and Hunter can complete the quest. I know you can."

"Maybe." Rasha averted her gaze, suddenly interested in a crack in a floorboard. "But I'm not going."

Aylin's jaw dropped. "Dammit, Rasha! You have to. Who knows what the demon will do to your baby? He could eat it, for all you know!"

Rasha hissed. "You think I don't get that? But I have to do what I must for our race, and that means not dying on some stupid demonic quest. Your weakness— and Hunter's—is making you blind to the practical side of this."

Irrational rage crashed down on Aylin like a rockslide in a mountain pass. "You heartless bitch."

Suddenly, Rasha was on Aylin, knocking her into the wall, her hand clamped around her throat. "How dare you question my decision? I've been groomed for leadership since birth, while you . . . your job is to keep your mouth and your legs shut until you're mated off and no longer our problem."

A twinge of hurt went through Aylin, but it was quickly buried in the rockslide of anger. "Believe me, I'm looking forward to that day as much as you are." Well, she would be, if she weren't mating with Tseeveyo.

"You have no idea what I've sacrificed for you, so I'd watch your mouth." Rasha shoved Aylin aside, and Aylin stumbled sideways into the coffee table. Her leg gave out, and she crumpled to the floor. She'd have thought she'd gotten over the humiliation of falling down all the time, but nope. Sprawling on the floor like a deer on ice was always embarrassing. "Fuck." Rasha rushed over and crouched next to her. "I'm sorry, Aylin. It's just . . . I'm not worried about it. I'm not going to have to give up my child. Father believes there's a loophole."

Aylin forgot her anger and indignity as she sat up. "A loophole?"

Rasha hesitated, as if trying to decide whether Aylin was worthy of hearing about this mysterious loophole.

"Rasha?" Aylin prompted. "What is this loophole?"

"You have to promise not to speak a word of this," Rasha said, a thread of warning woven into her words.

Stung, Aylin clenched her teeth. "When have I ever betrayed you?"

"Never," Rasha admitted. "But this could put us both in danger."

"Then I really need to know," Aylin insisted. "Tell me."

Rasha scrubbed her hand over her face, looking suddenly exhausted. "If Hunter dies before the baby is born," she said in a hushed voice, "the baby will be safe."

Aylin felt the blood drain from her face. "You wouldn't—"

"No," Rasha said, "I wouldn't. For a mate to kill a clan chief goes against the Way of the Raven. And the Way of the Crow, for that matter."

"I would think the ways of large black birds would be moot issues if the crow and raven story is utter bullshit."

"Clans need order. Ideology, even false ideology, provides structure and keeps people in line." Rasha offered Aylin a hand. "You're the history buff. You know how it works. Religious leaders have done it since the beginning of time."

Aylin shoved her sister's hand away. She had no doubt that Rasha believed what she was saying, but there was more to it than making sure vampires wouldn't lose their faith if Rasha slaughtered Hunter in his sleep or something. "I think it's even more important that you keep your hands clean so Moon-Bound's clan members will accept you as regent until your child is grown. So you can't kill Hunter, but I'm guessing that if he meets with a fatal accident while you're pregnant, you won't be too upset."

Rasha stood. "You can guess all you want. But keep it to yourself."

Aylin shook her head at the odd tone in Rasha's voice. "No. Something's off." Rasha offered her hand again, and this time, Aylin allowed her sister to help her to her feet. "You love a fight, and you love a challenge. I don't think you'd turn down a chance to best a demon and prove to Hunter that you're a worthy mate."

"Let it go, Aylin."

Yeah, something was definitely not right. "Remember when we were just learning to use our vampire gifts, and your ability to shroud yourself in silence kept failing?"

"No," Rasha said. "I don't remember that humiliating time at all."

Ignoring her sister's sarcasm, Aylin continued, "You always had a backup plan. You never did anything without a strategy to fall back on. Getting rid of Hunter while you're pregnant is your backup, isn't it? I've seen how you are with children, and I don't believe you'd risk your child's life if you didn't have to. So what's the real reason you're not going on this quest with Hunter?"

"Dammit, Aylin, you're a dog with a bone, aren't you?"

"I'm your sister," she said simply. "I don't always like you, but I do love you. You can tell me."

"Fine." Rasha threw up her hands in defeat. "I can't travel through portals, okay? Remember when I went with Father to meet with the Elders in Boynton Canyon? Passing through the vortex nearly killed me. The Elders said that the next time I try, I'll probably die. And naturally, Samnult's realm is accessible only through a portal."

"Oh, shit," Aylin whispered. She couldn't imagine being stuck in a position that left her helpless to save the life of her child. "There's got to be a way you can deal with this demon."

"There's not. Father has tried." Closing her eyes, Rasha inhaled deeply. "So yes, I have an alternative way of handling the birth of my firstborn with Hunter. I would never give up my baby to a demon or to anyone else, and if that means Hunter has to die, so be it." She crossed to the door but paused with her hand on the doorknob. "Speak a word of any of this, and you'll wish you'd remained at ShadowSpawn."

There was nothing Rasha could do to Aylin to make that happen, but she kept that thought to herself as her sister whipped open the door.

Hunter was waiting in the hall, and Aylin swore the temperature in the room dropped twenty degrees when he entered. His stormy gaze lit on Rasha and didn't waver. "Your decision."

"I'm not going with you." Rasha squared her shoulders in defiance, but a very subtle shift of her weight said she was worried about a violent reaction. She wanted to be prepared to defend herself, and Aylin didn't blame her.

A mix of anger, shock, and hurt crossed Hunter's face. "Do you understand that our son or daughter will be taken by a fucking demon? If we try to hide the child, he or she will die a horrible death. Was I not clear on that?"

Rasha's chin came up. "You were clear."

"Then there will be no children," he snarled. "I will never so much as *touch* you."

It was probably bad of Aylin to be happy about that.

"Don't be a fool." Rasha's words were sharp, but her tone was laced with regret. She truly wished she could go on the journey, didn't she? "Samnult will know, and I can only imagine how displeased he'll be."

"He'll only know if you tell him, Rasha," he gritted out. "I can't . . . I can't lose another child."

Another child? When had he lost one? Aylin could feel his pain from where she stood, a suffocating blanket of agony that made her want to reach for him. How could she let him suffer like that? Without thinking, she stepped forward.

"What about me?" she blurted. "Can I go with you in Rasha's place?"

Hunter and Rasha both wheeled around to her, but it was Hunter Aylin couldn't look away from. His dark gaze took her in, holding her in place with its intensity.

"That's impossible," Rasha said. "Only the chief's intended mate can accompany him on the quest."

"Unless the mate has an identical twin." Hunter stepped closer to Aylin, and her mouth went dry. "It'll be dangerous."

"I wasn't expecting it to be a stroll in the woods," she said. "But it needs to be done, and I'm more capable than people seem to think." There was no way she could allow a demon to take her newborn niece or nephew, and the idea that Hunter might die in an "accident" didn't sit well with her, either.

"This is ridiculous," Rasha said. "You'd be a liability." She rounded on Hunter. "You aren't honestly considering this, are you? She has no fighting experience, and she's lame. She can barely stand upright some-times, let alone run or trek over rough terrain."

Thanks for the vote of confidence, sis. The only thing that kept Aylin from saying that out loud was the fact that Rasha wasn't being intentionally mean. She was trying to keep Aylin safe.

"And yet," Hunter said slowly, "she's willing to fight for a child that isn't even hers. That kind of strength isn't a liability. But you wouldn't know any-thing about that, would you?"

At Rasha's gasp of outrage, Hunter's gaze swept Aylin up and down, taking her in from her face to her feet, and shame made her skin shrink. She could see the way he was weighing the pros and cons, and just as she was about to make things worse by pleading her case, he nodded.

"We leave in an hour."

16

HUNTER HOPED LIKE hell that he hadn't made a huge mistake, but even if he had, he could only be grateful that Aylin was willing to make the journey. *Why* she was willing baffled him. Clearly, she'd done it for her sister, but had she made the choice out of love, duty, fear, or something more ominous?

Because the fact was, Rasha was back at Moon-Bound, where there was possibly a spy in their midst, while Hunter was soon to be very much out of reach.

This was definitely not an ideal situation, made even more aggravating by the fact that Rasha wasn't willing to lift a finger to keep her own child safe. How the hell was he supposed to spend the rest of his life with someone like that?

On the upside, he probably didn't have to worry about having children with her, because he could barely look at her, and when he did, he felt nothing but revulsion. Sex might not even be possible.

Unless you think of Aylin.

. Man, he was fucked-up.

He looked back at her as she carefully navigated

the trail he left behind in the snow, and he found himself hoping she was strong enough for what was coming. Rasha was impossible to deal with, but she was nimble and fast, and she could fight as well as any of MoonBound's warriors.

They'd left immediately instead of the following morning, which had been the original plan if Rasha had been willing to go. But because of Aylin's leg, they needed the extra travel time, plus padding for breaks.

Rasha had thrown a fit, but since she hadn't offered to take Aylin's place, Hunter had left her behind and given Jaggar and Myne strict orders to keep an eye on her. Baddon, Riker, Katina, Takis, Tena, and Aiden accompanied Hunter and Aylin, but none knew the reason for the journey to the vortex. Riker asked, but Hunter had told him only that they had to make a trip to see the Elders. A lie, but Hunter had no other choice.

They'd traveled at Aylin's top speed for thirty-six hours, with only brief breaks to eat and rest. Half a dozen times, they'd had to take detours in their route in order to bypass groups of humans. Gradually, the snow gave way to rain and muddy ground, and by the time they arrived within a mile of the designated meeting place, Aylin was exhausted, her lips pale with the cold, her eyes ringed with dark circles. And Hunter had no doubt that under her clothing, she was covered in bruises and scrapes from all the falls she'd taken.

But she'd never once complained or asked for help. Hell, when anyone offered a hand, she flat-out refused. Gradually, the hard wariness in MoonBound's warriors' eyes was joined by admiration, and Hunter could feel his own feelings making that same shift. He had to keep reminding himself that she could be the enemy—that she could have volunteered to come with him as part of a ShadowSpawn plot.

He didn't want to believe that, but he also couldn't afford to let down his guard. Not when the future of his clan was at stake.

As they dropped into a sloping river valley, a powerful sense of awareness settled in his head. They were close. Samnult had told him he'd feel the vortex, and sure enough, it was as if something was tugging at his brain, leading him toward a stand of trees to the south.

"This way." He helped Aylin down a rocky path, and as the pull grew stronger, so did his misgivings. Aylin was clearly brave and smart, but with her lack of fighting experience and the bum leg, this was risky as shit.

"I can feel it," she murmured. "We're here."

Putting his back to a stand of ancient trees, Hunter turned to his warriors. "We have to do this alone." Riker opened his mouth to argue, but Hunter cut him off with a gesture. "This isn't open for debate. Wait for us, but if we haven't returned by the eve of the full moon, head back to MoonBound."

"Hunt—"

"Don't push me on this."

Riker's hard, defiant stare earned a harder one from Hunter. Riker was his friend, but he was also his subordinate, and when Hunter gave an order, he expected it to be followed. Without question.

Which was something Riker often had a problem with.

Fortunately, Riker didn't push. "After the moon fever, we'll come back for you."

"No. You'll carry on the way we've planned. You're in charge, with Baddon as your second."

"But I'm a turned vampire. The law—"

"I know what the law says about clan leaders being born vampires," Hunter said gruffly. "But everyone at MoonBound respects you, and with Baddon at your side, even the sticklers for custom should be mollified."

"You'll make it back," Riker said. "So leadership won't be an issue."

"I know."

"Sir?" Aiden cleared his throat as he approached. "Can I speak with you in private?"

Curious, Hunter nodded and drew Aiden a few yards away into the trees. "What is it?"

Aiden paused, as if he had changed his mind.

"Spit it out, man," Hunter said.

"I don't trust her." Aiden didn't need to gesture toward Aylin for Hunter to know who he meant. "I know you're traveling through a vortex somewhere with her, and I don't know why, but I don't like it. What if she leads you into a trap or is part of some ShadowSpawn plot to assassinate you?"

"And why would she go to all this trouble when Rasha could have killed me a dozen times over by now?"

"Because that would be obvious, and Rasha is too valuable to ShadowSpawn to risk. But Aylin is practically disposable to them."

Hunter's own thoughts had gone that way a time or two, but he couldn't come up with a reason for Aylin to want him dead. Then again, he couldn't figure out why she was willing to risk her life for a child that not only wasn't hers but wasn't even conceived yet.

Both twins would be the death of you. But only one of them will choose to bring you back.

Samnult's warning a couple of months ago rang through his head for the eight-millionth time. Instinct told him Aylin wasn't a threat, but centuries of living—and being betrayed—was proof that sometimes instinct wasn't enough. Hunter might be willing to give Aylin the benefit of the doubt, but he wasn't an idiot. He always took his warriors' thoughts into account.

"So what do you think Aylin would have to gain by doing ShadowSpawn's bidding?"

"What wouldn't she gain?" Aiden said, his voice grave. "Her life at ShadowSpawn has reportedly been hell. What if they promised her a place of prominence in the clan? Or a powerful mate?"

"ShadowSpawn has nothing to gain from my death. My mating to Rasha will bring more to the table than my funeral would."

Aiden shook his head. "Not if you refuse to share power with her. If she's inside our headquarters, she could sabotage the clan. With you out of the way, she could take advantage of the confusion and chaos, and she could lead ShadowSpawn warriors inside. I don't have all the answers, but I'm telling you, I don't like this."

Hunter didn't, either, but he wasn't going to operate on speculation and general "bad feelings." "I appreciate the concern," he said as he started back toward the rest of the group. "I'll be careful. And I'll trust you and the others to be my eyes and ears when I'm not there."

"We won't let you down."

"I know." He stopped a few feet away from where the others had gathered, and Aylin joined him at his side. "I don't know when we'll be back, but if we haven't returned by the eve of the full moon, Riker has his orders."

One by one, each wished them well. Riker was last, his expression grim as Hunter passed him the virtual torch of command.

"Good hunting, man." Rike clapped him on the shoulder with a gloved hand. "We'll be here when you get back."

"May Brother Eagle guide your path ahead and Cousin Coyote watch your back." Hunter turned away from Riker before they did something sappy, like hug.

As he took Aylin's hand and guided her to the stone circle in the small clearing, Riker and the others melted into the forest.

They paused outside the circle, and he turned to face her. "This is your last chance to refuse."

A breeze ruffled her hair, creating soft, golden waves around her face. "And this is your last chance to understand that I'm not as fragile as I seem. I have a bad leg, but there's nothing wrong with my mind."

The resolve in Aylin's eyes humbled him. She didn't have a stake in this, and yet she was willing to risk her life to save that of Hunter's future son or daughter . . . when even Rasha wouldn't. Remarkable. "Okay, then." He gazed up at the endlessly gray clouds and wondered if they'd fill the sky on the other side of the portal, too. "We do this."

"And what, exactly, is *this*?"

"Mutual feeding." Just the thought of Aylin's fangs in his throat again made him instantly, painfully, hard.

Aylin blinked. "Why?"

"Because demons are assholes," he muttered. "Samnult said we have to take each other's blood at the site, and we'll be transported to his realm."

"Oh." She glanced around and then shrugged. "Might as well get it over with, don't you think? Unless . . ."

"Unless what?"

She squared her shoulders as if preparing for battle. Trouble was, he was the one she was preparing to fight. "Unless you're afraid my blood is tainted by my deformity."

"A crippled bear is no less a bear." And Aylin was definitely no less female. Reaching out, he trailed the tip of his finger along the pulse in her throat. "There's one other thing. We have to be naked."

Drawing a sharp breath, she stepped away from him, and he braced himself for a refusal. So he was shocked as shit when she stepped inside the stone circle and shed her coat, dropping it onto the wet grass. Before he even had time to process what she was doing, she peeled off her sweater.

But it was when she dropped her bra on the ground, revealing creamy, strawberry-tipped breasts, that he understood just how difficult this quest was going to be. Screw the challenges and the danger and the demon.

He had a feeling that Aylin was the true menace to his future.

• • •

AYLIN HAD BEEN naked in front of males before, but only for punishment, and none of them had ever looked at her the way Hunter was looking at her. In the past, she'd seen only contempt and disgust in onlookers' expressions.

Now she saw hunger.

Hunter's gaze was as hot as the air was cold, scorching her as he scanned her body. The memory of being with him at the cabin flooded her, making her tummy flutter and her knees wobble. It also made her bold.

Back then, Hunter had believed she was Rasha. This time, there was no confusion. This time, he was very well aware that it was Aylin he was staring at.

And it was Aylin who had put the extremely large bulge behind the fly of his jeans.

Confidence swelled, and she shimmied out of her jeans and panties. She stole a few glances in Hunter's direction, and what she saw took her breath away.

He wasn't stripping. She should have been horrified that she was naked and he was fully clothed, but the way he was looking at her, his eyes dark, his teeth clenched, his hands balled into fists . . . it was as if he was mesmerized.

Aylin's confidence bloomed even more, and suddenly, she knew what her sister felt like when she was walking through ShadowSpawn's halls in her skimpy outfits, her hips swinging with extra flair when a male came into view.

This was . . . exhilarating.

Until she remembered how ugly and twisted her leg was. But Hunter didn't focus on her leg. His gaze was locked on hers, holding her in place as he shed his own clothes.

She didn't feel the cold air swirling around her or the snowflakes that began to fall. All she could feel was heat spreading through her muscles and her pulse pounding in her veins. Right now, she'd love for an arctic wind to scream out of the north and ease the hot ache that throbbed in her pelvis.

The pile of clothes at Hunter's feet grew larger as he stripped off his weapons harness, his black sweatshirt and matching T-shirt, and his boots. Next, with agonizing slowness, he shoved his jeans to his ankles and stepped out of them.

A whimper of pure admiration escaped her as he straightened. At his full height, he towered over her, and his broad shoulders blocked out the scenery behind him. His bare chest rippled with hard-cut muscles under smooth, tan skin that begged for her touch. He was so beautifully male, a savage beast that belonged out here in the wilderness, as bound to the forest as the wolves and the deer.

She knew she shouldn't look lower, but she only had so much willpower. Sliding her gaze down, over the rolling hills and valleys of his abs, she let out another whimper. He was magnificently hard, jutting upward in a dusky, thick column marbled with pulsing veins.

Her throat closed, and her breasts ached, and suddenly, she could picture herself taking him into her mouth. Of all the sexual acts she'd witnessed in the close confines of clan life, that was the one she'd found incredibly distasteful, especially the way males seemed to use it to dominate females. Pleasure and power seemed decidedly one-sided, but as Hunter stood there, a proud warrior with a rock-hard exterior, she understood that for a willing female, the power could be all hers.

"Are you ready?" The velvety purr of his voice was a stroke of pure ecstasy.

"Yes," she breathed. And it didn't even matter what it was he was asking if she was ready for. He could have been asking if she was ready to have her throat slit, and she was too far gone with lust to care.

Naked and fully erect, he came at her. She stood her ground, anticipating his touch so eagerly that she trembled.

He stepped inside the circle and stopped a mere whisper away, their bodies not touching but so close a feather wouldn't fit between them. She had to crane her neck to meet his gaze.

His palm came up to cup her cheek, and an instant, maddening pressure built under her skin. Good Lord, if he could do that to her with a simple caress on her face, what would happen to her if he touched her intimately?

There was a menacing glint in his eyes that didn't match the sensual undercurrent in his voice. "Before I put our lives on the line, I need to know if your offer to come with me was genuine, or if this is part of a ShadowSpawn plot."

Her first instinct was to get angry at the accusation, but almost instantly, she realized that his suspicion was warranted. ShadowSpawn didn't play by the rules, and they never had. She could be the enemy, one Moon-Bound would least suspect.

"On my honor," she said softly, "I only want to help."

His dark gaze searched her face, and she shivered at the cold resolve she saw lurking there. She was suddenly very glad she was telling the truth, because she had no doubt that crossing this male could end very badly for her. And worse for Rasha.

Finally, he nodded. "Then thank you, Aylin," he murmured as he lowered his head. His silky lips grazed her ear, drawing a shudder of pure desire from her. "You're as beautiful inside as you are on the outside."

A sob formed in her throat but never made it past her lips, lodged there by Hunter's fangs as they sank deep into her neck.

She gasped at the searing pleasure, her fangs punching down hard with an intense hunger that made her mouth water. Twisting, she flicked her tongue over the pleasure glands at the top of her fangs and opened her mouth over his shoulder. Warm, decadent blood filled her mouth as Hunter groaned and arched against her, pressing his erection into her belly.

Fluid heat unfurled between her legs and spread outward in electric tingles. It was as if her entire body was plugged into a giant erotic battery. Every cell vibrated and pulsed in a coordinated wave of euphoria that started at her scalp and ended at her curled toes. Was this what would have happened with Hunter back at the cabin if they hadn't stopped?

Great Spirit, now she understood the obsession with sex. If this was what it was like, she'd want it all the time.

Tightening her grip, she wrapped herself around

Hunter, her body moving on its own, rubbing against him, needing even more, although she wasn't sure what *more* could be. This was an orgasm, was it not?

Hunter's hand dropped to her ass and lifted her so his shaft slid between her folds. He didn't penetrate her, but in her mind, he was inside her, pumping deep, his cock sliding over places so sensitive that she jerked with every delicious stroke.

Something pulled taut in her core, a white-hot need that skated the edge of torment. She thrashed and cried out at the pain-pleasure, her body screaming for . . . she wasn't sure. All she knew was that she couldn't stop writhing, couldn't concentrate on anything but the relentless, building pressure in her sex.

What was happening? She'd already climaxed . . . at least, she thought she had. So what was this new torture? Panic welled up, but she couldn't stop moving or feeding or—

The pressure peaked, and without warning, the most intense explosion of bliss blasted through her, blowing apart her thoughts. Wrecking her. *Devastating* her.

This, she realized dazedly, was an orgasm. She surrendered to the *salisheye*, moaning and grinding against Hunter as the climax continued to pulse between her legs. As it waned, her legs went wobbly, but Hunter's strong arms tightened to hold her solidly against him.

But even as the last wondrous waves of pleasure ebbed, she noticed that something wasn't right. The warmth of the sun's rays beat down on her bare skin, and soft, warm grass tickled her feet. And at some point, she'd disengaged her fangs and buried her face in Hunter's throat. He was no longer feeding from her, either.

Exhausted, barely coherent, she cracked open her eyes, squinting at the bright sunlight. "Hunter?" she rasped.

"Yeah. I know. We're on the other side." He pulled away, his breathing as ragged as hers, and she felt a warm stickiness against her belly.

Hunter had orgasmed, too.

Savoring the feminine pride that arced through her, she looked up at him. Abruptly, her feeling of satisfaction died. She wasn't sure what she had expected to find in his expression, but what she saw made it very clear that he wasn't happy about what had just happened. Not at all.

17

WELL, THIS WAS humiliating as shit.

Not since Hunter was a youngling with his first female, a seductress his father had given him for his *salisheye*, had he gotten so worked up that he'd come without warning. And outside a female.

Now he had to reconcile that with the fact that it had been the most amazing orgasm ever.

But so . . . damned . . . embarrassing.

Hunter stepped back, cringing at the evidence of his climax on Aylin's belly. Naturally, their clothes hadn't made the trip through the portal, so he couldn't so much as offer a T-shirt to wipe up his mess. And didn't it just figure that there weren't even any fucking leaves on the ground, because apparently, this realm was nothing but endless green meadows and blazingly bright sunshine.

"I . . . ah . . ." Oh, great, he even *sounded* like a youngling with his first female. Summoning his command voice, he started again. "I'm . . . um . . ."

Excellent. Now he came off as flustered *and* authoritative. Nothing like sounding very sure that you couldn't put together a coherent sentence. Fuck. But then Samnult saved them both from more awkwardness by appearing from out of nowhere.

Hunter would never have believed he'd be happy to see a demon. Aylin, however, wasn't as thrilled, and she let out a squeak of surprise and made a futile effort to cover herself. Hunter stepped in front of her, allowing her some cover and also, selfishly, not wanting the demon to ogle her. If anyone got to ogle Aylin, it would be him.

Samnult looked mostly human today, with short black hair, tan skin, white teeth, and a pair of black jeans with some sort of leathery shirt. Then there were the ram-like horns that jutted out from his forehead and curled over his head and behind his ears.

So, yeah, *mostly* human.

"Maybe," Hunter suggested, "you could have mentioned the side effects of using the portal?"

One of Samnult's horns twitched. "If you'd known, would you have changed your mind?"

"No, but—"

"Then stop whining. The experience helps bond the two people who come to navigate the tests, and believe it or not, I want every couple to succeed. But this is the first time the female taking the challenge isn't the male's intended mate. Should be interesting." He craned his head to get a peek at Aylin, and Hunter shifted to block the view even as a growl rumbled in his chest. Shrugging in defeat, Samnult gestured to the ground, where two piles of clothes, a wooden bowl full of water, and two cloths had materialized from out of thin air. "Dress, and we'll begin."

He disappeared behind a copse of trees that hadn't been there a second ago.

Hunter pivoted around to Aylin and tried his best not to stare. Gods, she was gorgeous. She was tantalizingly, unintentionally sexy, with full, high breasts, a narrow waist that flared into rounded hips made for a male to grip, and delicate, sandy ringlets between her thighs that teased his gaze. Most born vampires lacked body hair, but not always, if one of the parents had been turned.

Hunter didn't mind at all, and his fingers itched to know how soft Aylin's feminine curls would be to his touch.

Way to not stare.

Cheeks heating, he crouched on his heels, dipped a towel in the warm water, and gently wiped Aylin's taut belly. When she gasped and stepped back, he caught her around the thigh and held her steady for the sweep of the cloth over her skin.

Her face turned the color of a ripe apple. "You don't have to do that."

"Yeah," he murmured, "I do."

His position put him at eye level with her navel, temptingly close to rosy nipples that made his mouth water. He lingered longer than he needed to, wiping away the last traces of himself as he admired the suppleness of her skin and the tight muscles that leaped under his touch. His fingers brushed the underside of her breast, and as if he hadn't just come all over her, his dick stirred to life again.

Before his errant cock embarrassed them both, he handed Aylin the buttery-soft buckskin dress trimmed with fringe and the knee-high moccasin boots that were clearly meant for her, leaving him to don the breechcloth, belt, buckskin leggings, and moccasins. He hadn't worn traditional Indian garb for anything nonceremonial in decades, and he wondered what, exactly, was in store for them.

As he pulled on the pair of moccasins, he glanced over at Aylin, who was tying her hair up in a high ponytail. Until now, when he looked at her, he had seen her mother's reportedly Scandinavian lineage in her blond hair, blue eyes, and fair skin. But standing there in the tan dress that fell to mid-thigh and knee-high boots that emphasized the curve of her slim calves, she was every inch the Comanche of her ancestors. Between her slightly parted lips, the glinting tips of her fangs brought all of her mixed heritage together into a mouthwatering combination.

He dropped his gaze low, taking in the expanse of bare leg between boot and dress that made his palm itch with the desire to caress it. And to keep going upward, because he knew she wasn't wearing panties beneath the dress.

With a fierce reminder that she wasn't his, he swung around to the grove of trees Samnult had disappeared into, and as luck would have it, the demon was walking toward them.

"Now," Samnult said, "the first challenge will test your self-control and willpower."

Hunter snorted. "I have that in spades."

"We'll see." A slow, toothy grin spread across the demon's face, and his eyes slid over to Aylin. "But keep in mind, Hunter MoonBound, that you are not the only one being tested."

18

Y*OU ARE NOT the only one being tested.*
Oh, shit.

Samnult might as well call her Aylin Second-Thoughts, because she was alternately holding her breath and taking shallow, rapid breaths. Before she could pass out from either a lack of oxygen or an excess of it, the demon snapped his fingers, and suddenly, they were no longer standing in a verdant meadow under the sun.

Now they were at the edge of a narrow canyon that cut a path through parched red earth that rose up into massive plateaus in every direction. They'd gone from lush, grassy lands to a desert with no vegetation. In the distance, a breeze blew a dust devil in a wide circle, but other than that, nothing moved.

Directly in front of them, a natural stone bridge spanned a canyon that was so deep Aylin couldn't see the bottom. On the other side of the fissure, a smooth ivory pillar, perhaps five feet tall and six inches in circumference, stood like a lone sentinel.

Then there were the bones and skulls littering the

bridge. Some were bleached and cracked with age, and others looked too fresh for comfort.

All belonged to vampires.

"What is this place?" she asked.

Samnult's skin had deepened into an inky black, and his eyes had gone crimson. Before, except for the horns, he could have passed for human.

Not anymore.

"This is the desert region of my realm. As you can see, nothing stirs during the day. At night . . ." He smiled, and a chill shot up her spine. "Let's just say that you need to do this before it grows dark."

Hunter swung around from where he stood at the edge of the canyon, and dressed as he was in native garb, his deeply tanned skin setting off his dark eyes and hair, he looked at home in the rugged land. Good grief, he was captivating, with a commanding presence even Samnult seemed to appreciate as the demon studied him.

"Do the bones belong to those who have failed this test?" Hunter asked.

"Not *this* test," Samnult said. "Besides battling for their firstborns, there are other reasons my children must participate in these challenges."

His eyes glittered with what Aylin could only decipher as excitement. He might want them to succeed, but the risk of death thrilled him the way it thrilled humans to watch someone walk a high tightrope without a net.

"Hunter, you cross first." The demon's voice was as deep as the canyon, and it echoed eerily, lingering too long in the still air. "Once you reach the other side, you'll grip the post and wait until Aylin is across."

Hunter's eyes narrowed. "That's it? We cross a bridge?"

"Of course that's not it," Sam said. "If you release the post before Aylin steps onto the other side, you fail the test. You'll be transported immediately out of my realm, and you'll offer up the firstborn child of your union with Rasha. And if, at any time during any of these trials, Aylin dies or is critically injured, you can choose to continue without her. If you die, she'll be sent back through the portal alone."

"What about weapons?" Hunter asked. "Will we need them?"

Samnult shrugged. "Probably." He disappeared, dissolving in a whirl of smoke, leaving Aylin and Hunter standing alone on the edge of the cliff.

"Asshole," Hunter muttered, and Aylin couldn't agree more.

"Well," she said, peering across at the other side, "this doesn't seem too bad."

"Sure." Hunter looked down into the endless chasm below. "Until something shoots out of the canyon and tries to eat us." He glanced over at her. "You okay with this?"

"Do we have a choice?"

His expression turned grim. "You do. This isn't your fight, Aylin."

She thought about her mother, and no, Hunter was wrong. This *was* her fight. Her father had thought her mother hadn't been strong enough to pass the tests, and he'd always believed Aylin followed in her footsteps. The difference was that he'd loved her mother . . . in his own twisted way.

He despised Aylin . . . in every way.

You're a cripple. Worthless. Too fucking weak to hunt for your own food.

She'd believed him for so long, but it was time to prove him wrong.

"I'm going to do this," she said. "Go. Let's get it over with."

A long silence fell as Hunter stared at her. Nothing in his expression gave away his thoughts, so she was shocked when he lifted his hand to her face. He skimmed the backs of his fingers over her cheek, and deep inside her chest, something stirred.

"You're not what I expected." With that, he strode to the bridge.

"Be careful," she blurted, as if he needed a reminder. He halted at the first step and shot her a look dripping with confidence so intense it stole her breath, and she suddenly had no doubt they'd make it through this.

Hunter stepped onto the bridge, his leather moccasins barely making a sound. Pebbles fell from the ledge as he walked, but aside from that, his trip from one side of the canyon to the other was uneventful.

Which meant that Aylin's journey across wasn't going to be as easy. Or maybe the challenge was in the post Hunter was supposed to hold while she crossed.

"Wait!" she yelled, as he reached for it. "What if it shocks you or something?"

He eyed the post and shrugged. "Then hurry!" he shouted back.

"Oh, gee, good idea." She rolled her eyes. "I would never have thought of that."

His laughter rang out, echoing in the quiet air. As the sound faded, so did his smile, and suddenly, they were reminded that they were in a demon realm, weaponless, and in a fight for their lives.

Talk about a reality check.

She held her breath as Hunter's hand hovered over the post. He closed his fingers around it, and when he didn't keel over and no giant monster appeared out of nowhere, she relaxed. At least, she relaxed until it was time for her to cross the bridge.

"Don't go until you're ready," he said, but Aylin didn't see any reason to put this off. How could she prepare for the unknown?

She stepped onto the bridge. Nothing happened. Another step. Nothing. Calming enough to unclench her teeth, she took another step. Suddenly, a rumble started beneath her feet.

Oh, crap, oh, crap . . .

A fracture appeared in the center of the bridge ahead, dividing it in half.

"Run!" Urgency cracked like a gunshot in Hunter's voice.

Aylin didn't argue. She sprinted as fast as she could go. Her right leg hindered her, nearly buckling several times as her foot came down on the uneven, trembling expanse. As she neared the halfway point, the bridge bucked, tossing her to the ground. Ahead, the fissure became a ragged, foot-wide gap, expanding rapidly as bits of earth and stone fell away into the chasm below.

Sharp rocks bit into her knees and palms as she tried to scramble to her feet, but the rolling ground knocked her down over and over, and her dress re-

stricted her movement. Hunter's voice became a drone
that blended with the pulse pounding in her ears and
the deafening roar of the upheaval surrounding her.

Desperate to cross the divide before it became im-
passable, she crawled, sometimes dragging herself on
her belly when the bucking became too intense for her
to remain on her hands and knees.

"I can do this," she murmured to herself.

You're a cripple.

Aylin uttered a breathless "Fuck you, Dad," and
hauled herself to the very edge of the fissure. A giant
chunk of earth broke out from under her, and she
screamed as she rolled away, barely avoiding plummeting into the void.

"Aylin."

"I'm okay," she rasped, although she wasn't sure if
Hunter heard her. She could barely hear herself.

"It's getting wider!"

She was well aware of that. Inhaling deeply, she
gathered her feet beneath her and launched. Her right
leg, far weaker than the left, might as well have been
rubber, and her body went off course. She twisted awkwardly in the air, striking the other side of the bridge
on her left side. The violent collision concentrated at
her hip, and she cried out as she clawed for purchase,
her legs dangling over the edge.

"No!" Hunter's deep scream rose above the other
sounds of chaos, and she risked a glance at him as she
strained to pull herself onto solid ground.

Hunter was barely gripping the post, stretched to
the limit as he reached futilely for her.

"Don't let go!" she cried out.

Damn him, he was going to do it. The need to save her glinted in his dark eyes. She couldn't be the reason he and Rasha would give up their child to Samnult—or the reason he refused to have children in the first place.

Gritting her teeth, she marshaled every drop of energy and determination, and with a cry, she hauled herself up and came down heavily on the bridge. The ground crumbled beneath her, and before it gave way, she dragged herself away from the crack. Her right leg screamed in pain, but she ignored it, pulling herself on shaking arms until they collapsed.

"Aylin!"

"I'm okay." She swallowed dryly . . . and realized the ground was no longer moving beneath her. Was the worst of the challenge over? Pushing herself awkwardly to her knees, she looked back at the path she'd taken so far, and holy shit, the entire half of the bridge she'd just crossed was gone.

Hunter's white-knuckled grip on the post eased, and although he no longer stretched his bones to the limits to reach toward her, he was still tense, his body coiled to break free.

"Come on," he urged her. "Only about twenty yards to go."

As Aylin studied the remaining distance, twenty yards looked like twenty miles. Grimacing at the ache in her leg, she shoved to her feet and started toward Hunter.

The uneven ground and loose pebbles left her stumbling with humiliating frequency. Rasha would have been able to leap nimbly over the mounds of earth piled on the bridge, and she'd have had no problem zigzagging between the stones that erupted spontaneously out of the earthen bridge for no apparent reason other than to scare the crap out of her and make her fall into the endless chasm below.

This challenge seemed almost tailor-made to cause Aylin problems, and she uttered a few nasty curses as she hurriedly picked her way across what remained of the bridge.

A harsh screech startled her out of her internal musings, and she looked up to see a fiery red lizard-like thing skitter up the cliff that loomed beyond Hunter. About the size of a beagle, it caught a tangle of tree roots and flicked the six-inch-long stinger at the end of its tail. The little animal seemed so out of place in this odd desolation.

Caw-whup.

What a strange sound it made. Aylin opened herself to her gift, preparing to let her mourning dove fly, but the lizard screeched with sudden urgency.

Caw-whup!

She had no idea what the creature was saying, but its alarm screamed through her as if she'd been jabbed in the spine with its tail stinger. Aylin put on a burst of speed, but when she brought down her right foot on what looked like stable ground, the earth gave way, and she slammed to her knees in a heap of pain.

Caw-squawk!

Son of a—

Aylin yelped as a claw-tipped hand, blackened and oozing with pus and blood, burst out of the ground and snared her around the ankle. The giant hand yanked, and she heard a snap, felt the agony of her bones breaking. She heard a scream, realized too late that it was hers, and as the world swirled around her and her vision grew dim, all she could think about was Hunter.

Don't let go of the post. Don't . . . let . . . go . . .

HUNTER'S STOMACH PLUMMETED to his feet as Aylin went pale with shock and her shriek of pain died out.

"Aylin!" Gripping the post with one hand, he lunged, the ridiculous futility of his action leaving him feeling like a helpless fool.

No, not helpless. He could let go of the post and go after her. His sweat-slicked fingers nearly slipped free of the ivory post as he called out to her again.

"Talk to me, Aylin!"

"Don't," she slurred. "Don't let go."

She kicked at the giant arm with her good leg, but the thing held her tight. What the hell did that giant, clawed hand belong to? He wasn't sure if he should be grateful or disturbed that the entire creature hadn't surfaced. But then, he supposed it didn't matter, because as he watched in horror, it began to drag Aylin into the sinkhole around it. Blood streamed from her leg, churning the dirt into mud.

"That rock next to you!" he yelled. "Use it! Crush the bastard!"

Still kicking at the creature but hindered by the restrictive nature of her dress, Aylin fumbled for the football-sized stone. She finally got a good grip, and with speed that surprised Hunter, she smashed it into the back of the creature's hand. The *thunk* of rock meeting flesh rang out. Aylin struck again, and a god-awful rumble vibrated the air, seeming to originate from somewhere far below in the canyon.

The hand flung backward, taking Aylin with it and slinging her like a broken rag doll. She slammed into the ground, and the crack of her skull as it hit the hard-packed earth was like a physical blow to Hunter's own head. He roared in frustration and anger at his inability to help.

Except, he *could* help. He could let Aylin die, continue the quest, and protect his firstborn child. Or he could save Aylin, fail the quest, and never have children with his mate.

He'd also never forgive himself for letting Aylin die.

"I'm coming—"

"No!" Aylin snarled, her fangs flashing, her blue eyes flaming. "I . . . need . . . to do this."

Blood streamed down her face from a gash in her temple, and he was pretty sure her left arm was broken, but she managed to close her fingers around the sharp end of a time-bleached bone. With a roar, she twisted her body and stabbed the bone beneath the creature's fingernail as its hand closed on her ankle.

An eerie shriek shattered the air. The hand released Aylin, but another burst through the rock, and then a massive snout punched upward. Almost in slow motion, a skeletal creature with the head of a vampire bat began to pull itself onto the bridge.

"Aylin, *run*!"

The creature lunged, catching Aylin's foot in its gaping maw. Blood poured down the thing's chin as

Aylin screamed in agony. Another raw scream joined hers, and he realized it was coming from him.

Hunter had felt helplessness before . . . as a child witnessing his father's harsh punishments leveled against enemies, clan members, and even Hunter's mother. Later, as an adult, he'd learned that there were a lot of things out of his control, but he'd never accepted powerlessness well.

But this . . . this was worse than anything he'd ever experienced, and as he prepared to release the post and fail the test, he reluctantly accepted the fact that he wouldn't be having children. He wouldn't sacrifice Aylin's life—or that of any child.

He was going to help her.

"Hold on!" he shouted. "I'm coming!"

"*No!*" Somehow Aylin summoned the strength and willpower to smash her good foot into the beast's snout. It jerked back in surprise, yanking her with it. She used the momentum to plunge the sharp bone deep into the creature's soulless eye.

The sound that emanated from the beast had surely been dredged from the deepest trenches in hell, and Hunter swore he felt the very air around him shudder. Aylin, her arm hanging at a wrong angle and both of her feet mangled so badly he didn't know how she could walk, let alone run, managed to leap away from the beast and dash, tripping and stumbling, to the end of the bridge. The moment both feet crossed the threshold onto solid earth, she dropped. Hunter cried out in both relief and fear, released the stone, and rushed to her.

Terror made his voice crack as he hit the ground

on his knees and pulled Aylin's trembling body into his arms. "You did it. Holy shit, you kicked that thing's ass."

"I told you," she moaned.

"Dammit, you could have died." He brushed her hair away from her eyes, being extra careful where it was stuck to her skin with blood—some of it belonging to the creature but most of it hers.

"I was supposed to have died at birth," she rasped. "Every day beyond that is a gift. If I die today, I still would have lived decades longer than I should have."

His heart quivered. There was something very special about this female, and the more time Hunter spent with her, the more time he *wanted* to spend with her.

She was nothing like Rasha.

A sinister tingle spread across the back of Hunter's neck like a rash, and a heartbeat later, Samnult materialized a few feet away.

"Congratulations," he said, all cheery and shit. "Nearly a fifth of those who take this challenge fail."

Hunter had to clench his teeth to keep from lashing out at the demon's casual attitude. "Did they fail because they released the post or because the monster killed the female?"

"There's not always a monster." Sam shrugged. "Every trial is different. They're all tailored to what the female fears most."

"Really?" Through the pain glinting in her eyes, Aylin glared. "Because I've never been afraid of a giant hand popping out of the ground to grab me before. But hey, thanks, *now* I am."

At Aylin's flippant response, Hunter casually shifted to shield her from the demon, but to Hunter's surprise, Sam merely laughed. "I was skeptical about Hunter's choice of companion for this quest, but I see I might have been wrong." He sobered, seemingly lost in thought. "Or not. Whatever. On to the next test."

"She's in no condition to continue." Hunter gently probed her distorted arm, doing his best not to hurt her. She trembled, but she didn't make a sound as he palpated the bulge midway down her humerus. She had what Nicole would call a closed fracture, but all it would take was one wrong move, and one end of the broken bone would puncture the skin. And her feet . . . holy hell, how had she walked on them? The right foot had to be crushed, and the left ankle was shredded along with the bloody boot. "She needs time to heal."

"Time?" Sam shook his head. "There is no time. The humans are knocking at your door."

Alarm, sharp and stabbing, shot through Hunter. "We've only been here for a couple of hours—"

"Not in the human realm. It's been days."

Hunter sucked air between his teeth. Days? Shit. "Send me to the next test. Let Aylin rest."

"Does an injured elk rest when the wolf is nipping at its heels?"

How did the demon know Hunter liked to spout that particular bit of Cherokee wisdom now and then? He wouldn't do that anymore. It was annoying as shit.

"Then give us a few minutes so she can feed." He held Aylin tighter in an attempt to calm her shaking body. Her pain radiated from her in tangible waves, and he ached to give her the kind of relief that would only come from taking his blood. She wouldn't heal fully without rest, but at this point, anything would be better than nothing.

"No." Samnult snapped his fingers, and in a flash of light, Hunter was ripped away from Aylin and left standing a few feet away, as she threw back her head and screamed.

19

AGONY RIPPED THROUGH Aylin as the bones in her arm, ankle, and foot shifted around, grinding together like someone was sharpening them against one another. Searing pain tore into her muscles and skin, and for a brief second, she wondered if she was being flayed alive.

Distantly, she heard Hunter's voice calling her name, but she couldn't see him . . . couldn't see anything. The world was a black hole of misery, and she was free-falling.

She didn't know how long the torment went on, but gradually, the pain faded away, and bright light and Hunter's handsome face filled her field of vision. She wobbled as the earth beneath her solidified. Hunter reached out to steady her, but his hand on her biceps wasn't needed. She found her footing quickly and, amazingly, without pain. In fact, she felt no pain from any of her injuries.

"You're healed." Hunter gazed at her in astonishment. "All of your injuries are gone."

She looked down at herself, and sure enough, all

evidence of her being attacked by a giant, clawed hand had vanished. Every cut, scrape, and broken bone had healed, and even her clothing had been repaired. Not a trace of blood remained.

"How are you feeling?" Hunter's touch lingered, as if he wasn't sure of what he was seeing and was afraid she'd keel over at any moment.

"I feel fine." Actually, she felt great, almost as though she'd slept for twelve hours straight. "Where's Samnult?"

"No idea. He must have taken off while you were going through that healing process." Hunter looked out across the sandy landscape, which was yellower in color than the last place they'd been. A green oasis sprouted out of the sand, and in the very center was a lake of the bluest water Aylin had ever seen. "Now, if we can just figure out what he wants from us in this test, we'll be set."

Hunter started toward the water, but she'd taken only a dozen steps when she realized something was off. The ever-present dull ache in her right leg was gone. She stopped. Squeezed her leg from hip to knee. No tenderness, no knotted muscles under the skin of her thigh. Her fingers probed deep, and her heart stuttered.

Her femur . . . dear Great Spirit . . . the bone . . . it was *straight*.

Afraid her fingers were deceiving her, she extended her leg and stared at the new profile. Her heart pounded in anxious, spastic bursts as she held her eyes wide, convinced that if she blinked, the next thing she'd see would be the curve in her thigh bone and a twist at the knee.

"Hunter," she gasped.

He swung around, his body coiled, his fists clenched, ready to strike at whatever had alarmed her. "What is it?"

"I . . ." She swallowed as tears flooded her eyes. "I'm healed." She moved toward him, and for the first time in her life, she didn't limp. For the first time, she walked without pain.

He stepped closer, as if concerned that she'd lost her mind. "Yes, I know."

"No, I mean . . . I'm *healed*. My leg is straight. It doesn't hurt. I'm not limping."

He blinked. Glanced down at her leg. A huge, broad smile spread across his face, and Gods, he was beautiful when he did that. "That's amazing."

Emotion clogged her throat. For the first half of her life, she'd prayed to any god who would listen that she would be made whole. Eventually, she'd realized her prayers wouldn't be answered, and she'd given up on even fantasizing about a life in which she was normal. In which she could escape the bonds of the savage Ravengelical clan life. Her wishes had morphed from wishing for a fully functional leg to simply surviving.

Now . . . now she could dream again.

Sheer, undiluted joy sang through her, and without thinking, she threw herself at Hunter, wrapping herself around him in a fierce embrace.

"I can't believe it." Her raspy voice barely broke above a whisper. "When I was a little girl, I used to fantasize about this, but I never thought it would happen." And she'd certainly never thought she'd find herself in the arms of a powerful, handsome male afterward.

Hunter pulled back, and his black eyes took her in, growing more intense as they stood motionless. Her body became increasingly aware of the fact that they were plastered together, and as if someone had lit a match, tension ignited, the same kind as before, when they'd been in the cabin, and later, at the portal.

Oh, this wasn't good.

Or maybe it was *too* good.

"Hunter?"

"Yeah?" His voice was low. Gruff. Sexy as hell.

"Thank you."

His lips were so close to hers that she could feel their heat, and she realized she'd gone up on her toes to get closer. She was such a fool, but at this moment, she was the happiest she'd ever been, and she wanted to share that happiness with the male responsible.

"Thank you?" He cocked his head to the side, as if confused. "For what?"

"For bringing me here," she said. "Even if I don't make it back to our world, I'll still have known what it was like to be whole for a little while."

She'd also have known what it felt like to be with a male, to reach that ultimate peak of pleasure she'd been denied her entire life.

Hunter had given her that.

She didn't think. Didn't hesitate. For once, she let impulse reign. Stretching upward, she kissed him. If he was startled at all, he didn't show it. He kissed her back, taking control with practiced ease. He was gentle with her, so not the male she'd seen putting down poachers with ease and grim satisfaction. She followed his lead, kissing him awkwardly but eagerly, opening up when he flicked the tip of his tongue between the seam of her lips.

His tongue delved inside her mouth, and heat licked between her legs. She inhaled sharply, unaccustomed to such a sudden, demanding sensation. But she wanted more. So much more.

And she couldn't have any of it.

All her life, she'd known her duty to the clan was to mate with whatever male her father arranged for her, and Hunter wasn't that male. Worse, Hunter belonged to Rasha.

This was wrong, and it didn't matter that it *felt* right. Felt right all the way to her lonely soul.

Abruptly, she broke off the kiss and tore away from him. The sight of him standing there, his bare chest glinting in the sun and heaving from the intensity of the kiss they shared, only made her want to plaster herself against him again. She ached to strip down to nothing and let his skilled hands touch her all over. Even though he hadn't taken her virginity, he'd taken her through her *salisheye* and awakened desires within her that she hadn't even known she possessed.

"What's wrong?" Concern hardened his expression, and his lips, glistening from their kiss, curved into a scowl.

"What's wrong?" She threw up her arms in frustration. "You belong to my sister."

He snorted. "I despise your sister."

"But that doesn't change anything. You're still hers."

Reaching behind him, he rubbed the back of his neck. "Then why did you kiss me?"

"I was excited. I got lost in the moment." Boy, had she ever. But the kiss hadn't been one-sided, and she narrowed her eyes at him. "Why did you kiss me back?"

"Honestly?" He dropped his hand to his side. "I don't know."

Ice filled her chest. That wasn't exactly what a female wanted to hear. Then again, she couldn't think of a single answer that would have put her at ease. But hearing that he was attracted to her would have been nice. Even if it had been a lie, she'd like to hear it. Just once.

"Don't worry," she said stiffly. "It won't happen again."

His nasty curse burned her ears, but if he had been planning to say something else, it was lost in Samnult's sudden appearance.

"What a lovely couple you make," Sam said as he walked toward them, his black jeans rasping, his cowboy boots kicking up dirt.

For once, he looked completely human from head to toe, and wasn't it strange that she actually preferred it when he was sporting horns or claws? There was just something unsettling about a demon not looking like a demon.

"What do you want?" Hunter growled.

Samnult's eyebrows shot up. "That's a fine thank-you for repairing Aylin's leg."

"Thank you," she blurted. "Is it . . ."

"Permanent?" he finished. "Yes. You'll need to be in top form to survive these next two quests."

Hunter gazed out at the sandy landscape. "Which are?"

Samnult waved his hand, and a rumble shook the land. As Aylin watched, a massive wall rose up out of the ground, stretching as far as the eye could see. Several openings lined the wall, revealing more walls and more openings.

"It's a maze," she breathed. Straight from the children's books she'd read so often.

Samnult nodded. "You and Hunter must find your way out."

"Sounds easy," Hunter said. "So what's the catch?"

"There are many," Samnult admitted, with a little too much relish. "As soon as you cross the maze's threshold, the clock will start. Move your ass to the exit. You have forty-eight hours to do it, and of course, there are beings in there who will try to stop you."

"Still sounds too easy."

"Yes," Sam purred. "It does." He gestured to one of the archways. "Inside you'll find a pack loaded with supplies. Your time starts now, so I'd get moving. Forty-eight hours isn't enough time for most, just FYI."

Samnult dematerialized in a smoky puff. Hunter turned to her. "You ready?"

She was. Even if she died in that maze, she'd die with a functional leg, and that, she thought, was a far better death than she'd ever hoped for.

YOU BELONG TO my sister.

I despise your sister.

But that doesn't change anything. You're still hers.

The conversation moments ago rang through Hunter's head as he and Aylin headed to the next challenge. He probably should be thinking about the dangers ahead, but dammit, he was still reeling from the kiss. It had been spontaneous. Pure. A meeting of more than mouths.

With all other females before her, kissing had been about lust. The first step in the journey to naked bliss. But what Aylin had done to him in those charged minutes before Samnult had showed up had changed everything.

She'd kissed him because she was happy, not because she wanted sex. He'd been startled at first and then eager to let her show him true joy. He'd taught her to kiss; she'd taught him to rejoice in the miracle of life.

It had been the best damned kiss in his two hundred years of living.

She'd asked why he'd kissed her, and he'd said he didn't know, and he didn't. He was finding it more and more difficult to believe she was part of a Shadow-Spawn plot, but he still knew he couldn't get involved with her.

You belong to my sister.

Mother. Fuck. He'd been okay about mating with Rasha—or at least, he'd been resolved about it. But Aylin had gotten under his skin, and for all his experience fighting enemies, he had no defense against a female whose strength humbled him, whose voice soothed him, and whose touch drove him wild.

Damn Samnult and his Portal of Bonding Orgasms.

Way to blame someone else for your attraction to Aylin. You've been aching for her since she fed from you at the cabin.

Yeah, well . . . whatever. Samnult and his portal still sucked.

Real mature, Hunt. Real fucking mature.

Cursing silently, he stepped beneath the maze archway. Aylin stopped next to him, but instead of checking out the endless walls before them, she stole glances at her leg.

"It doesn't hurt, does it?" he asked.

Wispy strands of blond hair whipped her cheeks as she shook her head. "I just keep making sure everything is still straight. Silly, I know."

"Not at all." He could only imagine how horrible her life had been because of her birth defect, and this was a huge development, one that could shape her future in ways that could only be good.

He just had to make sure she survived long enough to enjoy it.

She looked over at him, and he didn't like the lingering coolness in her eyes. He'd hurt her when he'd told her he didn't know why he'd kissed her, but maybe it was what they'd needed to douse flames that shouldn't be burning.

"Are we doing this?" she asked.

"Wait. We need to make your outfit more functional for fighting." He went down on one knee next to her, gripped the hem of her dress, and ripped the side seam up to mid-thigh. His knuckles brushed her creamy, smooth skin, and a shiver of awareness shot through him. "Turn around." His voice was humiliatingly hoarse, but she complied, and he did the same thing to the other seam.

Great Spirit have mercy, her legs were spectacular. Even before Samnult healed the twisted leg, they'd been beautiful—long and lean, the left a little more built-up from doing more work than the right. Now they matched perfectly, and he itched to span her thighs with his hands as he worked his way up to her feminine place.

He let his fingers stray, just for a moment, on her outer thigh. Beneath his fingertips, her toned muscles flexed and quivered, and unbidden, indulgent fantasies of leaning in and replacing his hands with his lips wrapped around him like a satin sheet.

He'd kiss her, right where her exposed expanse of flesh peeked through the gap in the torn dress. Slowly, seductively, he'd lick his way up until the material got in the way—and then he'd rip it with his teeth all the way to her waist.

Stop it. She's not yours.

Something wild and primitive growled at that. *Mine. Not yours.*

Fuck.

Reluctantly, angrily, he stood, clenching his hands into fists at his sides to keep from reaching for her again. She was forbidden fruit, and he dared not sample.

More than he already had, anyway.

He didn't meet her gaze as he stepped across the maze entrance's threshold. She joined him, and once they were both inside the maze, a soft *whoosh* stirred the air. The maze had sealed shut. Sealed so well that there weren't any lines in the walls to suggest that there had ever been an opening.

"Damn," he muttered. "Guess we're in it for the long haul now."

Aylin gave him a funny look. "Did you have any doubt?"

"No, but I'd hoped we at least had a way out if we needed it." He studied the forty-foot-high walls surrounding them, knowing there was no way to climb over. Not unless they grew about fifteen feet in height and developed springs for legs. A few grotesque, pulsing vines hung like tentacles from the wall tops, but the thorns that spiraled along the viny ropes promised pain. Or worse.

"Hey." Aylin tugged at his arm. "Over there."

He narrowed his eyes in the direction Aylin had indicated. Near a bend in the maze, he spotted the outline of what appeared to be a doorway. As they approached, the lines became clearer. Definitely a door. And at its base was a leather bag. The supplies Samnult had mentioned, he guessed.

"Do we dare open the door?" she asked as he crouched to inspect the contents of the bag. "Or should we stay on the main path?"

"That's the million-dollar question, isn't it?" He dug through the bag, finding four packaged pints of human blood—two O-positive, one AB-positive, and one superbly rare B-negative. At least Samnult had good taste in blood. There were also two bottles of water, six pemmican bars, and two slabs of dried venison. "What's your gut say?"

"That we open it." She bit her bottom lip in doubt. "Or maybe it's a trick. Maybe we're supposed to stay on this path."

Standing, he slung the bag over his shoulder. He figured they had an equal shot at survival either way, so they might as well go with Aylin's gut. Bracing himself for anything, he placed his palms in the center of the outlined rectangle and pushed. The grind of stone accompanied the opening of the door, becoming obscenely loud in the otherwise quiet landscape.

Before the door fully opened, he put his back to the wall and craned his neck to get a view of what lurked beyond the doorway. Nothing. Just more maze, creepy vines, and the rotting carcass of one of the lizard things they'd seen during the first challenge at the stone bridge.

Cautiously, they moved through the twists and turns, their moccasins whispering over the stone and earth pathway. Bones littered the ground, some animal, some vampire. And, as he found when he crouched next to a femur and tibia connected by withered threads of tendon, some were human.

"I'd say this is creepy," Aylin murmured as they skirted a sprung trap of razor-sharp spikes on which a vampire had been impaled, "but I've seen most of this at ShadowSpawn."

Hoping to avoid a similar fate to the poor vamp's, Hunter paused to study the trap's mechanism. The spikes had shot up from the ground, closing on the victim like a Venus flytrap's jaws. At least a dozen two-foot-long barbs had skewered the vampire, who appeared to have been dead for a few weeks.

"Have you seen a trap like this?"

Aylin rubbed her arms as if chilled. "No. My father would use fewer spikes. You know, to cause the greatest amount of suffering."

A green bird the size of a bald eagle, its feathers looking more appropriate for a porcupine than a bird, landed high up on a wall. Its golden eyes seemed to size them up, and then he swore it chirped at Aylin.

"Aylin?"

She ignored him, her concentration fixed on the creature. The bird cocked its head as if listening to something, and a moment later, Hunter he felt the whisper of wings brush his ear.

But there were no other birds in the air. Still, the porcupine-eagle began to chatter, its gaze following something invisible that seemed to be flying around it. Aylin stood silently, her gaze flitting between the bird and the empty air. The bird squawked at her, and she nodded as if understanding it.

Realization dawned. She *did* understand the creature. Which meant she was a mystic-whisperer. His gut twisted.

Mystic-whisperers are dangerous. Kill them. Kill them all.

His father's voice clanged around inside Hunter's skull. He didn't follow the Way of the Raven, but even the Way of the Crow preached wariness of those with the ability to either communicate with or become animals. Followers of the Raven believed that the animal-based gifts were evil, and while Crow followers weren't so rigid in their views, they still considered mystic-whisperers and animal shifters to be high-risk individuals in any clan setting. The animal-based gifts came with powerful animal instincts that often overrode rational thought. Hunter had seen it happen, and it wasn't pretty.

Aylin turned to him, but she didn't meet his gaze. "We should go. But not straight ahead. I think doubling back to the crossroads we just passed is our best bet."

"What makes you say that?"

Still not meeting his eyes, she shrugged. "It's a guess."

"A guess based on what that bird had to say?"

She flinched, just barely, but enough for him to know he'd struck his target. "How would I know what the bird said?"

"Because you're a mystic-whisperer."

She hissed. "That's forbidden—"

"Fuck forbidden," he snapped, annoyed and shamed by his own initial reaction to realizing she was an animal whisperer. "You should know by now that I don't run my clan the way your father runs his. I've only banished one person because of an animal-based gift, and it wasn't necessarily his gift that got him in trouble; it was what he did with it."

The mystic-whisperer, Lobo, used to belong to the clan but now roamed the forest with his wolf. The male had been so in tune with the animal world that he'd distanced himself from other vampires, and eventually he'd grown vicious, impossible to trust.

"What was his gift?"

"He was a skinwalker, so powerful that he could shift into people instead of only animals."

Aylin gasped. "That's . . . I've never even met a skinwalker, let alone heard of one being able to take humanoid form."

"Exactly. He used his ability to shift into another clan male in order to seduce the male's mate. If I hadn't sent him away, the female's mate would have killed him."

"Talking to animals seems pretty tame now," she muttered.

Maybe, but the more he got to know Aylin, the more he realized she wasn't as tame as she appeared. She was fierce but subtly so, her stubborn determination to survive permeating every fiber of her being.

"Never be afraid to reveal yourself to me, Aylin. I'm not your enemy."

"I know."

He looked up at the porcupine-eagle and started back the way they'd come. "I don't think you do."

She fell into step beside him, and he resisted the urge to smile. She no longer followed behind, no longer hesitated to walk next to him like an equal. "Things would be so much easier if you were an asshole," she said.

He laughed at that, but she was right. He could be a class A asshole, but sometimes he wished he could be even better at it. Nothing would bother him. Regrets wouldn't plague him. And he could wipe Aylin from his mind and pretend that the upcoming mating with Rasha wouldn't eat at his soul.

"Trust me," he said. "I can be a bastard when I need to be."

"I have no doubt," she said with a wry smile. "But I think it's rare. You're too smart to be a bastard."

"There's an old Cheyenne saying about how, when a man is as wise as a serpent, he can afford to be as harmless as a dove."

She snorted. "I'd say that 'harmless' is the last description that applies to you. But I like the sentiment. I've always believed that the more power or strength someone has, the less they should use it."

Ah, damn. He liked her. He really, *really* liked

her. "Unfortunately, it usually goes the opposite way. Power and strength too often are given to those who least deserve them . . . or who least can handle them."

Her gaze became distant, and he wondered if she was thinking of her father. Or Rasha. They were two of the least-deserving people he'd ever met, and Kars's abuse of power was staggering.

"I hope this isn't a sore subject," she began, "but I've heard your father, Bear Roar, was as cruel as mine. Is that true?"

Yeah, the subject wasn't just sore; it was an open, stinging wound. "He was, but in a different way. When he was calm, he was hard but reasonable. But his temper . . ."

Hunter inhaled, taking in fresh air in an attempt to cleanse the stale memories. Didn't work. He remembered every gritty detail about his father's homicidal rages, which could last for days, and when he came out of them, Bear Roar was often shocked by the swath of destruction he'd left in his wake. Now, every day, Hunter struggled with his own temper, avoiding triggers such as speaking the ancient language of the Elders and drowning his violent tendencies in alcohol and video games. He could not, *would not*, turn into his father.

"His temper was legendary," Hunter continued. "He was the reason humans fear us."

"I'm glad you didn't follow in his footsteps." She looked up at the endless blue sky, the tips of her hair rustling softly in the breeze. "You're pretty reasonable."

"I can be," he agreed. "At least, most of the time." And when he wasn't, Riker put him in his place. Sometimes gently, sometimes not. But the guy could usually bring Hunter out of whatever vicious mood he was in.

Usually.

Hunter had done things that still haunted him, that still shamed him. And he had no doubt that in the future he'd take many more actions that would do the same.

And as he watched Aylin lift her face into the sun and a breeze that smelled of juniper and sage, he prayed that bringing her along on this journey wasn't one of them.

20

To Aylin's surprise, she and Hunter navigated the maze for hours without incident. Which was a challenge and exhausting in itself. Who knew it took so much energy to be paranoid about what might lurk around the next corner?

To Hunter's credit, he never once settled into complacency or got sloppy. He kept watch to the front and behind, and before they rounded any bend in the path, he insisted they put their backs to the walls and survey the route ahead before he'd allow them to continue.

By the time the sun sank low on the horizon, casting long shadows inside the maze, they were both so tightly wound up that they were seeing monsters in every murky patch of shade. Really, the lack of activity, coupled with the numerous animal, vampire, and human remains, was its own special brand of hell.

"This is fucked-up." Hunter hefted the leather knapsack higher on his sun-baked shoulder as he eased around a corner. "I'd rather be fighting actual enemies than jumping at every sound."

He exaggerated; she'd not seen him jump once.

But she agreed, because she *had* jumped a few times. The anxiety over what *might* be lying in wait was making her insane.

"Samnult is a sadist." She eased the cramp-inducing grip she had on the thigh bone she'd picked up a while back to use as a club. Hunter had one, too, but he'd used a rock to grind one end into a sharp point. "I don't know how long my heart can keep beating at a thousand beats per minute. I'm pretty sure it's going to explode."

He turned to her, and in the waning light, she swore his eyes glowed as he cast a long, lingering look her way. Heat flooded her, and just when she thought her heart couldn't beat any faster, it went all kinds of crazy in her chest.

It was a blessing when he turned away, because she wasn't sure her body could take more sudden starts and stops.

The green bird reappeared every now and then, usually when they came to a crossroads in the maze. Hunter would watch as she sent her totem dove, invisible to all but her, out to speak with it, and while she sensed he wasn't entirely comfortable with her ability, he didn't condemn. Even now, as the spiky bird lifted off and her dove returned to her, he merely shook his head.

"Impressive. My totem bear would be as likely to eat that bird as talk to it." He skirted soccer-ball-sized purple bushes growing in the middle of the path and waited until she'd cleared them. The bushes could jump three feet into the air and spit acid, as the hole in the shaft of her boot could attest. "He's a grumpy son of a bitch."

She stared at him in astonishment. Special abilities and totem animals tended to be private things, rarely discussed, but she was learning that Hunter wasn't exactly a typical born vampire with pure American Indian breeding. Unlike her, a vampire with mixed human breeding, Hunter had instincts that would be deeply ingrained, woven into the fabric of his very soul. And yet he was by no means defined by his background.

It was . . . refreshing. She wondered if his openness extended to talking about his gifts.

A minefield of acid bushes lay ahead, and she fell behind to follow in his footsteps as they wove between the plants. As they forged ahead, she couldn't help but admire his bare back and the play of powerful muscles under his skin. And then there was the view of his ass, his bare cheeks flashing under the buckskin breechcloth every time he crouched to study a sprung trap . . . or something he suspected to be a trap.

"Hunter?" She cleared her throat of the lust that had lodged in it. "Can I ask you something?"

"Shoot."

A row of acid bushes blocked their path, quivering and rattling in excitement as she and Hunter neared. He jabbed his bone spear into the center of one, and the thing shrieked before shriveling into a fist-sized ball of straw. They quickly stepped over it, and Hunter narrowly avoided being sprayed by another agitated plant.

"Okay." She cleared her throat again, preparing to enter forbidden territory. "You know what my gift is, but I know nothing about yours."

The set of his shoulders became taut, and she

hoped she hadn't made a mistake. "You know, most people don't discuss this. You never want to give away your secret weapon." He cast her a pointed look over his shoulder. "Or your forbidden skill."

"Trust me, I'm aware of that," she muttered.

He spun his bone club around and whacked a vine slithering across the path. "Who besides me, and I'm guessing Rasha, knows that you can communicate with animals?"

"My father probably suspects, but he's never said anything." She leaped over the writhing vine, marveling at how her once-twisted leg didn't shake or ache. Strangely, she was tempted to be extra careful, for fear that injuring herself might reduce her to the same shameful state she'd been in her entire life. She couldn't return to that. She'd rather die. "I'm sorry if I offended you. You don't have to talk about it."

He shrugged. "I can read the weather, and if I try hard enough, I can manipulate it. Nothing wide-scale, but I can force a strong breeze or stop the rain from falling in a fifty-yard radius."

"That must come in handy," she said, feeling a little let down. With his background, he should possess far greater powers, like her father, who could project his voice into clan members' minds to give orders from a distance. His gift had delivered ShadowSpawn a major advantage during several battles they might otherwise have lost.

"Sometimes," he said with a shrug. "But I—*fuck!*"

Blood shot up from the earth in a fine spray—at least, she thought it had come from the earth, until she saw the wooden spike drilling up out of the top of

Hunter's foot. Lunging, he ripped his foot free and hit the ground in a messy sprawl.

"Hunter!" Dropping her bone club, Aylin went to her knees next to him, slapped her hands on both sides of the puncture wound, and lifted his leg onto her lap for elevation. "Lie down. We have to stop the bleeding."

Hissing, Hunter eased onto his back. "Son of a bitch," he bit out between clenched teeth. "Didn't see that one coming."

"The blood," she said, gesturing with a nod to the backpack lying at his side. "You need to drink it."

He shook his head. "Later. I don't want to waste—"

"Now!" she snapped. "I don't deal well with macho bullshit. You need to heal, and the blood will help. So open that pack, and down a pouch of O-pos."

Surprise flashed in his pain-filled black eyes, followed by a ghost of a smile. "Yes, ma'am."

It was her turn to be surprised as he fumbled with the pack's buckle. He might suffer from macho-itis now and then, but he was clearly smart enough to get over it when necessary. Or when scolded. Good to know.

He jammed his hand into the pack, but before he could retrieve a bag of blood, he froze. The fine hairs on the back of her neck stood up, and a heartbeat later, her ears picked up a sound that filled her with dread.

In the distance, but growing louder with every passing second, was a chuffing noise, the distinct sound of a large animal taking in scents. Tracking them, maybe.

The sound seemed to come from every direction, rendering all of their options down to a roll of the dice.

They could go back the way they'd come and run into the creature, they could take the path to the left and run into it, or they could go down the curvy path to the right and still run into it.

Suddenly, a flutter of wings accompanied a wash of air across Aylin's cheeks. The green spiny bird swooped down to land on the wall, gripping with sharp talons. Oh, damn, this couldn't be good. Urgently, she sent her dove to talk with the creature, and when it returned, melding with her to become part of her again, the images it transmitted scared the ever-living crap out of her.

"Aylin." Hunter's voice dropped, low and harsh. "What is it?"

"It's big," she breathed. "Really big." She glanced down at his injured foot, where blood still seeped between her fingers. "Can you run?"

Hunter didn't hesitate. In one smooth motion, he snatched up the backpack and his bone weapon and leaped to his feet with the nimble grace of an athlete. Although he grunted when his punctured foot hit the ground, he didn't favor it at all.

"Which way?"

She fisted her club, but if the images her dove gave her were accurate, her weapon would be as effective as a toothpick against a tiger. "The path to the right."

He grabbed her hand, and together they sprinted blindly down the curving path, running into dead ends when they took wrong turns. Naturally, the green bird hadn't given any directions other than an insistent *flee*, which had been pretty obvious, and the equivalent of *bear right*. After that, they were on their own.

A roar vibrated the air in a tangible wave that struck them from behind.

"It's close!" Hunter spun on his heel, and in a move so fast Aylin didn't see it until it was over, he slung her behind him just as a horror-movie monster wheeled around the corner.

The tank-sized beast looked like a cross between a lion and an iguana, but its serrated teeth were pure shark.

And it was coming right at them.

"Can you jump?" he yelled.

Confused, she yelled back, yes, she could jump, but—

The creature screamed like a banshee and lunged for Hunter. Just as she was sure he was going to be swallowed whole, he wheeled to the side and grabbed the beast around the throat. Jerked roughly off his feet, she thought he was going to be flung into the wall, but he twisted his body, flipping up onto the creature's shoulders.

"Jump on!"

Was he crazy? The thing bucked like a rodeo bronco, leaping and twisting as it tried to dislodge the vampire clinging to its neck.

"Aylin . . . *now*!"

"He's insane," she whispered to herself, even as she charged at the beast. It swung toward her, snapping its jaws. She skidded to a halt, throwing herself to the ground and barely avoiding being bitten in half.

"Bastard!"

She looked up in time to see Hunter double-fist his weapon and punch it, sharp end first, between the animal's shoulder blades. The thing screeched and twisted, striking at Hunter with claws and teeth.

Go! Now! Aylin dove for its hindquarters, finding purchase in its scraggly, wiry hair. She slipped as the thing spun, but when it fell back onto all fours, she managed to jam her foot into its knee and shove off, propelling herself onto its back. And dear Great Spirit, the thing reeked. Foul odors of rotten eggs, putrid meat, and voided bowels made her eyes water and her gag reflex kick in. She couldn't even care that her dress had hiked up to her hips, leaving her exposed and naked below.

Hunter yanked the bone spear out of the animal's flesh and replanted it at the base of its skull. Its roar of pain and fury tore through the air and, very nearly, Aylin's eardrums. Pain throbbed in her ears, but she didn't have the luxury of giving in to it.

"The wall!" Hunter shouted.

What the hell was he talking about? Digging deep into the creature's scaly skin to hang on as it bucked and whirled, she glanced at the wall. Hunter didn't want her to jump up there, did he?

"*Go!* When the thing bucks, jump!"

Shit. She could barely get to her feet, let alone find her balance. The thing threw itself into the wall, and she heard Hunter's pained shout as he was crushed between the animal and the wall.

"Hunter!" She scrambled toward him, but he waved her off.

"Jump!"

Dammit. Using all her strength, she catapulted to her feet and nearly slipped off the creature's back, and in a supreme stroke of badly needed luck, the animal bucked its back end. She pushed off, springing twenty feet into the air. She hit the top of the wall with her waist, knocking the air from her lungs.

Wheezing, she pulled herself onto the two-foot-wide ledge. Below, Hunter clung to the creature's wiry hair and scales in a desperate struggle to keep from being thrown or crushed between powerful jaws. Blood ran down his leg, streaming through gashes in his shredded leggings where the animal's teeth and claws had found flesh.

She'd dropped her club below, and she looked around frantically for a weapon, but the pockmarked wall top was clear of everything but dust and bird droppings.

Turned out she didn't need a weapon. Leaving the bone spear impaled in the creature, Hunter scrambled down its spine, and when the thing spun to grab him, he leaped. He landed on the wall in an easy crouch, as if he rode demon animals and hurtled onto forty-foot-tall walls every day.

Too bad he landed on the wall opposite her.

The beast roared in fury and tried its damnedest to scale the wall after them. Its claws gouged long, deep grooves in the stone, but with no real purchase, it couldn't make it more than halfway up before sliding back down.

"You okay?" Hunter asked.

"You're the one who's bleeding," she said.

He shot her a lopsided grin. "It's just a flesh wound." For some reason, he said it in an English accent.

"No, it's not," she huffed. "And why are you talking like that?"

"Not a fan of Monty Python, huh?"

She didn't even know who Monty Python was. "Um . . . guess not."

"When we get back, I'm making popcorn and introducing you to *Monty Python and the Holy Grail*." He sounded so casual, as if there was no doubt they'd make it back. He gazed into the distance, to the awesome bird's-eye view of miles and miles of walls that fit together like puzzle pieces. The maze seemed to go on forever, and maybe it did; the winding walls disappeared into a fog bank in the distance. "Let's get going. We can meet up at the next dead end."

She eyed him, assessing his wounds as well as she could with thirty feet between them. "How's your foot?"

"Healed."

"Bullshit."

"I'm a second-generation vampire," he said simply, and duh, they healed far faster than other vampires. As a third-generation vampire, Aylin would heal faster than turned vampires if her blood-clotting issue wasn't a factor, but even then, her body wouldn't mend wounds even half as quickly as Hunter's did.

They met up at a dead end a few hundred yards later. Without traps and monsters, their main concern now as they negotiated the walls on their way to the exit was avoiding plummeting back into the maze. For the millionth time today, Aylin thanked Samnult for giving her the use of her right leg, because staying on top of the wall would have been a serious challenge before.

But then, they wouldn't have ended up at the top of the maze anyway. Her leg wouldn't have allowed her to leap onto the beast, let alone jump *off* of it.

They passed dozens of horrors lurking in the maze below, horrors that would have caused them a lot of trouble, pain, and maybe even death. Steaming, bubbling pools of what appeared to be acid blocked several paths, and packs of furry wolf-like canines roamed the maze, their howls ringing out both close by and far away.

Hours later, under the light of two quarter moons and inside a bank of fog, the end of the maze finally came into view. They picked up their pace, threading their way through the mist and trying not to look down at whatever was cutting a path through the even thicker layer of fog that boiled below.

"We're almost there," Hunter said. "But this was too easy. I don't like it."

Aylin didn't, either. The terrain outside the maze had changed from desert to forest, with mountains rising up as far as the eye could see. But inside the maze, the darkness had brought out creatures so vile Aylin would forever have nightmares. Creatures with multiple glowing eyes. Tentacles. Teeth as long as her forearm. Those were the things they should have come up against, and she wouldn't be surprised if Samnult found a way to dump them back into the arena.

As they passed a group of humanoids with sharp teeth and black-tipped claws on their elongated hands, a screech rang out from somewhere behind them. Aylin swung around. There, maybe fifty yards behind them, a form took shape. A man. No, a snake.

"Fuck me," Hunter whispered. "Buweti."

Ice filled her chest cavity. She'd been raised on tales of the legendary snake man who appeared every fifty years to slaughter entire clans and gorge on their innards, but she'd never taken the fable seriously.

Time to reconsider the validity of all the legends.

"It's on top of the wall—" She didn't have a chance to say anything else. Hunter lifted her off her feet and swung her around so she was in the lead as they raced toward the maze exit.

Aylin ran as fast as she could, resisting the urge to look back even as she heard the pounding-slithering of the Buweti getting closer.

The snake man's hiss sounded just feet away.

Closer. She swore she heard its panting breath.

Suddenly, Hunter grunted. She put on the brakes, wheeling around as Hunter went down, the hideous, scaly thing with the body of a man but the scales, fangs, and cobra hood of a snake landing on top of him. Its fangs sank into his shoulder, and its claws ripped gashes in his arms as he struggled to keep from going over the wall.

"No!" Aylin attacked, kicking the thing in the face with all her strength. Blood spurted from its nose, and a powerful jab of her heel smashed it hard enough in its reptile eye that she felt the crunch of bone.

The Buweti released its bite and shrieked, blood and drool dripping from its nasty teeth. She kicked it again, right in its mouth, cutting off its scream and knocking it backward. In a heartbeat, Hunter was up and on top of the thing, his fists slamming into its head until it was nothing but a pulpy mess.

Out of the corner of her eye, she saw movement, and with horror, she watched as a dozen more snake creatures took shape in the distance.

"Hunter! We have to go!"

They'd lost the backpack, but neither of them gave a shit as Hunter kicked the Buweti's body into the maze below, where various other monsters tore it apart before it even hit the ground.

That could have been us.

It still could be if they didn't get the hell out of here. Like, *now.*

They sprinted, reaching the perimeter wall at the end of the maze in an uncoordinated rush. The pack of snake people had taken a wrong turn, buying Aylin and Hunter a few moments. Hunter crouched, gesturing for Aylin to do the same. Keeping one eye on the enemy behind them, she went down on her haunches, amazed at how easily she could do it now. And how much it didn't hurt. Great Spirit above, being normal was *awesome.*

"There's the exit." She pointed to an archway to their left. "Should we jump into the maze and go through it or jump down on the outside?" The fact that she was talking about leaping forty feet below would have made her giddy if they weren't in a life-or-death situation.

"I don't know," Hunter said gruffly. "What do you think?"

She froze. No one had ever asked for her opinion on a tactical matter. Actually, no one but Rasha had asked her opinion on anything, and even then, Rasha had been looking for a sounding board, not real advice.

Aylin thought back to an old warfare tactics book she'd read once, and while she couldn't remember the author, she remembered the battle. A Navy SEAL team had been pinned down on top of a building, and their choices had been to enter the building and fight their way down or to rappel down the side of the structure, exposing themselves to enemy fire from surrounding buildings. They'd chosen to go inside, where they'd been trapped. Only one had survived.

What if they jumped into the maze and the exit that was wide open right now suddenly closed?

"Hurry, Aylin," he said. "They'll be on us in thirty seconds."

"Outside," she said. "Something might come out of the woods and attack us, but the same thing could happen inside the maze. At least this way, we won't be trapped inside."

Hunter inclined his head in a sharp nod. "Then let's do it."

No hesitation. No questioning her. He simply took her hand and gave her a look that dripped with confidence and readiness.

Aylin was pretty sure that someday she'd look back and realize that this was the moment she fell in love with him.

Rasha, you bitch. You have no idea what you're getting.

"On the count of three," he said. "One . . . two . . . *three!*"

They jumped. A split second of terror gave way to exhilaration. Cool air swirled around Aylin as she plummeted toward the ground. Her stomach leaped into her throat, blocking her shout of absolute euphoria. This was freedom. This was what it meant to be a vampire, to use the natural strength, speed, and skills inherent to a healthy individual.

This was *life*.

They hit the ground in tandem thuds, and even though the impact was jarring to every joint in her body, Aylin reveled in it. She *wanted* jarring impacts. She *wanted* to leap from high places.

"We have to keep going," he said, glancing up at the wall. "The Buweti—"

"Won't harm you now." Samnult's voice rang out, and sure enough, the snake men stopped at the edge of the maze, their furious hisses making her skin crawl. "And bravo." Samnult materialized from out of the forest, walking toward them on two hooved feet and clapping theatrically. Aylin wondered if he would ever appear to them the same way twice. She wished he'd settle on one. His multiple personas freaked her out. "No one has solved the maze so quickly." He looked up at the wall. "But I guess you didn't solve it as much as you *bypassed* it."

Hunter's smile was part amusement and part in-your-face smugness, and if the wounds in his shoulder and arms left by the Buweti hurt him at all, it didn't show. "Pissed that we beat your little rat race?"

"No." Samnult's lips peeled away from yellowed, sharp teeth. "I'm pissed that you cheated."

Cheated? How could you cheat when you were fighting for your life? "We didn't cheat," she replied. They'd improvised, something she was used to doing to make up for her lack of physical ability. "You never said we couldn't get to the exit on *top* of the walls."

A deep rumble ripped up from Samnult's throat. "A mistake I won't make in the future." He clenched his hands into fists, and she wondered if he was having fantasies of wringing their necks. "But the maze did what it was supposed to do. Hunter, you've demonstrated your intelligence and resourcefulness."

Hunter snorted. "Without Aylin, I couldn't have done it."

"Using her spirit animal to talk to the bird was a good trick," he said, and Aylin swallowed hard. He knew? She shouldn't be surprised, she supposed, but she didn't like it. She'd spent too much time trying to keep it a secret. "But you didn't condemn her for it, which is smart. Because your *ways of the fucking big black birds* are fucking ridiculous." He grimaced. "Well, I'd be wary of skinwalkers. You got that right with your Raven and Crow crap."

Huh. It hadn't occurred to her that Samnult, who had created the vampire race, would have strong opinions about the lore vampires had developed to explain their origins. She wondered if the god who created humans viewed all the various religious dogmas the same way.

Apparently, Hunter's thoughts echoed Aylin's, because he glared at the demon and said, "You know, maybe if you showed yourself to our race and told everyone the truth, they wouldn't be living by bizarre lore that revolves around a raven, a crow, and two chiefs who never even met in real life."

Samnult smiled, but it was a cold one that chilled Aylin to the bone. "In time. For now, you'll continue to lead your flock the way you have been, and so will everyone who knows the truth. But first, you'll have to survive the next challenge."

Samnult snapped his fingers, and suddenly, they were inside a cave lit with smoky tallow candles. Silver moonlight streamed through the opening, bringing with it a cool breeze. Neat blanket rolls, food packets, piles of wood, and bottles of water sat on the floor of the cave, and along the back wall, a crystal pool bubbled softly, its surface nearly hidden by a layer of steam.

"Hot springs," Sam said. "If you wish to bathe."

Hunter and Aylin exchanged confused glances. "How is this a challenge?" Hunter asked.

Sam laughed. "This? This isn't the challenge. The second you step outside the cave, the test will begin. But it's night, and trust me, you want to wait until the sun is up. I've healed your wounds in preparation for the challenge, but what you'll truly need is good luck."

With that, he disappeared. Somewhere outside, something growled. Something *big*.

Aylin had a feeling that daylight was going to come far too soon.

21

As SAMNULT *POOF*ED away, Hunter cursed. Sure, a night's rest would be great, but more than anything, he wanted this to be over with. The sooner he was back with his clan, the better.

It wasn't that he didn't trust his clan members to behave while he was gone. If anything, Riker would keep everyone in line with a firmer hand than Hunter used. But Hunter didn't like unknowns . . . and Rasha was an unknown. Worse, humans were encroaching on vampire lands in numbers he hadn't seen since the white man had hunted Native Americans into the ground. If anything happened to MoonBound while he was gone, he'd never forgive himself.

If his clan was to be destroyed by humans, he wanted to die with them. And he wanted to take out as many of the enemy as possible before he went. He had priorities, after all.

Aylin checked the supplies on the floor as he moved to the cave entrance and peered out, careful to not step past the threshold. Beyond the opening, stretches of rocky ground and flat-topped hills defined the landscape. Cactus plants twice as tall as Hunter sat next to strange, twisted trees with skinny black leaves. Sagebrush and tumbleweeds dotted the land, and little critters scurried back and forth under the cover of the vegetation.

It was all relatively normal . . . except for the trail of clawed footprints in front of the cave. Footprints as long as Hunter's arm.

That couldn't be good.

"Hey!" Aylin called out. "Look what I found!" She held up a hatchet and a pocketknife, and he damned near let out a whoop of excitement.

"Toss the hatchet to me." She started toward him, but he shook his head. "Don't hand it to me. Throw it." He made a *come on* gesture with his fingers. "Do it."

With a shrug, she hefted the hatchet and launched it, but in the follow-through, her eyes shot wide. "Duck!"

The hatchet spun hard and fast at his head. He ducked to the side, felt a brush of air across his ear. The distinct *thud* of metal meeting bone rang out, and Hunter wheeled around in time to see a bald dude with a mouth full of sharp teeth hit the ground, the hatchet buried between his eyes. His fist was wrapped around the handle of a blood- and gore-stained machete.

"He slipped in behind you," she said breathlessly. "He was going to decapitate you."

"Holy shit. Thank you." He glanced between the dead creep and Aylin. "You're good. Real good."

"When you have a bad leg, you learn to excel at fighting in other ways." She was breathing hard, but her blue eyes glowed with predatory excitement in the smoky light. He liked that in a female. "Glad you ducked. I'm not used to not having to compensate for the unsteadiness of my right leg."

"It was a damned good throw. Better than anything most of my warriors could pull off." Crouching, he collected the machete from the dead guy and did a quick pat-down of his ratty clothing, which appeared to be fashioned from the skins of dozens of different creatures. "I'm going to get rid of him." Standing, he wrenched the hatchet free of the dead thug's skull and tossed it next to the machete.

While Aylin cleaned the weapons, Hunter disposed of the Neanderthal. Without crossing the threshold, he heaved the body outside and watched it tumble down the brush-covered incline and disappear.

Trash dutifully disposed of, he used a stick to draw a line in the earth from one side of the cave opening to the other, and using a simple protective chant he'd learned from the clan's mystic-keeper, he set up a basic proximity alarm. Anything trying to enter the cave would now trigger a warning that Hunter would feel on his skin like an electric shock.

When it was done, he went over to Aylin, who was sitting with her back to the cave wall, using a wet cloth to wipe the machete clean.

"Never thought I'd be fighting battles—in a demon realm, no less—and cleaning weapons." Something in her voice was off, but he couldn't tell what.

He moved closer, inhaling, seeking her scent. Bitterness wafted from her in a massive wave, and his stomach clenched. She'd volunteered to come on this journey with him, but he couldn't blame her if she wasn't exactly happy about it.

"I'm sorry you've had to do this. It should have been Rasha." Should have been, but some secret, shameful part of him was glad it was Aylin he was dealing with. And that made him a real bastard, didn't it?

"You think you need to apologize?" Aylin set aside the machete, stubborn bits of gore still clinging to its rusted and chipped blade. "Don't. Right now, in this dangerous freak show of a realm, I'm the most free and the strongest I've ever been."

He wasn't sure he'd heard that right. "Are you saying you like it here?"

"Oh, hell, no. But I don't really like our world, either." She reached for a bottle of water and twisted the plastic cap off with more force than was necessary. "I mean, I hate it here, and I'm dreading whatever we have to face tomorrow, but I think I'm dreading going back to the real world afterward even more." She smiled thinly. "How screwed up is that?"

Hunter had been around for centuries, knew that other clans had different customs, values, and regard for life, and he'd learned not to interfere or, frankly, give a damn. But he was too involved with Aylin now, and what she'd just told him broke his heart wide open. How sad was it that the shit they were dealing with now was better than the shit she had to deal with at home?

"Aylin?" He went down on his haunches in front of her, draping his forearms across his knees. "What happens after we get back?" *After Rasha and I are mated.*

Her smile was as bitter as her scent. "I'm supposed to be mated," she said, and a burning sensation spread through his gut, along with a healthy dose of anger.

Sure, he had no right to be jealous. None at all. And yet every fiber of his being screamed with it, as if he was being torn apart at the cellular level.

Mine.

"To whom?" He hoped she didn't hear the murder in his tone.

"No one in particular," she murmured. The way she said it didn't quite ring true, but he didn't know why she would lie. "But now that my leg is strong . . ." She trailed off, her smile and scent both losing the bitter edge. "I have options. For the first time, I'll outrank every female in my clan, and most males. I don't have to let everyone walk all over me." The predatory light lit her eyes again, but this time, Hunter didn't like what he saw.

"You're thinking about revenge, aren't you?" He cursed under his breath. "Don't waste your time on it, Aylin. Your father—"

"Is a monster!" she snapped so viciously that he rocked backward, surprised at the sudden rage that practically vibrated her body. "You have no idea what it was like to grow up at ShadowSpawn. To be thought of as a curse on the clan and the murderer of my mother. To be told every day that I should have been drowned at birth. To be reminded that Rasha was the worthy twin and heir, while I was not even useful as a spare." She threw down the bottle cap. "Well, now I'm whole. Now I don't have to put up with shit. If I want to leave, I can. And this time, I can run. I can escape my father's warriors when they come after me."

"This time?"

She made a sound somewhere between a laugh

and a growl. "I tried to run away once. A couple of decades ago." Her voice was soft, but it carried an undertone of fury that was tinged with cobwebs, as if her anger had finally broken free from the dusty box she'd carried it in for so long. "I was coming to you. To Moon-Bound," she added quickly.

His mouth worked soundlessly for a moment. "To me? Why?" As soon as the question crossed his lips, he knew. "Sanctuary. You wanted to escape from your father."

"Bingo." She downed half of the water, as if doing so would douse her anger. Instead, it only seemed to fuel her ire. "My sister and half a dozen warriors caught me before I could go ten miles. My father whipped me so badly that it took a week to recover. For three days, I thought I was going to die, and I was glad." She locked gazes with him, her eyes flat with what the Elders called the "warrior's wall," a hardness that couldn't be faked or broken through. When you saw it, you knew that the person you were looking at didn't fear dying. "Have you ever prayed for death, Hunter? Have you ever hated your life and what you were so much that death looked like the better option?"

He had, but he hadn't thought about it in a long time. He'd never spoken of it with anyone, either, but he suddenly wanted to. Maybe because here in a land where he might die tomorrow and with no alcohol or video games to distract him, he had no other way to silence his father's voice or the cries of his dead children. "I grew up with a father who lived the Way of the Raven. And I lost three children, any of which I'd have given my life for," he said. "So yes, I've been there."

The pity in her blue eyes was almost too much to bear. "I'm sorry." There was a long pause, and then, "What happened? Where are the mothers?"

A knot of sorrow twisted his gut. "Two died in childbirth, along with my son and daughter. One seventy years ago, the other more than a hundred and fifty." Closing his eyes, he let himself feel the pain of those losses, for the first time in . . . hell, he didn't even know.

The females had been skilled warriors and valuable clan members, and he'd loved both. But he'd known deep down that they weren't suitable mates for him. As a clan chief, he needed to mate only a born female he imprinted on, or he had to save himself for a mate taken for strategic reasons—like Rasha.

"What about the third?" Aylin's voice was a soothing balm on those raw wounds. "What happened to her and the child?"

Lifting his lids, he stared into the steam created by the hot springs at the back of the cavern. "Technically, she was the first. Standing Willow was the female my father sent to guide me through my *salisheye* when I was fifteen."

He'd been enamored of the born female's dark-haired beauty, had begged his father to let him mate with her. But Bear Roar had refused, had even forced Hunter to listen to the sounds of her making love with other clan males, hoping his infatuation would die.

His father need not have bothered; Standing Willow's behavior after the death of their newborn son had done that all by itself.

"She gave birth nine months later, but my son

didn't live through the night." His throat closed. "He died in my arms. The next day, she seduced the visiting son of DeathMist's clan leader. She left with him that eve."

"Oh, wow," Aylin murmured. "That's . . . heartless."

"She did what she had to do." Hunter could still feel the weight of his son in his arms, could feel the scars on his soul rip open at the memory of watching the boy's life slip away. "I couldn't protect him. I couldn't protect any of them. So believe me, I know what it's like to hate my life and what I am so much that I want to die."

Her hand came down on his, her slender fingers stroking his knuckles lightly. "But you also want to live, or you would have given up on clan life a long time ago."

"Only because my father is dead, and MoonBound deserves a better leader than he was."

Sometimes he wondered if he truly was any better. Oh, Hunter didn't mete out harsh punishments for minor infractions, and he didn't allow anyone to abuse anyone else, but he'd also made enemies out of clans that followed the Way of the Raven, and many had paid the price. The death of every MoonBound member at another clan's hand weighed on Hunter as heavily as the deaths of his children, because those, at least, had been preventable.

"From what I've seen," Aylin said, her fingers warm on the back of his hand, "you're a fantastic leader."

Her touch was as soothing as her voice, and he realized how selfish he was being, taking comfort in her when she was in more need than he was. His past was a murky mire of trauma, but the key word there was *past*. Aylin's *future* could very well be as bleak as her past.

"I wish I'd known you were coming to us back when you ran away. I could have done something—"

"If you'd helped, my father would have crushed you. It was stupid of me to try. I should have headed for Seattle. I could have hidden with other free vampires."

"You'd have lived like a rat with them," he pointed out. "You'd have been hunted by humans and forced to sleep in sewers."

"But I'll be free."

He sucked in a harsh breath. *I'll be free.* Not *I would have been free.* She was planning to run away again, and this time, she was fully capable. The suffocating sensation of panic squeezed his chest, and he blurted, "You can't do that!"

"I *can't*?" She leaped to her feet in an astounding blur of motion. Clearly, she was getting used to her new, improved leg. "Do you know how sick I am of being told that I can't do something?"

"I didn't mean it like that," he said. "You're resourceful, determined, intelligent. I have no doubt that you can succeed at whatever you put your mind to."

She jammed her hands on her hips and pegged him with a withering stare. "Then what *did* you mean?"

I meant that I don't want you to be far away from me.

Shit. That was dangerous thinking, given that he was due to mate Rasha in less than a month's time. But the truth was that he wanted Aylin. Even now, as she abandoned the scolding female pose and paced the thirty-foot width of the cave, he couldn't keep his eyes off her. The flex of her leg muscles with each silent step drew his appreciative gaze, and the mesmerizing sway of her hips made his body tense up in all the right ways.

He dragged his gaze up to admire the way her breasts bounced beneath the supple leather of her dress. They were small but firm, and his own chest burned in remembrance of them pressing into him when they'd been naked and feeding at the portal.

When he'd come all over her.

"Well?" she prompted, striking the hands-on-hips pose again. "What did you mean?"

Dammit. Grinding his teeth, he stood, accidentally kicking the packets of blood onto the ground. "Nothing." The blood sloshed around, something that should have made his mouth water, but all he wanted his lips to touch right now was Aylin. "We should feed," he said gruffly.

"I'm not hungry," she said. "Something about potentially dying tomorrow is killing my appetite."

Hunter had never had that problem. He could always eat. "You need to keep up your strength." He scooped up a packet of blood and held it out. "Eat."

"I said, don't tell me what to do! People have been ordering me around all my life. I hate it." Her face grew red with the force of her mounting anger, and while Hunter's first instinct was to gather her in his arms and hold her, he sensed that she needed to get this out. That she'd never truly let loose. "I hate ShadowSpawn. I hate my father. And right now, I hate Rasha so much I could beat her with that hatchet."

"Right *now*?" He was shocked that she hadn't *always* hated her sister. "Why?"

"Because she doesn't deserve you!" she yelled. "And she's not the one here fighting to save your child, but when all is said and done, *she* gets to mate with you and bear your children." Spinning, Aylin flung the water bottle into the wall with so much force that it shattered into half a dozen pieces and sprayed water everywhere.

Aylin might as well have punched him in the gut as the reality of the situation truly sank in. He was here, fighting alongside the female he wanted, but waiting for him back at headquarters was one of the most vile females he'd ever met.

She gets to mate with you and bear your children.

The very idea made his balls shrivel. He was going to have to spend the rest of his life with Rasha, and Aylin was going to disappear from it forever.

Emotion and helpless anger clogged his throat. He turned away from Aylin before she could see it, before she could witness how much this was affecting him. He had to stay strong, to keep things between them as distant as possible. The future of his clan was at stake, and one misstep could land MoonBound at war with ShadowSpawn. As much as he hated Rasha, he hated the idea of even one of his clan members dying because of his choices even more.

He heard Aylin padding toward him, and he tensed, excruciatingly aware of every step closer. When her palm came down between his shoulder blades, a tremor rocked him from the inside out, and he realized that the pain of losing her was going to be impossible to bear. He broke out in a cold sweat despite the burn of lust that radiated outward from her hand to every inch of his body.

"I shouldn't have said that." Aylin cursed under her breath. "I don't usually get angry like that, and I shouldn't be making your union with Rasha more difficult."

"Don't," he said roughly. "Don't apologize, and don't touch me. Never again."

Dammit all to hell, he didn't trust himself when she was touching him. Whoever said females were the weaker sex was a fucking idiot, because Aylin held more power over him than anyone ever had. It was time to minimize the hold she had on him, even if it meant hurting them both. "I belong to Rasha."

Those four words nauseated him.

Aylin's hand fell away, and the pain of the loss was almost physical. "I guess that says it all, doesn't it? Rasha will be thrilled to know you want her."

She strode away, and he lost it. Completely, utterly lost it. Before his brain could catch up with his body, he slammed into her from behind and hauled her against him, one arm around her waist, the other gripping her chin. Her slender shoulders bit into his chest as he put his mouth to her ear.

"I want *you*, Aylin," he growled. "I want you so bad I can't think straight. Or do you think this is for your sister?" He ground his hard cock against her ass and smiled when she let out an erotic, encouraging growl. "*That* is why I didn't want you to touch me. I want you, but I can't have you."

Craning her neck, she looked up at him. A hypnotic maelstrom of emotion swirled in her eyes, sucking him in so completely that he would willingly drown in them.

"Yes, you can," she whispered. "If only for tonight, you can have me."

In an instant, the atmosphere became charged. Her breaths, once shallow with anger, became deeper and more rapid. So did his. Her rear, pressing solidly against his crotch, rolled with each breath, and his cock swelled even more, cradled in the seam of her ass.

"Hunter," she gasped, pushing against him.

The scent of her arousal filled the air with her musky spice. He held in a groan, when what he really wanted to do was flip up the hem of her dress and drive into her. Just like this. From behind, his hands on her hips, his teeth buried in the crook of her neck to hold her steady for his thrusts.

Great Spirit above, it was tempting. To share one night of passion with her, to have this one memory to hold him for a lifetime.

"Please." She brought her hand up to slip behind his head, driving her fingers through his hair and holding him as he brushed his lips over the shell of her ear. "Make love to me. I want you to be my first."

He froze. "You're a virgin?" He should have expected as much, but he couldn't imagine how any male could have resisted her.

"Yes." Her voice trembled, but her left hand was steady as she wedged it between them to grip his thigh. "Take it. Take *me*."

He couldn't, for so many reasons. As tempting as it was to make love to her, she deserved better than to have her virginity ravaged on the floor of a cave by a male who would soon belong to another. And he knew, all the way to the depths of his soul, that sex with her would wreck him. He would claim her as his own, would be unable to let her go, and his clan would pay the price.

"I can't," he said in a broken whisper. "You deserve more than I can give you."

She cried out in frustration. "I've gone through my *salisheye* because of you. I need more now. I've never felt this way before. Help me, *please*."

Oh, hell, accidental or not, he was responsible for her sexual awakening, wasn't he? Pride and shame knotted in his gut. Pride, because of all of the males on the planet who could have taken her through the *salisheye, he'd* been blessed with that honor. Shame, because he should have made it more special than a dry hump during transport to a demon realm. Anguish radiated from her, and everything that made him male demanded that he make it better.

Slowly, he slid his hand downward, over her rib cage to her flat, hard abs. The tips of his fingers rested just above her pubic bone, caressing lightly, making her arch into his touch.

"I can't make love to you, but I can make you feel good. Will you let me do that?" He worked his way lower, down her thigh, until he reached the hem of her dress. "Let me touch you."

He slipped his hand under her dress, and she moaned. "Yes. Oh . . . yes."

Victory sang through him, speaking to both the warrior and the male inside him. And yet both recognized that victory came at a price. Tomorrow, he suspected, both he and Aylin would pay it.

22

AYLIN'S SENSES WERE on overload. Her skin was on fire, her breasts ached, and lightning danced along every nerve strand. And Hunter wasn't touching anything but her leg.

The fact that he didn't want to take her virginity stung, but his hand moving upward in a lazy, decadent climb eased the pain. For now.

Don't think about later, she told herself. *Nothing matters but . . . Oh, holy damn, yes!* His fingers brushed her core, wringing a strangled gasp from her. Pleasure zinged through her veins, and molten, liquid heat pooled in her feminine place.

Bracing her firmly against him, he wedged his foot between hers and nudged them apart. She held her breath as he cupped her mound and slipped one finger between her folds.

"You're so wet," he murmured against her throat.

She squirmed, suddenly embarrassed. Was she supposed to be that wet? Was there something wrong with her?

"Easy, sweetheart." His guttural voice dripped

with promise as he rubbed her in languid circles that somehow soothed her ache and made it worse. "I won't hurt you."

No, he was doing the very opposite, making her feel things she'd never felt, and those things could all be described as exquisite.

His finger dipped inside her, and her knees wobbled. "M-more," she breathed. She wanted him deeper, so deep she'd feel him there forever.

He obeyed, adding a finger and pushing deep. He hissed and rocked his hips into her ass. "Damn, you're tight."

He did something sinful with his fingers, stroked something inside that sent electric shocks of ecstasy through her entire pelvis. She clenched around him as he pumped in and out, and when he pressed his thumb against her clitoris, she cried out.

"That's it," he said hoarsely. "Ride my hand I want you to come so hard you scream."

Scream? She could barely breathe, let alone scream. He withdrew his fingers, and *that* made her want to scream, but he plunged them back inside and whispered hot, naughty things in her ear.

Would he say those things to Rasha? Would he tell her how beautiful she was, how he wanted to spread her wide and fuck her with his tongue? Would he tell her he wanted to mount her on the forest floor, deep in the wilderness where their primal instincts could be one with nature?

Guilt, confusion, anger . . . it all assailed her at once, waging war with the pleasure Hunter was giving her.

You should have thought about all of this before you

begged him to take your virginity. Maybe . . . but then, Rasha had the rest of her life to enjoy Hunter's attention. Aylin had only now. Besides, Aylin was here for her sister, so she deserved something for herself, right? And there were no guarantees that she was going to survive the challenge tomorrow. They weren't even in the real world.

What happens in a demon realm stays in a demon realm.

How easy it was to justify taking something that would very soon belong to her sister.

"Come on, Aylin." Hunter's guttural voice broke her firmly away from the lake of shame she'd been floundering in. "Stay with me. You're someplace else right now." How did he know? Before she could ask, he dropped to his knees and shoved her dress up over her hips. "Grab the wall."

His firm tongue stabbed her between her legs. Shocked by the sudden sensation and light-headed at the extreme intimacy, she fell forward, barely catching herself on the rocky cave wall.

"Hunter!" she cried.

His tongue swept along the length of her, from clit to core, plunging deep inside her as his hot breath caressed her most private places. Her own breath exploded from her lungs as he mimicked intercourse, thrusting in and out, finding a rhythm that made her dizzy.

Closing her eyes, she memorized every detail of what he was doing to her. From the delicious onslaught of licks to the almost unbearable pleasure of his tongue diving deep inside her and the light sucking when he opened his mouth wide against her entire sex.

Her legs and arms shook so hard she thought they might give out, but abruptly, he was on his feet again, his arm around her waist to hold her steady as he pushed two long fingers inside her. He stroked her faster and faster, until she was panting and quivering with the need for release. She was rocking her hips now, trying to reach her peak, but he denied her, changing up his rhythm and speed as she got close.

"Please," she moaned. "Please . . . now."

He flicked his thumb over her swollen knot of nerves, and pleasure cascaded through her. And then he was rubbing her flesh at the top of her cleft, the pad of his thumb just barely feathering over her clit as his fingers worked her core, and she saw stars.

The orgasm ripped through her, far more powerful than the one that had surprised her at the portal. Hunter's touch was seductive, ruthless, and so masterful that as her climax waned, another built behind it, battering her with new waves of ecstasy that went on and on.

As she came back down, her muscles gave out. Hunter caught her, lifting her into his strong arms as if she weighed no more than a house cat. She barely had the energy to cling to him, but she managed, burying her face in his throat as he carried her to the hot springs pool.

"I'm going to bathe you and feed you, and you aren't going to argue." His voice was both commanding and teasing, and she was too tired to argue anyway.

"What about you?"

"Don't worry about me. I'll eat and bathe when you're done."

"No, I meant . . ." Cheeks heating, she cleared her throat. "You didn't come. Let me help."

He went taut. "You've done enough already."

She frowned at the way he said it, as if it were an accusation. "Did I say something wrong?"

"Just the opposite," he said gruffly, leaving her even more confused.

He set her down next to the pool and removed her boots before helping her out of her dress. After what he'd just done to her, she shouldn't be nervous about him seeing her naked again, but maybe that was exactly *why* she felt so anxious. She'd been vulnerable in so many ways in her life, but never like this.

Making it worse, he'd gone robotic, his actions brisk and economical, as if he were unsaddling a horse instead of undressing someone he'd just given an orgasm.

As he helped her ease into the hot, bubbling pool, she was grateful for the steam that swirled between them. She'd just experienced the most magical moment of her life . . . but if the devastation on Hunter's face was any indication, he didn't feel the same way.

Not even close.

THERE WAS NOTHING like strained silence to make a male throw himself into mundane tasks with a vengeance.

While Aylin relaxed in the hot spring with a packet of blood, he built a fire, sharpened the weapons on a rock splashed with water, and sucked down his own nourishment. All the while, his dick throbbed and his balls ached, and what he wouldn't give to let Aylin "help" him with that issue.

But he'd already risked too much by giving in to his desire to touch her and taste her, to watch her come apart in his arms. He couldn't afford to create more of a bond between them. He was already dangerously close to entertaining idiotic fantasies—like running away with her.

And spending the rest of their lives being hunted by ShadowSpawn.

Brilliant, Hunt. That's just effing brilliant.

"Hunter?" Aylin's drowsy voice drifted to him as he tossed a stick onto the fire.

He didn't look her way. "Yeah?"

"Tell me about growing up. Your parents. How you became chief."

She couldn't have chosen more uncomfortable subjects if she'd tried. Had anyone else asked about those things, he'd have told them to fuck off. But this was Aylin, the female who had risked her life when her sister wouldn't, and she deserved answers to anything she asked, even the ugly things.

Sinking to the ground, he propped his back against the wall of the cave and slung his arms over his knees as he stared into the fire.

"My mother was a war prize." Closing his eyes for a moment, he wondered if they looked as glazed as they felt. "My father took her when he killed her mate—BlackRiver's chief."

Over the crackle of the fire and the soft gurgle of the water, he heard her sharp inhale. "How did she handle that?"

"She was a warrior, and her clan followed the Way of the Raven, so she accepted her fate." He smirked. "But that doesn't mean she was nice about it." The fights he'd witnessed between his mother and father had been vicious and sometimes violent. Pretty much how he imagined his union with Rasha would be. "My father made it worse by refusing to let her bring her two sons into the clan."

"My father would have done the same thing. He wouldn't want the offspring of another leader in his clan."

Exactly. As harsh as it was, those children could grow up and, with the mother's help, overthrow the clan chief. "It was a little more complicated than that," he said. "The boys weren't hers. They were her sister's. Her sister was mated to the clan chief before my mother was, and when her sister died during the second child's birth, my mother mated with their father and took over their care."

"What happened to the boys? Your cousins, I guess?"

The water swished, and he finally risked a glance in Aylin's direction. She'd moved to the edge of the pool and propped her arms on the smooth stone border. Her damp hair framed her face, and in the smoky firelight, she could have been a water nymph rising up to seduce him to his death.

What a way to go.

He tore his gaze away before he did something stupid, like join her in the pool. "They were sent to the Native American tribe of their ancestors. This was before the tribes separated themselves completely from vampires." Since born-vampire children appeared human and had human needs until their teens, many tribes accepted them . . . until their inner vampires made an appearance, and humans became food.

Another swishing sound. "How long was it before you were born?"

"I was born exactly nine months after my father killed her mate."

"He didn't waste any time, did he?"

"No." And Hunter could only imagine how *not* well that had gone.

More swishing and splashing. What was she doing in there? "Did your mother . . ."

"Did she resent me?" He stared up at the ceiling, hating going back to that time in his life. The clan had been such a dark place, its members little more than cavemen. "I think so. But she never treated me badly. She was just . . . distant. At least, until her sons reached puberty, and the tribe they were with kicked them out. They came to MoonBound, begging for a place to live."

"Did your father allow that?"

He closed his eyes. "He left the decision up to me."

It had been a cruel thing to do, and Hunter often wondered if his father had done it out of cruelty or if he'd been trying to teach Hunter about hard decisions. Maybe both. Probably both.

Aylin uttered something under her breath. "That's terrible. How old were you?"

"I was ten." An infant, by vampire standards. "I sent them away." He risked a look at her, expecting horror or pity or some equally awful thing, but all he saw was curiosity and patience. Still, he got defensive, maybe because he still questioned his decision. "I had no choice. If I'd let them stay, my father would have eventually killed them."

"What did your mother do?"

A lump formed in his throat. *Dammit*. He'd thought he was past what his mother had done to him, but nope. Apparently, trauma was the gift that kept on giving. "She never forgave me. Decades later, I started questioning the way my father ran the clan. Most of the members were loyal to him out of fear, but a few felt the way I did, that things needed to change. So my father told me to take a hike and start my own clan. The problem was that a lot of the members wanted to go with me. Obviously, my father was . . . less than pleased."

"What did he do?"

"He tried to kill me. We fought. He died." Sounded so simple and clean, didn't it?

But Hunter could never forget how, as years of verbal, emotional, and physical abuse boiled over during the battle, he'd become the very monster he'd sworn to avoid. And when he'd delivered the death blow, as his father lay bleeding out on the forest floor, he'd felt . . . satisfaction. And maybe a little joy.

Even now, he couldn't shake the guilty pleasure of the kill, and he wished like hell Samnult had included a bottle of vodka in the supply kit. Drowning the shame was a lot easier than remembering it.

"And your mother?" Aylin asked.

"Like I said, she never forgave me. She undermined my authority, tried to turn members against me. I had to banish her. She left during a snowstorm, and I never saw her again."

He finally looked over at Aylin again, and wished he hadn't. She was still facing him, her arms propping her out of the water from the shoulders up, but now her lower half floated, her feet kicking gently in the water. Her firm, rounded bottom breached the surface, drops of water beading on her smooth skin. What he wouldn't give to lick those beads away.

He wouldn't stop there, either. He could still taste her on his tongue, and he wanted more. So much more, and he couldn't have any of it.

AYLIN WAS GOING to turn into a prune if she didn't get out of the water, but despite the fact that she was in a dangerous land and she'd nearly been killed several times already, this was the most relaxed she'd ever been. She knew it was wrong of her to be enjoying her time with Hunter, but this was the first time any male had taken an interest in her, and she didn't want to waste a second of it.

"Enough about my parents," Hunter said, as he turned back to the fire. "Tell me about your mom, I know she was human when your father claimed her and that she died during childbirth, but that's all I've heard."

Okay, so maybe this wasn't as enjoyable as she'd thought. "My father's clan raided a railroad camp in the 1860s. They killed the men, kidnapped the women." She pulled herself out of the water and wrapped herself in a towel. "You can guess why."

Hunter nodded, the dancing shadows on his face emphasizing the disgust in his expression.

"Well, my father became infatuated with my mother, and he spared her life, keeping her captive long after the other women were dead." Aylin had heard the stories over and over, from her father and from clan members who were nostalgic about the "good old days," when vampires roamed freely, and their heinous acts could be blamed on the native human tribes. "Eventually, he turned her into a vampire, but according to some, she never really came around. By all accounts, she was the only thing my father ever loved."

Hunter looked up, and she swore his eyes darkened as he took her in. "Do you believe that?"

Even his voice had gone dark and husky, and warmth spread across her already warm skin. He'd said he wanted her, and now that he'd shown her the truth of that, she could see it, plain as day. Guilt and pleasure rolled through her, mixing so thoroughly that she couldn't latch on to one. He belonged to Rasha, but . . . he didn't want her.

He wants me!

More pleasure. More guilt.

This sucked.

"I believe my father loves Rasha," Aylin said, as she slipped into the filthy dress she'd worn all day.

"What about you?"

"He blames me for my mother's death." She snorted. "You know how followers of the Raven think. Second twin has an evil soul. And then, when I was born with a birth defect, it was a double whammy."

"Maybe," Hunter said from behind her, "that's proof that he loves you. Followers of the Raven destroy the second twin and any child born with a defect. The fact that he didn't—"

"Means nothing. He loved my mother, and before she died, she begged him to spare me. That's the only reason I'm alive." She turned back to Hunter, whose gaze burned hot, locked on her like a predator in the night. It was enough to steal her breath. To make her go liquid inside. To almost make her forget she had a sister who was waiting for him.

"I think there's more to it." Hunter stood, the magnificent muscles in his chest and abs flexing under skin that glowed in the light of the fire. "He risked a clan rebellion by sparing your life."

"Are you saying you wouldn't risk a rebellion for the female you loved?"

"I'd risk everything for the female I loved." Hunter moved toward her, mesmerizing her with the beauty of his form. He stopped a mere foot away, close enough for her to smell the smoke and sweat on his skin. Close enough to make her mouth water with the desire to taste him. "*Everything*. Which is why I can't fall in love."

"Can't," she whispered hoarsely, "or won't?"

For a long moment, he said nothing, but she saw a battle raging in his eyes, and she wondered if he was thinking about Rasha. It made her gut hurt. Just as she thought he wasn't going to answer at all, he turned away and started for the pool, his thick hair swishing across his broad back as he walked.

"Does it really matter?" he asked. "The clan is my priority. Period."

"But that doesn't mean you can't be happy."

Halting in his tracks, he shook his head. "How could you have grown up at ShadowSpawn and still be so naive?"

"How could I grow up in ShadowSpawn and not hope and dream for something better?" Fantasies and wishes were what had kept her sane. Without hopes and dreams of a better life, she'd have died of despair a long time ago.

"Are you still hoping for something better?"

She crossed her arms over her chest, digging in. No one could take her dreams away from her. "Yes."

"Then I hope you get it, Aylin. I truly do. But I learned a long time ago that hoping for something is a waste of time. I hoped for children. I hoped to mate with someone I loved. Now I just hope to survive the day tomorrow. We'll see how that goes." He worked on his belt, and she turned away as he dropped his clothing to the ground. "Get some rest. Maybe your wishes will work out better than mine."

She doubted it, since she wished Hunter could be hers.

HUNTER WOKE TO the sound of something dying. He sprang from the blanket he'd shared with Aylin and bolted to the cave entrance. Again, he was careful not to step outside, but he didn't need to go out to know what was happening. He could see the carnage very clearly from where he stood.

The weird thing was that the desert setting was gone, replaced by a lush jungle that could have been taken from the Amazon rain forest.

"What is it?" At any other time, Aylin's drowsy morning voice would have made him hard as a rock. Right now, it only highlighted how very vulnerable they were going to be once they left the safety of the cave.

"I don't know. But something really fucking big tore apart something else that's really fucking big."

She joined him, inhaling sharply when she saw the remains of a furry animal that had, when it was alive, probably resembled a carnivorous wooly mammoth. Its head sat on the forest floor, its blood dripping off broad leaves, its eyes glazed over but seeming to stare right at them.

Hunter turned to Aylin, wanting to shield her from the ugliness, but she sidestepped him and faced the blood and gore head-on.

"You don't need to protect me, Hunter. I'm tougher than I look."

He swept his admiring gaze over her. "Yes, you are." She was *so* much tougher than he would have guessed when they'd first met.

Oh, sure, before the journey to this hellhole of a realm, he'd known she was strong, but her quiet strength came from her heart. She'd transformed since arriving, and even though her healed leg probably accounted for some of it, there was more to it than that.

Last night, she'd lanced the festering wound that life at ShadowSpawn had given her. She'd said she never got angry, but the shattered water bottle might argue differently. Hunter had a feeling that she'd held in a lot of anger over the years and that for the first time ever, she felt empowered enough to let it out.

"My father is going to swallow his tongue when he hears that I accompanied you on this challenge, and he'll swallow it again when he sees me walk without a limp," she said. "I hope he chokes on it."

"I hope so, too." Hunter *really* hoped so. Kars's death would solve a lot of problems. He gestured to the stores of food and water. "We should eat something." Very soon they'd have to go outside and face whatever challenge Samnult had arranged for them. Hunter wanted to stall, wanted to hang out until they ran out of food, because even if they passed the test, the hell wouldn't end.

He'd have to say good-bye to Aylin eventually.

When they'd eaten the pemmican bars, half the jerky, and the rest of the human blood, Aylin sighed. "We should get started."

"I know."

She shoved to her feet. "No time like the present, I guess."

"Aylin, wait." Standing, he swiped the hatchet off the ground, leaving the machete. A crack in the blade made it useless. "Take this."

She shook her head. "You're stronger and faster, and you have more fighting experience. You can do far more with it than I can."

Maybe, but that was exactly why she needed it more than he did. "I won't argue about this," he growled.

"Good. Because I'm not arguing, either." Smiling brightly, she shoved the hatchet away when he tried to press it into her hands. "I'll take the pocketknife."

A pocketknife was not an adequate weapon. "Dammit, Aylin—"

"Trust me, I'm good with a small blade." If she was half as good with a knife as she was with a hatchet, she could still kick half his warriors' asses, but he didn't like it. "Best in the clan. Pisses my father off when I win throwing competitions. He's learned never to let me compete unless it's against another clan." She snared the pocketknife from the blanket and flipped it open. "Can't have me showing up ShadowSpawn males, now, can we?" She grinned. "But he always uses me as a secret weapon against other clans. I once humiliated NightShade by knocking competitors' arrows out of the air with nothing more than a butter knife.

Tseeveyo was so pissed that he executed one of his warriors right then and there."

Bringing up Tseeveyo's name made Hunter's rage meter hit the red zone. "Tseeveyo makes your father look like an angel," he said. "Sick bastard. I pity his harem of mates."

"Most of them don't have a choice," Aylin said, tucking the blade into her boot.

Too many females in the world were in that same boat. "He's willing to take pretty much any young female other clans don't want. The younger, the better." He cursed. "Those poor females would be better off dead."

The line of her mouth tightened, as if she was trying to decide what to say. "I suppose that's an option." She started toward the exit, and panic bubbled up in his chest.

"Wait." Rushing over to her, he grabbed her by the elbow and swung her around.

He wasn't ready to give up this moment with her yet. Wasn't ready to end their time together. This was the last chance they'd have to be alone, without the complications of clan life, Rasha, or some giant monster that wanted to eat them.

Aylin looked up at him, her sapphire eyes aglow with vitality. She truly had come into her own in the last couple of days, and if he'd been drawn to her before, now he felt like he couldn't escape her pull. She was a beautiful rose that had grown thorns, and he'd gladly let her draw blood.

"Please don't drag this out," she said. "Unless you're going to tell me that you'll break the deal with my father and mate with me instead of Rasha, don't say anything."

Pain jabbed him in the heart. He wanted to, Great Spirit above, he wanted to, but he'd signed a contract, in his own blood, stating that he'd mate Rasha. Unless she committed a grievous crime or ShadowSpawn was destroyed by humans or another clan, he was stuck.

"I can't tell you that." His voice sounded as if it had been scraped over sandpaper. "But you need to know that, as a clan chief, I've never met a female I *wanted* to take as a mate. Until you."

Her eyes flashed with outrage. "I told you not to say anything. Was that supposed to make me feel better at night, when I know you're in bed with Rasha instead of me? Am I supposed to be comforted by the fact that while you're screwing her, you'll wish I was the one wrapping my legs around your waist? Well, lucky you, because Rasha and I share a face. At least you can pretend."

She jerked away from him, but he caught her before she could take a single step. "I won't be pretending," he swore. "And you don't share a face. Twin or no, she's as ugly as you are beautiful."

For several heartbeats, he couldn't read her. Aylin, whose emotions seemed to play across her face like a neon sign, was as blank as a sheet of paper. And then her eyes iced over so completely he felt a blast of chilly air blow across his skin.

"Can we go now?" She turned away, putting her back to him and shutting him out. "I'm ready to leave last night behind us."

Yes, her thorns could definitely draw blood.

• • •

AYLIN FELT LIKE such a bitch as she strode through the cave's exit. Clearly, she and Rasha shared more than just looks.

But maybe it was time that she stood up for herself more than she had in the past . . . a past in which her way of fighting back had been subtle and behind the scenes. Something had happened to her since she'd arrived in this strange realm; a newfound confidence had risen up and given her a voice she'd always kept chained. Last night had been amazing, but this morning, reality had risen along with the sun. She and Hunter would never be together again, and the pain of that fact was so raw that her emotions felt abraded, stinging every time she so much as looked at him. It wouldn't have mattered what he'd said, she would have lost her shit.

It was about fucking time.

Too bad she was probably going to die in the next few minutes. That actuality tempered the residual anger enough for her to turn back around to Hunter when he murmured her name.

"What?" she asked tiredly. And damn him for looking every inch the warrior, as if nothing she'd said had bothered him at all. Then again, if he couldn't put aside his personal troubles when his life was on the line, he wouldn't make a very good warrior, let alone leader, would he?

"Let's make our way to the closest hill. The trees should give us some cover until we find a good vantage point and figure out what to do next."

Since she didn't have a better idea, she nodded in agreement, and they exited the cave. Instantly, as if they had passed through an atmospheric veil, they stepped into hot, humid air that nearly choked Aylin with each draw into her lungs. They picked their way across a spongy forest floor, walking carefully to avoid pools of blood and spattered fleshy bits of the animal that had been torn apart.

Strange screeches filtered down from the canopy overhead, but every time Aylin looked up, the creatures above went silent, leaving only the sounds of water dripping from leaves. As they stepped across a shallow gully, Hunter kneeled, hatchet in hand, to study a footprint that appeared to have been made by a cross between a bear and, as far as Aylin could tell, a pterodactyl.

"Damn, this thing is huge." He said something under his breath that sounded like "Fucking Samnult," but she couldn't be sure.

Mainly because right when he said it, something roared. Something close.

"What the hell?" Hunter rose fluidly to his feet as Aylin palmed the pocketknife. "Where is it? I don't see anything."

Aylin didn't see it, either, but she heard it. The unmistakable flap of wings. She looked up just as the pterodactyl-bear thing crashed through the thick green canopy, sending smaller creatures scattering and splintered branches and leaves raining down.

The size of a passenger jet, the creature had brown fur on its body, but glossy black wings that could lift a 747 into the air sprouted from its back. Red eyes focused like lasers on Aylin, and she swore its beak, lined with wicked teeth, turned up in a smile.

It was a flying death machine.

In her chest, her dove fluttered, ready for action. She'd never released it to communicate with something that looked like it wanted to make lunch out of her, but the thing coming at them, its massive maw gaping, its machete-sized talons outstretched, persuaded her to give it a try.

She released the dove just as Hunter slammed her to the ground. They rolled, him landing on top of her. She heard a screech, a tear, and Hunter's grunt, followed by the sharp tang of blood in the air.

"Fuck!" Hunter hissed. "The dinobear got me."

She scrambled out from under him as the dinobear, as he'd called it, shot upward, blood dripping from one talon. Hunter lurched to his feet, one arm wrapped around his rib cage. A nasty, deep gash stretched from beneath his armpit to his spine, exposing muscle and bone.

"Hunter!" She rushed toward him, but he shouted a warning, and she spun in time to see the dinobear swoop at them again.

This time, it had her mourning dove in its beak. Oh, shit . . . she hadn't thought spirit animals could die, but as she watched, the beast tore the little bird in half. Tiny gray feathers and droplets of blood rained down.

"No!" she screamed. "No!" Pain, as if someone had ripped one of her organs from her body, left her reeling. But as the dinobear came at her, shock and hurt yielded to rage. In a single, fluid motion, she flipped open the knife, took aim, and launched it.

The blade sank deep into the bird-bear's eye. The thing screamed and tumbled off course, careening off half a dozen tree trunks and flipping head-over-heels across the damp earth. Fur and feathers exploded into the air, and for a few heart-stopping seconds, Aylin held her breath, hoping like hell that the creature was finished.

And then, like the phoenix rising from the ashes, the monster shot upward and caught a draft. Wings spread, it rolled and came back at them in a smooth dive.

"Run!" Hunter yelled. "Toward the bushes!"

He had barely gotten the words out of his mouth when the thing put on a burst of speed and struck out with its feet. But Hunter was fast, and he swung the hatchet at the same time the bird-bear hit him. The weapon sank deep into its furry gullet, spraying blood across the thick foliage like a fire hose. It plummeted to the ground, bouncing and rolling in a bloody ball of fur and feathers until it came to rest against a bus-sized stone.

"You did it!" Aylin's voice was hoarse, her knees wobbly, but victory sang through her like a ceremonial chant.

She turned . . . and her heart skidded to a halt in her chest.

Hunter was lying motionless on a bed of moss in a puddle of his own blood. His chest had been laid wide open, his organs spilling from the gash that ran from his navel to his throat.

"Hunter!" She scrambled over to him. "No!" she screamed. "No, no, *no!*"

Lifeless eyes stared into the sky as she reached his motionless body and threw herself down. "Don't you die, you bastard! *Hunter!*"

Clumsily she gathered him into her arms. He was heavy, his limbs flopping, his skin ashen, as Aylin's gut told her what her brain didn't want to acknowledge.

Hunter was dead.

It couldn't be. Not after all they'd gone through. Not after she'd yelled at him for not choosing her over her sister, even though she knew there could have been no other choice. What if her anger had thrown him off his game? What if he was dead because of her?

Sobbing, she held him close, rocking his lifeless form as tears streamed down her face.

"He fought well." Samnult took form a few feet away, this time appearing as human as Aylin had ever seen him, dressed in a casual business suit, as if staged battles to the death were just another day at the office.

"Help him," she begged. "Please."

Samnult's expression was oddly tender, his voice mild. "Only you can help him now, Aylin."

Hunter was already growing cold . . . even in this heat, he was somehow losing precious warmth. "How?" she rasped. "I'll do anything."

"Anything?" the demon asked ominously. Gone was the compassion, and in its place was ruthlessness she chose to ignore. If she could help Hunter, she would, no matter what the cost. "Are you certain of that?"

Why was he asking such stupid questions and wasting time? Tucking Hunter's face against her chest, she cradled him as close as possible, as if her wildly beating heart could transfer life directly to him. "Yes."

Samnult bared his teeth, which included two vampire fangs as large as her thumb. "I want your dreams."

She blinked. "My . . . dreams?" That didn't sound too bad. Weird, maybe, but so what if she got a full night's sleep without dreaming?

"Your dreams of being normal. Of not being considered a curse and a freak." He cast a glance at her leg. "You will be crippled again."

Her gut twisted. He wasn't talking about dreams . . . he was talking about nightmares. She'd been given a glimpse into what it was like to be healthy and whole, and for twenty-four hours, she'd seen herself living a life of her own choosing. Even if that meant living in the sewers of Seattle and eating rats for dinner, at least she would have been free of the chains that bound her to her father's will.

But Samnult was asking her to give that up. To be crippled again. Crippled and stuck with Tseeveyo. If she agreed to this, she would be back where she had started, which was basically . . . screwed. But Hunter would be alive.

Ultimately, it wasn't a choice.

"Do it," she blurted. "Please."

Sam smiled. "Hunter chose well."

Chose well? He hadn't had a choice, and she suddenly wondered what choice Rasha would have made if Hunter's life was on the line.

No, she didn't have to wonder. Rasha would have let Hunter die.

"Come, Aylin." Samnult held out his hand. "I have something to show you."

24

HUNTER HAD HAD the strangest dream. He'd been riding a horse, a pinto he'd had as a child, across plains that went as far as the eye could see. Armed with a bow, he'd been following a herd of bison, but oddly, he wasn't there to hunt. He wasn't hungry, and the animals certainly weren't afraid of him.

He got the strange feeling that even if he'd shot an arrow at one of the animals, it wouldn't have been harmed.

The next thing he knew, he was at a table in a massive, noisy hall, dining with warriors who had died long ago. Music and laughter filled the room, as did the mouthwatering scents of all his favorite foods.

"It's good to see you, my friend," said a male sitting across from him. Soaring Jay, a human childhood friend from the Umatilla Indian tribe, held up a silver cup filled with something blue. "But you don't belong here."

"It's too soon," said a silver-haired female from Hunter's own clan. Leaf on the Wind, whom everyone had simply called Leaf, had been killed by humans a quarter of a century ago. She sat next to Soaring Jay, their fingers entwined.

Where the hell was he?

Confused . . . but strangely at peace, he sat there, watching dozens—no, hundreds—of friends and family from his past as they dined and drank, sang and danced.

This is a dream, he thought. It had to be. Unless . . . unless he was dead.

Where is Hunter?

The voice, so familiar and yet so distant, echoed in his ears. "Aylin?" he called out. Everyone looked at him with what he swore was pity.

He still doesn't understand.

Hunter has so much to do.

He's lost, but he'll find his way.

The whispers of the people in the room almost drowned out Aylin, and he couldn't figure out where she was. He shoved to his feet and shouted again. "Aylin! Where are you?"

Damn you, Samnult. Aylin's voice drifted to him, sounding as if it were being filtered through a tin can. *If you don't produce Hunter in the next five seconds, I'll gut you with my bare hands!*

Suddenly, he wasn't in the weird dining room anymore. He was standing in the middle of some sort of gladiatorial arena. Stone walls rose up around him, and beyond the walls were stadium bench seats filled with people armed to the teeth and dressed in traditional Native American garb representing dozens of tribes. Human bones and skulls littered the Roman-style arena, so many it would take days, maybe weeks, to count.

Seriously, what the fuck?

The distinct grind of metal gears vibrated the sand under his feet, and then the iron gate at the far end of the arena slid open. He crouched, waiting for some sort of beast or armored warrior to burst through the opening to kill him.

Instead, a blond female raced toward him, and his heart lurched. Aylin? But why was she limping?

Didn't matter. He didn't care. He took off at a dead run, covering the distance between them in three heartbeats. His heart soared as she flew into his arms. If he was dead, that was fine with him. He had Aylin, and that was all that mattered.

"Thank the Maker," she said over and over, as she kissed his cheek, his neck, his chin, and, finally, his lips.

He met her kiss with equal enthusiasm, growling deep in his throat as their tongues met and she clung to him so tightly he didn't think a molecule of air could fit between their bodies.

"Get a room, already." Samnult's deadpan voice broke the moment, but it didn't stop Hunter from holding Aylin close and burying his nose in her hair. He inhaled deeply, reassuring himself that it was her. That he wasn't completely crazy.

"I was afraid Samnult wasn't going to keep his word," Aylin whispered.

She stepped back, but she kept her hands on his bare shoulders, her nails digging in so deep he suspected he'd find blood later. Not that he gave a shit. He'd wear those marks with pride.

He looked between Aylin and the demon. "What happened? Where are we?"

"You died." Aylin's voice broke. "You died, and I thought you were gone forever—"

"But I saved your sorry life," Sam interrupted. "Well, Aylin did. An eye for an eye." He shrugged. "Or in this case, a leg for a life."

You don't belong here. It's too soon. All the voices crashed through his brain, and then came images of a weird flying bear thing attacking him. Of Aylin nailing it in the eye with her blade and of his chest being torn open.

He staggered backward, his mind a jumble of images and sounds and pain. Reality handed him his ass on a platter, and he realized that he hadn't been dreaming at all. He'd been dead.

And Aylin had sacrificed the one thing that was most important to her . . . in order to restore his life.

"Oh, Aylin." His voice was trashed, which was appropriate, given that he felt like she'd thrown away the only thing that might have made her life worth living.

"Yeah, yeah." Samnult rolled his eyes. "Sacrifice is always sweet." He made an encompassing gesture with his arm. "You asked where we are. We're in my training center."

"Training center?"

Samnult nodded. Behind him, through the gate Aylin had used, a tall blond male entered, his garb similar to Hunter's, except that he wore a leather harness loaded with deadly weapons. His boots crunched on the bones he stepped on.

"What did you think I did with all the firstborn children I take from first- and second-generation vampires?" Samnult's gaze swept the crowd. "You probably assumed I tortured them or ate them."

That was exactly what he'd thought.

"The people in the stands are those children," Sam said. "The bones belong to the humans who have oppressed your kind. Who have killed, abused, and enslaved vampires."

Aylin looked out over the crowd in awe. "You're saying that you've been taking children from their parents to . . . what? Hold gladiatorial battles with humans?"

"To train them to kill humans." Samnult snapped his fingers, and the bones disappeared. The blond man stepped next to the demon . . . and bared his vampire fangs at Hunter. "War is coming. And these children I've taken will lead the charge." He patted the newcomer male on his scarred shoulder. "Aylin Redmoon, this is your brother, Pale Wolf."

BROTHER?

Aylin stared at the male in front of her, his blue eyes, blond hair, and skin tone identical to hers, his square jaw, cruel mouth, and broad nose clearly belonging to her father. *Their* father.

His dispassionate gaze took her in with about as much interest as one might have upon seeing a cricket on the ground.

"I . . . um . . . hi." She offered a tentative smile, but his expressionless mask didn't change. At all.

"I watched you." His deep, gravelly voice was nothing like Father's, which, she supposed, was a good thing. "During the trials, I watched you." He whipped a blade from his weapons harness and presented it, hilt first, to her. "Your spirit sings, little one. Your heart is bigger than the challenges you've faced. I'm honored to call you sister."

Eyes stinging, she accepted the blade. The hilt, carved from some sort of ivory, fit her palm as if made for her. "I don't know what to say." She really didn't. What *did* one say to a brother she'd never met but who clearly knew more about her than she knew about him?

"Enough," Samnult said, and suddenly, they weren't in the arena anymore. Aylin, Hunter, and Samnult were where she and Hunter had begun the journey.

At the portal.

Bittersweet memories ricocheted around inside her skull. They'd made love without intercourse, exchanged lifeblood, and bonded in a way that Aylin would hold on to forever.

And yet, even after she'd saved Hunter's life, they could never be together.

With a brutal shove, she locked down those thoughts and brought herself back to the present. "Where's my brother?" she asked the demon.

"You'll see him again," Samnult said. "Soon."

Aylin wasn't sure she liked the sound of that. As much as she'd love to get to know the brother who was taken before Aylin was even born, she had a feeling that the next time they met, it wouldn't be under the happiest of circumstances.

Then again, neither was their first meeting.

"Are we done here?" Hunter glanced over at the stone circle that defined the portal, and she wondered if he also had to suppress the memories of going through it the first time. "Did we pass the tests? Or did my . . . death cause us to fail?"

Samnult's black eyes turned glassy, as if he was reliving the moment . . . and maybe savoring it. "You passed. You killed the creature. The fact that it killed you, too, is unimportant."

Aylin figured Hunter would disagree. "So what now?"

"Now?" The demon cocked an eyebrow. "Now you leave. But first, you can each ask a question. Anything you want." He held up his hand. "And the next thing out of your mouth had better not be 'Anything?' Because that'll count as your question. Also, don't ask about predictions. I don't know the future."

Aylin exchanged glances with Hunter, wondering what he would ask.

Finally, Hunter spoke. "I'm curious about imprinting and how it happens. What's the purpose, especially if it isn't voluntary and is one-sided?"

"Ah, yes. Good question." Samnult braced himself against a tree that hadn't been there a moment ago. Aylin couldn't wait to get back to the real world, where trees didn't move. "The imprint is a mark of genetic compatibility," he explained. "When a male imprints on a female and gains the mate mark, the chances of conception for the couple are vastly increased. The bond itself ensures that the male physically desires the female, therefore increasing the odds that children will be born of the union."

"Does that mean that there are multiple females in the world whom a male could potentially bond with? Not just one?"

"That's another question. But I'll answer. Yes. The idea of there being only one female in the entire world whom a male can imprint on is ludicrous. And I will say this: a male won't always imprint on a female he's compatible with. Timing is everything." He studied his nails with exaggerated casualness. "And I might have a hand in it."

"So you're saying I've been with compatible females before? That if the timing had been right, I could have imprinted on them? Who?"

"I've already answered your one question. Besides, you know the answer already."

Hunter frowned, and then he gave the demon a withering stare. "The mothers of my dead children. Had the 'timing' been right, I would have imprinted on them?"

"I won't answer more questions from you," Samnult said, a clear warning dripping from his words. "But keep in mind that those females are either dead or gone. Imprinting on any one of them would have destroyed you, so keep your anger to yourself." He turned to Aylin. "Have you got a question for me?"

There were millions of things she could ask, and all her life, she'd wanted to know why she was born with a twisted leg. But recent events had changed things. It no longer mattered—what was done was done. "During the third challenge, my totem animal was killed," she began, her voice hoarse, and Hunter pivoted around to stare.

"That's impossible. Our animals are spirits. They can't die." He glanced over at Samnult. "Right?"

The demon made a game-show loser buzzer sound. "Wrong. In my realm, everything can die."

"Do I get a new animal?"

"No. But the humans have an annoyingly appropriate saying about one door closing and another hitting you in the ass. Or something like that." He sniffed haughtily. "The portal just opened up behind you, so be on your way. You'll get out the same way you got in. Naked and feeding. See ya."

With that, the demon disappeared.

"I'm sorry," Hunter said. "Losing your spirit animal . . . fuck. That can't be easy."

Not easy at all. There was a void inside her that she couldn't describe. "I feel empty," she admitted.

"I'm so sorry," he repeated. "This is all my fault. You lost your spirit animal, and then your leg . . ." He looked like he wanted to touch her, to hug her, maybe, but a strange awkwardness sat heavily in the air between them now that they were heading back to the real world. The real world where Rasha would be part of his life, and Aylin would be nothing but a spectator.

"We've talked about this. It was my choice to come with you. I knew the risks." Well, losing her dove was a shock, but she'd expected to die, so the fact that she was alive was a bonus. "And my leg shouldn't even be part of the equation. I came with it like this, so I didn't lose anything."

But she had to admit that having full use of her leg and being pain-free, even for a little while, had been a gift.

Like the night in the cave with Hunter.

Hunter swallowed, and when he spoke, his voice was gruff. "The male who has the honor of mating with you someday is going to be the luckiest vampire on earth."

And there it was. Reality. Sucky, awful reality. But what else had she expected? That Hunter would come back to life, realize that nothing could keep him away from her, and risk his entire clan to be with her? Or that maybe he'd fall to his knees and beg her to run away with him?

"I hate him already," Hunter growled, and Aylin started.

"Hate who?"

"Your mate." His hands clenched and unclenched at his sides. "Whoever he is, I hate him."

Join the club. But for some reason, Hunter's words pissed her off. Before all of this, she'd have shrugged it off, but letting years of anger out in the cave had been freeing. Exhilarating. And a little empowering.

So she wasn't going to keep her mouth shut. She'd been a doormat for far too long.

"You don't have any right to hate him." She gestured to the vortex. "Should we go?" Not that she was in any hurry, but there was also no reason to stay here any longer. There was nothing left to say to Hunter, and she was a firm believer in ripping off the bandage fast.

Hunter hesitated, clearly preferring the slow, torturous method of removing the covering off a wound. But finally, he inhaled deeply and nodded.

Stay strong.

They undressed in tense silence. Aylin didn't even glance in Hunter's direction. It hurt too much to look at him. To know that after today, she'd never taste his blood again. Would never again kiss his firm lips. Would never feel his clever hands bringing her to pleasure.

Rasha would have all of that. Hunter might swear never to touch her, but by law, the mated couple must consummate the mating by sunrise on the second day. So no matter how much Hunter hated Rasha, how long would it be before he shared his bed with her again? And if he imprinted on her that first night, he wouldn't be able to hold out very long at all. His instincts and desires would be focused entirely on her.

Dropping her dress to the grass, she swung around to Hunter. He was already naked. Gloriously, beautifully, sinfully naked. His bronze skin, which had been marked with scars—not to mention the fact that he'd been eviscerated only hours before—was so flawless that if someone told her an artist had painted it on, she'd believe it.

All of her hard resolve pooled into jelly as he walked toward her, his gait stiff, his jaw unyielding. She hoped he was struggling as hard as she was to be detached.

When she dropped her gaze to his groin and the brutally hard shaft jutting upward, it became very clear that he was failing as miserably as she was.

25

HUNTER FELT LIKE such a jerk. Aylin had thrown up a wall between them, and he was trying to respect it, but his damned body had betrayed him.

Marshaling every last drop of self-control he had, he told himself this was no different than necessary feeding from humans. Arousal was involuntary, but it had always been easy not to act on it. He could do the same with Aylin.

Keep telling yourself that, dumbass.

Cursing silently, he halted in front of her before their bodies touched. Her gaze was averted, and he wished he could look away so easily. She was just so beautiful, so remarkable. He wanted to commit everything about her to memory, because soon that would be all he'd have left.

She tilted her head to the side, exposing her slender throat. Gently but firmly, he gripped her shoulder with one hand and used the other to support her head as he released the pleasure chemical and put his mouth to her vein. The moment her blood hit his tongue, he groaned in ecstasy.

Aylin tasted like sunshine and spring water, with a peppery zing on the swallow. Her blood was sweet and spicy, just like the woman.

Her pulse tapped against his fangs, and the fiery scent of her passion filled the air. She might be pretending to be detached and all business, but the beat of her heart and the musk of her arousal gave her away.

She sank her own fangs into the curve between his throat and his shoulder, and he groaned again as the pleasure-pain rippled through his body. He'd never been into pain the way Baddon and Myne were, but the sting of fangs in his flesh had always given him a burst of euphoria like nothing else.

The euphoria expanded, embracing him in a maelstrom of ecstasy. His entire body became erotically sensitized to every sound, smell, taste, and touch. In his mind, he saw himself sinking into her slick heat as she wrapped those long, toned legs around his waist. She clung to him, digging her nails into his flesh as she arched in ecstasy, taking his thrusts with wild abandon.

Ah, damn, she was perfect, fitting against him as if they were one unit, one soul. This damned vortex was messing with his head, telling him she was his mate in every way—fated, even.

He roared in both frustration and pleasure as he pumped into her, knowing this wasn't real, and yet he'd never felt anything so clearly in his life.

I want you.

I need you.

He felt Aylin's orgasm, her strong internal muscles clenching and rippling around his cock, and he came in a hot explosion so shockingly intense that his vision went dark and his brain shut down. Nothing mattered but the pleasure and the female he shared it with.

I love you.

He heard the words, but were they in his head? Had he said them out loud? Had he even been the one to speak them?

Consciousness slowly encroached on the bliss as cold air caressed his hot skin. The sound of someone clearing his throat seemed a little too real.

And a little too close.

Hunter popped open his eyes to see Riker standing there on the snow-covered ground, his beet-red face a mask of embarrassment.

"Ah . . . chief." He shifted his weight awkwardly. "We heard shouts." He spun around and barked a retreat order at the other MoonBound warriors who, Hunter realized with humiliating clarity, were also standing around, gaping as Hunter tugged Aylin close and tried to cover her.

As if they hadn't already seen everything. Motherfucking *everything*.

Aylin buried her face in his chest as the warriors melted into the surrounding forest. "I was really hoping we'd get through the vortex without the, um, *extras* this time. And I could have done without the spectators."

Hunter could have done without the surprise voyeurs, too, but he couldn't be sorry about the rest. Some secret, shameful part of him had wanted to experience that connection with Aylin again, even if it strengthened what he already felt for her.

So much for not liking pain, because you set yourself up for it like a champ.

Yeah, he was a dumbass.

Riker, who had remained at the edge of the forest, his back turned to afford them a little privacy, spoke up. "I hate to be a bastard, but you guys need to get dressed. Fast. Humans are swarming the woods. They're on to us." He gestured to a backpack on the ground. "I put your clothes in there to keep them dry."

Hunter peeled himself away from Aylin, the sticky evidence of his orgasm coating her belly and breasts. Quickly, he snagged his T-shirt from the backpack and started to clean her off, but she snatched the shirt from him and did it herself.

Her message was glaringly clear. *Intimate moment over. Don't touch me again.*

Right. They dressed hastily in the cold clothing. Just as Aylin shrugged into her coat and Hunter tied his second boot, a shot rang out. Movement exploded in the forest, followed by more shots and chaos.

"Hunter! This way!"

Hunter grabbed Aylin's hand and sprinted in the direction of Riker's shout. His warriors surrounded them, and then they were all running through the woods, while men on foot and horseback pursued. If Hunter's ears weren't deceiving him, there had to be fifty horses and twice that many humans.

"We can't outrun them!" Riker yelled. "Not at Aylin's speed. We need to split up. Hunter, take Aylin as fast as you can. Takis, Aiden, Tena, split right and double back behind the humans. I'll go—" An explosion rocked the ground, and fire blasted in front of them.

The blast wave knocked Riker and Katina off their feet and sent them smashing into tree trunks. Baddon's pained roar joined Aiden's curse and another spray of gunfire. Pain sliced through Hunter's arm—he'd either been shot or hit with shrapnel. Unimportant. He had to get Aylin the hell out of there.

"You're bleeding!" she screamed as he dragged her down a ravine.

"I'm fine," he gritted out, but he couldn't be sure about the others. He could hear all of them following, but he also smelled blood and pain, and the cadence of their footsteps indicated that at least two of them had severe injuries.

Shit. He and Aylin had managed to get out of Samnult's danger-filled realm, and they were going to die within minutes of returning to the real world.

But fuck if he was going down easily.

He summoned his anger, needing fuel for what he was about to do. He hadn't been exactly truthful with Aylin earlier when she'd asked about his special gifts. Deep inside his chest, an ice storm churned, and overhead, clouds billowed. With a roar to the heavens, he released the energy that sang through his body.

All around them, hail began to fall in the form of ice spears. Agonized screams shattered the air, but more shots rang out, showering Hunter and his crew with splinters of wood as tree trunks broke apart, victims of whatever massive slugs the humans were using.

And then, from out of nowhere, a shimmering circle of light opened up in front of them. Through the sparkly curtain, MoonBound's entrance beckoned.

A vortex? But how? It was impossible.

"Holy shit!" Riker and Baddon exclaimed in unison.

"It's gotta be a trick." Takis's labored breaths garbled his words, but Hunter understood, agreed, and didn't give a shit. They were all going to die unless they stepped through that portal.

Aylin put on a burst of speed and dragged Hunter toward it. "Hurry! Before it closes."

It could be a trap, and if it was, he wanted to test it first. Releasing Aylin, he leaped through, but she followed a split second later. The familiar sensation of being stretched like warm taffy swept through him in a wave of relief. It wasn't a trap. It was a genuine portal.

When they hit the ground in front of MoonBound's entrance, he grabbed Aylin and wheeled to the side as Tena came next, followed by Katina, who was limping and holding her ribs. Aiden and Takis darted into the vortex, both bleeding from various wounds.

But where were Riker and Baddon? Where the vortex stood, there was nothing but a silvery, swirling wall.

"Come on," Aylin whispered.

Hunter glanced over at her . . . and his heart skidded to a halt. The others were staring, too, astonishment leaving them slack-jawed.

Perspiration coated her skin as she stared at the vortex. Her teeth and fists were clenched, her body rigid. And her eyes, normally a piercing blue, swirled with silver, identical to the giant portal.

Aylin had created the vortex.

Holy. Shit.

"Can't . . . keep . . . it . . . open," she ground out.

Suddenly, Riker burst through, half dragging, half carrying Baddon's heavy ass. As if the air had been let out of her, Aylin collapsed, the portal crumpling like a ball of plastic wrap. Takis and Aiden rushed to catch her, but Hunter was there first, lifting her to her feet and bracing her against him.

"I . . . I can't believe I just did that," she rasped.

Riker's head whipped around to Aylin, but Baddon, who must have taken a bell-ringing blow to the head, merely looked dazed.

"You created the portal?" Riker asked.

Takis was still gaping. "How? Fuck me, that's impossible."

Not impossible, Hunter knew, but rare. So rare that he'd heard of only a single person, one of the Originals, who could summon portals at will.

"I think . . . I think I felt guilty about holding everyone back with my speed—"

"Fuck, Aylin," Riker said. "I'm sorry. I didn't mean to say it like that."

"I know, but it was true." Her face was flushed with excitement and shock, her blond hair blowing wildly around her shoulders. "All I could think was that I desperately wanted to help get everyone back to MoonBound, and the next thing I knew, the vortex opened." She glanced up at Hunter, and just like the vortex she created, her eyes drew him in. "I felt it inside me. It was where my dove used to be." She swallowed. "He was right. Sam was right about one door closing and another hitting you in the ass."

"Sam?" Katina asked. "Who is—"

"Someone we met on our journey," Hunter said, shutting her down hard. "Never speak of him again. Understood?" Hunter looked each of his warriors in the eye, hating that he had to be so harsh, but until Samnult said otherwise, his existence and the truth behind vampire origins must be kept secret. Even if the reason for keeping the secret was stupid.

"Yes, sir," Katina mumbled. A chorus of *yes, sir*s joined in.

Satisfied with their responses, he turned back to Aylin. "Can you open another portal?"

"I don't know. Why?"

"I want to make sure that wasn't a one-time thing." He glanced over at the others. "Get the injured inside." No one moved. Even Baddon had recovered enough to watch with interest, although he had to cling to Riker for balance. They all wanted to see what happened, and he didn't blame them. "You can stay, but only if Aylin says it's okay."

Aylin barely seemed to register anything going on around her. Hunter doubted he'd be any more capable of thought than she was. To potentially be able to control swiftwalking, the most powerful and coveted ability in vampire lore, was a stunner. A *holy shit* stunner.

"Fine with me," she said softly. "But I doubt it's going to work. I'm thinking of someplace I want to go, like I did to get us here, but nothing is even stirring."

"Where are you thinking of?"

"The beach." She smiled, the smile that made him think of sunshine. "I saw a picture of Haystack Rock on the Oregon coast once, and I've always wanted to go."

He'd been there, and he'd love to take her. Ruthlessly shoving aside wishes that would get him nowhere, he offered an alternative destination. "Try to open a path to the cabin where we spent the night. It's possible that you can only travel to places you've been."

Waputuxne, the Elder who had possessed the gift of swiftwalking, had spoken about the journeys he'd taken, because every new destination opened up more swiftwalking possibilities. Hunter, only thirty years old at the time, hadn't understood what the guy meant, and he hadn't truly cared. His father had dragged him to the twice-per-century Meeting of Elders in Boynton Canyon, and he'd been far more interested in the females in attendance than in tribal politics.

Closing her eyes, Aylin concentrated. At first, nothing happened. But when she opened her eyes, they swirled with silver, and a split second later, a vortex opened a dozen yards away, its shimmery transparent surface revealing MoonBound's hunting cabin behind it.

"Fucking awesome." Baddon's gaze swept from the portal to Aylin, a new spark lighting in his dark eyes. An appreciative spark Hunter didn't like at all.

Jealousy is a bitch, isn't it?

The vortex snapped shut, and Aylin slumped against a tree, brushing aside Hunter's hand when he attempted to steady her. He tried to ignore the rejection, just as he tried to pretend that Baddon wasn't most likely mentally undressing Aylin.

Neither was successful, and both disappointment and resentment ran through his veins like acid.

"No one speaks a word of this to anyone," Hunter said. "If this gets out, Aylin will be a target for every clan with an agenda." He lowered his voice, determined to make everyone understand the gravity of the situation. "And I will hunt down those responsible and peel their flesh from their bones while they scream. Am I clear?"

Everyone nodded. Good. Because while Hunter had always considered himself to be a fair, easygoing leader, he also knew he'd come from vicious stock. Hunter's father had committed atrocities that, until now, Hunter hadn't thought he was capable of.

But when he looked at Aylin, he knew the truth about himself.

Like father, like son.

26

AS AYLIN ENTERED MoonBound's headquarters with Hunter and the others, she was still reeling from the discovery—and the potential benefits and complications—of her new ability. Once a year, her clan celebrated its ancestors, one of the few events Aylin actually enjoyed. The weeklong observation was full of festivities and competitions, and in the evenings, the entire clan would sit around a massive bonfire to share tales from both Native American and vampire lore.

Stories of how deer got their antlers, legends that explained why beavers built dams, and yarns about vampires who created portals were staples on those nights. Aylin had absorbed every word the way she absorbed writing in books, and she'd fantasized about how wonderful—and freeing—it would be to possess the long-lost powers of her ancestors.

Now she was the bearer of one of the rarest and most coveted of vampire abilities, and she wasn't sure how to process that fact.

And what was up with Hunter's ability to rain

spears of ice down on the enemy? He'd definitely downplayed what he could do with the weather. But why?

She was so lost in her thoughts as they walked through the narrow halls that she didn't notice they'd arrived at the huge common room until she heard a commotion. From the screeched "Where are they?" and "Why the fuck wasn't I told they were here?" it was clear that Rasha was throwing a fit because no one had announced her sister and her "mate's" arrival.

He's not your mate yet.

The petty words almost fell out of Aylin's mouth as Rasha hurried toward them. She bit down on the inside of her cheek to keep herself in check, not because she was afraid of her sister but because it was time for Aylin to forget Hunter. To finally accept that he wasn't hers, would never be hers, and that wishing for it would only make things worse for both of them.

Sadly, her little pep talk went out the window when Rasha hugged Hunter. He stood stiffly, hands at his sides, but if Rasha noticed his blatant rejection, she didn't show it. She smiled like a dutiful mate and welcomed him home.

Aylin growled low in her throat. Yep, so much for the pep talk.

Rasha finally peeled herself away from Hunter and threw her arms around Aylin. "I'm so glad you're back. I was afraid for you."

"You didn't need to be," Hunter said. "She fought as well as any of my warriors."

Rasha stepped back and gave them both a placating smile. "Yes, I'm sure." She might as well have been speaking about a toddler who won a mock battle with a wooden sword.

Hunter's gaze bored into Aylin with such intensity that she couldn't look away. "If not for her, I wouldn't be here."

"In that case, I'm proud of my sister." Rasha leaned in and lowered her voice to a conspiratorial whisper. "We'll talk later, Aylin. I want to know everything that happened." Oh, wouldn't that be fun? Turning her back to Aylin, Rasha hooked her arm through Hunter's. "I'll have a celebration of your return prepared in our chambers. Come. Let's drink to your victory."

Hunter's gaze lingered on Aylin, but his expression fell, became almost despairing. Aylin knew the feeling. And as he walked away with Rasha, a leaden heaviness centered in her chest.

This sucked.

A hand came down on her shoulder, momentarily lifting her out of the pit of depression she was sinking into.

"Hey," Riker said. "Nicole is heading to the lab with Baddon and Katina. You should have her check you out, too. At the very least, she'd love some company."

It was nice of Riker to recognize that Aylin needed someone right now, but she wasn't sure she was in the mood to chat. Still, it couldn't hurt to clean up and see what Nicole was up to.

That would be far better than obsessing about what Hunter and Rasha would be doing in the privacy of their quarters.

• • •

A SHOWER AND a change of clothes did wonders for Aylin's mood . . . until she walked by Hunter's chamber on her way to the lab. She couldn't hear anything from inside, but she knew he was in there with Rasha, and her stomach soured.

Knock it off. Let him go.

Aylin picked up speed and practically ran to the lab, where Nicole was just sending Katina out, covered in bandages and sucking on a bag of human blood.

"Light physical activity only," Nicole called after Katina. Katina gave Nicole the finger and a toothy grin, and Nicole rolled her eyes. "Vampires are impossible."

"I hate to be the bearer of bad news," Aylin said, "but you're a vampire."

Nicole sniffed. "I'm a very young one. I think the impossible factor comes with age."

Laughing, Aylin wandered around the lab, endlessly fascinated by the equipment. Advanced technology was something she never saw at ShadowSpawn, and she wished she knew more about it.

"How was your trip?" Nicole asked. "Everyone's talking about how you and Hunter went off together through one of the vortexes. People seem to think you went to see the Elders. Is that true?"

Aylin pretended to be extra interested in a rack of vials filled with orange gel. "I can't really talk about it."

"Are you at least glad you went?"

Aylin didn't hesitate. "Absolutely."

The journey had been rife with danger, but she didn't regret anything. Plus, she now possessed a priceless ability, one that could change everything for her. She just wished she hadn't lost her dove. The gentle creature had been a comfort to her, the only constant in her life that she could trust.

"Good," Nicole said brightly. "So . . . what happened between you and Hunter?"

Aylin wheeled around so fast her leg nearly buckled under her. "What do you mean?"

Nicole looked over with a sly smile. "I mean that Riker might have mentioned that you two were . . . ah . . . sort of intense when you got back. He hopes it means things will change between Hunter and Rasha."

I wish. "Nothing can change with Rasha," Aylin said. "Not unless you guys really enjoy war." And from what Aylin had seen, MoonBound's residents weren't warmongers like everyone at ShadowSpawn. "But there have been some new developments I wanted to talk to you about."

One ginger brow arched. "Really? What?"

Hunter had warned against telling people about her gift, but since Riker knew, Nicole would probably soon know, too. Besides, Aylin trusted the female with her life. Still, she hesitated as she glanced around the room.

"Aylin? What is it?"

"I lost my totem animal." Her chest cavity tightened as if trying to fill the empty space inside. "Can that affect my health? You know, the way not feeding a male during moon fever can?"

Nicole frowned. "Not that I know of . . . From what I can gather, only born vampires have totem animals, and I've never heard of one losing it, but I'll do some research." She tucked her hands into the pockets of her lab coat. "I'm very sorry."

"Thank you, but it isn't all bad. I have a new ability. One that will make me very valuable to a clan. And one that could help me escape if I need to."

"Seriously? That's . . . amazing."

"There are limitations," Aylin admitted. Like the fact that she could only transport to places she'd been, and as of right now, she'd only been to MoonBound, Hunter's cabin, ShadowSpawn, and Samnult's vortex. She might be able to transport herself to any of the places she'd been in the woods, but how much good was that going to do her? No, in order for her gift to be truly effective, she needed to travel. "But maybe I can get out of the mating with Tseeveyo and find a male who isn't a complete horror show now."

Nicole appeared to consider that. "Let me talk to Riker. He's more familiar with clan workings than I am. He might be able to help."

Gratitude warmed Aylin, filling her with a sense of peace she hadn't felt in a long time, if ever. She'd never had a real friend before, but Nicole had, in the short time she'd known her, become as valuable to Aylin as Rasha was.

"Thank you." Aylin cleared her throat of the emotional hitch in it and glanced at Nicole's belly. "And how have things been for you?"

"Actually, I need to thank you, too. When you came to me about your bleeding disorder, it made me think about the similar complications female vampires suffer while giving birth. I don't want to jinx myself, but let's just say I'm hopeful that I might be on to something."

Great Spirit, Nicole had already made it possible for vampires to easily conceive; if she could reduce the dangers of giving birth, she'd be revered, pretty much *worshipped*, in vampire society.

"I have faith in you," Aylin said. "Is everything going well with *your* pregnancy?"

Touching her swollen abdomen, Nicole beamed. "Perfect. But I'm craving root beer. I hate root beer, but for some reason, I just can't get enough."

They settled into a chat about pregnancies, babies, and, finally, Nicole's recent past as a human, which Aylin found to be incredibly interesting. When Riker's son, Bastien, came into the lab and reminded Nicole that it was time for their checkers match, Aylin bowed out. She'd spent almost two hours with Nicole already, and besides, she'd seen on the schedule outside the common room that the movie on the big-screen TV was going to be an old classic, the very first Harry Potter movie.

A strange sensation stayed with her as she walked through the halls, and it took a while before she could identify it.

Happiness. Even if it only lasted for the rest of the day, she was going to enjoy it. MoonBound was full of life, laughter, and people who didn't scorn her for her limp. She had a friend, a library at her disposal, and movies. It was heaven, and nothing was going to ruin it for her. Not tonight.

Smiling to herself, she rounded the corner and nearly collided with Hunter.

An unwelcome tingle of excitement went through her at the sight of him, followed by a sinking sensation when she noticed his clean jeans, sweatshirt, and wet, slicked-back hair. He'd showered. Maybe with Rasha. A stabbing pain in her chest made it hard to breathe.

A wordless, awkward silence settled between them. She had no idea what to say, and clearly, neither did he. One thing *was* clear, though: she had to get away from him. The longer she stood there staring at him, the more she remembered the things they had done together. The feeding. The kissing. The orgasms.

"I need to go." Blindly, she rushed past him, her skin burning when her arm brushed his.

"Aylin, wait."

Stupidly, she halted in her tracks, but she was proud of herself for having the willpower not to turn around. Instead, she stared straight ahead.

"Nothing happened." His voice was a broken whisper, as fragile as she had ever heard it. "With Rasha, I mean. Nothing happened." She heard him take a step toward her, and she went taut. He stopped. "She had champagne and chocolate and . . . other shit I don't care about. I couldn't . . . I didn't . . ." He exhaled on a juicy curse. "Nothing happened, Aylin."

She should be thrilled, jumping with joy, and a secret, selfish part of her was. But more than that, there was a bleak hopelessness that obliterated her earlier happiness. No one was a winner here. Not even Rasha. In a small way, Aylin could empathize with her sister, because she knew how it felt not to be wanted.

"You don't owe me an explanation." She squared her shoulders. "Maybe something *should* happen. It's going to, eventually. You might as well get it over with."

"I don't want her."

"Then do something about it."

He took a deep, shuddering breath. "You know I can't."

Yes, she did, and it had been a shitty thing to say. Still, her eyes stung as she swung around to him. "Then leave me alone. Please. It hurts too much to be near you. Go screw my sister, or don't. But don't come near me again."

With that, she walked away. Didn't look back.

And didn't go see the movie.

27

HUNTER WASN'T HAVING the best day, which seemed to be a theme lately. Rasha was driving him batshit.

So was Aylin, but for different reasons.

Every time he was with Rasha, his desire to destroy something—namely, her—made his entire body taut. Just seeing Aylin at a distance made his body taut, too, but not with violence. With lust.

She did things to his insides that had never been done before.

The logical part of him said she had to go, and the sooner, the better. The rest of him snarled like an angry bear at the idea.

Go screw my sister, or don't. But don't come near me again.

Aylin's words two days ago had nearly killed him. He didn't know what he'd been thinking when he'd gone all confessional on her, admitting that nothing had happened with Rasha, but he knew what he'd felt.

He'd felt as if he'd cheated on Aylin when he was sitting in his chambers while Rasha poured sparkling wine and tried to feed him chocolate and strawberries. She'd stripped down to only a pair of sheer panties and a fur shawl as she worked to seduce him, but aside from his skin crawling, he'd felt nothing. Only when she'd climbed onto his lap and he'd closed his eyes and thought of Aylin had his body stirred. Naturally, Rasha had assumed his hardening cock was for her.

The moment her hand cupped his crotch, he'd shot out of the chair, dumping her on her ass. She'd sprawled on the floor like a doe on a frozen pond, while he made a beeline for the bathroom, saying he needed to shower.

She'd tried to join him.

Holy Maker, forget the deer; she was like a cat in heat. Once again, he'd escaped, had been evading her come-ons ever since, but it was taking a toll on both of them. He was exhausted and grumpy, and she had destroyed almost everything in her chambers with her temper tantrums.

There wasn't enough alcohol in the world to deal with her. The icing on top of this shit cake was that tomorrow night was the full moon, which meant he couldn't keep avoiding her.

And he couldn't stop picturing Aylin feeding another male.

A rap at his chamber door brought him out of the dark place in his head. Then the thought that it might be Rasha put him back in it. Until he remembered that Rasha used the door between their bedrooms instead of the main entrance. And she didn't knock.

"Come," he called out as he poured himself a bourbon.

Riker strode inside, his blond hair grooved and spiky, no doubt from running his fingers through it. "Hey, chief. Got a minute?"

Hunter gestured for Rike to take a seat and handed him a shot of the warrior's favorite tequila. "'Sup? Is this about the humans?"

"No change. They're still infesting the woods like fleas, and as far as we can tell, the files Nicole leaked to the media haven't made their way to the public yet." Riker knocked back the drink and sank into the leather chair. "I'm here about Aylin."

Hunter's heart skipped a beat. He recovered with a gulp of whiskey and hoped Riker didn't notice that his hand shook. "What about her?"

"She needs help."

Hunter froze with the glass to his lips. "What's wrong? Is she okay?"

"She won't be okay if we don't do something." He blew out a breath, and Hunter nearly went mad with impatience. "Did you know she's going to be mated next month?"

Relief slammed into him, relief that she would soon be out of his sight, relief that he'd no longer be distracted and tempted by her sweet scent. Her soft skin. Her sexy fangs. No, some other male would have the pleasure of bedding her.

A snarl threatened to rise up and make him look like a fool, so he drowned it in a wash of bourbon.

"So?" he managed calmly, when what he really wanted to do was pull a Rasha and destroy the room.

"So . . . her mate is Tseeveyo of NightShade."

This time, the snarl clawed its way through the

whiskey burn. "*What?*" He stared at his second in command, sure the guy was fucking with him. But no, Riker wasn't one to poke bears with sticks for fun. He was serious, and Hunter felt his inner grizzly roar to life. *Shut it down, man. Stay cool.* "Tseeveyo is a fucking *monster*. He likes little girls, and he has a fucking harem." Aylin didn't deserve that. No one did.

Well, maybe Rasha.

"That's why we need to help her."

"We could kill Tseeveyo," he growled. "That would help."

Riker gave him a *let's be serious* look, but Hunter *was* serious. He'd take out that fucker in a heartbeat.

And doing so would put MoonBound at war.

Fuck. Maybe he could make it look like an accident. Or maybe Tseeveyo could have a run-in with human poachers. Surely Nicole had connections . . .

"Hunt? Yo, Hunt." Riker snapped his fingers in front of Hunter's face, drawing him out of his homicidal fantasies. "Nicole and I talked about this. We think we could find a mate for her here."

Hunter sucked in a harsh breath. The idea of seeing Aylin on a daily basis with one of his warriors, knowing what they were doing in their chambers . . . His fingers tightened on the glass in his hand. He could barely restrain himself now, when she was merely chatting with males at the dinner table or in the common room. To see someone touching her, kissing her, whispering sexy things in her ear . . . he growled loudly enough for Riker to set down his drink and settle into a defensive posture.

Forcing himself to relax, Hunter swirled the whiskey in his glass and tempered his tone. "Kars will never agree. Tseeveyo is a clan chief. He's not going to downgrade his daughter's mate."

"What if we get a born male from our clan? We could offer something else, too. Money, land, a truck full of packaged human blood if Baddon can hijack one—"

"And who do you propose to mate her to?" Hunter interrupted. "Myne?" He snorted. "He's a bastard on the best of days. Baddon? He likes his females bound in leather and chains."

Hunter could picture Aylin now, her tender skin broken by Baddon's toys and teeth, her beautiful eyes hidden behind a blindfold.

The glass in Hunter's palm cracked.

"They're good men," Riker said. "Not the best fit, maybe, but better than Tseeveyo."

A drop of liquor squeezed through a fracture in the glass and ran down Hunter's finger like blood. "And what do you think Myne and Baddon would say about this?"

"The same thing I said when I mated Terese. The same thing you said when you agreed to mate Rasha. It's for the clan."

Except it wouldn't be. It would be for Aylin. Hunter already knew Myne wouldn't do it. Baddon would, and if the way he'd looked at her when they'd returned from Samnult's portal was any indication, he'd be thrilled to have her.

The bastard.

"Kars isn't going to go for it." He slammed the glass down on the coffee table and reveled in the sound of it shattering. He wondered if Tseeveyo's skull would sound the same. "We don't have anything he'd want."

"There *is* another option to get Tseeveyo out of the picture."

That got his attention. At this point, Hunter was willing to try anything except mating off Aylin to someone she didn't want or who didn't want her. "What do you suggest?"

Riker hesitated, and Hunter went on instant alert. The other male was usually a straight shooter, which meant Hunter wasn't going to be on board with whatever Riker had to say. "She could lose her virginity."

Hunter swiped the bottle of bourbon off the bar and drank straight from it, but no alcohol burn was going to scorch away where this conversation was headed.

"Unless . . . she lost her virginity recently." Riker shot him a meaningful stare, and Hunter knew he was thinking about what he'd seen at the vortex.

"Fuck off."

Riker continued as if Hunter hadn't spoken. "According to what she told Nicole, her virginity was the linchpin in the deal with Tseeveyo. Without that, he might let her go."

Hunter snorted. "And her father would kill her."

"Not if she asks for sanctuary."

"That doesn't apply to relatives or mates of chiefs."

"Dammit, Hunt!" Riker barked. "We have to do *something*. She helped us. She helped Nicole escape from ShadowSpawn. She might even have saved Nicole's life."

She *had* saved Hunter's life. "Trust me," Hunter said, "I'd give up my soul for her. I won't let her go to Tseeveyo, even if I have to offer up my own head."

"But?" Riker prompted. "I know there's a 'but' in this."

But he didn't want to think about Aylin having sex with another male, let alone be a part of arranging it. "But we have to be smart. Consider all options *and* their consequences." He sank into the worn leather chair behind his desk and kicked up his feet. "Her new ability changes the game."

"Not if no one knows about it, and she can't tell anyone. Can you imagine what Kars would do with her if he found out?"

Yeah, Hunter could imagine. Kars would likely keep her for ShadowSpawn, and with her history of running away, he'd have to keep her chained to prevent her from opening a portal and escaping. She'd be forced to travel in order to memorize locations, and then Kars could use her to transport his entire clan anywhere he wanted to in a matter of minutes. He could attack enemy clans before they even knew what hit them, and then he could use a portal to get out as quickly as they got in.

He could change the balance of power with Aylin's gift, and no one could stop him.

"Have you been working with her on using her ability?" The question was sour on his tongue. He wanted to be the one helping Aylin learn to explore the extent and limitations of her power, but he didn't trust himself around her. And he didn't want to hurt her any more than he already had.

Riker took a swig of his drink. "She's experimenting with the size of the portal and how long she can keep it open. So far, we've learned that she can't open one indoors, and that the farther away the destination, the harder it is to open one and keep it open. I think it's going to be a while before she can operate one for more than a few seconds. Also, anything that gets caught in the portal while it's closing gets chewed up. She closed it on a melon. Let's just say that you do *not* want to get a body part caught in that sucker."

"Talk about a splitting headache, huh?"

"Funny." Riker tapped his fingers on the rim of his glass. "So? What do you think?"

Hunter hadn't been thinking, and that was the problem. At least, he hadn't been thinking like a clan chief. Somehow he had to protect both his people and Aylin.

"Put out some feelers with males you trust," he said quickly, before he changed his mind. Or before he vomited. "Maybe one of them would want to . . ."

Riker laughed. "*One* of them? Just about every unmated male in this place has already asked if she was feeding someone tomorrow. They'd all jump at the chance to take it a step farther."

Hunter was pretty sure the alcohol he'd consumed had turned to steam and was coming out of his ears.

The door to the adjoining chambers opened, and Rasha swept in. "Hello, boys."

Riker bared his teeth at her, not even trying to be polite. "I'm out of here. Hunt, let me know." He made a speedy exit as Rasha poured herself a drink and sank into the chair opposite Hunter.

"What were you talking about?" she asked, curiosity gleaming in eyes that matched Aylin's in color but were different in every other way.

His first impulse was to tell her it was none of her business, but hell, he might as well use her for information. "Aylin's mate."

Rasha raised an eyebrow. "Tseeveyo. What of it?"

"It doesn't bother you?"

"She'll be mated to a clan chief." Rasha's words were careful, measured, as if reciting from a book. "It's an honor, especially for someone like her. She's very lucky."

"Lucky?" he asked, incredulous.

"She's weak and crippled. She's bad breeding stock. Who else would have her? Certainly not any other clan chief."

Hunter sat stunned. Rasha truly believed what she was saying, and she honestly saw the mating as a great opportunity for her sister. "Aylin isn't weak. She's one of the strongest warriors I've ever met," Hunter snapped. "She held her own in Samnult's realm, and she deserves far better than Tseeveyo."

"I know." Swallowing hard, Rasha turned away. When she met his gaze again, genuine fear had glazed her eyes. "It's her only shot at getting away from ShadowSpawn, Hunter." Now her voice was strained, almost pleading, as if she was trying to convince them both that mating Tseeveyo was for the best. "Without me there . . . I don't think she'll survive."

"And you think she'll fare better with Tseeveyo?"

"He won't kill her," she said urgently. "He'd be a fool to risk my father's wrath."

Hunter doubted there'd be any wrath, but whatever. "What if she were offered a pureblood male from another clan?"

Rasha shook her head. "Nothing will sway my father. I've tried. In trade for Aylin, we're getting another midwife to replace the one you got killed." Yeah, he really appreciated the reminder. "Even more important, NightShade will pledge allegiance to my father."

If Rasha had whipped out a pistol and shot him in the chest, he couldn't have been as shocked. Clan leaders made treaties and formed alliances, but they *never* swore allegiance to another.

Never.

To do so was to give up authority and lose independence. So why in the hell would Tseeveyo, leader of the third-largest clan on the West Coast, swear to follow Kars?

"Surely you see the importance of this deal." Rasha tapped her long fingernails on the desk. "War with the humans is only a matter of time, and vampires need to join forces."

The big picture was starting to become clear, and Hunter had to hand it to Kars—he wasn't a fool. He was getting the clans in line by strategically placing his daughters. Did he have alternative plans to bring other clans under his thumb? Kars was dangerous now, but if he had more than one clan at his side, no clan in the world would challenge him.

More than ever, Hunter had to prevent an alliance between ShadowSpawn and NightShade. "What if the thing Tseeveyo wants Aylin for was taken away?"

"Her virginity?" Rasha shook her head. "Who would fuck her?"

I would. And according to Riker, so would everyone else in the clan. Another growl bubbled up. "Let's just say it happened."

She rolled one shoulder in a skeptical shrug. "My father would demand the head of the male who defiled her. Tseeveyo might negate the deal, but do you really want to face my father's fury? Why do you give a shit about this, anyway?" she asked. "Someday we'll have to make mate matches for *our* sons and daughters. We'll have to make political decisions based on what's best for the clan."

Screw that. He braced his forearms on the desk, leaning forward so she got, real clearly, how he felt about this subject. "We won't be having any children, and even if we did, I would never send a child of mine away to mate with someone they don't like, simply to gain friends and allies."

One blond eyebrow cocked up. "And that is why my father considers you to be a weak leader."

"And I consider him to be a brutal dictator. Not a leader." He glared. "Tell me, do you think I'm a poor leader? Are you ashamed to take me as a mate? Maybe you'd rather have Tseeveyo?"

"Don't be absurd. He keeps a harem. I wouldn't tolerate other mates." She gave him a pointed look. "Or mistresses."

No, he didn't plan to take mistresses. He'd seen what his mother had done to some of his father's bedmates, and he had a feeling Rasha would make his mother's bloodbaths seem tame. Still, he couldn't resist pushing some buttons.

"You know the law," he drawled, with the nonchalance of someone planning to take advantage of said law.

"Of course," she snapped. "After the mating ceremony, a clan chief can announce his intention to take more mates or to sleep with a mistress. The female he just mated with can either accept his decision or fight him." Her glass clinked on her fangs as she gulped a drink and then leaned toward him, her eyes glinting with murder. "I will fight until every one of my bones is broken and I'm not able to lift my head off the ground. If you want mistresses, you're out of luck. I will destroy every female I merely *think* you want."

And that, he knew, would include Aylin.

28

MOON FEVER HAD a different vibe at Moon-Bound than it did at ShadowSpawn, and even though it wasn't night yet and things could change, Aylin could only marvel at how much more civilized these people were.

Tension was high, sure, and tempers ran hot. By mid-afternoon, Aylin had seen four fights break out, three of them between males and one among three females. But there were no serious injuries and, better yet, none of the bloodsport events that had always haunted Aylin.

Rasha was probably right about Aylin being the worst vampire ever.

As she finished drying the last of the dishes in Rasha's kitchen sink, her sister came out of the bathroom in a slinky leather dress that didn't leave a lot to the imagination. A plunging neckline would allow Hunter to feed from anywhere he wanted from her cleavage up, and the crotch-short hemline would allow him to feed from her femoral artery—or to put his mouth anywhere he wanted—without disturbing her dress at all.

Aylin wanted to throw up.

Two more weeks, she told herself. *Two more weeks, and then I'll be out of here.* If Riker and Nicole's plan worked, she wouldn't be expected to mate with Tseeveyo. But that would just mean she had to go home to Shadow-Spawn.

Except she wouldn't. She didn't care if she had to spend the rest of her life leaping through portals and scrounging for food where she could. She would *not* go home, and she would *not* be mated to a scumbag like Tseeveyo.

Rasha rushed over and took a wet glass from Aylin's hand. "I told you not to clean my apartment. You did enough for me by going with Hunter on Samnult's quest."

Aylin snatched the glass back. "I don't have anything else to do."

Rasha let out a frustrated curse, but relented. "What happened during Samnult's trials, anyway? I know you aren't supposed to talk about it, but Hunter says you fought well."

Grabbing a dry towel, Aylin wiped down the glass with short, brisk strokes.

I saw Hunter naked. I practically begged him to have sex with me. But don't worry, he turned me down. Aylin settled for a clipped "I did what I had to do."

"Well," Rasha said softly, "whatever you did, I'm grateful."

If you knew everything, you wouldn't be.

Shifting gears, Rasha strutted over to the full-length mirror on the bathroom door and struck a few slinky poses. "What are your plans for tonight?"

Oh, I'm probably going to be having sex with some random stranger. "Nothing."

"Why don't you join the other females who aren't feeding a male? I hear they're going to watch some sappy romantic comedy in the common room."

There were more females than males in the clan, so not every female needed to participate in the full-moon fever, but Rasha made it sound as if the extra females were all losers no one wanted. It was *so* tempting to say that Riker was arranging for a partner for Aylin, but knowing Rasha, she'd sabotage the plans.

For Aylin's own good, of course.

Sometimes Aylin wasn't sure what to believe.

She gave a casual shrug. "Maybe." She glanced up at the clock on the wall. Nicole's shift in the lab would end in a few minutes, and she wanted to get a "before feeding" blood sample to compare with an "after feeding" sample. The tests would determine whether Aylin's blood-clotting difficulty was, indeed, an issue caused by a lack of feeding males. "I need to go. Do you need anything else?"

"No." Rasha frowned, a pretty pout that drove males nuts. "I don't suppose you've seen Myne around."

"Myne? No. Why?" That was one scary male. He kept to the shadows, and he seemed to have two moods: pissed off and more pissed off. Then there were his fangs. *Titanium*, Nicole had said when Aylin asked. Aylin shivered.

"No reason." Rasha waved Aylin off, but before she could even put down the dry glass, Rasha called out, "Wait."

Sighing, Aylin turned around in time for Rasha to slam into her with a huge hug. Stunned, Aylin could only stand there and wonder if her real sister had been abducted by aliens.

"Don't say anything," Rasha murmured into her ear, "but I have a plan to save you."

Aylin jerked backward. "Excuse me?"

Genuine affection glittered in Rasha's eyes. "I was talking to Hunter yesterday, and he made me think. The match with Tseeveyo is wrong. I mean, it's good for ShadowSpawn, but the thought of you and him . . ." She gripped Aylin's shoulders in an almost bruising hold, and to Aylin's surprise, her sister's hands shook. "You can't speak a word of this to anyone, but I'm planning to be pregnant tomorrow. I'm taking Nicole's conception potion."

Aylin stumbled back a step, feeling as if she'd been shot through the heart. But at the same time, the fact that Rasha was so concerned about Aylin left her speechless, grateful, and feeling more guilty than ever about what had happened with Hunter in Samnult's realm.

"Rasha," she squeaked. "I—I don't know what to say. Thank you, but . . . why? Can't you wait until you and Hunter are officially mated?"

She shook her head. "If I get pregnant, I can tell Father I need you to help. Then you can stay here."

Somehow Rasha had just made staying at Moon-Bound sound worse than mating with Tseeveyo. "He'd never go for it."

"Trust me," Rasha growled, "he will."

Aylin doubted it, but even if Rasha was right, it

would only buy her nine months. "And what happens after the baby is born? I'll be shipped off to Tseeveyo."

"But we'll have time to come up with a plan." Releasing Aylin, Rasha hooked a strand of hair around her finger and twirled it, something she only did on very rare occasions when she was stressed. Was she really that worried about her night with Hunter? Or was Aylin's future a concern? Either way, it was good to see Rasha's heart beating like a normal person's.

"Don't do it, Rasha." Aylin placed the glass, now extra dry, in the dish rack and rounded on her sister, desperate to stop the crazy pregnancy plan of hers. Yes, someday Rasha and Hunter would have children, but Aylin didn't want to be around to see it. "I'm taking care of Tseeveyo my own way."

Rasha frowned. "How?" Realization dawned, and her eyes shot wide. "You . . . you're planning to sleep with someone tonight, aren't you?"

Aylin didn't confirm or deny, knowing that Rasha would see through a lie and jump all over the truth.

"Just . . . be careful, Aylin," Rasha said quietly. "There's only so much I can do to protect you. I can handle Father, but anything else is a gamble."

Aylin had no idea what to say to that. Hell, the entire conversation had been weird, as if they'd both been discussing the same book but Aylin had only read the CliffsNotes.

She needed to get out of here. Her head was spinning and her emotions were raw and tangled, and she suddenly had no idea what to think anymore.

Excusing herself, Aylin went to the lab, but Nicole was already gone. The salt-and-pepper-haired male named Grant took Aylin's blood instead. Just as he was finishing up, Hunter entered.

Maybe she was dizzy from the blood draw. Maybe she hadn't eaten enough at lunch. Or maybe she swayed drunkenly simply at the sight of Hunter sauntering toward her, his dark gaze locked on her, his broad shoulders rolling under a weapons harness, his thigh-length leather jacket billowing out with every step.

As he approached, he flashed his fangs at Grant. "Leave." The single word sent Grant scrambling out of the lab, leaving her alone with MoonBound's leader.

"That was rude."

"He'll get over it." Hunter stopped in front of her. "I'll make this fast. Why didn't you tell me you're supposed to mate Tseeveyo?"

Ah, crap. She'd given Riker and Nicole permission to find her a male for tonight, but she hadn't thought Hunter would be involved.

"Because it's none of your business," she said.

"Bullshit. Is it because you didn't want me to know what Tseeveyo promised your father?"

She blinked. "What? I have no idea what you're talking about."

He narrowed his eyes at her. "Then why didn't you tell me? You told Nicole, and it wasn't any of her business, either. So what gives?"

Abruptly, anger steamed in her veins. Funny how easily the emotion kindled in her now, and how freeing it was. "I was ashamed, okay?" she snapped. "My own father thinks so little of me that he'll sell me off to a fiend. How can I not be humiliated by that?" She looked past his shoulder at the door. "Can I go now?"

He scrubbed his hand over his face. "Shit. I'm sorry." He dropped his arm. "Do you know what kind of alliances your father has made with other clans recently?"

"No, why?"

"I think he's up to something. He might be trying to unite the clans."

"Wouldn't that be a good thing? Samnult said war with the humans was coming."

"Uniting the clans is vital if we want to save ourselves from extinction. But your father wants more than allied clans. He wants the allied clans under his control."

"Like a king? That's crazy." But was it really? Kars had always been power-hungry, and she'd often wondered why he spent so much time digging into the affairs of rival clans. "You know, now that I think about it . . . Remember I told you about the competitions ShadowSpawn has been holding? We've had more than usual, and clans have been coming from farther away than ever before. JaggedSky from Montana and BoneSworn from New Mexico. They'd never been to one of my father's competitions before, but they've both been twice in the last three years. He's even arranged for truces with sworn enemies. Like you."

"Damn," Hunter breathed.

For some reason, she pictured him saying the same thing, just as softly, against the skin of her throat. Her breasts. Her inner thighs.

As if he knew, his dark gaze sparked. He swore again and inhaled raggedly. "You okay? How have you been?"

"Do you really want to chitchat?"

A low, pumping growl vibrated the air and rumbled through her in an erotic wave. "What I want to do is strip you, throw you onto the counter, spread your thighs, and lick you until you scream. That's what I want to do. *I* want to be the male who takes you for the first time. And every time after that. The thought of you being with someone else tonight is killing me, to the point where I'm tempted to have Riker lock me up so I don't do something stupid. I don't understand it, and frankly, it's pissing me off. But there it is."

His stark, raw honesty stole her breath. She wanted all of that, too, could relate to everything he'd said. Here he was in front of her, and she couldn't have him. And in this moment, she was ashamed to admit that if he offered her even the smallest scrap of his attention, she'd take it. Without thinking, she reached for him, but he stepped back with a hiss, his massive fangs bared.

"If you touch me, I'm lost." His big body trembled as he continued backing up. He took panting breaths, and his eyes were as wild as a cornered cougar's. "I . . . have to go."

"Hunter, wait." She moved toward him. He stopped, and she had a feeling he was fighting a battle with himself deep inside. Good. Now he knew how she felt every time she saw him. "Don't have sex with her. Not tonight."

He barked out a laugh. "Really? Just yesterday you told me to get it over with. *Now* you get jealous?"

"This isn't about jealousy," she said. Okay, it was, but there was also the fact that Rasha mentioned getting pregnant. "You can't . . ." *You can't trust Rasha.* Aylin didn't say it. She couldn't. As true as it was, she wouldn't sell out her sister like that.

"Can't what?"

Aylin closed her lids. "Nothing. Just trust your instincts."

"I got news for you," he said roughly. "I can't trust *myself* right now."

He took off in a rush, and something told her he was heading straight to Rasha.

HUNTER HAD ALWAYS been one to play with fire, had never minded the burns. But Aylin burned hotter than any flame, and if he hadn't left when he did, he'd have turned to ash.

Holy Spirit, she tested his self-control. Samnult's trials were a piece of cake compared with the challenge of keeping his hands off Aylin.

He bolted through the halls, the moon fever licking at his heels. He wasn't sure where he was going, and he didn't care. As long as he got away from Aylin before the demands for blood and sex became too much, he didn't give a shit where he ended up.

Except that somehow he found that he'd circled back around to the lab, where Aylin's scent still lingered inside. Like an idiot, he peeked in, but she wasn't there.

Lifting his face, he inhaled, caught her grass-and-sunshine aroma, and started to track her.

Dammit! Panting, he dug his heels into the ground. He bent over and braced his hands on his thighs in a desperate attempt to get hold of himself. It didn't work. He could smell her. See her in his mind. And practically taste her in the back of his throat.

His fangs throbbed with the desire for blood— her blood. Maybe Rasha's would be the same. Maybe it wouldn't taste like battery acid the way he imagined.

You have to try. Aylin is lost to you. She'll be with someone else shortly, if she's not already.

He straightened with a snarl. Made a mental note to tell Riker never to reveal the name of the male who spent the night with Aylin. As much as Hunter would like to say he could be objective and logical . . . yeah, when it came to Aylin, his civil side was pretty much nonexistent.

The need for blood began to cloud his thoughts in a haze of red. It was time, and he couldn't put it off. Most vampires could miss a moon feeding . . . two or three if they really had to. But as a second-generation vampire, his instincts were too strong, and he'd learned the hard way that missing a feeding on the full moon meant a month of viciousness he sometimes couldn't control. Fourteen years had passed since the last time Riker had been forced to chain him in the prey room, and he didn't want to end that streak.

His father, as a first-generation vampire descended from the Originals, had been even worse. When he missed a feeding, he'd been the epitome of the word *monster*. He'd even changed physically into a horrific skeletal creature with a gaping maw of sharp teeth and serrated claws that could slice through steel. It had been terrifying, a beast so mindless and bloodthirsty that it had once tried to eat its own infant son.

Sometimes Hunter wondered if he'd have even cared about killing his son when he turned back to normal. And as much as Hunter despised his mother, he had to give her credit for her willingness to go to the creature on the next full moon and allow it to use her.

He questioned whether Rasha would have done that, but he had no doubt about Aylin.

With a nasty curse, he headed toward his chambers. Rasha wasn't expecting him yet, but he didn't give a shit about inconveniencing her. He needed to get this over with while he still possessed a thread of self-control. He'd take her blood, but he wouldn't take anything else from her.

But what if, in the fever madness, he thought she was Aylin? What if he was so far gone with bloodlust that he couldn't control himself? Again, normal vampires were better with self-control, but during the moon fever, Hunter was little more than an animal feeding its basest desires.

Even now, his senses were zeroing in on what he needed, identifying the location of nearby females with the accuracy of Doppler radar. There was one in the room he'd just passed. Six gathered in the common room. Two—with a male—in the storeroom ahead. The scent of blood and sex billowed from it like steam, ramping him up a dozen notches. Sweat bloomed on his hot skin, his mouth watered, and his cock ached like a son of a bitch.

Aylin.

No.

He shoved open his chamber door. And went on instant alert.

The scent of blood and arousal was coming from the rear of his quarters.

A chill of foreboding rippled up his spine as he eased his way through his office and living area toward the bedroom. He instinctively palmed the hilt of a dagger as he shoved the door open.

He stepped through the doorway and came to a sudden, stunned halt.

Rasha was pinned against the wall, panting softly at what Hunter was pretty sure was the edge of orgasm, her barely clothed body undulating against the big male whose teeth were buried in her throat.

Titanium teeth.

Hunter couldn't believe what he was seeing. His vision went ebony and crimson, like blood dripping down a black wall, and rage awakened the primal beast inside him. A male he hated on a good day, wanted to kill on the bad ones, had invaded Hunter's den and was feeding from Hunter's female. Didn't matter that Hunter didn't *want* the female. She was his, like it or not, and as clan chief, what was his was sacred.

With a roar, he seized Myne by the back of the neck and ripped him away from Rasha. Blood sprayed from the torn wound in her throat, but he barely gave it a thought.

She'd recover. Unfortunately.

Surprise flashed in Myne's coal eyes as Hunter bashed his fist into his jaw and slammed him into the wall before the guy could recover. "Bastard." He wrapped his hand around Myne's throat and pounded his fist into Myne's face again, savoring the crack of his nose breaking.

Myne pitched to the side to avoid another blow. "It's not what you think."

Crack. Fist to the face. "Were you feeding from her?"

Myne spat blood—Rasha's and his own. "Yes, but—"

Crack. Myne was going to need a good dentist. Maybe the one who had given him the titanium fangs. "Then it's exactly what I think!"

"He . . . he forced me," Rasha said from behind Hunter. Myne's head whipped around to her, his incredulous stare telling Hunter all he needed to know. Rasha was lying. Myne was a bastard, but he wasn't a rapist.

"You understand what you're saying." Hunter ground out the words between clenched teeth. "If Myne forced you, it's a death sentence."

She lifted her chin. "I'm the firstborn daughter of a second-generation vampire and clan chief." In other words, she was daring him to call her a liar. Her hand came down on his shoulder, and he shrugged out from under her touch.

"Stay here," he told her, as he hurled Myne out of the bedroom and slammed the door behind him.

Myne wheeled into the couch, his heavy body cracking the frame. "Dammit, Hunter, listen to me."

"You were feeding from my mate!" Snarling, Hunter dived, hitting Myne with a full-on tackle. They crashed onto the floor in a tangle. Myne tried to get up, but Hunter was faster, flipping the male onto his back and slamming two hard blows into his ribs.

"She's not your mate," he wheezed. "You don't even want her."

The truth of that was as infuriating as it was humiliating. And leave it to the one male in the clan Hunter hated most to voice it out loud. In one quick, seamless move, Hunter straddled Myne and decked him hard enough to feel a bone crack. "You disrespected me in my own fucking chamber! We took you in when you were broken. I trusted you. And this is how you repay me?" Fisting Myne's T-shirt, he shook him hard enough that his skull cracked on the floor. "Did you fuck her?" *Say yes and die.* And why in the hell was Myne not fighting back?

"No."

"You told me that once before. Remember that, asshole?" Hunter slipped a dagger from his harness, the soft hiss of metal clearing its leather housing the sound of impending death. "You lied then, so why should I believe you now?"

Myne's black eyes went dead. "You shouldn't."

Hunter put the tip of the blade to Myne's jugular. There was no fear in Myne's gaze, no resistance in his body. He expected to die and was prepared to go out like a warrior.

And for all of Myne's faults, he *was* a warrior. A damned good one. An image of Myne as a boy flirted at the edges of Hunter's anger. A boy only a few years older than Hunter's ten-year-old self, standing at the edge of the forest with his brother, both waiting for a decision that would determine the rest of their lives.

Hunter had had to make that decision. To this day, he wondered whether he'd made the right one all those years ago, and it was that doubt that stayed his hand now.

Sheathing his blade, he popped to his feet and stared down at Myne. "Get the fuck out of my sight, because I don't know how long I can keep myself from eviscerating you."

Myne didn't look at Hunter as he staggered to his feet and out of the chamber.

The bedroom door whispered open, and the soft sound of footsteps came toward him.

He smelled fear.

"Please, don't kill him." Rasha's unsteady voice rang with alarm. "And please, don't let this affect our mating. My father will only blame you."

"Well, that's one hell of an apology," he snapped. "And why in the ever-living fuck would he blame me?"

She had the decency to look away while she explained away her behavior. "Because you've ignored my needs. I was forced to do what I must—"

"Forced? You keep using that word. I do not think it means what you think it means," he said, mimicking a character in one of his favorite classic movies. *Gotta love* The Princess Bride. *So many good lines, so many cool ways to die.*

Rasha slid the spaghetti straps of her dress off her shoulders. "Let me make it up to you."

"Make it up to me?" he sputtered. "You've made me look like a fool in my own house!"

"No one has to know." The skimpy slip slid down her curvy body and pooled at her feet, leaving her naked and nowhere near as beautiful as her sister.

"I'll know." He couldn't deal with this, couldn't deal with anything right now, and he headed for the door.

"Where are you going?"

"To feed." Looking back over his shoulder, he gave her his coldest, cruelest smile, the one his father had had down to an art. "I came to be with you, but it looks like you've already been used."

29

THE TREMOR STARTED so subtly that Riker didn't notice until the pictures on the common-room wall began to rattle. He looked up from the pool table, where he, Jaggar, Bastien, and Baddon had been finishing one more game before they went their separate ways to feed.

Well, not Bastien. He hadn't blooded yet—a miserable event in a young vampire's life, when he or she felt the first yearnings of moon fever.

Jaggar put the eight ball in a corner pocket. "Earthquake?"

The ground shook under their feet. Baddon's head whipped up. "I don't think so."

"Hunter," Riker whispered. "Shit."

He tore out of the room and jogged down the hall toward Hunter's chambers. Myne, bloody and holding his ribs, came around a corner and slammed into Riker. He snarled and shoved Riker into the wall.

"What the fuck?" Riker held his fists at his sides, but only because someone had already beaten the holy hell out of the other male.

Myne stared, his gaze as empty as it had been when he'd first come to the clan. For a long time, he just stood there, his eyes haunted, his face pale.

"Myne? Buddy?"

Myne released Riker and stumbled backward. "Sorry," he rasped. "I . . ." He shook his head. "Sorry." He took off, leaving Riker baffled and staring down the hall.

A sudden, dark suspicion spurred Riker on faster now, but he skidded to a halt when the door to Hunter's chamber flew open. The clan chief stormed out of his quarters, his knuckles shredded, his dark eyes radiating a crimson glow. Instantly, Riker's suspicion was confirmed. Hunter and Myne had gotten into it.

But this wasn't like the other times, when both Hunter and Myne walked away with similar injuries. This had been one-sided, and where Myne had smelled like shame, Hunter smelled like murder.

"Hunt." He grabbed the vampire's arm, halting him in his tracks. "Obviously, you're pissed—"

"You have no idea," Hunter snarled.

Oh, Riker had an idea, all right. "What happened?"

A rumble boiled up from deep in Hunter's chest. "He fed from Rasha."

Riker sucked in a sharp breath, his thoughts immediately going to what he knew about Rasha, which was that she was an evil skank. Maybe she'd lied to Hunter. "Who told you that?"

"I saw them!" he roared. "They were in my fucking *bedroom*."

Holy shit. So it was true? And Hunter had let Myne live? "Hunt, listen to me. Myne didn't mean to disrespect you."

"He betrayed me!" Hunter's expression was thunderous, his eyes flashing like lightning from a summer storm.

"I know. But I guarantee he's punishing himself harder right now than you ever could."

"I doubt that." Hunter jammed his hand through his hair. "What was he thinking?"

"He was thinking he was hungry."

"And of all the females he could choose from, he chose mine?"

Riker cursed this situation, not wanting to betray Myne like this but also not wanting Hunter to destroy the guy. "He didn't just decide at the last minute to screw you over. He's been feeding from Rasha for years."

"What?" Hunter's voice throbbed with warning. He wasn't happy that this had been kept from him, and Riker didn't blame him. "Why?"

"No one else will have him," Riker said carefully. He didn't want to end up with a rearranged face and broken ribs à la Myne. "Myne's bite is too painful for other females. No one in our clan will feed him. I'm not sure how he hooked up with Rasha, but it's the only way he's been able to feed."

Hunter scrubbed his hand over his face. "Why didn't he—or *you*—say something when Rasha first got here?"

"Because he made arrangements for a female at the Velvet Fang. One who didn't know how painful his bite is. But when he went into town today, he found out she was killed by a hunter. He got back an hour ago." Myne had been snappish and jittery, and Riker wished he'd stuck closer to the guy. "He was going to try to find another female. He wanted to stay away from Rasha, but he's missed a couple of feedings. He was starving. I should have known he couldn't resist." Riker squeezed Hunter's biceps. "Hunt, you need to know that he wouldn't have approached Rasha. She would have gone to him."

A muscle in Hunter's jaw twitched. "Did he lie about not fucking her?"

Riker shook his head. "He knew her father would rain down hell on our clan. He refused to put us in danger."

Hunter closed his eyes and breathed deep. When he lifted his lids, his eyes no longer burned with anger, but Riker wasn't sure the icy composure was any better. "Keep him away from me, Rike. Keep him away, or so help me, I'll kill him."

FUCK.

The only thing worse than feeding from the chief's mate would have been to sleep with her. The fact that Hunter and Rasha weren't formally mated wasn't important. According to vampire law, touching a clan leader's potential mate without the leader's express permission was a grave trespass.

It was within Hunter's rights as clan chief to slay Myne for what he'd done. He probably should. Many would simply see it as putting down a rogue cur, and no one would question it. Hell, killing Myne would send a strong message to the clan that betrayal wouldn't be tolerated.

Myne was such a piece of shit. It didn't matter that his blood feud with Hunter went so far back that no one in the clan was even aware that he and Hunter had clashed long before he became MoonBound's chief.

Shame tore at him. He had betrayed a pureblood chief. Betrayed the clan that took him in when was barely alive. He couldn't call himself a warrior. He didn't deserve that title. Honor gave him only one choice, and that was to leave.

Well, he could kill himself, but that wasn't going to happen. Myne had learned a long time ago that his sense of self-preservation was extreme.

He shoved the last of his clothes into a duffel and looked around his chambers. Nothing here belonged to him. It never had, he supposed. Hunter had merely allowed him to stay here. Myne had never *lived* here.

Which, really, was Hunter's fault. If Hunter had made a different decision all those decades ago, things would have been different. Myne's brother would still be alive, and Myne wouldn't be the titanium-toothed freak he was now.

So, really, he could lay the blame for all of this at Hunter's feet.

Yep, he'd go with that.

There was a light tap on the door, and then it whispered open, and Rasha slipped inside. Mother. Fuck. Seriously? At least she'd changed into a much more modest outfit of jeans and a fluffy blue sweater that matched her eyes.

"Get out," he growled. If Hunter knew she was here, there'd be no second chances for Myne.

Her demeanor was uncharacteristically subdued, her gaze averted, her stride hesitant. "I only need a minute."

"Just long enough to make *sure* Hunter kills me?"

"I'm sorry about that." She moved forward, her eyes pleading, which had to be an act. "I panicked."

"So you told him I forced you," he said flatly. "What the fuck?"

"I said I'm sorry!" she snapped, her moment of contrition expired. "I freaked out—"

"And have you admitted that you lied? Have you told Hunter the truth?" Her pursed lips and silence were enough of an answer. And it wasn't the answer he'd wanted. "So even now, Hunter could be rounding up a team of warriors to drag me to my execution ceremony." He had to get the hell out of there. Now.

Rasha shook her head. "If he'd wanted to kill you, he'd have done it in his chamber like any other chief. And even if he was still thinking about it, don't you think he'd have you chained in the pit right now?"

Maybe.

Or maybe he was trying to make Myne sweat a little before he hauled him off to the chopping block.

"Why are you here, Rasha?" He zipped his duffel and tossed it onto the chair by the door. "To apologize for being a lying bitch? Mission accomplished. So get the hell out."

Rasha's cheeks flamed red. "How dare you?" she snarled. "I'm the daughter of a chief, soon to be First Female of a clan. You do not speak to me that way." She sniffed, going from batshit pissed to calm in a heartbeat. "I came here to apologize. But I can't have you ruining my future. You need to leave."

Had she missed the fact that he was packing to do exactly that? But her command rankled, and he found himself pushing back. "And if I say no?"

One corner of her mouth curved into an evil smirk as she grasped the collar of her sweater and ripped it far enough down to reveal cleavage. "I'll tell everyone you attacked me."

"You . . . *bitch*." In an instant, he had her by the throat and shoved against the wall. "I despise Hunter to my very marrow, but you know what? I actually feel sorry for him right now. You're poison, Rasha, a scorpion that can't change its nature, and not even Hunter deserves to be mated to you."

She hissed, her fangs extending as her eyes glittered with crimson flecks. "Leave now, *wenputi*, or I will see to it that you're executed before sunrise."

He'd never liked Rasha. Had only tolerated her because she liked pain, and he gave that in abundance when he fed. But whatever small part of him had allowed him even to tolerate her died the moment she called him *wenputi*, a vampirized Nez Perce word that combined several insults. Orphan. Bastard. Outcast. Beggar. Parasite. Burden. Untrustworthy. Freak.

It had taken him years to accept a place here at MoonBound, and while he'd always remained detached from the other clan members—with the exception of Riker, whom he considered a friend—he'd recently begun to settle in, to participate in clan functions. Riker had played a huge role in that, but so had Bastien. Myne had become the kid's mentor, teaching him to fight and hunt and ogle females without getting caught. And in return, Bastien had taught Myne how to laugh again.

For the first time ever, Myne had started to feel like he had a home.

Now that rug had been yanked out from under his feet, and, just like it had been for more than two centuries, he was going to be homeless and alone.

Way to feel sorry for yourself, wenputi.

A wintry void hollowed out his chest, ruthlessly scouring away all the warm fuzzies that had been filling the empty places inside him. With a vicious shove, he pushed away from Rasha and slung his duffel over his shoulder.

He didn't look back as he opened the door and walked out of his chambers. Didn't look back as he exited clan headquarters and stepped out into the cold night air. Didn't look back when someone called his name.

Because the truth was that someone would only call after him in his dreams.

30

THE TAP ON the door almost made Aylin cry. Someone was here to feed from her, and the joy was
almost overwhelming.

But so was the anxiety. What if the male on the
other side of the door was only here because he was
ordered to be? Riker promised that he'd find a willing partner, but what if this "willing" male didn't know
about her birth defect? Would she feel his disgust radi-
ate off him while he took her vein? Could she stand the
humiliation?

What if, by some miracle, he'd agreed to more than
blood? The moon fever wasn't just about feeding; it was
about breeding. Sex. Putting all pretense of civility aside
to assuage carnal hungers that couldn't be contained.

Aylin wanted that so badly.

With Hunter.

Right now, he was probably rolling around in his
luxurious bed with Rasha, his fangs in her throat, his
naked body moving with hers.

Nausea bubbled up from her belly, and the tears
that had threatened earlier stung her eyes.

Stop it. He isn't yours. He never was. He never will be.

Ruthlessly, she banished his name from her mind. The knock sounded again, this time louder. Harder. More urgent. Someone was hungry.

Inhaling deeply, she opened the door.

Baddon stood there, his shiny sable hair shoved away from his face in wild waves, his mocha eyes gleaming with barely contained hunger, his fangs glinting through full, parted lips. Erotic energy pulsed from his leather-clad body in waves she could feel on her skin and deeper, all the way to her core. She nearly swayed with the intensity of it.

This was what a male in the throes of moon fever was like.

Obviously, she'd been around males on the night of the full moon, but she'd never been the focus of a male's attention. She'd never known what she was missing.

Damn, but she'd been missing.

"Hi," he said. Such a short, simple word, but behind it was a whole lot of promise. "Can I come in?"

She swallowed. Instantly, Baddon's gaze snapped down to her throat, and his fangs lengthened even more, until they were putting dimples in his lower lip.

"Um, y-yes," she stuttered, feeling like a fool.

Slowly, with a casual swagger that belied the intensity in his expression, he sauntered over to her, his black boots striking the floor with heavy thuds. When he was mere inches away, he hooked his finger under her chin. Was he going to . . . surely not . . .

Dipping his head, he pressed his lips to hers. For a long moment, Aylin was too freaked out to be anything but shocked. Eventually, her senses came back online, and the warmth of Baddon's lips penetrated her stunned brain. His kiss was firm, not gentle, but not brutal, either. Not that Aylin had much in the way of comparison.

Only Hunter.

And oh, Great Spirit have mercy, Hunter could kiss.

Baddon's mouth moved over hers as he backed her up against the wall and covered her body with his. "Don't be afraid," he murmured, his husky voice rolling through her like the first stirrings of orgasm. "I won't hurt you."

You already have. I want you to be someone else.

Baddon couldn't have known what she was thinking, but he pulled back and frowned down at her. "If you don't want this, tell me now. The moon fever is rising, and it won't be long until I—"

"Can't control yourself?" She'd seen males at ShadowSpawn turn into little more than animals during the full moon.

One corner of his mouth turned up in a lazy, lopsided grin. "I was going to say I get grumpy, but whatever."

Charmed, she relaxed enough to nod. "I want this."

"What about Hunter?"

She started. "What about him?"

"He's my chief, so if this is going to cause problems, I need to know now."

Oh, sweet Maker, what did Baddon know? "Why would this cause problems?"

"I saw you at the portal. I see the way he looks at you." Again he hooked his finger under her chin and forced her gaze to meet his. "More important, I see the way you look at him."

She held in a groan. How many people knew about them? Everyone who'd gone to the vortex, obviously, but had anyone else in the clan noticed these "looks"? "He's mating my sister."

"That doesn't answer my question."

She huffed. "There's no answer, because there's no Hunter. You need blood, and I'm willing to give it to you. End of story."

He cocked an eyebrow. "What about what *you* need?"

The virginity problem. Right. She felt her face heat. "Let's . . . just see how things go. And no more talk of Hunter." She swept her hair away from her neck, and as if she'd flipped a switch, Baddon let out a low purr, his gaze zeroing in on her jugular.

"Hunter?" Baddon's warm breath swept over her throat, sending shivers across her skin. "Fuck Hunter."

No, she thought, as Baddon's tattooed arms hauled her against him, *that won't be happening.*

HUNTER STALKED DOWN the halls, melting snow dripping off his bare skin as he walked. He wore only a deerskin loincloth, and even if the passages had been bustling with people, he wouldn't have been given a second glance.

For two hundred years, he'd run off his anger, his anxiety . . . any emotion that got too intense to contain. Usually, he ran naked, so yeah, the loincloth wouldn't draw attention at all. Clan members were all too familiar with his uncontrolled sprints through the forest.

The difference between all those other times and now was that before, a top-speed run until he was exhausted took the edge off whatever was bothering him. Tonight it was as if he hadn't run at all. As if he hadn't come across a group of vampire poachers and taken them apart.

What was truly coming apart was his life.

He was about to be mated to a female he hated. A high-ranking clan male had betrayed him. The forest was crawling with humans who wanted to slaughter or enslave vampires. He suspected that someone in the clan was a spy. And the female he wanted . . . he couldn't have.

He let out a vicious snarl and stormed toward his chambers, hoping for Rasha's sake that she wasn't there. His footsteps echoed in the passage, which was empty of people but rife with the erotic tension of moon fever. His skin tightened, almost as if forming a shield against the maddening lust in the air.

He needed to feed, but Rasha had already been used. There were more females than males in the clan, so he could easily find a partner, but dammit, he didn't want any female but Aylin.

With a curse, he slammed his fist into the wall and kept going. And going. Until he found himself heading in the direction of Aylin's quarters. Heat flooded his veins, and his heart beat faster. He breathed deep, tracking Aylin like a wolf.

She was in her room.

Lifting his face, he inhaled again, seeking her scent as he got closer. He caught it, stronger now, a tangle of grass, sunshine, and dew that made his nostrils tingle and his body harden. Damn, but something about the way she smelled made him fantasize about taking her in a sunlit meadow, the sounds of a rushing river softening her passionate cries.

Twenty feet away, he forced himself to stop. More than anything in the world, he wanted to knock on her door. The driving desire to touch her, to kiss her, to feed from her, raced through him like burning gasoline.

Resist.

He inched forward.

Come on, asshole, you're stronger than this.

Another step. Her door was within reach.

You're . . . stronger . . . than . . . this.

Sweat beaded on his brow, but he managed not to take another step. Or to grab the doorknob and rip it out of the door in his urgency to get to Aylin. He couldn't make things worse for her.

Pivoting on his heel, he spun around. Deep inside, he swore his bear roared. And then it went dead silent as Baddon's scent filled the air. And with it, the unmistakable aroma of arousal.

It was coming from Aylin's room.

Instant, possessive rage overcame him.

He was going to break down the door if he had to. Rational thought fled, leaving behind only the primal desire to make the female his and destroy whatever— or whoever—stood in his way.

31

BADDON'S LEAN, MUSCULAR body pressed against Aylin's, his tattooed hands brazenly stroking her hips as he kissed his way up her throat and jaw. He'd nicked her skin with his teeth instead of going for a full feed right away, and her pulse thudded painfully hard inside her veins as her own body reacted to his blatant seduction.

But even as her skin heated and her breasts began to throb, her mind was looking for a way out. This was wrong. It was something she'd wanted for so long, and maybe if she hadn't fallen for Hunter, she could go through with it. But now there was no way she could give herself to another male. Not while she was under the same roof as Hunter.

Bizarrely, this felt like cheating.

A hysterical laugh threatened to spill right into Baddon's mouth. How could she cheat on a male who was going to be mating her sister? Who was probably, right now, in bed with her?

Aylin was a fool, but she couldn't control how she felt. When one hand slid beneath her sweatshirt, she cried out in both pleasure and regret. "Baddon," she breathed. "I—"

Suddenly, everything went cold and still, as if an arctic air mass had settled over them. Baddon's head came up, and he barely had time to whisper a harsh "Fuck" before the door burst open with a crack of exploding wood.

He spun around, keeping his body between her and . . . *Hunter?*

Her heart screeched to a halt. Hunter's massive shoulders spanned the width of the doorframe, his lips were peeled back to reveal sharp fangs the size of her pinkie, and his entire body threw off lethal menace as he zeroed in on Baddon.

His entire *nearly naked* body. Spirits have mercy, the skimpy loincloth only made it worse. She knew what the deerskin flap concealed, and she wanted to rip it from his hips with her teeth.

Her fangs tingled in anticipation.

"Leave, warrior." His gravelly voice was so deep and powerful that the vibrations got her heart going again . . . but in an unstable, terrified rhythm. "Now."

Baddon took a single, heavy step toward Hunter. "She's not yours."

Oh, shit. This was not going to end well. On the best of days, a confrontation between two angry alpha-male vampires could end in disaster, but when moon fever set in and everyone was jacked up with the need to feed and mate, people could die.

"It's okay," she said quickly, but as if she hadn't spoken, the two males snarled like beasts out of hell and met in the middle of the room, nose to nose, chest to chest.

Both were born vampires, but Hunter was taller and probably outweighed Baddon by twenty pounds. But she'd seen Baddon fight. He was fast, and he reportedly ran a motorcycle gang that was notorious for torturing and killing its rivals. He definitely fought dirty.

"Get. Out." Hunter's hands clenched into fists. "Last warning."

Baddon's answering growl spurred her into action. Desperate to prevent bloodshed, even as a small part of her reveled in the fact that two males were competing for her—well, for her blood, anyway—she laid her palm lightly on Baddon's biceps. His leather jacket creaked as she squeezed to get his attention.

"I think it's for the best if you go," she said softly. "Please. Thank you for coming by."

It was an eternity and a half before Baddon stepped back. He flung one last, defiant glare in Hunter's direction and then turned to Aylin. "My door will always be open to you." He stalked out of the room, slamming the destroyed door behind him.

Hunter rounded on her before the sound even faded in her ears. "Did you feed him? Have you fed any of my warriors tonight?"

Annoyed by his arrogance and intrusion into her private life—even if part of her secretly loved it—she folded her arms over her chest and glared. "You interrupted before that could happen."

He raked her with his gaze. "Did you fuck any of them?"

Abrupt anger doused the warm fuzzies of being fought over. "That's none of your business. And if I'd participated in an orgy with a dozen of your warriors, it would still be none of your business."

His expression went flat. Cold. "You're mine."

"*Yours?*" She gaped at him in disbelief. He seriously thought he could just take what he wanted, when he wanted. As a clan chief, he was apparently no different from the rest. "Where's Rasha?" she mocked. "You know, your mate. The twin who *is* yours."

"She fed another tonight."

Aylin sucked air. Even though Rasha and Hunter weren't officially mated, Rasha had made a stupid choice. She wondered what male would have been dumb enough to risk Hunter's wrath. She also wondered what had happened to that male. "Well," she said, "I've always been second to her in everything. I will not be second to her in this." She pointed to the door. Such as it was, anyway. "Now it's time for you to leave. I won't be a consolation prize."

Maker help her, if she wasn't so angry, she'd probably be happy to be a consolation prize for Hunter, and how sad was that? But dammit, all she wanted was to rid herself of her pesky virginity with someone she chose to be with. Someone she loved. She wanted those memories to hold on to when she was miserable in another clan chief's cold bed.

"Consolation prize?" Hunter's eyes shot wide. And then they narrowed to slits, and in the blink of one of those ebony eyes, he had her on the bed, his body covering hers and his mouth sealed against her lips. "You could never be a consolation prize." His voice was fierce, the force of his conviction ringing through her. "I want you, Aylin Redmoon."

Tears stung her eyes. She wanted him, too, but aside from Rasha being a fool of the highest order, nothing had changed. Her heart was all in, but her brain was screaming warnings.

Wedging her hands between them, she palmed his chest and shoved. "That's the moon fever talking."

He looked down at her, his eyes glowing, his jaw a hard, aggressive line. "It wasn't the moon fever talking when we were at the vortex. It wasn't the moon fever talking when we were in the cave and I made you come. And it sure as hell wasn't the fucking moon fever chatting you up yesterday when I told you I wanted to strip you, lick you, and be the one who makes love to you for the first time." His gaze fell to her throat, where the tiny nick Baddon had made was still bleeding, and he cursed. "I don't know how things are going to play out, but I do know I'm not letting you go." He dropped his head to her throat and dragged his tongue over the little cut. "I can taste him. I want him gone." One hand dropped to her hip and hauled her hard against his erection as he sealed his mouth over the wound and then drove his fangs deep.

Her gasp of pain eased into a moan of pleasure. He drew deeply, the erotic sensation spreading through her body and all the way to her core. It was like at the vortex, when she'd felt a climax building from out of nowhere. Rasha had always said that with the right male, moon feedings were sex without getting naked.

Yup.

Hunter undulated against her, rubbing his hard length against her sex. A shock of pure arousal streaked through her, and any doubts she'd had a moment ago were silenced. The future was something to worry about later. She needed to feed a male for health reasons, and she needed to lose her virginity to lose any appeal she held for Tseeveyo.

More important, she was dying for this experience. She had no doubt there would be real consequences, both for her heart and for Hunter, but right now, as his hand slipped beneath her shirt and caressed its way upward, she didn't care.

HUNTER HAD NEVER been this turned on before. Oh, he'd shared a lot of wild nights with a lot of females, and truth be told, the two occasions he had been with Aylin at the vortex and the time in the cave had overshadowed all those other nights.

But this . . . this was going to blow everything apart.

Her silky blood cascaded down his throat, satisfying the biological demand for nourishment, and as the hunger waned, a deeper, darker craving bloomed. There was more of her to taste, and he wasn't going to waste another second.

Disengaging his fangs, he sucked gently on the punctures he left behind. Aylin moaned in response and arched against him, twining her legs around his as her hips rocked upward. His cock slipped out from the loose buckskin covering him, and the little vixen found it with her hand.

It was his turn to moan as her inexperienced fingers explored with light, tentative strokes. "Is that okay?" She sounded breathless and nervous, and so sweet he couldn't resist smiling against the satin skin of her neck.

"More than." He kissed his way down her throat, nipping at her collarbone and then soothing the bites with his tongue.

"Mmm . . . that feels good."

"Baby, you ain't felt nothin' yet." He pulled back just enough to strip off her sweatshirt, leaving her upper body gloriously bare. He loved that she didn't wear a bra. And that she blushed as he admired her. He dipped his head to kiss both nipples, letting his lips linger on the stiff tips.

Aylin made a sound of surprise and pleasure, both hands coming up to hold his head as he deepened his kiss to suckle one swollen peak. She liked this, and as he worked the fly of her jeans, she arched her back, seeking closer contact.

Chuckling softly, he opened his mouth wider and swirled his tongue in lazy circles. His body buzzed, high from her blood and her response. He didn't see how he could possibly get any higher, but when he slipped his hand inside her jeans and found her soaked panties, he felt like he'd been plugged into an electrical outlet.

"Aylin," he breathed. "I need to taste you."

His desire burned out of control as he leaped up, and in one quick move, he yanked her pants down to her ankles. The damned things caught on her feet, but she kicked them off, apparently as impatient as he was. Her damp panties, plain white cotton, were nearly see-through, revealing two plump hills and a deep, shadowed valley he couldn't wait to part with his tongue.

Mouth watering, he climbed onto the mattress and kneeled between her legs. Aylin watched him, wide-eyed, her lips glistening from his kiss as he smoothed his hands up her calves. The fragrance of her arousal filled the room, and he purred with approval.

He feathered light strokes over the skin of her thigh and followed with nibbles and licks that lingered the higher he went. She squirmed on the mattress, panting, making her impatience clear.

"If anything I do makes you uncomfortable," he said softly, "I'll stop."

"If you stop, I'll kill you."

"Noted." He should have known she'd leap into this fearlessly. This was the female who had volunteered to travel to a dangerous demon realm and fight to the death. Sex certainly wasn't going to scare her.

More eager than ever, he spread her thighs wider and opened his mouth over her center. She inhaled raggedly as he licked at her through the fabric of her panties, tracing the contours of her sex with the tip of his tongue. When he probed her cleft, she dug her heels into the mattress and pushed against him, seeking more.

More? No problem. He was a gentleman that way.

With a throaty purr, he tore her panties away with his fangs. She was open to him now, her center pink and swollen, and wet with arousal. Greedily, he slid his arms under her hips to hold her while he kissed her deeply. Her plump lips parted for the sweep of his tongue from her core to her clit. She let out a soft mewl as he rubbed one fang back and forth over the sensitive nub.

She tasted like rainwater and apples, like sugar and sin, and he knew he'd never get enough. Replacing his fang with his finger, he plunged his tongue inside her, loving how she arched up and called his name.

"That's it," he murmured against her succulent, tender flesh. "Take what you want." He tongued her again, deeper this time, and was rewarded with another cry of pleasure.

Using the pad of his thumb, he circled her clit as he made love to her with his mouth, alternately licking and sucking until she was panting uncontrollably. He could feel her on the verge, and his body responded, tightening and aching with the need to get inside her and take them both over the edge.

But he would have to wait. He wanted her to come, to be completely open to him when he broke her barrier.

"Hunter," she rasped. "I'm . . . I . . . oh, *yes*."

She bucked and twisted, her beautiful face contorted in sweet agony as her climax took her. His cock felt like it would break as he reared up and poised himself at her entrance. He hesitated only a moment, and then he rocked his hips and sank to the hilt inside her.

She cried out in surprise, but a heartbeat later, she moaned as the brief moment of pain gave way to pleasure.

Gritting his teeth, he held himself in check as she pulsed around him, her inner walls spasming and squeezing as her orgasm rode her. As she started to come down, he began to move, slowly at first, but he was too worked up, his body too ready for this, and he doubted he lasted thirty seconds before he was pumping his hips wildly. He drove into her, reading her breaths and sounds as she began to climb again.

"Aylin," he groaned. "You feel . . . so . . . fucking . . . good."

He dropped his face to her throat and bit down, not enough to puncture her skin but enough to hold her for his frenzied thrusts. Every part of his body was inflamed with passion for this female, so much so that he couldn't think beyond how she made him feel and how badly he wanted to feel this way every day.

The sexy sounds she uttered as she rocked her pelvis to meet his plunging hips added to the building heat, until he couldn't take it anymore. The rush of ecstasy crashed over him as he emptied himself into her. Her tight sheath contracted with her second climax, milking every last drop he had to give.

When it was over, he collapsed on top of her, shifting slightly to the side to avoid crushing her. The room, its air thick with the earthy scents of their lovemaking, filled with the sound of their labored breaths.

Nothing could be more perfect.

"You're in my bloodstream, Aylin. Literally." He brushed his lips over hers, then lingered there for a moment, showing her with a kiss just how serious he was. "I'm not letting you go. We'll find a way." If he had to give up everything, including his clan, he would.

That was when he felt it. The localized burn all males both desired and dreaded.

He lifted his arm, and there on the back of his hand was an inch-long red mark, and as he watched, it began to take the shape of a feather. His heart pounded, and his pulse raced, and holy shit, he'd imprinted.

So much made sense now: his intense physical attraction to Aylin, his possessiveness, his jealousy. Samnult had said the whole thing was genetic, so it made sense that he'd have an extreme reaction to a genetically compatible female.

Abruptly, he broke out in a cold sweat. He'd had an extreme reaction to Rasha, too. Granted, he'd had the opposite reaction from the one he had to Aylin, but with them being twins, he was pretty sure that Rasha was genetically compatible, too.

Which meant that if he'd slept with her, he might have imprinted on her.

He'd dodged a bullet. A big one. A fifty-millimeter. With a hollow point.

"Hunter?" Aylin's voice was groggy and husky, a welcome interruption. "What now?"

What now, indeed. He stroked her hair, his gaze focusing on the feather on the back of his hand. "Now we face the music."

She squirmed away from him and propped herself up on one elbow. "Face the music?"

"We tell Rasha. And then we tell your father."

The color drained from her face. "We can't. You need to mate with her, and—"

He quieted her with a finger on her lips. "I told you that you're mine. I meant it. I don't care if we have to run away together and live in the middle of nowhere. I'm not giving you up."

"The middle of nowhere? Such as?"

He shrugged. "Dunno. Canada?"

Her blond eyebrows rose. "Isn't that where Baddon is from?"

"That's why it's so funny."

She laughed, the tips of her fangs glistening, her clear-water eyes sparkling.

He liked that. He wanted to see her this happy every day. She'd known too few joyful days in her life, and he wanted to make sure every single one from now on made up for her shitty past.

"Promise me you won't do anything . . . mean to him."

He had to hold back the jealous growl condensing in his chest. Had he not arrived when he did . . . There went the growl. "I won't do anything mean."

She gave a doubtful snort. "Why don't I believe you?" She poked him in the sternum. "Promise me. He really was a gentleman. You know, as much as he could be with the moon fever riding him. And he was here to help me."

It was Hunter's turn to snort. "My ass. It wasn't a sacrifice for him." At her stern expression, he sighed. "Fine. On my honor as a clan chief and pureblood vampire, I won't cause him any trouble."

"Thank you."

"But if he so much as looks at you wrong, I'll lay him out." He gave her his best innocent look. "What? He'd expect as much from an imprinted male. I can't disappoint my people."

"I guess. But—" She sucked in a harsh breath. "What did you just say?"

He feigned ignorance. "I said I can't disappoint my people."

"About the imprint." She sat upright, her entire body trembling, and he couldn't tease her anymore.

Taking her hand in his, he kissed her fingers, allowing her a primo view of the back of his hand and the feather that marked it. "See," he said softly. "You're mine. On some level, I think I knew from the moment I met you."

"I don't know what to say," she whispered brokenly. "Are you okay?"

He laughed. "Am I okay? You make it sound like I broke a bone or took a bullet." He swept her into his arms and held her tight. Her hair smelled like apples, but the rest of her smelled like him. "You're the best thing that's ever happened to me. I'm honored to bear this mark."

"You're sure?"

He arched against her, pressing his cock into her belly. "I'm sure." Sliding his hand over the plump globe of her ass, he let his fingers dip between her legs. "And now I'm going to show you just how sure I am."

32

H UNTER?"

"Hmm?" He kissed Aylin's forehead as she lay tucked against him with her head on his shoulder, her palm resting on his sweat-dampened chest.

"Have we made a huge mistake?"

He shifted so she was lying on the pillow and he was propped on one elbow, looking directly into her gorgeous eyes. "I've made a lot of mistakes in my life, but this isn't one of them."

"But this is going to have huge repercussions."

Yeah, it was. "I don't want you to worry about it. I always manage."

She gave a skeptical sigh. "This is huge. Tsee-veyo . . . my father . . . my sister." Closing her eyes, she groaned.

"Hey." He palmed her soft cheek until she opened her eyes again. "We'll work through it. Everything happens for a reason."

She cocked an eyebrow. "And what is the reason for what we just did?"

Hunter blew out a long breath. "Remember when

I told you that I had to make a decision to refuse my cousins entry into MoonBound?" When she nodded, he continued. "In a way, that decision is why all of this happened."

She blinked. "You've lost me."

Smiling, he brushed her hair back from her brow. "A couple of decades after they left, I took a female into the forest to hunt. And . . . you know."

She rolled her eyes. "I get the picture. Too clearly, really."

"Well, my cousins had apparently decided it was time to make me pay for refusing them entry into the clan. My mother had been communicating with them all along, and they all figured now was the time to take the clan from me. They ambushed me while I was hunting and beat the ever-living fuck out of me. If they hadn't been interrupted by a MoonBound patrol, they would have killed me. As it was, they took the female. We searched behind every damned tree and under every rock for the bastards, but we never found them. I still don't know where they went or what they did for a full century, but I do know that after the humans learned about us and began to enslave us, they were captured."

"Killed?"

"Worse."

Aylin cursed softly. "The female, too?"

"She was turned into a pleasure slave and shipped overseas."

The sheets rustled as she shifted to face him more fully. "Wait . . . how do you know all of this?"

"Because one of my cousins escaped. Riker found him and brought him back here."

"And you allowed that? After what he did to your female?"

"Trust me, there's no love lost between us."

"He's still here?"

"Yup. But we no longer call him by either his given name or his chosen name. We call him by his slave name."

"Which is?"

He paused, feeling the weight of a lot of bad blood between them. "Myne," he said finally. "The warrior who fed from your sister tonight."

33

MYNE? WAS RASHA insane? As Aylin climbed out of bed, she had to wonder. She'd known for years that Rasha secretly met a MoonBound warrior on the nights of the full moon, but she'd assumed Rasha would be smart enough to let that relationship go when she was promised to Hunter.

When would Rasha learn that every action had a consequence?

"I'm going to tell Rasha about us," Hunter said. "I want you to stay here."

"Not a chance." She headed for the shower. "I need to be the one to tell her."

"I don't trust her," Hunter called out.

He said something else, but Aylin turned on the water, drowning him out. This wasn't something she was going to back down on. Rasha was Aylin's sister, and she deserved to hear what had happened from Aylin's own mouth.

Aylin washed, letting the cool water soothe her heated skin. Hunter hadn't been rough with her, but she wasn't used to intimate activity. Not that she was complaining. She'd be happy to feel that special ache every day.

After her shower, she found Hunter in jeans and a maroon T-shirt, his gaze glued to the TV. "Rike brought me clothes," he said. "And a heads-up that we made the news. Nicole's video leaks are all over the screen."

Ugly scenes from some kind of sprawling, prison-like facility flashed on the screen. Her gut churned as horrific images of dead and dying vampires in cells and on autopsy tables scrolled to the commentary of a beautiful dark-haired news anchor.

"I can't watch this," Aylin said. "I'm going to go talk to Rasha."

Hunter turned to her. "I still don't like it."

"I've survived more than a hundred years with her," she reminded him. "I can handle this. I have to."

Closing his eyes, he inhaled a deep, ragged breath. When he opened them again, the admiration in them made her own eyes sting. "I need to meet with Riker about the developments in the human world . . . and between us. Let me know as soon as you're done talking to her. I don't care how busy I am. Got it?"

She nodded. Dipping his head, he kissed her. It was brief but brimming with significance she felt all the way to her soul. He'd imprinted on her, but he'd also marked her in a way she couldn't explain. All she knew was that no matter what happened from here on out, he would always belong to her.

"By the way," she said, stepping back from him. "Why did you lie to me about what you can do with your ability? Was it because you didn't trust me?"

"No." He reached out and cupped her cheek, reassuring her with his touch. "What I told you was the truth ninety percent of the time. I can only bend the weather to my will under certain circumstances. There has to already be energy in the atmosphere. I can't create rain out of blue skies or snow on a summer day. But if the conditions for hail or lightning or a blizzard already exist, I can help them along, but only for a short time." His hand fell away. "And once I use my gift, it's lost to me until the next full moon."

"There's a price for everything, isn't there?" she murmured, thinking that the price for her ability was silence. She just had to pray that everyone who was privy to her secret would keep it.

"Some things are worth any price," he said softly, his eyes gleaming with the kind of affection she'd only read about in books. How very lucky she was.

Hunter's phone beeped, so she left him to handle business while she handled her sister. She was both terrified and eager, ready to begin a new journey in life . . . but not at Rasha's expense.

She didn't bother to knock on her sister's door. She found Rasha sitting on the floor, an empty vodka bottle next to her and smashed glass everywhere else.

"I fucked up." Rasha's bloodshot eyes focused on Aylin.

No shit. Rasha had sent Hunter straight into Aylin's arms. "Why would you allow another male to feed from you in Hunter's quarters?"

"It's a long story." Rasha flipped her hair over her shoulder, going from self-loathing to alcohol-fueled arrogance in a heartbeat. "But damn, you should have seen Hunter. He was so jealous. I'm surprised Myne isn't dead."

"He wasn't jealous," Aylin ground out. "No male would want another to disrespect him like that."

"It was more than that." Rasha's words were as alcohol-soaked as her mood. "He could barely contain his envy."

Even though Aylin knew Rasha was lying, probably to herself more than to Aylin, she couldn't suppress the twinge of doubt and the lash of hurt. Because the fact was that Hunter had gone to Rasha before he'd come to Aylin. She knew the *why* of it, but logic had no say when it came to what she felt.

"Ay?" Rasha's tone dropped from her haughty high-pitched voice to the soft one she reserved only for her sister. "What's wrong?" For all Rasha's faults, she read Aylin like a book and never wanted to see her upset. Unless, of course, Rasha was the person who'd caused it.

Aylin's stomach got all tied up in knots. Maybe Hunter should have come along, because she had a feeling this wasn't going to go well.

"There's something I have to tell you." She swallowed, but it didn't help relieve her suddenly dry mouth. "I've spent a lot of time with Hunter. You know, the cabin . . . and the demon's challenges . . ."

Rasha frowned, and then her eyes shot wide. "Spirit strike me," she said. "You have a crush on him."

"It's not a crush."

Snorting, Rasha came to her feet, a little off balance. "You think you love him?"

"Yes. And he loves me."

Amusement and pity flickered in Rasha's expression. "And what makes you think that?"

There was no easy way to say this. Aylin doubted that saying it while Rasha was drunk was a good idea, but with Hunter's imprint mark so blatantly visible, there was no putting it off.

"He imprinted on me," she blurted. "Tonight."

Rasha barked out a laugh. "I've never understood your sense of humor, but *that* was funny."

"It's not a joke."

Rasha laughed harder, and the anxiety Aylin had experienced a moment ago turned to smoldering anger.

"Rasha!" Aylin kicked the bottle aside. "For once, can you look at me like I'm more than a twisted leg? Like I'm a female vampire, born from the same dam as you?"

Rasha's laughter died away, leaving her looking confused. "You're serious." She shook her head. "You couldn't be. There's no way Hunter had sex with . . . with *you*."

Now Aylin was pissed. Straight-up furious, and she stepped right up to Rasha. "Maybe if he hadn't caught you with Myne, he never would have come to my chambers. But he did, and I don't regret a single second of it." She swept her hair away from her neck so her sister got a good look at the puncture marks. "He fed from me. Drank my *cripple blood* right down." She took perverse pleasure in watching Rasha's expression fall as the truth settled into her alcohol-logged brain. "It happened, Rasha. Ask him. *Ask the imprint mark on the back of his hand.*"

That last part was unnecessary, but it felt good. Felt good right up to the point where Rasha's fist slammed into Aylin's face.

Aylin wheeled backward, the loss of balance twisting her bad leg and sending her tumbling over the back of the couch. She hit the floor hard, and the breath rushed from her lungs.

"You traitorous bitch!" Rasha's shrill scream pierced the pounding in Aylin's ears as she struggled for a breath. Suddenly, she was yanked off the ground and slammed hard into the coffee table. She heard a crack, and agony tore through her torso.

Blood spurted from her mouth, and then she felt what she was pretty sure was a kick to the gut. She tried to breathe, but she choked on blood as she curled in on herself to stop the pain. Distantly, she heard her sister's voice, a buzz in the haze of her brain.

Aylin? Aylin! Shit, I'm sorry . . . oh, Ay, I'm so sorry . . .

Aylin tried to speak, but nothing came out. Black spots filled her vision, expanding as she struggled for air. Then there was nothing.

AYLIN WAS HURT. Hunter could feel it as if her pain was his. The imprint didn't work that way for most males, but the closer the male was to the original vampire bloodlines, the more intense the bond was to the female he imprinted on.

So yeah, he felt Aylin's distress as he tore through MoonBound's halls and hit Rasha's quarters at a dead run. The door tore off its hinges as he burst through it.

Rasha let out a surprised scream, but instantly, upon seeing his face, she settled into a fighting stance.

It didn't do any good. He clamped his hand around her throat and lifted her into the air. It took every ounce of self-control he had not to squeeze until she was no longer breathing.

"Where's Aylin?" he rasped.

"I-I took her to the lab. She's okay," she added quickly.

He shook her. Hard. "What did you do to her?"

Rasha bared her fangs, but it was a defensive move, not an aggressive one. She was scared. She should be. "She . . . she betrayed me."

"The way you betrayed me with Myne?" he snarled.

"Listen to me, Hunter—"

He got right up in her face, his temper near cracking. "She risked her life for the sake of *your* firstborn child!"

"I know," she rasped. "I was wrong. I thought she owed me for protecting her for decades. For making sure she got enough food and clothes. I made sure her beatings didn't kill her. I let her have a place at the fire in the winter. And then she took you . . . and I lost my temper."

"You seriously thought she *owed* you for that? If she *killed* you for it, no one would be surprised." He practically shook with rage. He *did* shake Rasha. "You and your clan have treated her like a stray dog, tossing her scraps and relegating her to the very edges of your society. Has she ever had anything that made her happy?"

He felt her throat work beneath his palm. "She had a pet rabbit once."

Hunter blinked in surprise and finally released Rasha. "Kars let her keep it?"

"When he learned about it, he made her eat it."

What. The. Fuck. Hunter took a step back from Rasha before he made her pay for what Kars had done. "Your father is a fucking fiend. I can't imagine that she willingly ate her pet."

"He held her down and forced it down her throat."

Hunter closed his eyes. What a nightmare existence Aylin had endured. "So she went through all of that, and you still tried to destroy her tonight."

"I did warn you," she said softly. "I told you I wouldn't tolerate another female."

"No, Rasha, you don't understand." Lightning-fast, he gripped her chin and forced her to look into his eyes. "I love her. *You* are the other female. Forget that at your own peril."

He left Rasha to stew in her own bitter juices and rushed to the lab. He caught Nicole as she was on her way out.

"How's she doing?"

Nicole tucked her hands into her lab coat's pockets. "It could have been bad, given her blood issues, but—"

"What blood issues?"

"Her blood wasn't clotting right. It's a problem in vampires who aren't fed from during the appropriate moon phase. I told her she needed to participate." Nicole shrugged. "Looks like she did, because her internal bleeding has slowed far faster than it would have just yesterday."

"So she's going to be okay?"

Nicole nodded. "She's tough."

"I know." He shot an impatient glance at the door. "Can I see her?"

"She's asleep," Nicole said, "but she should wake up any minute."

"Asleep?"

"I gave her a sedative." Nicole held up her hand. "Don't worry, it was mainly a precaution. I wanted to help boost her clotting ability, and vampires heal best when they're out."

He relaxed, but only a little. "You're sure she's okay?"

Smiling, Nicole patted him on the arm. "I promise. Go see her. And if that mark on your hand means what I think it means . . ." She trailed off, her expression going fierce. "Get Rasha the hell out of here."

He dared anyone to try to stop him.

Leaving Nicole, he found Aylin resting in one of the patient beds, her silky hair spread out over the pillow, her ivory skin marred by the faint shadow of a bruise along her cheekbone. She was healing, but the sight still ramped up his anger.

She stirred as he approached, opening groggy eyes with a smile. "Hey."

He didn't waste time with pleasantries. "I should have been there when you told her."

She reached out to pat his hand. "I didn't think she'd react so violently. She's never hurt me before. Not like that. But I don't blame her. I'd react the same way if I lost you."

"I'll never let anyone hurt you again." He lifted her hand to his lips, and with the tenderest of kisses, he pressed his lips to each finger and then lingered with his mouth in her palm, telling her without words that what she held in the palm of her hand was more than a kiss.

She held his heart and soul.

34

A S HUNTER'S ANCESTORS would say, it was time to look the wolves in the eye.

For all of Hunter's authority and years of successful leadership, he was still unsure how his senior warriors were going to react to his news. The developments between him and Aylin were going to have some serious repercussions for the clan, and he needed his people to be on board.

When he arrived in the meeting room, Jaggar, Takis, Katina, Riker, and Baddon were already seated. As he strode to his seat at the head of the table, Baddon shot him a glare. Hunter returned it, holding the other male's gaze until Baddon finally looked down with extreme interest at the skull ring on his right hand.

Took for-fucking-ever, though.

"Where's Aiden?" Hunter took a seat.

"On patrol," Takis answered.

Damn. Hunter had really wanted everyone here. Takis, as if reading his mind, added, "He gave me his voice."

Meaning that Takis had Aiden's permission to speak for him. The pair's thoughts had been in sync from the day they'd met and became a couple a few years ago. Hunter was glad; Takis had been alone for far too long.

"Okay, let's get to it." Hunter looked each of his warriors in the eye, lingering a little on Baddon as the memory of the big male in Aylin's chambers flickered in the back of his mind. "There's no easing into this, so I'm just going to say it." He held up his hand, revealing the raven feather marking his skin. "I imprinted on Aylin."

Three sets of eyebrows shot up.

Riker blew out a breath.

Baddon let out a whispered "Fuck."

That's right, buddy. She's mine.

"So what now?" Riker asked. "Don't get me wrong . . . I'm happy for you, man. But *dayum*. Kars and Tseeveyo are going to blow a gasket."

"Tseeveyo?" Katina scowled. "NightShade's chief? What's he got to do with anything?"

Hunter's chair squeaked as he leaned back. "Aylin is supposed to mate with him next month."

A chorus of curses and groans made their way around the table. "I'm guessing that's not going to happen now," Jaggar said. "And I'm also guessing that's going to be a huge problem."

"Which is why I called you here," Hunter said. "I'm supposed to mate with Rasha in two weeks, but I'm not giving up Aylin."

"So basically," Riker said, "you have two choices. Mate with Rasha *and* keep Aylin, which isn't going to go over well with either of the other clans. Or you can refuse Rasha and keep Aylin, which will go over even worse, since you'll be breaking the contract with Kars."

"That about sums it up."

Baddon flexed his fingers on the tabletop, leaving grooves in its surface. "So you fucked Aylin *and* us."

Hunter didn't remember shoving to his feet. Didn't remember diving across the table and taking Baddon down to the floor in a tumble of bodies and chairs. But he remembered slamming his fist into the male's face. Several times.

And he'd remember the knee to the gut Baddon gave him for a while.

"Knock it off!" Riker's bellow echoed in the chamber as he and the others hauled Hunter off Baddon.

Blood blazing with anger, Hunter struggled to land a few more punches. He managed two hard hits and one kick that would have shattered a lesser male's thigh bone, and then he was wrestled to the ground and pinned there by Katina, Takis, and Jaggar. Riker tackled Baddon, knocking him into the wall.

"You stupid son of a bitch!" he yelled at Baddon. "You should be happy for him."

"It could have been me." Baddon's furious tone carried a note of pain Hunter knew wasn't physical, and his own anger eased a little.

Long ago, Baddon had lost a female he loved, and after decades of mourning, he'd gotten back into the game with a vengeance. He was desperate to find a mate, was desperate to imprint on a female, but he'd already slept with pretty much everyone at MoonBound. Outside the clan, worthy females weren't easy to find.

"You know that's unlikely," Riker said. "So let it go." When Baddon ground his molars and said nothing, Riker gave him a little shake. "Hey. I said to let it go. This is your first warning. There won't be a second. You'll go straight into the pit. Feel me?"

Baddon inclined his head in a single sharp nod. Riker released him and turned to Hunter. "Let's get this figured out."

Although Hunter's blood still ran hot, he wasn't a complete fool. Baddon was right, and he'd probably voiced what everyone else had been thinking.

"Thanks, Rike, but Baddon isn't wrong. I put the clan in a dangerous position. I intend to accept full responsibility, and I'll do whatever it takes to keep everyone at MoonBound safe, even if that means stepping down as chief." Swallowing his pride, which felt like a flint arrowhead was lodged in his throat, he said grimly, "I'm sorry. I've let you all down."

Baddon swore, and Hunter braced himself for the others to jump all over this. If Hunter were them, he'd be pissed as hell, and he wouldn't blame them if they dragged him before the clan and forced him out.

"Fuck that," Riker said quietly. "You've led us through wars with other clans and battles with humans, and you've done what you needed to do for our survival. You deserve to be with a female you love." He glanced at the other warriors in turn. "I'm standing behind him."

Katina stepped forward. "Ditto."

"You aren't going anywhere, man," Jaggar said. "You've saved this clan more than once. We're in this together."

Takis bowed his head deeply. "My loyalty has always been yours."

Hunter didn't bother looking at Baddon. He'd be the dissenting vote, and it was what Hunter deserved.

"Mother. Fuck," Bad muttered. "Yeah, you fucked up, but I'd have done the same thing. You're not going anywhere, chief."

Son of a bitch. Damn, but their loyalty touched him, humbled him, *honored* him. There had been occasions—not many, but a few—in the past when he'd wondered if his father's methods of leading the clan had garnered more respect than Hunter had earned, but he would never wonder again.

His father would have demanded devotion; these warriors gave it freely.

"Thank you," he croaked. "I promise—"

The chamber door flew open, and Aiden burst into the room, panting, his blond hair damp with sweat. "We have a problem," he blurted. "Tena and I ran into ShadowSpawn warriors—"

"ShadowSpawn?" Hunter interrupted. "Here? In our territory?"

Aiden's voice lowered ominously. "There are dozens of them. They've set up camp not far away. Kars is with them."

"Why the hell would they be here?" Katina's dark skin flushed even darker with anger. "The mating isn't for two weeks."

"It gets worse." Aiden jammed his hand through his hair. "NightShade is here, too. And Tseeveyo is demanding Aylin."

• • •

HUNTER DIDN'T LIKE surprise visits. He especially didn't like surprise visits from enemy asshole visitors. And now he had to choose which enemy asshole visitor to confront first.

While Hunter assigned a permanent shadow for Rasha—no way was he letting her have full run of the compound after what she'd done to Aylin—Riker and Baddon went to scout out the enemy camps and determine the threat level. Barely half an hour later, they returned with a message from Kars.

Apparently, the ShadowSpawn leader wanted to meet right away.

"Both clans are camped out a quarter of a mile from here." Riker addressed Hunter and the others now that they'd reassembled around the massive battle table. "There are approximately thirty enemy warriors in the ShadowSpawn camp and forty in NightShade's."

"That's a lot of damned vampires gathered in one place," Katina said. "How are they concealing themselves from the humans?"

"ShadowSpawn brought a mystic-keeper to piggyback off our wards."

"Bastards," Baddon growled. "We'd be within our rights to demand payment."

Yes, they would. But until Hunter knew what ShadowSpawn was up to, there was no point in antagonizing them. Besides, their mystic-keeper could only strengthen MoonBound's wards, which were intended to repel humans so subtly that they didn't even know why they would feel the need to turn around and go in the opposite direction.

"Is NightShade doing the same?"

Riker shook his head. "They concealed their camp from human eyes by themselves. Seems that one of Tseeveyo's mates is a dark shaman."

Hunter drew a sharp breath, and so did pretty much everyone else. MoonBound's mystic-keeper drew from positive natural energy to create wards and to activate a spell that concealed the entrances to the clan's headquarters, and maintaining the wards and the spell took up every drop of his power. Dark shamans used negative natural energy to spin up their magic, and even weak dark shamans were generally more powerful than the strongest mystic-keepers.

But for a dark shaman to hide an entire camp from humans, even if those humans were standing right next to a tent, took more power than Hunter had known existed.

"Both chiefs are demanding an audience with you," Riker said. "They're waiting for an escort."

Hunter stood. "There will be no escort. I'm going to them."

"Sir," Riker said, "I strongly advise against that. Bring them here, where we have the advantage of numbers and the comfort of our home."

"They're already in our home," Hunter pointed out, thinking of Rasha. "Now they're on our property, and I won't cower behind walls."

Riker's vile curse rang out. "Then give me an hour to get teams of warriors posted around their camps. They won't even know they're there."

Hunter gestured to a framed Lakota quote on the wall and shook his head. "'Force, no matter how concealed, begets resistance,'" he said. "No. I'll go with no more than two warriors to accompany me. And don't argue." He crossed the room to the closet where he kept his battle gear and grabbed his weapons harness. Where's Myne?" He might despise the male, but he was one of the best fighters in the clan.

Riker's pause sat heavily in the air, and Hunter knew he wasn't going to like the answer. "He's gone."

"What do you mean, gone?"

"His chamber is empty." The worry in Riker's eyes said it all. Myne wasn't off on one of his usual unannounced solitary disappearances.

Hunter's first reaction was to wish the fucker good riddance. But dammit, the clan needed him. "When this is done, find him." He buckled his harness to his chest. "Now, let's see why these bastards are here."

35

Hunter met with Tseeveyo first. Strategically, it made the most sense; NightShade was the lesser threat to MoonBound, and if Hunter played his cards right, he might gain vital information he could use against ShadowSpawn.

But it still pissed Hunter off that the bastard was on MoonBound property.

NightShade had erected several crude lean-to shelters around a central campfire, but Tseeveyo's shelter was the largest and most private. When Hunter entered, he found several fur bedrolls on the floor, some containing sleeping females.

In one corner of the tent, a young female, who appeared to be no more than eighteen, tended to a toddler with pink ribbons in her jet-black hair.

Hunter had heard that Tseeveyo didn't travel anywhere without at least five of his mates, and it looked like that rumor could be confirmed as true.

Tseeveyo, a born vampire with muddy brown eyes and long black hair that was just starting to go silver at the temples, took a seat in one of two folding camp chairs. The table between them held a bowl of nuts and berries, a skin of what Hunter guessed was blood, and a plate of steaming corn cakes.

"You can sit or not." Tseeveyo squeezed the contents of the wineskin into a wooden cup. "I don't give a fuck."

Pleasant guy. Hunter remained standing, angling his body to keep one eye on movement outside the tent. "Tell me why you're camping on my land without permission."

Tseeveyo snorted and took a swig from his cup. "Didn't think I needed it, since I've come to collect my promised bride."

Hunter's hand drifted toward the dagger at his hip as he entertained fantasies of driving it through the bastard's heart. "Did you alter your deal with Kars to take Aylin sooner?"

"Fuck him." Tseeveyo wiped his mouth with the sleeve of his buckskin tunic. "He promised me that virgin bitch, and I want her."

Hunter's fingers curled around the hilt. "What if she's no longer a virgin?" Not that Tseeveyo was going to get Aylin. But this shit would go down a lot easier if Tseeveyo gave up Aylin willingly.

The other chief hissed as if Hunter had just thrown a poisonous snake in his face. "I still want her. I'll beat her to within an inch of her life for fucking someone else, but I want her."

Hunter *so* wanted to knock Tseeveyo's teeth out. And *then* stab him. "If we all got what we wanted, you'd have a blade through your heart."

"And your clan would be extinct," Tseeveyo said,

almost pleasantly. "But as you pointed out, we don't all get what we want. Now, hand over Aylin. My clan is moving, and I want to move her with us."

"Your deal is with Kars. You need to talk to him."

Tseeveyo leaned back in his chair and stared down the bridge of his broad nose at Hunter. "That bastard will require an outrageous payment."

"Not my problem."

Tseeveyo's oily smile made the hair on Hunter's head stand up. "How about an incentive?" He curled his finger at the young female in the corner, and she came over, the toddler in tow. "I'll offer my daughter to you." He snatched up the child and held her out as the mother fell to her knees and sobbed. "I was saving her for myself, but the trade for Aylin will be worth the loss."

Raw fury scorched Hunter's throat. The sick bastard was going to mate with his own daughter? And he was willing to hand over an innocent baby to a strange male who could do who knew what with her?

Hunter had seen enough. Even if he hadn't fallen for Aylin and the mating with Rasha was still on track, he'd never have handed Aylin over to this monster. And if Tseeveyo hadn't been holding a baby, Hunter would have knocked his teeth out the way he'd wanted to a moment ago.

"You," Hunter growled, "are a twisted abomination. You have until nightfall to get off my land."

"Don't threaten me, asshole. My dark shaman can more than defend our camp."

"Not if your dark shaman is dead." Hunter spun on his heel and headed toward the exit. "Be here after the sun goes down, and you'll see." Every male and female at MoonBound would happily join in the battle to rid their territory of NightShade's infestation.

Tseeveyo's roar of fury followed Hunter out of the tent and all the way to the edge of camp, where Riker and Aiden were waiting. When he heard the child whimper and one of the females cry, he wheeled around, dagger drawn, and both Aiden and Riker had to hold him back.

"Easy, chief," Riker said, eyeballing the wall of Tseeveyo's armed warriors who had closed around the tent. "Going back would be suicide."

Aiden nodded. "His day will come."

Yes, it would. And Hunter would be front and center.

HUNTER SAT CROSS-LEGGED on a plush bear pelt on the floor of Kars's teepee. Modern clans, like MoonBound, had long since found that human-made camping equipment was superior to—or at least more portable than—Indian native equipment, but some clans, like ShadowSpawn, never caught up to modern times.

Sitting across from Hunter, Kars offered him a wooden cup of hollywine. Careful to keep the imprint mark on his hand hidden, Hunter took the cup to be polite, but he didn't drink. Kars was rumored to have poisoned rivals in the past, and Hunter wasn't taking any chances.

"This is a surprise, Kars." Hunter searched the other chief's expression for any hint of what he was thinking, but the male's face was a blank. Like his personality.

Kars shrugged. "I missed my daughters and wanted to make sure you're treating them well."

Liar. "Is that so."

"Mmm." Kars's noncommittal response made Hunter grind his teeth. "How's it going with Rasha?"

"It's not," Hunter said, figuring that where he could, he might as well be straight.

Kars smiled fondly. "She can be difficult."

Difficult? She was foul-mouthed, psychotic, callous, and abusive. "She's more than difficult."

Another shrug. "You'll grow to appreciate her."

Only if she was thousands of miles away. He'd appreciate *that.* "You didn't come all this way to ensure that your daughters are happy. So why are you really here? And at the same time as NightShade?"

The smile fell off Kars's face. "Tseeveyo shouldn't be here until after the new moon. After you and Rasha are mated. It was agreed."

This was getting weird. What were the odds that both clans would show up for the same female at the same time if they hadn't arranged it?

Hunter put the cup to his lips, but he didn't drink. "Why do you think he's here?"

"For Aylin, obviously." Kars waved his hand in dismissal. "Doesn't matter. I'm going to take her home."

Hunter's hand jerked hard enough to spill blood-red wine on his hand. "Aylin is supposed to tend to Rasha until the mating ceremony." Which obviously wasn't going to happen, but he needed time to figure out how to avoid outright war.

"I changed my mind. She belongs at Shadow-Spawn."

Hunter took a deep, controlled breath. *Stay calm.* "Tseeveyo isn't going to take that well." No, the guy seemed to want Aylin in a bad way.

"I'll handle Tseeveyo."

"You should have done that a long time ago."

Kars went taut. "Meaning?"

"Meaning Tseeveyo is a rabid dog." Hunter leaned forward, wanting the other male to see every flicker of emotion that crossed Hunter's face. "And you promised your daughter to him, which makes you even worse than he is."

Kars snarled, spitting wine and flashing stained fangs. Had he never heard of a toothbrush? "I promised her a life! Without Tseeveyo, she'd have nothing and no one. If I died, the other clan members would tear her apart."

Did he truly believe that what he'd done was done out of concern for Aylin? That handing her over to a fiend was for the best?

If so, something wasn't adding up. "If life is so bad at ShadowSpawn for Aylin, why do you want her back? And don't give me some sob story about how you miss her. We both know that's a bunch of elkshit."

Kars gazed at Hunter with shrewd eyes, as if he was trying to decide whether to tell the truth. Finally, he chugged the last of his wine and tossed the cup over his shoulder. "I've found another mate for her."

Kars's blunt announcement was like an icicle through the chest. "Who?"

"One of my warriors," Kars said. "By mating her to Fane, I'm guaranteeing her safety and assuring that when I'm gone, my clan will be led by a worthy male."

"Fane?" Hunter shook his head in disbelief. "You want to mate her to that asshole?"

"He's strong. Brave. Aylin is deformed and weak. He'll protect her, and with the Raven's help, their children will inherit Fane's strength of character instead of hers."

Hunter wanted to leap across the space between them and beat the ever-living fuck out of Kars. But something wasn't sitting right, and until he knew what it was, he had to proceed carefully and with fewer homicidal thoughts.

According to Riker, it was called diplomacy. *Di-plo-ma-cy*, he'd said. The smartass.

"Come now, Kars. We both know there's no damned mystical Raven."

Kars shifted uncomfortably and spoke in a hushed voice. "We don't speak of these things."

"You don't. I do." He leaned forward, resting his elbows on his knees. "I've been through the trials. I've passed the fucking tests."

Kars shot to his feet, fangs bared. "And you dishonored Rasha to do it! How dare you take her unworthy sister?"

"Dishonored Rasha?" Hunter asked incredulously as he came to his own feet. "She dishonored herself by refusing."

"That was her choice."

"And it was a choice I couldn't accept," Hunter snarled. "I would never give up my child to a demon. Aylin was willing to fight for what Rasha wasn't. And she was magnificent."

Kars jabbed his finger at him. "You took a foolish chance."

"I— Wait." Hunter frowned. "How did you know I took Aylin instead of Rasha?"

Kars's eyes flared, but a heartbeat later, he waved dismissively. "You traveled outside your territory. You think I don't have scouts everywhere?"

Plausible, but Kars's tiny eye flare stuck in Hunter's craw. Something was very, very wrong about this entire situation, from two clans arriving at the same time and both demanding Aylin to the reasons they were giving for wanting her.

Neither Kars nor Tseeveyo had any respect for Aylin, so the keen interest in her meant that something had happened to spur them to this.

Oh . . . *oh, fuck*. There was only one logical answer.

Somehow they knew about Aylin's new ability. They knew she was now one of the most powerful vampires in existence.

Which meant that neither clan was going to let her go.

36

AYLIN HAD BEEN summoned to Hunter's chamber. Apparently, he'd gone to the lab to find her, but she'd gone to the library. There was something so hugely calming about a room full of books, and right now she needed calm. She wasn't ready to see Rasha again . . . didn't know how she'd react when she *did* see her. And the news that her father and Tseeveyo were both camped out just a quarter-mile away had rattled her.

Now, with Hunter asking her to his chambers, she couldn't help but wonder if he'd decided to hand her over for the sake of his clan.

She rapped tentatively on the door, and a heartbeat later, Hunter was there. Sweet Spirit, he was gorgeous, his hair pulled back with a leather thong to reveal the angled planes of his face, his black T-shirt stretched over layers of muscle, and black leather pants that fit him like a glove.

Anxiety wracked her . . . until he tugged her into his arms. His mouth found hers in an almost desperate kiss that left no doubt how glad he was to see her.

When he stepped back, she felt dazed, both from

the arousal he so easily called from her and from relief that nothing had changed between them after his visit with the two enemy clans.

"Join me," he said. "I'm playing video games."

Baffled, she followed him inside, where he plopped down on the couch and picked up a controller. "Video games? Did my father and Tseeveyo leave?"

His expression went dark, but oddly, he dived into the game with a vengeance. "Nope."

A knock at the door startled her before she could get him to elaborate.

"Enter," Hunter called out.

The door opened, and Bastien swept in with a huge tray of something covered in cheese and red chunky stuff.

"Thanks, kid," Hunter said. "Just leave it on the coffee table."

Bastien gave a silent, shy nod, his face turning bright red when he noticed Aylin. He ran out of there like his feet were on fire.

"Bastien is just discovering females," Hunter said, amusement lacing his tone.

"Just now? How old is he?"

"He's twenty, but until three months ago, he lived in a cage inside a Daedalus lab, so he's a little behind the curve." Hunter winked at her, and she would have been charmed if she wasn't still hung up on what he'd just said. "He's catching up fast, though. The females love him."

A cage? In a human laboratory? Aylin would never complain about her life again. "How did he get free?" She blinked. "Wait . . . isn't he Riker's son?"

Hunter nodded. "Riker's first mate, Terese, was pregnant when she was killed while in human captivity. Riker thought his son died with her until he and Nicole found Bastien in a Daedalus laboratory."

Great Spirit have mercy. "There really are no words for how awful that must have been for everyone involved."

"I know. That's why we don't talk about it much." Hunter removed his feet from the table and patted the cushion next to him. "Take a load off, and have some totchos."

"Some what?"

He gestured to the plate of stuff Bastien had brought. "Totchos. Tater tots with nacho toppings. Awesome."

Aylin had no idea what nacho toppings were, but the smell was making her mouth water. She sank down onto a cushion next to Hunter . . . but not too close, which made his mouth quirk with amusement. He reached out and lifted a tot off the plate and popped it into his mouth. She watched him chew for a moment, watched the way his throat muscles worked with every swallow. Damn, even when he was doing nothing but eating, he was the sexiest thing she'd ever laid eyes on.

Stomach growling, she followed his lead and ate one of the little things. An explosion of flavor burst onto her tongue . . . creamy, tangy, sharp. Onions, tomatoes, cheese, and other flavors she couldn't identify made her moan with delight.

"Good, huh?" Hunter asked, and all Aylin could do was nod as she shoved another into her mouth.

She ate a dozen more bites, chewing slowly, but all

she was doing was delaying the inevitable. Finally, she wiped her hands on a napkin and turned to Hunter. "Okay, so what's going on?"

He did something on screen that caused an explosion. "Obviously, you know ShadowSpawn and Night-Shade are here."

"That's all anyone is talking about." The totchos suddenly weren't sitting well. "Why are they here?" *Please don't say Tseeveyo is here for me.*

"They're here for you."

She was going to throw up. "Why would my father be here for me, too?"

Pausing his game, Hunter shifted on the sofa to face her, his expression alarmingly serious. "I think they might know about your ability. Who did you tell?"

"No one."

"Not even Rasha?"

"I don't trust her," she said, the ache of her admission eating at her like a betrayal. "Her loyalty is to ShadowSpawn, not me."

Hunter's raw curse scorched her ears. "I was sure she'd gotten the word out."

Aylin couldn't blame him for thinking that, but she doubted even Rasha would tip off Tseeveyo about Aylin's newfound gift.

"Where is she? I haven't seen her." She assumed Hunter would have tossed her into the pit or the dungeon, it was what her father would have done in a similar situation. But deep down, Aylin couldn't help but hope for mercy. Rasha was hard-hearted, but given her upbringing, how could she have turned out any other way?

Hunter's dark eyes burned with anger, but his voice was strangely gentle. "She's confined to her chambers, with Katina as her guard."

Relief spread through her. "Thank you," she said, aware that Hunter's mercy was out of consideration for Aylin. "What are you going to do about Kars and Tseeveyo? You have to give me up, don't you?"

"Fuck, no." He threw down the controller and took her hands in his. They were so warm and strong, so capable of both fighting and pleasuring. What if she'd found him only to lose him because of what was going on outside MoonBound's walls? "If I have to hand over MoonBound to Riker and take you halfway around the world to keep you from those bastards, I will."

Aylin's heart fluttered, and warmth spread through her veins. Hunter was willing to give up everything for her. Everything.

Which was why she wouldn't let that happen, even if it meant she had to run away by herself. He belonged with his clan, not hiding from both humans and vampires while trying to protect her.

But she also knew that an imprinted male wasn't going to just let his female take off without him. And a male like Hunter would chase her to the ends of the earth. Obviously, running away, together or separately, would be a last resort. Hunter would have another plan.

She brushed her thumbs over his knuckles, still amazed that he'd chosen her. Not just chosen her but dedicated himself to her. "So what are we going to do?"

"I *was* going to kick them both off my land, but if they know about your gift, they're not going to go easily. So I want you to practice handling portals, and I'm going to lay it all out to Kars and Tseeveyo. They should be here any minute."

She stared. "That seems a little . . . reckless."

His grin was heart-stopping. "Riker said the same thing. He's a planner. I'm better when I have to think on my feet." Releasing her, he picked up the controller from the sofa and unpaused the game. "And when I'm kicking virtual ass."

She glanced over at the TV screen. "What are you playing?"

"Grand Theft Auto: Vampire Clans. You get to be a human or a vampire."

"And you are . . . ?"

He winked playfully. "Vampire."

"Do you get to kill humans?"

"Yup."

She picked up a controller. "Will you show me?"

After a brief moment of surprise, Hunter grinned again. "You bet. Come on, let's steal some cars and whack a few humans."

MY QUARTERS. NOW.

Hunter glanced at Riker's text . . . and then he did a double-take and stared hard. What the hell could be so urgent?

"Stay here," he told Aylin as she sat on his couch, game controller still in her delicate hands. "I'll be back as soon as I can."

Tucking his phone into his jacket pocket, he high-tailed it to the apartment Riker and Nicole shared on the opposite side of the compound.

The door was open, so he burst inside, no announcement, no polite hello. Nope, he was all about the "What the fuck is going on?"

Riker's expression as he stood in the living room amid piles of paperwork, computer printouts, flash drives, and files was bleak. Downright dire.

"It's bad." Riker gestured to the mess. "This is the stuff Nicole stole from Daedalus. She's been going through it for anything we can leak to the media about Daedalus's practices."

"And?" Hunter prompted, his adrenaline still juicing him, thanks to Riker's urgent text.

"And it's been sitting out for months." He picked up a file and flipped it open. "Do you remember when I said that Rasha had been gathering intel on our warriors? Remember how I told you she knew things about Myne she couldn't have known?"

"Yeah," Hunter drawled hesitantly, afraid he knew where this was headed, and it wasn't good. It was as far from good as it could get.

"Even though it was a long shot, I hoped like hell that ShadowSpawn had a spy inside Daedalus who gave her the info on Myne." Riker shoved the file at him. "But Nicole found this today. It's all right here. The surgeries. The experiments. The torture." Riker's voice grew strained. "The humans took one of his kidneys while he was still conscious."

Hunter's stomach turned over as he scanned the reports. The shit the humans had done . . . Great Spirit above, it was a wonder the guy was still sane.

"Hunt, Myne didn't tell *anyone* about what happened to him. Someone broke into our apartment, went through these files, and fed this shit to Shadow-Spawn. We *do* have a spy in the clan."

Hunter's stomach stopped turning over, but only so it could plummet to his feet. "Son of a bitch," he growled. "Son of a *fucking bitch*!"

Riker's hands formed fists at his sides, and his lips peeled back to reveal his long-ass fangs. "I don't think we can deny it anymore. Someone from MoonBound told ShadowSpawn that we lost their midwife three months ago. And they've been giving ShadowSpawn personal information on our warriors."

Hunter closed his eyes. "Kars knew I took Aylin to the vortex instead of Rasha, and he gave me some bullshit story about how his scouts saw us, but I knew he was lying. It had to have been the traitor who told him. And it's a safe bet that whoever this spy is, they also told both ShadowSpawn and NightShade about Aylin's gift." Rage, thick and hot, ran through Hunter's veins like lava. "Which means we can narrow down our suspects to those who were with us when we returned from the portal."

Riker nodded. "I understand. I'll step down from the investigation—"

"You aren't a suspect," Hunter blurted. No way. What spy would have revealed where he'd gotten the information?

That Riker wasn't considered a suspect should have been good news, but the guy shook his head sadly. "But several others are."

"Katina, Takis, Aiden, Tena, and Baddon," Hunter said numbly. "One of them betrayed us."

The rapid pounding of boots thumped in Hunter's

ears, pulling him out of his shock. Baddon skidded to a halt in the doorway, his face red, a vein at his temple throbbing.

"What is it?" Hunter barked, his nerves already on edge, and damn how he wanted to kill something right now. The spy would be a good choice.

As he stared at Baddon, he felt sick, hoping the male wasn't the one Hunter would have to put down. He would, but damn, he'd hate to lose the fighter.

He'd hate to lose any of them.

Baddon held up his hands, which were coated in blood. "I found Katina unconscious in Rasha's quarters. Someone fucked her up. Bad."

"And Rasha?" Hunter ground out.

"Gone." Baddon's hands clenched into fists. "She escaped."

37

"WHERE ARE YOU going, warrior?"

Myne had barely made it to the eastern edge of MoonBound's border when a silver arrow pierced the ground in front of him. Wrapping his hand around the shaft, he yanked it out of the dirt and looked up at the female crouched in the tree branches overhead. Man, it pissed him off that he never sensed her presence. Never heard her, never smelled her. She could have put that arrow through the top of his skull, and he'd have been dead before the pain hit.

"I'm taking a fucking vacation."

Sabbat, a human bounty hunter, cocked a pale blond eyebrow. "With all these humans swarming the woods?"

"Maybe I'm hunting them." He tossed the arrow upward, and she deftly snagged it out of the air.

"Maybe you're full of shit." She cast his duffel a pointed glance that he could see even through the wraparound sunglasses she wore.

"And maybe," he suggested, "it's none of your business. So unless you have a contract out on me, why don't you let me pass?"

Her ruby lips curved into a sinister smile. "Today you're safe. I'm after a city vamp who went blood-lust." She scowled, losing the evil grin. "Assuming the damned poachers don't get him first."

Myne didn't give a rat's ass either way. But if a poacher got in his way, the poacher was going to die. Sabbat . . . she could live. As far as human hunters went, she didn't suck. She went after rogues who attracted too much attention to other vampires, the clan in particular, so everyone left her alone. But the day she started pull-ing the same shit as trophy hunters and poachers was the day someone at MoonBound took her out.

Won't be you, asshole. You don't belong there anymore.

Guess he never had.

"Good luck," he said.

"Yeah, you, too." She stood upright on the branch, which looked way too skinny to hold her, her black, foot-forming shoes gripping the wood as if they'd been coated with glue. Her tight camouflage bodysuit shifted color to match the background as she eased along the branch with an unnatural grace. She was like a fucking Predator from the old movies, practically in-visible and deadly as fuck.

Suddenly, Sabbat froze, and Myne wheeled around, trusting her instincts. The scent hit him instantly.

Rasha.

She slipped through the trees in silence, her dark clothing concealing her as she moved from shadow to shadow. He'd never seen anyone but Sabbat move as silently as Rasha could.

"What the fuck?" he growled. "What are you doing here?"

Frowning, Rasha looked up.

He followed her gaze, expecting to see Sabbat with a weapon trained on Rasha, but the hunter was gone. The freakishly quiet bitch had disappeared like a ghost, leaving no trace that she'd ever been there.

"I want to go with you," Rasha said. "And I could have sworn I saw something up there."

"You didn't, and you can't. And why in the ever-living realm of fuck would I take you with me?"

She looked down her dainty nose at him, which was quite the feat, given that she was eight inches shorter. "You need me for the moon fever."

Snorting, he wheeled away. "Go back to Hunter. I don't need him coming after me."

"He won't." She grabbed his arm and spun him back around. "He's taking Aylin as a mate."

Myne blinked. Holy shit. And holy shit again. "What about the deal with ShadowSpawn?"

"War, probably. They're camped outside Moon-Bound now, along with NightShade."

Adrenaline hot-loaded into his veins. "They're *what*? Why? Because Hunter tossed you out on your ass?"

"I don't know," she admitted. "But if I go back . . . I might end up mated to Tseeveyo."

He laughed. "So that bastard was good enough for your sister but not for you?"

"It's not like that," she ground out.

"Yeah? Because here's the thing. Only an asshole leaves their family in danger, and that's what you're doing to Aylin, isn't it? Leaving her to die in a war that MoonBound can't possibly win."

Her mouth fell open. Closed. Opened again.

"That's what I thought." He cursed. "Come on. Changed my mind. You are coming with me." He bared his fangs. "Willingly or not."

A SWEEP OF the compound didn't turn up a single shred of evidence that Rasha was still inside. According to Katina, who was barely coherent, someone, presumably Rasha, had struck her over the head with something before jamming a blade into her ribs. The next thing Katina knew, she was waking up in the lab, with Nicole and Grant frantically working to stop the bleeding.

Aylin's sister or not, if Hunter got hold of Rasha, she was going to be the first in centuries to feel the full brunt of his wrath. He was too worked up right now to give a shit that his father's influence was surfacing, churning inside him in a caustic brew of fury and betrayal.

But as pissed as he was at Rasha, she, at least, had an excuse for her behavior; she was the enemy and always had been.

Somewhere inside MoonBound's walls, there was another enemy, one who had pretended to be a friend.

Someone in their midst was a motherfucking spy, and he wished he had time to dig more deeply into their identity. Unfortunately, it was time to meet the other clan chiefs. Riker had wanted him to deal with Kars in private, especially given the fact that Rasha had disappeared, but Hunter had another plan.

Chaos.

"'The weakness of our enemy makes our strength,'" he'd told Riker. He hoped the old Cherokee saying would hold true.

The other two clans were volatile, their chiefs arrogant and overconfident. It was a long shot, but if Hunter could exploit those qualities and set the other clans against each other, MoonBound might make it out of this without bloodshed.

Kars, flanked by the Mohawk-haired Fane and another warrior Hunter didn't know, emerged from the woods, arriving on time at the meeting spot outside MoonBound's headquarters. But where was Rasha? Had she not gone to her father? Or maybe she was back at camp while Kars played dumb?

Tseeveyo came from the opposite direction, two large males also accompanying him. And again, no Rasha.

Hunter had no doubt that not far away, each chief had a contingent of warriors on standby . . . just as Hunter did. Next to him, Riker tensed. Jaggar flipped a blade into the air, his carefree attitude deceptive. As an ex–CIA operative in his human life, the guy had a lot of tricks up his sleeve.

Such as the bomb rigged to explode behind the other two chiefs, to be triggered by a single throw of the dagger if needed.

"Where is my daughter?" Kars barked, and Hunter wondered which one he was talking about.

Tseeveyo, his hair in twin braids that fell forward over his chest, scowled. "My mate, you mean."

"The deal is off." Kars stepped closer to Hunter, the implication that Hunter had already chosen sides made very clear. At least he now knew this was about Aylin. For now.

"You can't do that." Tseeveyo's lip curled. "You need my allegiance."

So Hunter had been right. Kars was trying to get the tribes aligned under him. How many did he already have?

"What can I say?" Kars said with a shrug. "A daughter's love is more important than alliances."

Hunter nearly laughed. Not even Tseeveyo could be buying that line of bullshit.

Tseeveyo rounded on Hunter. "You will give Aylin to me. Hand her over right now, and I'll pledge my support to you against ShadowSpawn."

"Hmm," Hunter mused. "Let me think on that. Oh, wait. Fuck, no."

As Tseeveyo turned several shades of angry purple, Kars grinned. "You've made the right choice, Hunter."

"So you're willing to break your deal with Tseeveyo?" Hunter set the trap, and now Kars needed to step into it.

"I would break any deal to keep my daughter safe and happy."

Hunter could practically hear the trap snap shut. "I'm glad to hear that," he said. "Because Aylin will be safest and happiest here with me. You can have Rasha, since you feel the need to have a daughter with you."

Hunter watched Kars closely for any sign that he knew Rasha had escaped from MoonBound, but ShadowSpawn's chief was concerned with Aylin, his color rising to match Tseeveyo's.

"W-we had a deal!" Kars sputtered.

"Didn't Tseeveyo just say the same thing?"

Tseeveyo's mouth twitched in amusement, but his humor was fleeting. "The female was promised to me."

"She is my daughter!" Kars roared. Next to him, Fane tightened his grip on his bow.

Jaggar's knife flipping slowed, his concentration becoming more focused.

"And she will be my mate." Hunter flashed the imprint mark on his hand.

Kars and Tseeveyo cursed in tandem, knowing damned well that no imprinted male would allow his female to be taken from him.

Riker cursed, too, but for a different reason. The two clan chiefs now understood that taking Aylin wouldn't be a matter of negotiation; it had become a matter of killing Hunter.

"This," Kars snarled, "is unacceptable." He thrust his finger at Hunter. "I will see you dead before I allow you to mate with her. Rasha is a far worthier mate—"

"Then take her back, and let me have the 'less worthy' daughter," Hunter countered smoothly. "Our peace agreement can remain intact, and you'll have another chance to make an even better political match for Rasha. It's a win-win."

A win-win unless Hunter was right and the two chiefs knew about Aylin's ability. And on this, Hunter wasn't wrong.

Murder blazed in Kars's eyes. "I will destroy you and your clan down to the last child," he swore. "You have twenty-four hours to hand Aylin over, or your clan will burn."

"And I will be there to dig your bones from the ashes," Tseeveyo said, hatred dripping from his voice like blood. He turned to Kars. "And yours as well."

Kars bared his fangs, and with a vicious snap of his wrist, he sank a blade into the snow between them all. Tseeveyo's blade landed next to it, and Hunter's mouth went dry.

The two enemy clans had just declared war.

On each other . . . and on MoonBound.

THE ATMOSPHERE AT MoonBound had gone from warm and welcoming to tense and cold, with a tinge of fear dancing on the edges of the friction.

Aylin had waited anxiously in Hunter's chambers for his return from the meeting, and the news he brought had been devastating. Now they were sitting in his battle room, his senior and second-tier warriors gathered around.

Hunter had insisted that she take a seat next to him, but try as she might, she couldn't help but feel that this was all her fault. No one had consciously made her feel that way, but she sensed speculating eyes on her, and as battle plans were discussed, she felt more and more guilty.

Especially given that her sister had seriously injured a MoonBound warrior and left her to bleed out on the floor before fleeing like a coward. And according to Hunter, there was a strong possibility that Rasha hadn't gone back to ShadowSpawn. So where was she?

Hunter took Aylin's hand in his and addressed his clan members. "We have twenty-four hours to give Aylin over to either ShadowSpawn or NightShade, or we face a battle. I want suggestions, no matter how crazy." His voice deepened with a solid warning, and maybe it was her imagination, but he seemed extra tense, as if anger was churning deep inside his very marrow. "But if anyone suggests that we give Aylin up, they will be very, very sorry."

Everyone exchanged glances, and finally, Takis shrugged. "What if we smuggle Aylin out of the clan? If she's not here, NightShade and ShadowSpawn will look for her instead of attacking us."

It was a good idea, but Hunter voiced what Aylin was thinking. "They won't believe she's gone. Even if they do believe it, looking for her will be pointless unless they can put pressure on us to reveal her location. And by pressure, I mean an attack. Either way, they won't leave us alone."

"This is our territory," Jaggar said. "We know it in ways they don't. We can get out there tonight and set traps. It won't win a war, but we can even the odds."

"Do it," Hunter said. "Take whoever you need to get it done." He looked around the room. "Anyone else?"

They tossed around ideas, some of which Hunter approved and others, like the suggestion to barricade everyone inside the compound, held as last resorts.

Finally, with precious few courses of action, Aylin spoke up. "I have an idea."

Accustomed to being either scorned or dismissed outright, she was shocked when everyone just looked at her, curious. How long would it take before she got used to being accepted? What a great problem to have.

Hunter inclined his head in a sharp nod. "Speak."

She opened her mouth, but at the last second, she remembered what Hunter had said about a spy. "Can I talk to you alone?"

He nodded and led her away from the group, leaving them with orders to keep brainstorming. "Whatcha got?" he asked, turning his back to the others and blocking her from their view.

"What if I use my ability to help? I can't see how it would be useful in a fight, but I could use it to evacuate everyone to safety if it becomes necessary."

"That's an excellent plan," he mused, but the frown on his face said something different.

"What is it?" she asked. "What's the matter?"

"Nothing. In fact, I think you're on to something." He gestured to Nicole, who had entered a moment ago. "Do you think you can get a message to your brother?"

If Aylin remembered right, Nicole's brother was the CEO of Daedalus . . . so what was Hunter up to?

Nicole blinked, apparently as perplexed as Aylin. "Chuck? Why the hell would I do that?"

An evil smile turned up the corners of Hunter's mouth, revealing the sexy points of his fangs. "For once, the humans are going to do us a big favor. *We* are the alpha predators on this planet," he said darkly, "and it's time we proved it."

38

HUNTER DECIDED TO move on ShadowSpawn and NightShade before the deadline was up. There was no point in waiting, and a surprise attack could only work in MoonBound's favor. Both clans had brought in more fighters—Riker and Jaggar had both reported seeing dozens of vampires moving in to join the camps, leaving MoonBound badly outnumbered and outgunned. They now needed every advantage they could get.

Jaggar had set up trip wires attached to small but deadly explosives, all carefully mapped out for Moon-Bound's residents. Hunter just hoped their mysterious spy didn't alert one or both of the enemy clans.

But even if the worst happened, Jaggar had also set up some special traps that delivered a dose of deadly boric acid. No one but Jaggar, Riker, and Hunter knew the locations of those traps, but they carried vials of the antidote, manufactured by Nicole, in the event that a MoonBound member fell victim.

NightShade and ShadowSpawn were on their own. Every male of fighting age and all trained females had been outfitted with weapons and were, under the cover of early-morning darkness, slipping into the woods. Hunter hesitated at the exit, his fear for Aylin holding him back. She was the secret weapon in this crazy plan, and at some point, he'd be putting her in danger.

"No matter what happens, don't leave the compound," he said. "Stay here until either Riker or I come for you."

"Be careful," she whispered. "Unlike Rasha, I'd really like to keep you around for a while."

Laughing, he kissed her. He didn't linger, though. This wasn't good-bye. And she didn't need to know that he'd met with his senior warriors just moments ago to ensure that she would always have a place in the clan should something happen to him. No matter what, Aylin would be safe.

He jogged out of the compound and joined Riker before he could change his mind about the quick kiss and turn it into something he couldn't pull away from.

"Rike." He spoke in hushed tones, and the two made their way toward NightShade's camp. Half of MoonBound's team was taking on ShadowSpawn, but Hunter and Riker had both wanted a piece of Night-Shade. Hunter despised Kars, but Tseeveyo had earned a special place on his Need to Die list.

Riker eased a dagger out of the sheath at his hip as they neared the camp. "'Sup?"

"When you're away from Nicole, does it feel like . . . I don't know, an ache?" He rubbed his sternum, but it did nothing to get rid of the weird tug that got more insistent the farther they went from MoonBound.

"Yep," he muttered irritably, but Hunter knew it was a testosterone show. The guy was completely besotted by his mate. "And the bitch of it is that she doesn't have that same ache. The one-sided imprint thing sucks."

"But you wouldn't change anything, right?"

Riker grinned. "Hell, no. I—"

An explosion rocked the forest, and in an instant, all hell broke loose.

War cries rang out, followed by shouts, grunts of pain, and screams. The woods came alive with enemy warriors, and suddenly, Hunter and Riker were in a fight for their lives.

Five huge NightShade males came out of nowhere, tomahawks and daggers flying. An arrow punched through Hunter's left biceps, but he ignored it to slash the throat of the nearest warrior. Another male hit him from behind, knocking him to the ground. He rolled, lost track of Riker, and kicked his feet out to catch his assailant in the knees. The vampire went down with a grunt, but he maintained his grip on his hatchet, and as he hit the snow, he aimed it at Hunter's head.

Hunter dodged, barely avoiding a very close haircut. Scrambling to his feet, he broke off the arrow sticking out of his flesh. The hatchet dude got a little too close with another swing of his weapon, and Hunter ducked, leaped, and drove the arrow shaft through the bastard's right eye.

As the enemy fell, Hunter crouched, prepared for another attack, but Riker took down his last male as Takis leaped out from one of the trees to drive his Ka-Bar through the skull of the fifth warrior.

"Shit," Hunter breathed. "Did they know we were coming?"

"Looks like!" Takis snapped, as pissed as Hunter had ever seen him. "I think someone triggered the explosion intentionally to warn the camps. There's no body near the blow site, but there's an arrow at the trip-wire line."

"When I catch this son of a bitch, I'm going to rip out his fangs and gut him with his own teeth." Hunter had seen his father do exactly that, and at this moment, Hunter could feel his sire's influence rising up in the anger of betrayal.

"Remind me never to betray you," Riker muttered, just as another explosion, this one close by, ripped through the air.

Something hit the tree next to Hunter, and he whirled, expecting a weapon, but nope. A severed arm marked with NightShade's poison-leaf symbol lay in a bloody pool on the ground.

"Remind *me* to give Jaggar a raise." Hunter gestured for Takis and Riker to follow him. They had to get to NightShade's camp. If they could take out Tseeveyo, the rest of the clan might stand down. And if they didn't . . . well, at least the sick fuck would be dead.

As they approached, the sound of fighting got louder, and the stench of fear, pain, and death became almost overpowering.

"Holy fuck," Riker swore. "It's a slaughter."

The carnage was beyond the scope of anything Hunter had seen in at least a century. NightShade's fighters were tearing apart MoonBound's warriors, their numbers far greater than anyone had anticipated.

Enraged, Hunter charged toward the fight, but before he hit the clearing, a shot rang out. He skidded to a halt as rapid-fire gunshots filled the air. NightShade's warriors broke off from the battle with MoonBound's fighters to deal with the new and deadlier threat.

Nicole had come through. Humans had arrived.

"Rike!" Hunter yelled. "You told our warriors to hightail it back to the clan if humans showed up, right?"

Riker shouted an affirmative, but even as his voice faded away, Hunter watched his surviving warriors sprint in the direction of the compound.

"Get out of here!" he told Riker and Takis, but neither moved.

"We're staying with you," Takis said. "And don't fucking argue."

"I'm scheduling pit time for both of you," he growled. He turned, ready to run back to the clan for Aylin, but out of the corner of his eye, he saw something he couldn't leave behind.

Riker grabbed his arm. "Come on, chief."

"Go," he said. "That's an order. Get Aylin. I've got something to do."

Leaving Riker and Takis behind, he launched himself through the forest at a dead run toward Tseeveyo's tent.

NightShade's chief was about to understand that Hunter was his father's son.

NO MATTER WHAT happens, don't leave the compound. Stay here until either Riker or I come for you.

When Takis showed up at MoonBound's entrance to take Aylin to Hunter, she planned to refuse. Aylin trusted her instincts, and Takis didn't ring any internal alarms, but she also trusted Hunter, and if he told her to go somewhere only with himself or Riker, she wasn't going to argue.

Fortunately, Riker was on Takis's heels, bow at the ready, and she had no doubt that he was prepared to take out any threat, even if that threat was another MoonBound member.

Together the two males led Aylin safely along the outskirts of the battle, where she needed to be in order for her plan to work. The sounds of distant fighting echoed through the forest, the screams, gunfire, and occasional explosions making her stomach clench. Nerves made her twitchy, but thanks to her experience in the demon realm, she'd learned to control her fear. And she'd also gained a lot of confidence. Twice her leg gave out, but for the first time in her life, she wasn't ashamed of her disability. It was part of her, but she was so much more than a twisted limb.

Anxious to get to Hunter, she protested when Riker made them stop under the cover of a tangle of fallen trees.

"Why are we stopping?" She gripped the blade her brother had given her with white-knuckled tenacity, her only concern to find Hunter. "We need to find him."

"He'll be here," Riker assured her.

As much as she liked Riker and respected his abilities as a warrior, she couldn't help but snap, "You shouldn't have left him! He could be injured. Or worse."

Riker jammed his hand through his hair, leaving

spiky grooves that somehow managed to look annoyed. "I know. But he gave an order." He crouched low, his gaze fixed in the direction of the sounds of fighting. "Your safety is the priority, and only you can deal with the humans."

Riker made sense, but it didn't ease her worry. "Where *are* the humans?"

Gently, Takis palmed her shoulder and forced her behind a fallen log that was almost as thick as she was tall. "Baddon and Aiden are luring them this way."

She cursed. "That could take forever, if it even works." She slipped away from the two males before either of them could grab her. "I'm going to them."

"The hell you are."

Riker came after her, but she wasn't going to sit around and do nothing when she could help. Their only shot at surviving a war on three fronts was for her to get closer to the humans before they wiped out every vampire in the forest.

"Aylin," Riker said, as he and Takis flanked her. "Hunter will kill us for this."

Her foot slipped on a patch of ice, and although she didn't fall, the strain on her bad leg made her clench her teeth in agony. "I'll accept full responsibility."

"Great," Takis muttered as he tugged his Seattle Seahawks baseball cap low on his forehead. "Then he'll kill us knowing we're not responsible. Either way, we're dead."

"Not if this works." Sure, it was a big *if*, but they had no choice. If she could open a portal in the right place at the right time, she could turn the tide of the battle.

They moved as fast as they could, given Aylin's reduced speed and the necessity of keeping well out of the thick of the fighting, but even so, Riker and Takis both took down a few human snipers who had concealed themselves on the outskirts.

As Riker finished off a burly human male, he froze, staring into the trees.

"What is it?" she whispered.

"Could have sworn I saw Myne." He gestured beyond a forest-fire-thinned patch of scrub brush. "Over by those dead guys."

Holy . . . shit. Not just dead guys but a lot of dead guys. Or, more accurately, a lot of parts of dead guys.

And all around, closing in fast, dozens of vampires were engaged in battle with hundreds of humans. On a level playing field, vampires were the superior beings, but here, dressed in military garb and helmets and carrying more weapons than she could count, let alone identify, the humans held the advantage, not only in weapons but in numbers.

Riker grabbed her and threw her to the ground just as a dozen men started their way. "Fuck. I think they saw us."

Takis crouched next to them and raised his bow. Not that he had much hope against men armed with automatic weapons.

"No." She grabbed his arm. "I got it."

Breathing deeply, the way Riker had taught her to do during their practice sessions, she reached inside herself, to the place where her dove used to roost. Now it was filled with a new energy that writhed like a living thing as she called it forth. Before, she'd had to concentrate. This time, it shot out of her in a rush of wind that nearly blew Riker and Takis off their feet.

Quickly, she pictured a destination . . . and the portal shot open mere feet in front of the men coming toward them.

Six humans, their momentum carrying them forward too fast to reverse course, fell into the opening, trapped as she snapped the portal shut. A chorus of curses, shocked shouts, and confusion froze the remaining men in place, their inability to believe their own eyes giving Aylin a chance to throw open the portal again, this time on top of them. They disappeared as quickly as the others, and once again, she slammed it closed before they could escape.

"Jesus," Takis breathed. "That's fucking scary." He turned to her, his usually tan skin a shade whiter. "Where are you sending them?"

Aylin grinned. "Someplace where they'll get the fight they want."

She opened up the portal again, this time right in the center of the massive group. When it flashed wide, she wondered if anyone else saw the arena on the other side of the vortex—Samnult's arena in his realm, where vampires chanted from the stadium seats while others closed in on the panicked and terrified humans she'd sent there.

From the other side, a familiar blond male raised his hand, and although Aylin couldn't hear him, she could read his lips.

Well done, my sister. Well done.

• • •

HUNTER CUT THROUGH Tseeveyo's guards with an ease that would have astonished him had he taken the time to give a shit. But as he neared the NightShade chief's camp, his mind clouded with only one thought.

Kill.

All around him, the screams of the injured and the moans of the dying—humans and vampires—rose up, filling him with power. This was what he'd both feared and craved, the berserker-like strength, speed, and insanity that came with being a second-generation vampire whose DNA was forged from demonic energy.

His father had reveled in it. Hunter had denied it. Now, as he focused on Tseeveyo, who was driving the sharp end of a hatchet between a human male's shoulder blades, Hunter embraced it.

"Tseeveyo."

The other chief spun around, his native clothing dripping with blood and gore, his fangs coated in crimson, his black eyes burning with bloodlust.

He, too, was in the grip of the ancestral vampire savagery, and with a grin that revealed a mouthful of sharper-than-normal teeth, he came at Hunter.

They met with the force of two bulls, the shock wave rocking the earth around them. Tseeveyo struck Hunter first, his fist smashing into his jaw, but the pain was fleeting. Hell, it was *welcome*.

Spurred by the throbbing, Hunter laid the bastard out with two rapid strikes to the face, another to the throat, and another to the gut. Tseeveyo hit the ground with a grunt, but he was up again in a flash, hand curled around a machete he must have pulled from his ass, because it hadn't been there a moment before.

The older male spun in a blur, whipping the blade low for a deep strike into Hunter's hip. Agony wrenched through him as his leg folded beneath him. A flash of silver was his only warning as the machete arced downward once more, striking him a couple of inches below the first gash. Blood sprayed across the snow, the trees, the dead leaves clinging to dying branches.

Groaning, Hunter rolled to the side as Tseeveyo abandoned the blade to kick the ever-living fuck out of him. Tseeveyo's boot crunched into his ribs, his shoulder, his neck.

Shit, this bastard was strong, and his extra two centuries of experience showed in every blow. But Hunter wasn't going to give up easily, not when he had a clan to run and a female to protect. Even now, the raven feather on his hand burned, a reminder that he had more to live for than he could ever have dreamed possible.

Fuck. This.

As the sole of Tseeveyo's boot filled Hunter's vision, a death blow that would have crushed his skull, Hunter rolled. He snapped his hand out, catching Tseeveyo's ankle with a tug that brought the son of a bitch down into the snow, which had grown slushy with their mixed blood.

But as Hunter shoved to his knees, his injured leg buckled again under his weight, the ice beneath his knee sending him sliding down a gully with Night-Shade's chief scrambling after him. Tseeveyo's hand clamped around Hunter's throat as he pinned him to the icy ground.

"You fucking whelp!" Tseeveyo snarled. "I knew

Bear Roar. He was powerful. Strong." His fist slammed into Hunter's skull so hard he saw stars and heard bells. "He would be ashamed of you."

Invoking Hunter's father's name was like summoning a demon, and deep inside Hunter's chest, an evil shadow flickered to life. Even as Tseeveyo lifted Hunter to his feet by his throat, he smiled, feeling an ice storm gathering overhead.

Suddenly, they were wrapped in a tornadic blizzard so fierce that frost formed on the other male's eyebrows, his lashes, even his lips, which turned pale blue as he tried to squeeze the breath from Hunter's body.

"My father's . . . shame . . . makes me . . . proud."

Summoning his last, desperate breath and taking a page straight from his father's book of dirty tricks, Hunter whipped a blade from the sheath at his back and drove it deep into Tseeveyo's groin.

Tseeveyo screamed, then screamed again when Hunter yanked the knife upward, slicing through the bastard's balls as if coring an apple.

"That's for every one of your child-brides," Hunter snarled.

Tseeveyo threw himself backward, gripping his crotch as blood spurted between his fingers. Eyes wide with pain and horror, he scrambled, stumbling, away from Hunter. The bastard could try to get away, but Hunter was the predator now, and he'd tasted his prey's blood. His fear.

And he could smell death coming.

The knife was slippery with blood, but Hunter gripped it like a lover he would never let go.

Like Aylin.

With every step closer to Tseeveyo, he relished the male's terror. He knew he should be horrified at his own bloodlust, but Tseeveyo was a monster who deserved to die a far worse death than Hunter was going to give him.

The male stumbled over a broken branch and fell awkwardly to the ground, his skin growing ashen as blood loss took its toll.

All around, humans and vampires were fighting, but Hunter ignored it all, allowing only a tiny portion of his senses to alert him to anyone who came too close as he crouched over the fallen chief.

Something flashed in the corner of his eye. One of Tseeveyo's mates, a girl with a black eye and a swollen cheek, peered at them from behind a tent flap, her gaze filled with hatred for the bastard on the ground.

For a moment, Hunter watched her, waiting to see if she was going to fight for her mate, but her eyes caught his, and in them he saw encouragement and victory.

"I'd like to cut off your dick and shove it down your throat, you sick fuck," Hunter growled, "but that's what my father would do, and I'm nothing like him." With that, he brought his blade swiftly across Tseeveyo's throat, opening it from ear to ear.

Behind the tent flap, the female acknowledged Hunter with a solemn nod.

Leg throbbing, head aching, ribs screaming, Hunter stood. The wind around him died down, and vaguely, he heard someone call out his name.

"Hunter . . . chief . . . *Hunter*." A MoonBound warrior, a female named Trish, jogged toward him, flanked by another female and a young male who had only graduated from battle training a month ago.

"The humans are fleeing," she said through split lips and a swollen jaw. "ShadowSpawn is broken." She broke off to fire an arrow to her right, and he heard a grunt and the thud of a body hitting the ground.

"Aylin," he breathed. "Where is she?"

"I don't know," she said. "But I saw Riker to the south."

Gathering his weapons, he limped toward them. "Take care of NightShade's females and children. They're not to be harmed." With one final look at Tseeveyo, whose last dying breaths were whispering over his lips, Hunter headed south.

The monster was dead.

And now, Hunter knew, so was the monster inside him. His father was gone, and would never again have a hold on him.

39

Hunter was in a panic. He'd made his way to the designated meeting spot, but Aylin wasn't there. He could feel her, but he'd been badly wounded, and through his own pain, he couldn't sense Aylin's. If she was hurting, he had no way of knowing.

Inhaling deeply, he caught her scent. She was with Riker and Takis, but there were so many other odors in the air that tracking them led to a lot of wrong turns.

He moved as quickly as his wounds would allow, but that wasn't nearly fast enough. Not when he saw vampires rushing through the forest, completely ignoring him when they should have been trying to kill him. The humans had to be right on their tails.

Pain lanced him with every step and every breath as he negotiated the uneven ground. But as he came around a hill, the reason the vampires had been running for their lives was swirling in a huge circle between two trees. And as he watched, the shimmering portal moved. It actually fucking chased the humans bolting away from it. The thing was like a giant vacuum, swallowing people up as it went.

Finally, it collapsed. Except for the cries of the wounded and the stray sounds of an occasional skirmish, the woods were quiet.

"Hunter!" Aylin's beautiful voice came from thirty yards away. He loped toward her as fast as he could and caught her in his arms. "We did it," she breathed. "I can't believe it."

"I never doubted." He looked out over the devastation left by the battle. So many had died, and more had been wounded. They'd won, but the price was never easy to pay.

Scowling, she pulled back from him. "You're hurt. We have to get you to Nicole."

"Not until I've located all of my warriors and we've secured all of NightShade's females and children." He nodded his thanks to Riker and Takis, who had started scouring the battlefield for fallen Moon-Bound members. Surviving humans would become blood donors, and enemy clan members who survived would be given a choice. They could join MoonBound or die. Simple as that. "I want to get you back to the clan, though."

She shook her head. "I'm staying with you. I can help. Besides cooking, the one thing I got to do a lot of at ShadowSpawn was patch up wounds. And I can help with the females and children." He was about to refuse her offer when she jammed her fists on her hips. "Hello, I can whip out a portal and take care of anyone who tries to attack us. Or I can go through it myself to escape. Don't treat me like an invalid."

She was right. He wanted to protect her, but she was doing a fine job of that on her own. "You win." He pressed a kiss into her hair. "But don't expect to win often. I hate to lose."

She grinned. "You'll learn to love it."

The brush rustled, and he wheeled around to see Tena emerge. She had Rasha with her, her hands bound behind her back, her feet loosely hobbled with wire. She looked as pissed as a wet cat.

"Sorry, chief," Tena said. "But I found her tied to a tree, and the bitch wanted to tell you something. Said it was important."

Rasha sneered at Tena, but when she turned to Hunter and Aylin, her expression turned contrite. "Is Kars dead?"

"Unfortunately, no." Hunter tugged Aylin more firmly against him. "But Tseeveyo will never hurt anyone again."

Aylin squeezed his hand. "If my father is still alive, he'll never stop coming after you."

Rasha closed her eyes, and when she opened them, they were liquid with what Hunter would swear was defeat. "Let me handle our father. I'll get you out of the contract."

"I think it's far more likely that you'll help him plot against us," Hunter said.

Hunter expected a defiant comeback, so the fact that she merely sighed told him how defeated she truly was. "Does that mean you plan to hold me prisoner?"

It was tempting. But now that both clans had been soundly trounced, there was no point. Holding Rasha would only make Kars even more volatile and prone to revenge. Aylin was right; Kars would never let this go, and even if he could no longer launch a full-scale attack on MoonBound, he could still cause a lot of damage. A wounded bear was far more dangerous than a healthy one. He turned to Aylin. "She's your sister. This needs to be your decision."

For a long time, Aylin stared down her twin. It wasn't until Rasha, once the alpha of the two, looked away that Aylin nodded. "Let her go. But Rasha? After this, our father is dead to me, and if you betray us, so are you."

MOONBOUND HAD WON. And just as important, no one had seen Myne helping from the periphery, slaughtering humans and enemy clan members alike. Rasha probably hated him more than ever for tying her to a tree for Tena to find, but he couldn't care less.

What he did care about was whether she was going to keep her word and help Aylin and MoonBound, too.

He followed her from a distance, staying far back until she finally located her father. Kars was several miles away from the battle, one hand badly broken and clutching a human head in the other.

Very carefully, Myne eased close to the pair as Kars held up the head. "This should be Hunter's. It *will* be Hunter's."

"Father," Rasha said, sounding saner than she ever had, "you need to let this go."

"Let this go?" he bellowed. "Hunter has no honor! He went back on his word. He humiliated our entire clan and shamed you. I swear to you, I will destroy every MoonBound male, and I'll force him to watch as his females and children are dragged to ShadowSpawn in chains. Then I'll skin that bastard alive and wear him like a coat in every battle from the day of his death on." He snarled. "And Aylin, that traitorous whore. I'll beat her daily for the rest of her sorry life. She'll never see another day in the sun for as long as I live."

"No, Father," Rasha said, knocking the gruesome trophy out of his grip. "You won't do any of that. You're going to leave Aylin and MoonBound alone."

He stared, speechless, before his face went crimson and his eyes flashed with fury. He struck out, slapping Rasha so hard she rocked backward.

What a great father. Kind of reminded Myne of his own late sire.

"You will never speak to me that way." He leaned forward aggressively and practically snarled his words. "No female *ever* speaks to a clan chief with such disrespect, not even my own daughter."

Rasha spit blood on the ground, splattering pink drops on a patch of snow. "See, that's where you're wrong. You *will* listen to me, and you *will* accept Aylin and Hunter's mating." She smiled, a sneaky, knowing smile, and Myne wondered what card she held in this game. "Or I'll tell Aylin that you've been lying to her since the day she was born."

Lying? About what? Must be a fucking *great* card.

He snorted. "You wouldn't."

"I would, and I will. I promise you, I'll tell Aylin how *she* was the firstborn, not me. She'll know that when you saw her twisted leg, you considered drowning her in the bucket you had ready to drown the second twin. But it's bad luck to kill a firstborn twin, so you had to keep her. When I was born, you told everyone I was first and that you decided not to kill the second twin, Aylin, because a raven appeared and told you not to." She smiled around wicked, bared teeth. "And the fools who hang on your every word believed you. Well, except the midwife, who knew everything. Funny how she was killed by *humans* a few days later, isn't it?"

Every drop of blood drained from Kars's face. This just kept getting more and more interesting, didn't it?

"Lies," he rasped.

"You told me yourself. One night when you were drunk and pining for my mother, you confessed it all. I kept quiet all these years, because, like every other fool at ShadowSpawn, I believed that you always do the right thing for the clan. So I let Aylin think she was a curse on our people, like you said. I let her believe that she was the reason our mother died. I treated her like shit to make you happy. But I've seen how things can be different, and now I know how poorly you've led our clan."

He hissed. "Hunter has brainwashed you. Filled your head with insanity—"

"Hunter has nothing to do with this. He's too soft on his people, and he runs MoonBound like it's a big theme park. But his clan is in far better shape than ours, and his people love him, which is more than can be said for you."

Some of the color came back into her father's cheeks, leaving them splotchy with anger. He raised his hand to strike her again, and she dared him with her stare. Myne might despise the bitch, but he had to admit, she didn't back down from a fight. It was her lone admirable trait. For some reason, that made him think of Sabbat, whose lone *negative* trait was that she was human. Well, that, and she killed vampires for money.

"Do it," Rasha said quietly. "Do it, and I swear it'll be the last time you *ever* touch me."

"You ungrateful, spoiled little bitch. I should have drowned you. I should have drowned you both."

A quick flash of hurt crossed Rasha's face but was gone a heartbeat later, replaced by the familiar, ever-present icy mask of indifference. "And I should have stood up to you a long time ago," she shot back. "For me *and* Aylin. But whatever. I'm doing it now, so here's the deal. Things are going to be a little different for ShadowSpawn from now on. And you're going to let Aylin and Hunter live in peace."

Fury darkened Kars's gaze. "Or you'll tell her the truth."

"Oh, I'll do more than that. I'll tell *everyone* in our clan the truth. I'll tell them how you've been lying for a century. That you named a second born twin as heir and killed the clan's midwife in order to keep your secret. Best-case scenario? Some will desert Shadow-Spawn, and those who stay will never trust you again. They probably won't listen to you, and you'll have to defend every decision you make. Worst-case scenario? They'll rise up and banish you."

He swallowed. Hard. "They'll do the same to you. Maybe worse."

"Maybe. But I have options. There isn't a clan out there that wouldn't take me, a born female from a second-generation vampire." Oh, Myne could think of one clan that wouldn't take her. Shrugging, she stud-ied her father, who suddenly looked very old and very tired. "So what's it to be? Are you going to leave Aylin and Hunter in peace or not?"

For a long time, a storm cloud brewed in Kars's expression, and Myne thought the chief was going to refuse. But finally, he let out a gruff curse. "I'll agree to your terms," he said. "But you are a huge disappointment."

"Then don't look in the mirror, Father, because I turned out just like you." Pivoting on her heel, she walked away, heading in the direction of Shadow-Spawn's territory.

Myne flicked his tongue over his titanium fangs, his brain working to process everything he'd just heard. Aylin was the firstborn and true heir to ShadowSpawn. It was a revelation that, in Hunter's hands, could destroy Kars.

Or Myne could use it to his own advantage. But how? And to what purpose?

Pressing his tongue against the tip of one fang, he drew blood, the tiny prick delivering a dose of pain-pleasure that made him shiver. Pain and pleasure. Two sides of the same coin. It was what gave him joy, and what made him miserable.

Funny, that.

Movement drew his attention away from his peculiar preferences, and he looked over to see Kars kick the human head across the clearing before limping off after Rasha. Myne supposed that was his cue.

It was time to get the hell out of MoonBound's territory. Out of Washington. Maybe out of the Pacific Northwest.

Or maybe he'd just hit the city scene, see what

Seattle had to offer. Because one thing was certain: Myne didn't belong in a clan. He never had, and when he thought back to that day all those years ago when Hunter had sent him and his brother packing, he realized that the guy had done him a favor.

Because ultimately, pleasure and pain were the only family he needed.

40

TWO WEEKS AFTER the battle that destroyed Night-Shade and decimated ShadowSpawn, Aylin was still amazed that she belonged to such an incredible clan.

Hunter had gladly taken in NightShade's survivors, mostly females and children, so the compound was bursting at the seams, but no one seemed to mind. Baddon was, even now, arranging for needed supplies to expand the living quarters and common areas. The biggest challenge would be getting the provisions to MoonBound without human notice.

And that was where Aylin came in.

The supplies would be delivered to the cabin where she and Hunter had stayed on the first night they'd met, and from there, MoonBound members would haul the provisions and building materials through an Aylin-created portal to the clan's compound. She'd spent hours each day learning to hold the portal open, and now she could keep it gaping wide for nearly ten minutes before she had to close it and rest. Even the time she needed to recover was decreasing, and she could reopen portals about an hour later.

Pretty cool.

Even better, the human threat had taken a significant turn. The information Nicole had leaked to the media had caused a political shitstorm, and not only had Daedalus's practices come under fire, but all vampire hunting had been temporarily banned.

The loss of hundreds of humans had raised protests everywhere, and while some protesters called for an immediate extermination of vampires, the majority wanted all violence to stop. Newspapers and magazines had begun to interview anonymous vampires, and the leader of a hidden city clan had come forward with a request to begin a peaceful dialogue between the two races.

Unfortunately, he was found nailed to a cross in the center of the city a couple of days ago, igniting violent responses on both sides. Still, Nicole was hopeful that this was the beginning of change.

Change was definitely on the horizon for vampires, anyway. The most stunning developments of all following the battle were still happening.

Four clans from around the Pacific Northwest had sent representatives to Hunter. Word of the battle had spread, and MoonBound was becoming something of a legend. Kars had been on the right track when he tried to rally clans behind him—vampires were ready for a leader. But he wasn't it. Now clans were lining up behind Hunter and Aylin, their desire for a united vampire nation spurring them on.

But the situation with ShadowSpawn was the thing

Aylin found the most amazing. Kars had sent a peace offering, a white dove that had to have been Rasha's idea. And with it was a message:

I, Karshawnewuti Redmoon of ShadowSpawn clan, declare eternal peace and allegiance to MoonBound clan, so long as I live.

Holy. Shit.

Rasha had been true to her word, but how she'd accomplished such a feat was a mystery. And Aylin figured it would remain that way.

The one dark cloud hanging over the clan was the presence of someone who had given away secrets and put MoonBound in danger. But she, Hunter, and Riker had agreed that right now, the risk of sabotage was low, given the growing peace among the clans. So for the time being, they thought it best to play it cool, to give the person a chance to think he or she was off the hook. The traitor would eventually screw up, and in the meantime, Hunter and Riker could devise a trap. They would get their spy—they just wanted to do it without hurting anyone else.

A tap at her chamber door came right on time, and Aylin opened it to find Nicole standing there in a lacy green knee-length dress. She grinned when she saw Aylin.

"You're gorgeous," she said. "Hunter is going to flip out."

Aylin hoped so. Hunter's Cherokee background had fascinated Aylin, so she'd researched traditions and clothing, and with only days to prepare, she and several clan members had put together an ensemble fitting for a mating ceremony with a clan chief.

Hard to believe that just a month ago, Aylin had thought her future was lost. Now she was about to officially mate the chief of the largest clan in the Pacific Northwest. A chief who now commanded the respect of multiple clans. A chief who wasn't just mating with her for political reasons.

He loved her.

She couldn't wait to make it official. Especially because she'd insisted on keeping separate chambers until the ceremony, and tonight would be the first night she and Hunter spent together since the full moon.

Tonight was the new moon, when the female moon fever would rule, and she could already feel the pull tugging at her.

She cast a final glance in the mirror, wondering if the feather and turquoise headdress was too much. She adjusted it. Took it off. Put it back on.

Finally, a deep male voice made the decision for her. "If you wear that," Hunter said from the doorway, "we won't make it all the way through the ceremony."

Smiling, she pivoted to face him. Nicole had conveniently disappeared, leaving Aylin alone with the male she was about to commit to.

And if she'd had any doubt before, the sight of him, his dark gaze glittering with excitement and admiration, demolished it. His ebony hair fell in a shiny curtain over his broad shoulders and chest, which were bare except for a silver and amber necklace fashioned in MoonBound's symbol of the half-moon circled by a serpent. A single braid woven with a leather thong and eagle feathers hung from his right temple, secured by a miniature version of the MoonBound pendant.

And hanging low on his hips were supple buckskin leathers that hugged his muscular thighs as if they'd been painted on.

Reaching out, she put her palm on his chest. "We don't have to wait until after the ceremony."

"We'll be late." He stepped close and pressed his lips to the pulse in her throat. "But I'm sure everyone expects that."

Heat flooded her veins, and beneath her hand, his heartbeat raced. "Then let's not disappoint them."

His hands circled her hips, and as if she weighed nothing at all, he lifted her so she could wrap her legs around his waist. "Thank you, Aylin," he whispered in her ear.

She clung to him, rotating her hips against the hardness of his erection. "For what?"

"For saving my life."

"You've already thanked me."

"For bringing me back from the dead, yes." He tugged on her earlobe with his teeth, sending a shock of arousal straight to her core. "But not for saving me. I was headed down a path that wouldn't lead anywhere. Then Rasha happened, and if I'd mated with her, my path would have turned . . . ugly. You did more than bring me back from the dead, Aylin. You resurrected me."

Emotion clogged her throat. "You did the same for me. I wouldn't have survived being sent to Night-Shade."

"I think," he said roughly, as he slid inside her, filling her, completing her, "that you'd have done fine. You're strong, Aylin, and it's your strength that saved me. Saved us both."

She moaned at the delicious possession. "You broke me out of ShadowSpawn's chains and gave me the freedom to be strong," she whispered. "I didn't think I could belong to a clan and still be free, but here I am."

He braced her between his big body and the wall and moved against her, his hips pumping slowly, sensuously. "I would never chain you, sweetheart." He gave her a naughty smile. "Unless you want me to."

"Mmm . . . maybe later."

Leaning in, he scraped his fangs over her clavicle, and she shuddered with pleasure. "I have dreams about that," he said, his voice dripping with erotic promise. "Having you at my mercy."

"Before you came along, dreams were all I had. And you've made every one of them come true." She reconsidered that. "Well, most of them."

He froze. Pulled back. Looked down at her with heartbreaking worry. "What dream haven't I fulfilled?"

Reaching up, she cupped his cheek. "Just one. But it'll happen."

He scowled. "What is it?"

"Children," she murmured. "All my life, I was told I wouldn't be allowed to have them. And in a way, it was a blessing. I couldn't raise a child in a clan like ShadowSpawn or NightShade. But I can't think of a better place to raise them than here, with you as their father."

Hunter's dark eyes grew liquid, and his throat worked over and over on swallows. When he finally spoke, his words were edged with emotion.

"Only if Nicole finds a way to make giving birth

safe. I can't lose you. I love you, Aylin. Samnult is a bastard, but he was right about one thing." Dipping his head, he brushed his lips over hers. "I chose wisely."

Yes, he had.

They both had.

ACKNOWLEDGMENTS

HUGE, SINCERE THANKS to everyone on the Pocket Books team who helped bring this book to publication under less than optimal circumstances. Your patience and understanding kept me sane, and I appreciate you more than I can say. Extra huge hugs to Lauren McKenna and Elana Cohen for all your hard work. You went the extra mile for me, and I can't thank you enough.